"IS THAT THE BEST YOU CAN DO?"

"You know better than that, darlin'," he said with a wicked grin.

"Show me."

His kiss was like silken fire and lightning, sending heat shooting through every fiber of her being. Cara pressed herself against him, wanting more.

"Here, now," Vince said, "what do you think you're doing?"

"Nothing," she said innocently.

"Nothing?" He drew her body tight against his, letting her feel his arousal.

She smiled at him, a decidedly sexy, wanton smile.

"You keep looking at me like that and I'm going to take you upstairs and have my way with you."

"Really?"

"Really."

"Better hurry," she said, "I have to be back at work in half an hour."

Books by Amanda Ashley

DEAD SEXY

DESIRE AFTER DARK

NIGHT'S KISS

A WHISPER OF ETERNITY

AFTER SUNDOWN

Published by Zebra Books

AMANDA ASHLEY

NIGHT'S TOUCH

ZEBRA BOOKS
Kensington Publishing Corp.
www.kensingtonbooks.com

To Candace Camp
who gave me the idea for
writing a sequel to Night's Kiss.
Thanks, Candace!

And to Ronda Thompson
for brainstorming with me
in the wee small hours
of the morning.

And to the ladies in my critique groups
for their invaluable help.

Prologue

It was at a very early age that Cara Aideen DeLongpre realized her mother and father weren't like her friends' parents. For one thing, she never saw her mom and dad during the day, and they never ate dinner together, the way families did on TV. As far back as Cara could remember, she had eaten all her meals in the company of her nanny, Charlotte Ray, until Charlotte retired. Cara's new nanny, Melissa Kent, had been much younger than Miss Ray, and although Cara missed her old nanny, Miss Kent quickly found a place in Cara's affections.

Cara was homeschooled by Miss Louise Byrne until she turned twelve. On her birthday, Cara's father informed her that she would be going to public school so that she might associate with other children. Cara wasn't happy about that, but her father assured her that it was for her own good. She needed to learn how to get along with people her own age. To that end, Miss Byrne was dismissed and Frank Di Giorgio was hired. Mr. Di Giorgio had thick black hair going gray at the temples and gray eyes that, when he was angry, looked as cold as stone. He was built like a wrestler and had a face like a bulldog. It was his job to drive Cara to school and pick her up afterward.

Going to public school had been a trial. After spending the first twelve years of her life with adults, Cara had found it hard to relate to children her own age. It had also emphasized, once again, the differences between her parents and the parents of the other kids. Her mother and father didn't attend parent-teacher conferences or school plays or any other functions, unless they were held at night.

Until Cara went to school, she had assumed that everybody opened their Christmas presents at night and hunted for Easter eggs after the sun went down. Thanksgiving was a holiday that was never celebrated in her home. Valentine's Day meant a big candy heart from her daddy.

Cara's favorite holiday was Halloween. She always dressed up as a witch, and her mother and father always went trick-or-treating with her. Her mom dressed as a witch, too. Her dad didn't dress up, though he did wear a long black cloak that made the other kids ask if he was supposed to be a vampire.

When Cara turned sixteen, she was allowed to go out with boys, but only if they went out with a group or with another couple. To her chagrin, Mr. Di Giorgio was always nearby and Cara came to understand that he was no longer just her chauffeur, but her bodyguard as well, though she had no idea why she needed a bodyguard. Bodyguards were for presidents and rock stars, not for ordinary people.

She put the question to her mom and dad the night after it occurred to her.

Roshan DeLongpre considered his reply for several moments before he answered his daughter's question. He wasn't surprised by it, only amazed that it had taken her so long to ask.

"I'm a wealthy man," he explained patiently, "and I have many enemies. Frank is there to make sure that no harm comes to you."

"What kind of enemies?" Cara asked.

"Ruthless ones."

She digested that a moment, then asked, "Why don't I ever see you or Mom during the day? Why don't we eat together? Where do the two of you go every day, and why can't I ever go with you?"

Roshan looked at his wife, one brow arched in a silent plea for help. He and Brenna had both known this day would come sooner or later, but how did a man tell his adopted daughter that her father and mother were vampires and, more than that, that her mother was a witch?

"Brenna?"

Brenna took her daughter's hand in hers and gave it a squeeze. "Years ago, while traveling in Africa, your father and I contracted a rare disease. The sun is like poison to us now, so we sleep during the day."

Cara nodded. She knew she was adopted. Her parents had told her that as soon as she was old enough to understand. It explained why she wasn't affected by the same disease that plagued her mom and dad.

"Maybe we could eat dinner together?" Cara suggested. "Like other families. You know, like the ones on TV."

Brenna and Roshan exchanged glances.

"Due to our ailment, your father and I are on a rather strict liquid diet," Brenna said after a moment, "but we'll be happy to sit at the table with you while you eat, if you like."

"I'd like that very much," Cara said, smiling. "At least once in a while."

"Then that's what we'll do," her father said.

"Are we very rich?" Cara asked.

"Yes," her father replied soberly. "Very."

"Do you think I could have a car?"

"When you're eighteen," her father said.

Cara sighed. "Lily got a new car for her sixteenth birthday. So did Jennifer. Why can't I have a car now?"

Brenna looked at her husband, one brow raised as she, too, waited for his answer.

Roshan glanced from his daughter to his wife and back again. "We'll compromise," he said. "You can have the car of your choice when you turn seventeen."

The car she chose was a baby blue convertible with black interior.

Cara was twenty-two years old when she finally discovered why her parents weren't like everyone else's.

Chapter 1

Cara Aideen DeLongpre sipped her drink, too preoccupied with her own thoughts to pay any attention to the crowd and the noise that surrounded her. She had grown up knowing her mother and father weren't like other parents. Once she had started going to school, she had discovered a whole new world. Other kids went on vacation with their parents when school was out. They went out to dinner and to the zoo and to Disneyland and Sea World. They had birthday parties at Chuck E. Cheese's. Other kids had brothers and sisters, aunts and uncles, and cousins and grandparents. When Cara asked why she didn't have brothers or sisters or aunts and uncles, her father had explained that her mother couldn't have children, and that he and her mother didn't have any siblings, and that her grandparents had all passed away.

It was a perfectly logical explanation, but it didn't make her feel any less lonely. It would have been nice to have an older brother, or a sister she could share confidences with.

What wasn't logical was the fact that, in over twenty years, her parents hadn't changed at all. She told herself she was being foolish, that she was overreacting, imagining things, but there was no arguing with the proof of her own eyes. They both looked exactly the way they had when Cara was a little girl. Her mother never gained or lost an ounce. Her face was as smooth and clear as it had always been. The same was true of her father. Roshan DeLongpre looked like a man in his mid-thirties, and he had looked that way for as long as Cara could remember. He had taken her to the movies one night last week and they had run into a couple of Cara's acquaintances. Before she could introduce her father, her friend, Cindy, had taken her aside and asked how long she had been dating that "good-looking older man."

Cara stared into her drink, wishing she had the nerve to ask her parents why Di Giorgio aged and they didn't and why their lifestyle was so different from everyone else's. She knew about their aversion to the sun and their liquid diet, but why did that keep them from other normal activities? Why did they encourage her to make friends but discourage her from bringing them home? Why did they keep the door to their bedroom locked during the day? What were they doing in there?

She looked up as a man sat down beside her. He smiled, then pointed with his chin at her drink. "Can I buy you another?"

"No, thank you."

He lifted a hand. "Hey, no problem. You just looked a little down. I thought you might like some company."

He had a nice voice, blond hair, and dark brown eyes. What harm could it do to share a drink with him?

"Are you sure you won't change your mind?" he coaxed, as if sensing her indecision.

"Well, I would like another."

"What are you drinking?" he asked, signaling for the bartender.

"A virgin pineapple daiquiri."

He ordered her drink and a scotch and water for himself, then held out his hand. "I'm Anton."

"Cara." She hesitated a moment before taking his hand. Though she had been on her share of dates, she tended to be shy around strangers. She wasn't sure why—maybe because she had never forgotten her father's warning that he had "ruthless enemies." Still, she told herself there was nothing to worry about. Frank was here.

Anton's grip was firm, his skin warm. "Do you come here often?"

"No, this is my first time. I was just passing by and I heard the music and . . ." She shrugged. "I thought it might cheer me up."

"If you tell me what's got you feeling so blue, I might be able to help."

"I don't think so, but thanks for offering."

Cara glanced out at the dance floor as the lights dimmed. The music, which had been upbeat, changed to something slow and sensual with a dark, sexual undertone. It called to something earthy deep within her.

"Would you like to dance?" Anton asked.

Again, she hesitated a moment before agreeing.

Anton took her by the hand and led her out onto the floor. "So," he said, taking her in his arms. "Tell me about yourself."

"What do you want to know?"

"Let's see. What do you like to do for fun? Do you work, or are you an heiress? Who's your favorite singer? And, most important of all, are you a chocoholic like every other woman I've ever met?"

She laughed. "Guilty on the chocolate," she said, and then frowned as she realized she had never seen her mother eat or drink anything chocolate. Even the most rigid dieters cheated every now and then.

"Did I say something wrong?" he asked.

"No. I work at the library, and I don't really have a favorite singer." She didn't tell him that she was, in fact, an heiress. After all, he was a stranger and she wasn't a fool.

Not that she had anything to worry about, not with Frank Di Giorgio sitting at the far end of the bar watching her like a hawk.

"You're a librarian?" Anton exclaimed.

"Is something wrong with that?"

"No, no, but . . . well, you're a knockout. I sort of thought you might be a model or an actress."

Cara smiled, flattered in spite of herself. "Disappointed?"

"Not at all."

When the music ended, he escorted her back to their seats. Their drinks were waiting for them. Cara sipped hers, thinking how glad she was she had stopped in here tonight. Di Giorgio had tried to dissuade her, but she had insisted. Once inside, she almost hadn't stayed, it was such a strange place. For one thing, she was the only one in the place who wasn't wearing black. Voodoo masks and ancient Indian burial masks decorated the walls. Tall black candles flickered in wrought-iron wall sconces, casting eerie shadows over the faces of the patrons; a good number of them wore long black cloaks or capes with hoods.

"So," Anton said, "what do you think of The Nocturne?"

"I'm not sure. Why is everyone wearing black?"

"This is a Goth hangout."

"Oh! Silly me, I should have guessed."

He grinned at her. "I take it you're not into the Goth scene."

"Not really," she replied, and then frowned, thinking that her father would be right at home in a place like this. He had an affinity for dark clothing, and he had a long black cloak. It was more than that, though. From time to time, she had sensed a darkness in her father that she couldn't explain and didn't understand.

Cara finished her drink, then looked at her watch, surprised to find it was so late. "I should be going," she said reluctantly. "My folks will be worried."

"Don't tell me you still live at home with mom and dad!"

Cara shrugged. "I like it there." And she did, although sometimes, especially when the days were long and the nights were short, it was like living alone.

"One more dance?" he coaxed.

"I don't think so. I really need to go," she said, and then wondered why she had to be home before midnight. She wasn't a child anymore. Why did she still have a curfew? Lately, she'd had so many questions about the way she lived. Why did she still live at home? Why did she still need a bodyguard? She was twenty-two years old and no one had ever tried to kidnap her or molest her or so much as give her a dirty look. Of course, Di Giorgio was probably responsible for that. A man would have to be crazy to try anything with the Hulk lurking in the background. Still, maybe it was time to sit her folks down and ask the questions that had been plaguing her more and more in the last few months.

"Thank you for the drink and the dance," she said, rising.

"Any chance you'll be here tomorrow night about this time?" he asked.

She canted her head to the side, considering it, and then smiled. "I'd say the odds were good."

"Great. I'll see you then."

Leaning back against the bar, Anton Bouchard watched his enemy's daughter leave the bar, followed by a big bear of a man who looked as if he could easily take on every other man in the place without breaking a sweat.

Anton grunted softly, thinking how pleased his mother would be when he told her he had put the first part of her plan into operation.

Chapter 2

Serafina Bouchard beamed when Anton told her that he had made contact with DeLongpre's daughter. Serafina had waited over twenty years to avenge herself on DeLongpre and now the time was at hand, so close she could taste it. She wasn't powerful enough to destroy the vampire or his witch wife, but destroying their daughter would hurt them far worse than any physical pain she could inflict, and they deserved to be destroyed. They had killed Anthony Loken, the only man she had ever loved, and Myra had been killed that same night. Serafina didn't know how Myra had died, or who had killed her, but she was certain that, one way or another, Roshan DeLongpre had been responsible for her death.

Serafina smiled. She wasn't sorry that Myra was gone. She had always been jealous of Myra, jealous of her power, jealous of her association with Anthony. With Myra's death, the Wiccan Way Coffee Shop and Book Store had closed and the coven had been without a leader, but not for long. When no one else seemed inclined to take over, Serafina had stepped in and taken charge. She had opened a new bookstore on the other side of town and offered it to the coven for a place to meet. Now, twenty years later, she was the undisputed head of the coven and The Wiccan Heart was thriving. When Anton grew old enough to work, she had made him her partner in the bookstore.

Later that night, alone in her room, Serafina spoke to her beloved's photo. "Soon, Anthony, soon your death will be avenged and you'll be able to rest in peace."

She pressed his picture to her breast. She had fallen in love with Anthony Loken the first moment she had seen him, so tall and blond, like one of Satan's angels. She would never forget the day Myra had introduced her to Anthony. He had smiled at Serafina, and she had known that he loved her in return. One night, during a spring ritual shortly before his death, she had offered herself to him. Anton was the result.

Anthony had never known of her love for him or about the child she had conceived. By the time she knew she was pregnant, he was gone. She had raised her son alone, teaching him everything she knew about Magick and witchcraft, whispering to him late at night that he would be the instrument that would bring down the people responsible for his father's death. And always, in the back of her mind, she clung to the sure knowledge that Anthony had loved her, assured herself every day that if he had lived, he would have married her and claimed Anton as his son. She believed it with every fiber of her being, her surety growing more unshakeable with every passing year, until she had convinced herself that Anthony had not only loved her, but married her before he died. If DeLongpre and his witch wife hadn't destroyed her beloved, Anthony would have been hers for all eternity.

Even though her beloved was gone, Serafina refused to let him go. His clothing filled her closet. His books and journals were in a trunk in her basement. Each Beltane, she made a list of seven reasons why she loved Anthony Loken. When her list was complete, she drew a circle of power on the floor of her bedroom. She sat on one side of the circle and on the other she placed a life-sized rag doll that she had dressed in Anthony's clothes. Sitting in the circle, she read her list. The reasons were different each year. When she finished reading her list, she took her make-believe Anthony's hand in hers and said, "I will love you forever because you're you."

She kissed his image, then placed the photograph on her dresser. Soon his death would be avenged and when the deed was done, she would join him in the After World where they would finally be together forever.

With that thought in mind, Serafina crawled into bed, one of Anthony's handkerchiefs clutched to her breast.

She would dream of him again tonight.

Chapter 3

Roshan DeLongpre looked up as his daughter entered the room. She was a lovely child, he thought, though at twenty-two, he supposed she was no longer a child. Still, she would always be his little girl. Her hair, the color of ripe wheat, fell to her waist in soft waves. Her eyes were as blue as sapphires, her skin smooth and unblemished. How had she grown up so fast? It seemed like only yesterday that Brenna had found Cara's mother in an alley giving birth. Roshan had spread his cloak beneath the girl; Brenna had helped bring the child into the world.

He remembered that night clearly, especially the look of wonder in Brenna's eyes as she wrapped the tiny, new-born infant in her cloak.

"You have a beautiful little girl," Brenna had said.

"Take her," the mother said. "I don't want her. I don't want to see her."

Brenna had looked up at him, her arms tightening around the infant.

He shook his head. "Don't even think about it."

"But she does not want it."

"Brenna, what would we do with a baby?"

"Love her."

"No. It won't work. There's no way . . ."

The mother glanced at Brenna. *"If you don't take her, I'm just going to dump her in a trash can somewhere. I can't take her home with me."*

"Surely the baby's father . . ."

"I don't know who he is." The teenager was pulling on her discarded jeans as she spoke. Taking a deep breath, she stood up, one hand braced against the wall behind her.

"What are you doing?" Brenna asked.

"I'm leaving." A sob rose in the girl's throat. *"Do whatever you want with the baby."*

How quickly that baby had grown, Roshan thought again. It was hard to believe he had not wanted her. Now, he couldn't imagine their life without her. She was vibrant and alive and he loved her more than his own life.

"Did you have a good time tonight?" he asked as she sat down on the sofa beside him.

"Yes."

"Where did you go?"

"I went for a drive and then I stopped at a nightclub. It was a strange place."

Warning bells went off in Roshan's mind. "Strange?"

She nodded. "Everyone was dressed in black, like something out of an old horror movie, if you know what I mean. I met a guy there. He seemed nice."

"What was the name of this place?" Roshan asked.

"The Nocturne. It was like Halloween inside, you know? Lots of people wearing black. The valet wore a black suit and a hooded cloak. And then, to get into the club, you have to walk under this black canopy, and then down some stairs. Talk about a creepy atmosphere! The door was carved with all these mystical signs. It was awesome. I'll have to take you and Mom there sometime."

Roshan nodded. It was all he could do not to demand

that she never go there again. The Nocturne! There was
no telling what kind of man she had met in that place. It
was a hangout for vampires and other creatures of the
night. Of course, he rarely let any other vampire remain
in his town too long. Like all of his kind, he was a terri-
torial creature, not disposed to sharing his domain or his
food source.

"Where's Mom?" Cara asked.

Roshan smiled inwardly. His wife was outside, dancing
under the stars. She did that from time to time. He enjoyed nothing more than watching her, but tonight she
had wanted to be alone.

"Why don't you go up to bed," he suggested. "I'll find
her and send her up to you. I know she'll want to hear
about your evening."

"All right." Cara kissed him on the cheek and then,
humming softly, she went upstairs.

Roshan stared after her a moment and then, muttering, "I've got a bad feeling about this," he went out the
back door.

A wide path lined with night-blooming flowers wove its
way through the yard. Wrought-iron benches were placed
here and there along the way. A small white headstone
occupied a small bower, marking the final resting place
of Brenna's cat, Morgana. He had expected Brenna to
find another cat to take Morgana's place, but when he had
asked her about it, she had simply said that Morgana
couldn't be replaced, and that had been the end of it. Of
course, they'd had their share of pets once Cara got old
enough to want one. Dogs and cats, birds and turtles, mice
and fish had all come and, thankfully, gone.

Roshan found his wife in the middle of the yard in the
midst of a circle of tall trees. He paused in the shadows,
watching her dance. It reminded him of the first night
he had seen her. She had been dancing in the nude
then, too. It was one of his favorite memories, burned
forever in his mind.

Tonight, her fiery red hair shimmered like flame in the silvery light of the full moon. Her deep green eyes were flecked with gold and sparkled with delight as she twirled in the moonlight, her only covering the waist-length hair that fell down her back and over her shoulders like veils of crimson silk as she dipped and swayed to music only she could hear. A necklace of amber and jet circled her slender throat. She was the most beautiful creature he had ever seen.

After a moment, she stopped dancing, a seductive smile playing over her lips as she turned to face him.

"Come," she beckoned, holding out one slender hand. "Dance with me."

"Another time," he said, stepping out of the shadows. "Our daughter is home and asking for you."

"Oh." Moving toward a stone bench, Brenna pulled a velvet gown the color of the midnight sky over her head and smoothed it over her hips in a sensual, feminine gesture. "Is she all right?"

Roshan nodded. They had ever been overprotective parents, but perhaps that was to be expected. Cara was their only child, the only one they would ever have. "She's fine. She met a man."

"Really? Where?"

"At The Nocturne."

Brenna stared at him in disbelief. "The Nocturne! What on earth was she doing there?"

"I have no idea."

"Roshan, you have to talk to her. Tell her she mustn't go there again. The Nocturne!" Brenna pressed a hand to her heart. The Nocturne. Merciful heavens!

"Go on up and tell her good night," he said, kissing her on the cheek. "I'm going out to talk to Di Giorgio."

The bodyguard lived in a small house in the rear of the property. He was a solitary man, seemingly content with his own thoughts and his own company. Roshan knew Frank Di Giorgio had been connected to one of the crime families in Italy when he was a young man, but that had been a long time ago.

At Roshan's knock, Di Giorgio opened the door, gun in hand.

"Evening, Frank."

Grunting softly, Di Giorgio shoved the gun into the waistband of a pair of expensive looking trousers, then invited his boss inside.

The bodyguard's report was brief. Cara had been sitting at the bar in The Nocturne when a young man approached her. He had bought Cara a drink. They had talked and danced one dance. The man seemed harmless enough. He hadn't said or done anything out of line.

Roshan listened carefully, some of his worry ebbing as he listened to what Di Giorgio had to say. Bidding the man good night, Roshan returned to the house.

Brenna was waiting for him in the living room. She had turned the lights down low and started a fire in the hearth. Smiling, she patted the seat beside her.

Sitting down, he draped his arm around her shoulders.

Brenna sighed. This was her favorite time of the night. Cara was home and safely tucked into bed and all was right with the world.

A wave of her hand turned on the TV. She surfed through the channels until she found a movie she liked, then settled back once again, her head resting on her husband's shoulder.

Roshan stared into the flames as scenes from the past paraded across his mind. He had fallen in love with Brenna Flanagan when he happened across her image in a book titled *Ancient History and Myths, Fact or Fiction*. It had been a small pen-and-ink drawing depicting a woman bound to a wooden stake, surrounded by a mob of angry men waving torches over their heads. The caption under the drawing had read: *The Burning of Brenna Flanagan, Accused of Witchcraft*.

He had become obsessed with that drawing, so much

so that he had traveled back in time to the year 1692 where he had saved her from a fiery death. He had brought her back to his time, helped her learn her way around his world. She had blossomed here, free to practice her witchcraft if she wished to do so. While exploring the city, she had come across the Wiccan Way Coffee Shop and Book Store. It had been there that she met Anthony Loken, an evil warlock who had been obsessed with discovering the secret of immortality. Convinced that the blood of vampires held the secret of eternal life, Loken had frequented The Nocturne in search of vampires, luring them to his laboratory where he took their blood and their lives. Due to Myra's treachery, Roshan had found himself strapped to a table in that lab, bound with heavy silver chains that had burned his flesh and weakened his powers. Only his concern for Brenna, who had also been Loken's prisoner, had given Roshan the strength he needed to free himself. In the end, Roshan had forced Loken to drink his own potion. The warlock had died a horrible, excruciatingly painful death.

Feeling suddenly restless, Roshan went to stand in front of the hearth.

"What's wrong?" Brenna asked, switching off the TV.

"I don't know."

Rising, she went to stand behind him; her arms slipping around his waist. "Is it Cara? Is there something you're not telling me?"

"No." He shook his head. "It's probably nothing."

"If it was nothing, you wouldn't be so worried."

Turning in her arms, he brushed a kiss across her cheek. "I'm going out for a while."

"Where are you going?"

"Just out for a walk. I won't be long."

Grabbing his cloak, Roshan left the house. Standing in the shadows, he let his preternatural powers probe the night. Although he sensed nothing amiss, he couldn't shake the feeling that danger lurked nearby.

* * *

Anton Loken Bouchard stood across the street from DeLongpre's house. Hidden by the darkness, he watched the vampire walk down the long driveway and stop at the gate in the high fence that surrounded the property. Hatred rose up within Anton as he stared at the creature who had killed the father he had never known. Ever since Anton had been old enough to understand, his mother had told him stories of his father. Anthony Loken had been a great man, a wizard without equal. He had been on the verge of a fantastic discovery that would have benefited all mankind when Roshan DeLongpre killed him in a jealous rage.

Every year, on the anniversary of his father's death, Anton accompanied his mother to the site of his father's grave, where he lit a black candle and vowed to avenge his father's death. As someone had once said, revenge was a dish best served cold. Over the years, Anton's grief and anger had coalesced into a hard icy lump in the core of his being. Avenging his father's death was the only thing that could melt that painful lump. Revenge. It was so near, so near he could almost taste it. It would be sweet, indeed.

Humming softly, he turned and headed for home. He would be at The Nocturne again tomorrow night. He had a feeling he would find Cara there. It wouldn't take much to seduce her. She had been sheltered her whole life. A show of interest, a few chaste kisses, and she would be his for the taking.

Cara thought about Anton at work the following day. She couldn't decide how she felt about him. He was polite and handsome, and yet there was something about him that bothered her. She wasn't sure what it was that rubbed her the wrong way, but it made her wary and distrustful. Her father had told her to always trust her instincts, though in her sheltered life she'd had little need.

With a shake of her head, she laughed it off. She was just being silly and overly suspicious because she had so little experience with men. Instead of looking for questionable behavior where there was none, she should be flattered that a handsome man found her interesting and wanted to see her again.

He had seemed amused when she told him she worked in a library, but she loved her job—not that she had to work. After all, her father was a rich man, but if she didn't work, what else would she do with her days? Besides, as far back as she could remember, she had loved books and loved to read; it didn't matter what. If it had words, she read it. She was certain that a good part of her love of books had been inherited from her father. His library at home was enormous, with bookcases that reached from wall to wall and floor to ceiling. The shelves were filled with a variety of books, many of them rare first editions. Some were so old they were in danger of disintegrating. A few were truly ancient, like the medieval Psalter that dated back to the fourteenth century. It was Cara's favorite book, a beautiful work of art, carefully written and illustrated by hand. Her father also owned a Bible handwritten by monks. Each page was in itself a work of art. He had other books and writings that were also truly unique. Some were written on tree bark, others on bamboo or cloth or silk. One had been engraved on metal plates. He had a folding book that came from Burma. It was called a *parabaiks,* and it told the life of Buddha in words and pictures.

Yes, she loved books. They were more than just words and pictures. When she had been a child, they had been her companions during the day when her schoolwork was done. They had taken her to faraway places and fueled her imagination. She had lost herself in the pages of her favorite stories. She had been Sleeping Beauty and Cinderella and Snow White. She had been the beautiful fairy princess, the valiant heroine who saved the prince, the benevolent queen who overcame the evil wizard and freed the slaves.

One of the reasons Cara loved working in the library was the hope that she could instill her love of books in the hearts and minds of the children.

She glanced up at the clock, then plucked one of her favorite books from the shelf. It was story time, the best part of the day. Taking her place, she smiled at the children sitting in a half-circle on the floor. They smiled back at her, their eyes alight with anticipation.

Cara opened the book and began to read. "Once upon a time, in a land far, far away . . ."

The library closed at nine. Cara bid good night to her coworkers and left by the side door. After getting into her car, she sat there a moment, trying to decide if she should go home or go to The Nocturne. She had told Anton the odds were good she would be there tonight, and she always kept her word. Of course, she hadn't really given him her word . . . she tapped her fingertips on the steering wheel, puzzled by her ambivalent feelings about him. Last night, she had been excited by his attention, but now . . .

She shook off her doubts. What was she worrying about? She was just going to meet him for a drink after work, for goodness' sake. What harm could there be in that? Besides, she had to see Anton again so she could decide how she really felt about him, and Frank the Hulk would be close by.

With her mind made up, she put the key in the ignition and drove to The Nocturne.

Chapter 4

Vince Cordova sat at a booth in a back corner of The Nocturne, idly sipping from a glass of what looked like red wine. He was new to this town, to this place. New to the nocturnal life. He looked at the wannabe vampires that filled the club. Men and women alike, they were all clad in black—black shirts or blouses, black pants or skirts, long black cloaks, some lined in white, some in blood-red satin. The women wore black eye shadow and eyeliner and wore matching lipstick. Here and there he caught a flash of fang—fake, of course.

Vince ran his tongue over his own teeth, felt the needle-sharp prick of his fangs. They were the real deal and he still wasn't used to them. Or the ever-present yearning for blood.

He stared into the glass in his hand. The liquid soothed the craving but he found no real satisfaction in it. There was nothing like drinking from the source, inhaling the scent of it, feeling the warmth slide over your tongue and trickle down your throat. Damn! Just thinking about it stirred his hunger.

Draining the contents of his glass, he went to the bar for a refill.

* * *

Cara threaded her way through the crowd toward the bar, conscious of Di Giorgio entering behind her. Sometimes she wished he would just disappear, although in a place like this, she was glad he was there.

She glanced around the room but she didn't see Anton. Maybe he had changed his mind, and maybe the fact that she felt relief instead of regret answered the question of how she felt about him. It was probably just as well that he hadn't shown up, she thought, since she was certain he had a lot more experience with women than she did with men. Still, she couldn't help glancing toward the door every now and then.

Upon seeing an empty bar stool, she sat down and ordered her usual, a virgin pineapple daiquiri. Her friends at work teased her because she didn't drink alcohol, but it was a taste she had never acquired. Maybe it was because her parents didn't drink, either.

Sitting there, she ran her finger around the rim of the glass while she watched the couples on the dance floor. She really was out of her league here, she thought. As soon as she finished her drink, she'd go home. No more walking on the wild side for her.

"You get stood up?"

Cara looked at the man who had taken the seat to her left. He wore a black T-shirt, tight black jeans, and a pair of black leather boots, and he was far and away the most gorgeous man she had ever seen. Thick black hair brushed his broad shoulders. His eyes were dark brown under straight black brows; his nose was thin and sharp. His lips were full and sensuous. She had the strongest urge to run her fingertips over them to see if they were as warm and soft as they looked.

"Are you talking to me?" she asked coolly.

"I asked if you'd been stood up. You keep looking toward the door."

"No, I haven't, not that it's any of your business."

He shrugged. "Sorry. Just trying to make conversation."

"I'm sorry, too," she apologized. "I didn't mean to be rude."

"No problem." He gestured at her empty glass. "Can I buy you another drink?"

"I guess so."

"What are you drinking?" She hesitated a moment, reluctant, for some reason, to let him know she didn't indulge. She was over twenty-one, after all. It wouldn't hurt her to have one drink.

He was watching her, waiting for her answer.

"A pineapple daiquiri."

Vince gave the bartender her order and asked for a glass of red wine for himself. It was not his usual drink of choice; ordinarily, he ordered a Bloody Mariah.

"I'm Vince."

"Cara."

"Nice to meet you, Cara."

"Thank you."

"You don't seem like the type to frequent this joint."

"Why not?"

"Look around, honey. I don't want to hurt your feelings, but you don't fit the profile."

She wanted to be offended, but how could she when he was right? She was the only one in the place who didn't look like they had just stepped out of a cheap horror flick.

"I just sort of stumbled into the place," she admitted. "Until last night, I never knew The Nocturne existed."

He nodded. "You met someone here, didn't you? And you came back hoping to see him again."

"How did you know that?"

He shrugged. "I used to do the bar scene a lot."

"Used to?" She smiled at the bartender when he placed her drink in front of her. He winked at her, then moved on down the bar. She wondered what the wink was for until she tasted her drink. He had thoughtfully left out the rum.

"I've been a little off my game the last year or so," Vince said. "Been spending a lot of time by myself."

"Were you sick?"

"In a way."

She found it hard to believe he had ever been ill. He looked the picture of health, strong and fit. His T-shirt stretched over a broad chest; his arms were long and well muscled. He reminded her of a bodybuilder except that he wasn't bulky. He looked solid, though.

He jerked his chin at the dance floor. "Care to take a whirl?"

Her heart skipped a beat at the thought of being in his arms. Nodding, she followed him onto the dance floor, felt her cheeks grow hot as he took her hand in his and slipped his arm around her waist.

Dancing with Vince was far different from dancing with Anton. Vince moved with a kind of fluid grace that made her wonder if he was a professional dancer. Her skin tingled where his hand rested on her waist, her whole body throbbed with an unfamiliar longing when she looked into his eyes. He didn't hold her too close, didn't say or do anything the least bit suggestive, and yet she was aware of him with every fiber of her being.

She hated to hear the song end, felt bereft when his hand fell away from her waist. No other man had ever made her feel the way he did. A smile, a touch, and she felt beautiful, desirable. When she looked into his eyes . . . it was like looking into the far reaches of eternity. For a moment, she forgot where they were, forgot that they weren't alone.

For a moment, she wished he would kiss her.

A wistful smile curved his lips, as if he knew what she was thinking. When he spoke, she wondered if he was reading her mind.

"I know," he said quietly. "I feel it, too."

Taking her hand in his, he led her back to the bar.

A man was sitting on her stool.

"Hi, sweet cakes," Anton said, smiling. "Sorry I'm late."

Cara glanced from Anton to Vince and back again. "Hi. I . . . I didn't think you were coming."

"Hey," Anton said, looking offended, "would I let a pretty girl down?"

Cara had never been in a situation like this before and she didn't know what to do. She had sort of a date with Anton, but it was Vince she wanted to be with.

Her upbringing made the decision for her. With an apologetic smile, she looked at Vince and said, "Thank you for the dance."

"Anytime." Dropping her hand, he picked up his drink and walked away.

"Who was that?" Anton asked.

"I don't know. Just a guy who asked me to dance." Cara didn't like the look in Anton's eyes as he watched Vince settle into a booth in the far corner of the room.

"How about a late movie?" Anton asked. He checked his watch. "If we leave now, we can just make the ten o'clock show."

"No, I don't think so."

"You're angry because I was late."

"Oh, no," she said quickly. Quite the opposite, she thought. If he had been on time, she wouldn't have met Vince. She wondered if he came here often. Sitting on the stool next to Anton's, she sipped her drink, wishing she could think of a way to find out if Vince was a frequent patron.

With a sigh, she looked at Anton. "You never told me what you do for a living," she remarked.

"I'm part owner of a bookstore. That's why I was late. Something came up and I had to take care of it."

"A bookstore!" she exclaimed. "Sounds heavenly."

"I knew we had a lot in common when you told me you were a librarian," Anton said, grinning. "Who's your favorite author?"

"Oh, gosh, I have so many, I wouldn't know where to begin, but Tolkien is right up near the top."

"*Lord of the Rings,* eh? Got a thing for wizards and elves, do you?"

"Well, I have a thing for Legolas," she admitted with a grin. "And Aragorn, of course."

Anton smiled, wondering what she would think if she knew she was talking to a practicing warlock. His powers had come to him late, but his abilities were growing stronger and more proficient each day. Given time, he knew his magick would be as powerful as his father's had been, perhaps more so.

For a while, they talked about books. She liked fantasy, he liked science fiction; she liked humor, he liked murder mysteries. Somehow, it didn't surprise her that their tastes were so divergent, but no matter what they were discussing, Cara was always aware of Vince sitting in the back of the room. Even when he was just sitting still, there was something about him that drew her gaze again and again. Now and then, she caught him watching her. Each time that happened, a pleasurable tingle of awareness skittered down her spine.

She was acutely aware of Vince's gaze when Anton asked her to dance. Once again, she found herself comparing the two men and her reaction to them. Dancing with Vince was a sensual experience that had made her very much aware of the fact that she was a woman and he was a man. Dancing with Anton was just . . . dancing.

"Would you like another drink?" Anton asked when they returned to their seats.

"No, thank you. I've got to go. I'm a working girl, you know." She didn't start work until three in the afternoon, but he didn't know that, and it made for a good excuse.

"Come on," he said, "I'll walk you to your car."

She didn't want him to, but she couldn't think of any plausible reason to refuse.

From the corner of her eye, she saw Vince lift his glass in a farewell salute as she made her way toward the door.

Cara went up the outside entrance to her room when she got home. She felt a little guilty for not going in to tell her folks she was home and kiss them good night, but she wasn't in the mood to answer a lot of questions about where she'd been and what she'd done. Besides, Di Giorgio would give them a full report and let them know that she was home safe and sound before he retired for the night.

She often wondered about Frank Di Giorgio. Being her bodyguard didn't give him much time for a life of his own. He lived in a house out back. To her knowledge, he never had any visitors, he never took a vacation, and he rarely had a night off.

After undressing, she slipped into a pink T-shirt and a pair of comfy pajama bottoms, then opened the French doors and stepped out onto the balcony. It was one of her favorite places. During the day, she had a view of the backyard and the mountains beyond. Taking a seat in one of the two wicker chairs, she stared up at the sky. It was a beautiful night, warm and clear. Stars twinkled brightly overhead. Moonlight bathed the leaves of the trees with a pale silver sheen.

The night. There was something mesmerizing about it. Her parents loved it. They went out for a walk together every evening; sometimes they were only gone for a short time, sometimes for hours. At home, they frequently sat outside in the gazebo, holding hands. Sometimes, her mother and father seemed so wrapped up in each other, Cara felt like an outsider in her own home. It was more than the fact that she was adopted. Sometimes, it seemed like they were communicating silently, sharing secrets she would never know. She told herself it was just a part of their being married, but she knew it was more than that. She just didn't know what.

Sighing, she was about to go inside and go to bed when she had the oddest sensation that she was being watched. She glanced over her shoulder, thinking maybe her father had come upstairs to say good night, but there was no one there.

Rising, she looked over the balcony railing, then thought how foolish that was. Even if there was someone down there, it was too dark to see anything lurking in the shadows. Frowning, she leaned forward. What was that? Was she imagining things, or was that a pair of eyes— a pair of glowing red eyes—staring back at her? She might have thought it was a cat, but she'd never seen a cat with eyes that color!

Spooked, she turned on her heel and sprinted into her bedroom. She locked the door behind her and closed the curtains over the windows, then she stood there, breathing hard, one hand pressed to her heart.

That was how her father found her when he knocked on her door a moment later.

"Cara, may I come in?"

"Yes!"

Stepping into the room, he took one look at her face and asked, "What's wrong?"

"Nothing." She gestured toward the balcony. "I . . . I thought I saw . . . I don't know what it was."

He moved toward the French doors, opened them, and stepped outside. "Think, Cara. What did you see?"

"I'm not sure." She went to stand beside her father, unafraid now that he was there with her. "It looked . . . it looked like eyes. Red, glowing eyes."

He looked at her sharply. "Red eyes? Are you sure?"

"Yes, why? Does that mean something to you?"

He took a breath. "No, of course not." Putting his arm around her shoulders, he led her back into the bedroom, then closed and locked the doors. "Probably just a cat."

"With red eyes?"

"A trick of the moonlight," he said with a reassuring smile. "Di Giorgio tells me you went to The Nocturne again."

Nodding, she sat on the edge of her bed.

"Two men spoke to you tonight."

She tried to subdue her annoyance at having her every move watched and reported, but it came out in an angry breath. She was twenty-two years old! Was she never to have any privacy?

"Yes, Dad," she said irritably, "I saw two men. I danced with two men. They bought me drinks. I came home alone. Is there anything else you want to know?"

"I don't care for that tone, young lady."

"I'm sorry." She was instantly contrite, and a little confused by her growing resentment.

He sat down beside her. "I know having Di Giorgio follow you is wearisome. I know you don't fully understand or appreciate the necessity of having him there, but it's for my peace of mind and for . . ."

"My own good," she finished, having heard it all a hundred times before.

"Cara . . ."

"Dad, I'm twenty-two years old! No one's ever even looked at me sideways. What's the big deal? What are you really afraid of? I think I have a right to know."

"Perhaps it's time," he allowed. "I'll discuss it with your mother."

"You promise?"

"If you think it's necessary, then you have my word."

She smiled at him. "Thanks, Dad."

With a nod, Roshan kissed his daughter on the forehead, then left the room, closing the door behind him.

Brenna looked up when he entered the living room. "Is everything all right?"

"She's starting to chafe at having Di Giorgio trailing after her, and she's starting to ask questions." He shook his head, surprised that it had taken her this long.

"Maybe we're worrying for nothing. It's been over twenty years. Surely if the coven meant to take some kind of revenge, they would have done so by now."

"Maybe." Roshan sat beside his wife, his expression grim. "We should have moved years ago."

"I know, but I love this house."

He was as guilty as she. It was a big old place located on a quiet street in a respectable part of the city. Once, it had been a dark and lonely place, but Brenna had changed all that. She had brought light and color into his home just as she had brought it into his life.

He blew out a sigh that came from the very depths of his being. "We can't hide the truth from her forever."

"I'm afraid," Brenna said, clutching his hand. "This isn't like telling her she was adopted. That's normal. But what I am . . . what we are . . . what if she refuses to accept us? What if we disgust her? I can't bear the thought of losing her."

"I know." It was a fear he had lived with since the night Cara had wrapped her tiny, dimpled finger around his thumb and captured his heart and soul. He had rehearsed ways to tell her the truth over and over again in his mind, but how did you tell your only child that her mother and father were vampires, and that her mother was a witch? Telling Cara the truth would only lead to more questions, questions with ugly answers. There were parts of his past that he wanted to forget, parts of his existence best left unmentioned. He could lie to her, of course, sugarcoat the truth, leave out the gruesome details, but there was always a chance, however unlikely, that she would learn about it later, and that would be even worse.

Vince stood in the deepening shadows across the street from a house big enough and fancy enough to qualify as a mansion. He had followed Cara home, not because of any dark or depraved intentions, but simply because he was bored and she was pretty and he was curious to see where she lived.

He had been surprised to find that he wasn't the only one who followed her from The Nocturne.

A man built like a bull had followed her out of the parking lot in a silver Lexus.

The jerk from the nightclub had followed her in a gray BMW.

Vince had brought up the rear in a hopped-up black Mustang convertible.

The first man had followed her through a wrought-iron gate and up to the house.

The jerk with the BMW was standing directly across the street from the driveway, studying the upstairs windows.

Vince stood a little farther down the road, his curiosity growing by the minute.

Keeping to the shadows, he crossed the street and vaulted over the wall that surrounded the property. Dissolving into mist, he drifted up the driveway to the house. He was about to peer into one of the windows when waves of preternatural power swept over him.

Apparently he wasn't the only vampire around.

He floated up through the air and hovered over a second-story balcony. He sensed Cara in the room beyond. Materializing, he listened at the door. He could hear her moving around inside, perhaps getting ready for bed.

He was about to leave when Cara opened one of the French doors.

For a moment, the two of them stood there, staring at each other.

"You!" she exclaimed. "What are you doing here?"

"I followed you home," he said, thinking quickly. "I noticed two other guys following you out of the club, and . . . I wanted to make sure you got home safely."

"Two guys?" she asked, obviously not believing him. "What two guys?"

"A really big character and that jerk who stood you up." Mr. BMW had hung back far enough to keep from being seen by either Cara or the big guy in the Lexus.

Cara crossed her arms under her breasts. "He didn't stand me up," she retorted. "Anyway, I don't believe he followed me home."

"Believe what you want," Vince said with a shrug. "I just wanted to make sure you were all right."

She stared at him a minute, as if making up her mind whether to believe him or not, and then frowned. "How did you get through the gate?"

Damn, he thought, she had him there. The wrought-iron gate was set in the high stone wall that surrounded the house. It could only be opened electronically, and it had been locked, so he'd vaulted over the wall, just like Superman.

"Well?" She tapped her foot on the floor, waiting to catch him in a lie.

"I ducked inside behind the big guy's car. Who is he, anyway? Not your father?"

"He's my bodyguard, and he'll break you in half if he finds you here."

"Then I hope you won't call him."

Cara laughed in spite of herself. "You're despicable."

"So I've been told."

He was too close. Even though they weren't touching, she was aware of the attraction that hummed between them. It was primal, sensual, and a little scary. He felt it, too. She could see it in his eyes, feel it in the tension that hummed between them, so thick it was almost palpable.

She should go back inside and lock the door. She should have him arrested for trespassing. She should call her father. She didn't do any of those things and she wasn't sure why, except that she was attracted to him in a way she didn't understand. Beyond that, she was grateful to him for bringing a bit of excitement into her otherwise unexciting life. You only had to look at him to know he was the kind of man mothers warned their daughters about, thereby making them more appealing—and he was very appealing, with his long black hair and tight-fitting jeans.

"As long as you're here, you might as well sit down," she said, gesturing at one of the deck chairs.

"Thanks."

He sat where she indicated, and she sat in the chair across from him. She wondered what her father would do if he came to check on her again and found her sitting out here with a stranger, then shrugged her worries aside. Her father had already checked on her once; he wasn't likely to return at this time of the night.

Cara bit down on the inside corner of her bottom lip. Now that she had invited Vince to stay, she was at a loss for words. She was basically shy around strangers and had never been any good at making small talk.

Searching for a safe topic of conversation, she said, "Tell me about yourself. I don't even know your last name."

"It's Cordova," he said. "As for my life story, there's not much to tell. I'm a mechanic. I own my own shop. I've got three brothers, a sister, and a bad-tempered cat."

"A cat? Most guys don't like cats."

"I don't like this one, either."

"Then why do you have it?"

"Somebody ran it over. I found it in some bushes, half dead. I couldn't just leave it there." He didn't tell her that the cat had turned up the night after he'd been made, or that, driven by an unholy hunger, he had licked the blood from the cat's wounds. Surprisingly, the cat had recovered. "What about you?" he asked, glancing around. " It's obvious that your folks are well-off. I guess that explains the bodyguard."

She regarded him warily. What if Vince wasn't the nice, easygoing guy he seemed to be? What if he was only showing interest in her because he knew her father was rich? What if he had come in hopes of kidnapping her and holding her for ransom? What if he was a robber, or a murderer, or worse? Maybe she did need a bodyguard!

"I think you'd better go," she said, hating the sudden tremor in her voice. She told herself there was nothing to be afraid of. One scream would rouse the household and bring Di Giorgio and her father running.

"Did I say something wrong?" Vince asked, frowning.

"Why did you really come here?"

His gaze moved over her, as hot and tangible as a summer breeze. "Because I was afraid you might never come back to the club, and I'd never see you again."

At his words, Cara's heart skipped a beat.

"I know we've just met," Vince said, "and you have no reason to believe me, or trust me, but . . ." He shook his head. "I just wanted to see you again."

Right or wrong, foolish or not, she believed him.

Vince gained his feet. "I'm sorry if I was out of line. Go on back inside. I'll leave and you'll never see me again."

She stared up at him, her heart pounding, and then she whispered, "Don't go."

Chapter 5

As soon as she uttered the words, Cara had second thoughts. What was she doing? Vince was a stranger to her. They had shared nothing more than a drink and a dance in a nightclub. She knew nothing about him save what he had told her, and for all she knew, everything he'd said could be a lie. How many times had her father and mother warned her to be careful of strangers?

She bit down on her lower lip. Maybe she was an idiot; maybe she was no better than those foolish girls who got into cars with guys they didn't know and then wound up dead in a ditch with no one to blame but themselves.

She lifted her gaze to his. If eyes were the windows to the soul, then his soul was dark and haunted, and yet she had no sense of being in danger. He might be dangerous, she thought, but not to her. She had never been more certain of anything in her life.

"Cara." His voice was thick with an emotion she couldn't identify. "I think I'd better go."

"Why?" She reached out, as if to stop him, then let her hand fall to her side.

"It's late. You should get some rest."

"You, too. You probably have to open your shop early in the morning."

He didn't answer, but merely grunted softly.

"Will you be at The Nocturne tomorrow night?" she asked.

A faint smile played over his lips. "I will if you will."

"I'll be there." As if drawn by an invisible hand, she took a step toward him.

He moved toward her, his gaze burning into hers. "What time?"

"Nine-thirty." They were only a breath apart now.

"Nine-thirty," he repeated. "I'll see you then."

Heart pounding so loud she was sure he could hear it, she waited for him to kiss her.

Instead, he turned and walked away.

Cara stared after him as he went down the winding staircase, disappointed that he hadn't kissed her good night. It wasn't until he disappeared into the shadows that she wondered how he was going to get through the gate.

Vince ghosted through the darkness to where he had left his car. He noted in passing that the man, Anton, had gone. Anton. There was something about the man that rubbed Vince the wrong way. Of course, it might be nothing more than a bad case of good, old-fashioned jealousy, but he didn't think so. There was something dark and sinister about the man.

Vince laughed. Dark and sinister. That was rich! There weren't many things walking around that were darker or more sinister than what he himself had become.

Vince the vampire. Even now, almost a year later, he still couldn't believe what had happened to him.

He slid behind the wheel of the Mustang and pulled away from the curb. Vampire. He supposed he had been like everyone else on the planet, assuming vampires were creatures of myth and legend, until the night he had the misfortune to pick up the wrong chick. He shook his head. She hadn't looked like a vampire, he thought glumly, let alone one that was thousands of years old! She'd had the body of a siren and the face of an angel, and he'd been helpless to resist her.

He laughed softly, bitterly. As the old saying went, he had chased her until she caught him. They had been in the middle of the best sex he'd ever had when she'd sunk her fangs into his throat. That was his first hint that she wasn't an ordinary female. The second had come when he tried to fight her off. She was just a little thing, hardly more than five feet tall, and couldn't have weighed more than a hundred pounds soaking wet, but she'd held him down with one hand, and when he had gotten desperate and drove his fist into her face, she had laughed at him. Then she had drained him to the point of death and given him a choice—live or die.

Looking back, he wondered if he would have chosen death if she had told him just what being a vampire entailed. Not that it was all that bad. True, he could no longer eat brunch with his folks on Sundays, but his senses were so acute he could hear the flutter of a moth's wings. He couldn't go surfing early in the morning anymore, but he could bench-press a bus. And even though he couldn't go outside during the day, he'd been surprised to discover that he wasn't compelled to sleep when the sun was up. He wasn't sure why. He had even doubted that he was a true vampire until he foolishly went outside one morning. That was a mistake he hadn't made again. The sun had burned him like acid. He was weak during the day, and so he usually rested until early afternoon and did the brunt of his work after dark. Even drinking blood wasn't as bad as he had expected it would be. Bad? Hah! It was like the nectar of the gods.

And there was no denying the thrill of the hunt. At first, he had been shocked and shamed by the kick he got out of it, but that hadn't lasted long. There was nothing else like it, finding prey, smelling their fear, knowing that you held their life in your hands, that you could take only what you needed to survive or you could drain them to the point of death. He had done that only once, but he had never forgotten the ecstasy of drinking a human life, of absorbing the man's essence, listening to the beat of his prey's heart grow weaker as his own grew stronger. As exhilarating as it had been, he had never done it again, afraid that if he did, he would turn into the kind of ravening monster that vampires were reputed to be. It was hard enough to hang on to what remained of his humanity.

The only real downside to being a vampire had been moving away from his family. They had always been a close-knit bunch and he missed rough housing with his brothers and babysitting his nieces and nephews, but moving had seemed the easiest solution. He couldn't tell his kin what he had become and couldn't keep thinking up new excuses for why he didn't show up for brunch or why he couldn't eat dinner, or go to the park with his sister's kids, or watch his nephew play Little League anymore. It had just been easier to sell his business, move away, and start a new life. He'd hated to leave Georgia, but he'd had to move far enough away that his parents couldn't just hop in the car and drive over for a visit. It hadn't been easy leaving his friends behind, either, or starting a new life, especially a life with a lifestyle he didn't know anything about.

The other drawback to being Undead was finding things to do to pass the time late at night. He couldn't work all the time, and once the movies, the bowling alley, and the bars closed, there wasn't a whole heck of a lot to do except visit The Nocturne.

He parked the Mustang in the garage and lowered the iron security door. Cat was waiting for him at the bottom of the stairs. With a gravelly meow, the cat followed him upstairs. At one time, the room had been a large office, but Vince had converted it into a combination living room–bedroom. He no longer needed a kitchen, or much of anything else. He had furnished the place with a black leather sofa and chair, a coffee table, a couple of end tables, a home theater system with surround sound, and a stereo. He'd had the windows plastered over so he didn't have to worry about the sun finding him. As long as he avoided its light, he was safe inside. On really sunny days, he closed the security door and just left the side entrance open. Satellite TV and a couple hundred DVDs provided entertainment in the wee hours of the morning.

He turned on the TV, and even though the volume was turned low, he could hear it perfectly.

Dropping down on the sofa, he stared at the screen; his thoughts turned inward as he idly scratched Cat's ears. He had been an easygoing guy not too long ago. He'd had friends, played softball on the local team once a week, gone dirt biking with his buddies, had his share of women. He grinned inwardly. Maybe more than his share. Of course, all that had changed when he did.

He had left all his old friends behind because it was easier to move than try to explain the unexplainable. He didn't really trust himself with women, though they seemed to gravitate toward him more than ever. Since becoming a vampire, he could have scored every night, but he had no interest in meaningless sex. Of course, it made satisfying his other hunger easier. Talk about a quickie! He smiled at the women who came on to him, mesmerized them, took what he needed to satisfy his hellish thirst, and sent them on their way, none the wiser.

But Cara was different. He didn't want to drink from her . . . well, he did, but that wasn't all he wanted. There was something about her that called to him. For all that she had money and lived with parents who seemed to love her, he sensed she was just as lonely as he was.

And she lived with vampires.

He mulled that over for a time, wondering if the vampires were her parents, and if so, how such a thing could be possible. He'd been told that the Undead couldn't create life, but if they weren't her parents, who were they?

Cara. She occupied his thoughts until the rising of the sun made his mind and body sluggish and he sought his bed for a few hours' sleep.

He would see her later, after the sun went down.

Smiling, he closed his eyes and took his rest.

Cara woke the next morning with a smile on her face and a fluttery feeling in the pit of her stomach. Tonight, she would see Vince. She giggled at the thought. Was this what it was like to be in love? She bounded out of bed and then, arms outstretched, she twirled around and around, then fell back on the bed again. She was going to see Vince in . . . she glanced at the clock and groaned. It was only ten-thirty! Eleven hours until she would see him. If she knew where he worked, she could stop in and surprise him, she thought, and then sighed. He might not like that. Some men didn't like to be bothered at work, so it was probably just as well that she didn't know where his shop was.

She took a quick shower, dressed, and went downstairs to fix breakfast. As usual, the house was quiet. The words "quiet as a tomb" whispered through the back of her mind. Frowning, she wondered where that thought had come from.

She read the paper while she ate a leisurely breakfast, then lingered over a cup of coffee. After putting her dishes in the dishwasher, she went upstairs to brush her teeth and put on her makeup.

Di Giorgio was waiting for her when she went out to the garage. He nodded at her, then got into his car and followed her to the library.

She had often wondered what her parents paid him to be her bodyguard. He rarely got a day off. It had to be the most boring job in the world, following her around, sitting in the library when she was at work, sitting outside her house on her days off. She doubted he had much of a social life. He certainly wasn't married. After all, what woman would be content with a husband that was hardly ever home? She suddenly felt ashamed of herself. Di Giorgio had been her bodyguard since she was twelve years old and she didn't know a thing about him except that he had come to the United States from Sicily when he was in his mid-twenties. She had always thought of him as a necessary evil, like going to the dentist.

She pulled into her parking space, waved at Di Giorgio as she got out of the car, and almost laughed out loud at the surprised look on his face. She vowed then and there to be nicer to him in the future.

She nodded at the other workers as she moved through the library. They were a nice bunch of ladies. Most of them were in their forties or fifties and they all mothered her. A couple of them flirted with Frank. They grilled her about his private life and asked her to give Frank their phone numbers. Cara found it amusing. Secretly, she wished that Frank would call Mary Garfield, but Frank didn't seem interested in Mary or any of the other women.

Cara spent the better part of the afternoon returning books to the proper shelves. As the day wore on, she caught herself constantly looking at the clock.

"You must have a big date tonight," Sarah Beth Coleman remarked with a smile. Sarah Beth was Cara's best friend. She was married to a police officer and pregnant with their first child.

"Why do you say that?"

"I've never known you to be a clock-watcher before. Have you met someone new?"

The ladies in the library were always asking her that,

hoping she would find a "nice young man" and settle down.

"I have," Cara said, unable to keep from smiling at the mere thought of him.

Sarah Beth took her by the hand and drew her deeper into the stacks. "What's his name? What's he like? When do I get to meet him?

Cara laughed. "I really don't know anything about him. I just met him last night, but he seems wonderful. He's so nice, and so handsome . . ."

"Sounds like love at first sight to me," Sarah Beth said with a teasing grin.

"Was that how it was with you and Dean?"

Sarah Beth nodded. "Yes. I took one look at him and I knew he was the one."

"I'm meeting Vince tonight after work. I can hardly wait."

Sarah Beth gave her a quick hug. "I'll expect a full report tomorrow."

Around eight-thirty, things slowed down. Cara sat at her desk, idly drawing hearts and writing her name and Vince's inside. It was such a high-school kind of thing to do, but she couldn't seem to stop, couldn't help noticing how well their names looked together. She drew a new heart and wrote Mr. and Mrs. Cordova inside.

Vince. She didn't know anything about him except how he made her feel.

At five minutes to nine, she cleared her desk and grabbed her coat, told the ladies good night, and practically bolted out the door. Frank Di Giorgio wasn't far behind.

It was nine-thirteen when she pulled up in front of The Nocturne. No doubt she would get a serious lecture from Di Giorgio about the dangers of speeding sometime in the near future, but she'd worry about that later.

Looking in the rearview mirror, she applied fresh lipstick, ran a brush through her hair, took a deep breath, and then got out of the car.

Di Giorgio followed her as she walked under the black canopy and down the stairs. The man in the hooded black cloak looked her over carefully, then murmured, "Welcome back, mistress."

Cara smiled faintly, thinking his raspy voice sounded like it belonged to someone who had been dead for a hundred years.

She stopped inside the entrance, letting her eyes adjust to the dim light, then walked around the edge of the dance floor to the bar. There was a vacant stool at the end and she sat down, her gaze moving around the room.

What if he didn't show up?

"Hey, it's about time you got here."

Startled, she almost fell off the bar stool. "Vince! Where did you come from?"

"My mama?"

"Very funny. How did you sneak up on me like that?"

"Dunno. Just quiet on my feet, I guess." He smiled a roguish smile. "You're early."

"So are you."

"I know. I couldn't wait." His gaze moved over her from head to foot. She looked good enough to eat, he thought. Literally. She smelled good, too, like a fragrant breeze on a warm summer day.

"Me, either."

"How was your day?" he asked.

"Not very productive. I kept returning books to the wrong shelf."

"Why is that?"

Her gaze slid away from his. "I couldn't concentrate. All I could think about was meeting you."

"Ah, Cara."

She looked up at him, her eyes wide and innocent. Damn, he wanted to take her home and make love to her all night long, and that was just wrong, because she wasn't the kind of girl to settle for a one-night stand and he couldn't offer her any more than that.

Damn! What was he doing here? There was no way they could have any kind of relationship. She was everything that was good and pure and he . . . he should be staked for what he was thinking!

"Vince, what's wrong?"

"Nothing."

"Did I say something to make you mad?"

"No, darlin'."

Darlin'. The word wrapped around her like a warm blanket on a cold night. No one had ever called her darlin' before.

Vince muttered an oath. He had to end this now, before he did something he would regret for the rest of his life—and that could be a hell of a long time. "I've got to go."

"Go?" She looked up at him. "But I thought . . ."

The disappointment in her eyes was like a dagger piercing his soul. "I'm sorry, Cara. I . . ." Dammit, what could he say to wipe that little girl lost look from her eyes?

"It's all right," she said quickly, and he could almost see her defensive walls springing into place.

"Cara, listen . . ."

"Hey, Cara, I was hoping you'd be here."

Turning her back on Vince, she pasted a smile of welcome on her face. "Hello, Anton. It's *so* good to see you," she said with feigned enthusiasm.

Vince ground his back teeth together. Damn the man. The jerk's timing couldn't have been worse.

"Cara . . ." Vince laid his hand on her arm.

She glanced at him over her shoulder. "Oh, are you still here? I thought you were leaving."

Vince nodded. Maybe it was better this way. Turning on his heel, he stalked out of the club.

Cara stared after him a moment, the ache she felt inside

almost too much to bear. She had spent the whole day looking forward to being with Vince. She had hoped . . . what
had she hoped? That he would be her knight in shining
armor? That he would fall head-over-heels in love with
her and carry her off to his castle? What a fool she had been.
Things like that only happened in fairy tales.

"It's a beautiful night," Anton remarked.

"What? Oh, yes, it is."

He ran his forefinger up and down her arm. "Would
you like to go for a drive?"

It was the last thing she wanted, but her bruised ego
wouldn't let her refuse. Vince Cordova might not want her,
but Anton found her attractive and wanted her company.

Forcing a smile, she said, "sure". Any second thoughts
she had about going out with Anton were put to rest by
the knowledge that Di Giorgio wouldn't be far behind.

Anton escorted her to his car, a late model BMW. Ever
the gentleman, he held the door for her before going
around to the driver's side.

A glance over her shoulder confirmed that Di Giorgio
was right behind them.

Anton tuned the radio to a station that played soft
rock, then leaned back, his arm resting along the back
of the seat. "Any place you'd like to go?"

"No."

"Are you in the mood for a hot fudge sundae? I know
a place that makes the best ones in town."

Determined to have a good time, she said, "Sounds
good to me." As any woman could tell you, chocolate
healed a multitude of hurts.

Cara frowned when he pulled up in front of a bookstore. "They sell ice cream here?"

"Among other things."

He got out of the car and came around to open her door.

"The Wiccan Heart," Cara murmured. "Are you into
witchcraft?"

"Who, me?" He shook his head. "I just like good ice cream."

She felt a shiver of unease as she stepped inside. She didn't know why. It was a lovely place, filled with books and trinkets, crystals and candles in a wide variety of colors. There was an old-fashioned soda fountain in the back corner, complete with stools covered in shiny red leather.

Cara sat down and Anton sat beside her. He smiled at the waitress. "Two hot fudge sundaes, Lucy Mae, and don't spare the chocolate."

"Whatever you want," Lucy Mae replied with a saucy grin. "Your mother was asking for you earlier. She wants you to call her at home."

"Okay, thanks." Anton grinned at Cara. "My mother owns the place," he explained with a wink.

"Oh. How nice."

"Sit tight. I'd better call and make sure she's okay."

"All right." Cara watched him walk to the other side of the room, pull out a cell phone, and punch in a number, and all the while she had the feeling she should get up and go home.

She was about to do just that when Anton returned.

Moments later, Lucy Mae placed two enormous hot fudge sundaes on the counter.

"Goodness!" Cara exclaimed. "I'll never be able to eat all that!"

"That's what you say now, but wait until you taste it."

It was everything he said it would be and more. "I've never tasted anything like this," she said, licking a bit of chocolate from her lower lip. "What do they put in it?"

"I could tell you, but then I'd have to kill you."

She knew he was joking, but his words sent an icy chill down her spine. She didn't know why, but she had always been superstitious about talking about death.

"So, tell me about yourself," Anton said. "All I really know about you is that you're a librarian, you like hot fudge sundaes, and you live at home. What are your parents like?"

"They're just parents like . . ." She started to say like everyone else's, but couldn't make herself say the words. "They worry about me and want what's best for me. I'm sure your mother is the same."

"My mother," he murmured. "Yes, of course."

"Is she a witch?"

"Why would you think that?" he asked, his voice gruff.

"No reason. I mean, well, it's a normal assumption, isn't it? I mean, she owns a Wiccan book shop, after all."

He laughed, but it sounded forced. "Witchcraft and the occult are all the rage now, that's all. If onions and artichokes are popular next year, she'll change the name and the decor."

Cara grinned. "I'd like to see that."

"I'd like to meet your parents," Anton said. "Any chance I could wheedle a dinner invitation for, say, Sunday?"

"No, I'm sorry."

"Some other night?"

She shook her head. "My parents don't entertain."

"Why not?"

"They just don't."

"That seems odd. I mean, they live in that huge old . . ."

Cara put her spoon down as she remembered something Vince had said. "Did you follow me home from The Nocturne the other night?"

"Me?"

"Did you?"

"Why would you think that?"

"Just answer me, yes or no. Did you?"

He shrugged. "What if I did? I just wanted to make sure you got home all right. Is that a crime?"

"No, but . . ."

"Lots of crazies hang out at The Nocturne. I was worried about you, that's all."

"You needn't worry. I'm perfectly safe wherever I go."

"Yeah? Why is that?"

"I have a bodyguard."

"You do? Why?"

"My parents are very protective."

"No sh . . . no kidding. I don't think I've ever dated a girl who had her own bodyguard." Anton glanced around the shop. "Where is he?"

"Probably peeking in a window somewhere. He's very discreet." She glanced toward the door when it opened, letting in a blast of cool air and two women wearing long gray cloaks.

Cara leaned closer to Anton. "Are they witches?"

"How would I know?"

"Well, they certainly look like witches." She glanced at her watch. "I should go, it's getting late."

"Since I can't convince you to invite me to dinner on Sunday, how about if I pick you up and take you out? Just one thing," he said with a grin, "your bodyguard has to pay for his own meal."

Cara considered it a moment. When she said yes, it was more to soothe her bruised ego than because she wanted to go out with Anton.

As they left the shop, Cara noticed the two gray-clad women with their heads together. She couldn't help wondering if they were talking about her.

Chapter 6

Serafina waited until Anton had gone to bed, and then she left the house, her destination Anthony's secret lab located in an abandoned brick building on the outskirts of town. The front door was made of heavy steel. The windows were boarded up on the inside and barred on the outside, but she had a key. After unlocking the door, she stepped inside, then closed the door behind her.

She wandered from room to room before entering Anthony's laboratory. Save for a new state-of-the art computer and printer that Anton had bought to replace his father's old ones, the lab was just as Anthony had left it. Serafina ran her hands over the glass jars and test tubes, the beakers and flasks and funnels, and as she did so, she imagined she was touching him. She paused in front of a shelf that held several books on witchcraft, anatomy, and hematology. A small refrigerator, a microscope and an incubator shared space on a counter that stretched across half of one wall. A large gray metal file cabinet stood on one side of the door. A circle of power had been drawn on the floor in the center of the room. A gray metal table stood in the middle of the circle. A splotch of blood, now a dark, ugly brown, stained the floor.

She moved around the room, walking where he had walked, touching what he had touched. She didn't know what had happened the night her beloved Anthony died, but from reading his notes, she was certain that Roshan De-Longpre and his witch wife had been involved.

The story of Anthony's death had made all the papers. Speculation ran wild as to the cause of his demise and what had happened in the house the night he died. Myra's body had been found cocooned in plastic. There had been blood on the sheets on the bed, but it hadn't been Anthony's blood and it hadn't been Myra's. The newspapers had had a field day. The headlines screamed, "Witches Run Amok in City."

She had crossed the yellow police tape under cover of darkness, gathered up all of Anthony's journals, personal effects, and clothing, and taken them home. After the funeral, she had placed an enchantment on one of the gravediggers, directing him to return that night, dig up Anthony's coffin, and transport it to Anthony's lab where a stone crypt waited. When it was done, she had erased the memory from the man's mind and sent him on his way.

Nights when she was lonely for her beloved, she came here to the lab to talk to him. If only he had discovered the secret of immortality, he would be with her now.

She made her way down a flight of stairs and unlocked the door to a large, windowless room that had once been used for storage. Anthony's tomb rested inside. Sometimes she opened the coffin and looked at him, and when she did, she saw him as he had been in life.

"Where are you now?" she murmured "Is your soul still in Summerland?"

She wondered if he was resting peacefully, recovering from the trials of his most recent life, or if he was reflecting on all the lives he had lived in the past. Perhaps he had rested long enough and he was already planning his next incarnation.

Hopefully he had not already been reincarnated. If so, her spell would most certainly fail.

The thought brought tears to her eyes. Sitting on the floor, she laid her head on his tomb and wept.

Chapter 7

Vince moved silently through the dark city streets. Who would have thought that being immortal would be boring? He had always been a night person, but this was ridiculous. He hadn't expected to miss ordinary things like eating a hamburger or just walking down a sunny street. Not that he had taken that many walks when he had the chance, but he sure as hell missed it now that it wasn't an option.

His thoughts turned to Cara, as they so often did of late. She had brought a little color into his world, made him yearn for a normal life. He wondered where she was, what she was doing.

Almost without conscious thought, he found himself standing on the balcony outside her room. His senses told him the vampires who lived here weren't home, and he wondered again how a mortal happened to be living with the Undead. Was she their daughter? Had they been turned after she was born?

One of the French doors leading into her bedroom was partially open. Prevented by some vampire mumbo jumbo from entering without an invitation, he peered into her room. She was in bed, lying on her side facing his way, one hand tucked beneath her cheek. Her hair fell over her shoulder like a river of molten gold.

She made a small, sleepy sound and rolled onto her back, and he knew she was awake.

Cara bolted upright, her gaze darting around the room. "Who's there?"

"It's me, Vince."

"Vince! What are you doing out there?"

"I came to apologize for hurting your feelings the other night."

She folded her arms across her breasts. "I don't know what you're talking about."

"Don't you?"

"No. I think you'd better go."

"Is that what you want?"

"No." The word was little more than a whisper. She peered at him through the darkness. What was there about him that attracted her so? She hardly knew him, yet he had been constantly in her thoughts since the moment they met. "My father will have a heart attack if he comes in and finds you out there."

"I doubt it," he said dryly. "Besides, he's not home."

"How do you know?" She glanced at the clock beside her bed. It was three AM. Where would her father be at such an hour?

She thought Vince shrugged, though she couldn't be sure. It was silly to sit here in the dark, she thought, and turned on the light on the bedside table. "You might as well come in."

"You sure?"

"I'm sure."

He pushed the door open all the way and stepped inside.

Cara looked up at him, her eyes widening. "You're bleeding!"

"What?"

"There," she said, pointing, "on your lower lip."

He wiped it away, thinking he would have to be more careful when he fed in the future. "I guess it's too late to go for a walk."

She laughed softly. "Just a little. Besides, I'm not dressed for a midnight stroll."

"Can I see you tomorrow night?"

"I'd like that."

He liked it that she didn't play hard to get, and that she didn't hold a grudge for the shoddy way he had treated her at the club. "What time should I pick you up?"

"Nine, at the library."

"What are you, a bookworm?"

"No, I'm a librarian."

"Really? I don't think I've ever met a librarian before."

"I love books. It's the perfect place to work."

"So, what does a librarian do?"

"Since our library is small, I do a little bit of everything."

"Like what?"

"Well, I read book reviews and publishers' announcements and catalogues to keep informed on current literature. I buy books from publishers and distributors. I keep an eye on Sarah Beth, who's my assistant, and make sure she keeps our database up to date. I'm in charge of the story hour, and sometimes I invite authors to come and speak. When there's nothing else to do, I help put books away."

"Sounds like you're pretty busy."

"Most of the time, but I like it that way."

He nodded. "So, where would you like to go tomorrow night?"

"Any place is fine with me."

"How about a late movie?"

She nodded. She didn't care where they went, so long as they were together. She gazed up at him, willing him to kiss her, disappointed once again when he didn't.

Tomorrow night, she thought; she would get that kiss tomorrow night or know the reason why!

Roshan paused in the shadows and drew his wife into his arms. "It's a beautiful night. Why do you look so glum?"

"I'm worried about Cara."

"Still?"

"I can't shake the feeling that something terrible is going to happen."

"What do you mean?" He had great respect for his wife's intuition. "Is she in danger?"

"I don't know. I just have this bad feeling and I can't shake it. It's dark energy . . ." She shivered. "Like Loken's. I always felt dirty when I was around him and that's how this feels." She looked up at him, her eyes wide and scared. "You don't think he's come back from the dead?"

"Brenna."

"I know, I'm being silly, but . . . I want to go out to the lab."

"Why?"

"I just need to see it, to prove he's not there."

"All right, if it will make you feel better."

A thought took them across town to the laboratory. Roshan sensed the magical energy that surrounded the place immediately.

"Someone's been out here," he said. "They've put a protective spell around the building."

"Can we cross it?" Brenna asked.

"I don't know."

He dissolved into mist and tried to slip under the door, but the spell was strong and it pushed him out. After resuming his own form, he walked around the perimeter of the building. In addition to the protective spell, the threshold shimmered with power. The lab wasn't a home, but someone loved the building and what it contained. Combined with the protective spell, it made a powerful, impassable barrier, one he couldn't cross even though he had been there before.

"Now I'm really worried," Brenna said. "Who would be interested in this place?" She frowned thoughtfully. Who indeed? Before Myra had showed her true colors, Brenna had spent a lot of time in her bookstore. Brenna had seen the way Serafina Bouchard looked at Anthony Loken when she thought no one was watching, but that seemed pretty far-fetched. Loken had been dead for over twenty years. That was a long time to carry a torch, especially for a dead man.

"Come on," Roshan said, taking her by the hand, "let's go home and check on our girl."

Cara was sleeping peacefully, as Roshan had known she would be. He was about to leave the room when his nostrils twitched with the scent of vampire.

Hands clenched, he glanced around the room. Not only was there a new vampire in his city, but the man had been in his house—in his daughter's bedroom, this very night.

Moving closer to the bed, Roshan examined Cara's throat and neck, relieved that there were no telltale bite marks. Of course, not all vampires drank from the same place. Some preferred a vein in the wrist, others liked the inside of an elbow, or the inner thigh where the marks were not so obvious.

Leaving the room, he went downstairs to tell Brenna to keep listening to her feelings.

Eager to see Vince again, Cara was waiting outside the library when he drove up the following night. "Wow," she exclaimed, "nice car!"

"Thanks."

"I guess I shouldn't be surprised, since you own a garage. Where is it, anyway?"

He didn't want to tell her, didn't want her dropping by some afternoon or morning when he was taking his rest and wondering why he wasn't at work. Not that he couldn't come up with a plausible fib if he had to, but he didn't want to lie to her. "Over on Seventh and East Streets."

He opened the door for her, then slid behind the wheel. "I checked the paper. The late show starts at nine-twenty. I figure that gives us just enough time to get there."

Cara nodded, her gaze moving over him. Tonight he wore a long black coat over a white shirt and black jeans.

He was the most handsome man she had ever met. Just looking at him stirred a longing deep within her.

Vince pulled into the parking lot a few minutes later, bought two tickets, and handed them to the guy inside the door. He was walking down the corridor toward the theater when he noticed Cara wasn't with him.

He was turning around to look for her when she tapped him on the shoulder.

"I'm a little hungry," she said. "I think I'll get some pop-corn."

"Hey, you're with me. I'll buy. What do you want to drink?"

"Lemonade."

He put in her order, paid for it, and followed her down the aisle to theater number three. They found two seats in the back.

The lights went down and the theater closed in on him. So many beating hearts. The scent of blood flowing through a hundred veins. The stink of popcorn and candy and soda. It was like being on sensory overload. He wondered if he would ever get used to it. He wondered about so many things that had to do with his new lifestyle—death-style? Whatever they called it.

"Do you want some popcorn?" she asked.

"No, thanks."

"Lemonade?"

"Too sweet."

"Sorry."

"It's okay, I'm fine."

Numerous commercials and previews flashed across the screen before the movie started.

He couldn't really concentrate on what he was watch-ing. He was all too aware of the woman beside him. Every breath she took, every beat of her heart resonated in his being. Even though there were a hundred other people in the theater, his senses honed in on Cara—the scent of her shampoo and soap, the flowery fragrance that clung to her hair, the fried chicken she'd eaten for dinner, the hot buttery popcorn on her breath. But overall, the sweet scent of her life's blood called to him. It would be so easy to take. If he leaned toward her just a little, and tilted his head just so . . .

Damn! What was he thinking?

He shifted in his seat. Maybe this hadn't been such a good idea, after all! He glanced up at the screen and prayed that the movie would soon be over because he needed to put some space between them pretty darn quick.

Whispering, "I'll be right back," he practically bolted out of his seat.

He went to the entrance of the theater, opened the door, and took several slow, deep breaths. Better, he thought, that was better. Breathe in. Breathe out. In. Out. He would be fine now. He wondered if there was a way to block all the sensory input that plagued his every waking moment, and if it was possible, how long it took to master such a thing. All in all, he liked being immortal. He liked the fact that he was impervious to practically everything, that wounds healed overnight, that he could move faster than the human eye could follow. He liked his preternatural senses, too; he just wanted to be able to control them. What he needed was a guidebook for new vampires. He had looked for one online but with no luck. Hell, maybe he should write one!

After taking a last deep breath of fresh air, he returned to his seat.

"About time you got back," she whispered. "I was beginning to think you found another date. What kept you so long?"

"Sorry, darlin'. It won't happen again."

"See that it doesn't," she said, and then she smiled at him.

Slipping his arm around her shoulders, Vince knew he would do just about anything to have her smile at him like that just once a day for the rest of his existence. That sobered him. Barring some unforeseen accident, he would be around a lot longer than she would. The thought depressed the heck out of him. He hardly knew her and he already couldn't imagine the world without her in it.

"It was a good movie, wasn't it?" Cara remarked as they left the theater.

"Yeah." To tell the truth, he didn't really know. He had spent the last half of the movie thinking about how dreary the world would be when she was gone. But she was still young, he thought, looking on the bright side. She would be around for a good long time.

"I love movies," she said. "I think I'd go every night if I could."

"Every night?" He shook his head. "You really are a movie junkie."

"And a book junkie," she said, grinning. "And a chocolate junkie. And a computer junkie. So, what do you like?"

"My Mustang." They were standing beside it now, and he patted the roof.

"That's it? You don't like anything but your car?"

His gaze moved over her, long and slow. "I can think of one or two other things," he said with a wicked grin.

Cara felt her cheeks grow hot under his sensual gaze. She cleared her throat. "Like what?" she asked breathlessly.

"Like hair the color of spun gold, and eyes the color of a peaceful mountain lake, and a smile that's brighter than the sun."

"I had no idea you were a poet."

"I'm not."

He opened the door for her, then walked around to the other side and slid behind the wheel.

"Do you want to go home?" he asked.

"Not really, why?"

"I thought we could go for a drive."

"I'd like that."

He started the car and the engine came to life with a low growl. Once he got out of town, he found a long straightaway and goosed it up.

It was like flying, Cara thought, one hand clutching the edge of her seat.

"Do you want me to slow down?" he asked.

"No, I love it!"

"Hang on!"

It was exhilarating, flying through the dark night. She knew it was an incredibly stupid thing to do. A flat tire, a rut in the road, a skid, anything could be fatal at this speed, but it felt wonderful and a little bit wicked.

Vince muttered an oath when he heard the siren. A glance in the rearview mirror showed flashing red lights coming up fast behind him.

Had he been alone, he might have tried to outrun the law, but not when Cara was with him. He had already put her life in danger by driving like some reckless teenager.

He pulled off the road, rolled down the window, and waited.

A cop approached him a moment later. "Can I see your driver's license, sir?"

Vince had it out and ready.

The cop looked it over, then shined his flashlight in Vince's face. "Do you know how fast you were going back there?"

"Yes, sir."

The cop tucked his flashlight under his arm and flipped open his ticket book. "This is going to cost you big bucks."

"Officer, you really don't want to give me a ticket."

The cop looked at him. "Is that right?"

"That's right." Vince gazed deep into the cop's eyes. "A warning will do just as well this time, don't you think?"

"Yes," the cop said, nodding. "A warning will do just as well this time." He closed his ticket book. "Have a nice evening, folks."

"Thank you, officer."

Cara stared at Vince, her eyes wide. "How did you do that?"

"I don't know. Just my winning personality, I guess."

She laughed. "You are so lucky. I'll bet that ticket would have cost you at least four hundred dollars."

"At least."

After pulling onto the road again, he drove a mile or two and then turned off on a one-lane dirt road flanked by shrubs and tall trees.

Cara glanced around, a little shiver of unease snaking down her spine. Was she going to be one of those girls who wound up dead in a ditch? "What are we doing here?"

"There's a pretty little pond down the road a ways. Not afraid of the dark, are you?"

"I don't know." She could hear the news flash now. Girl's body found in the woods. Film at eleven. She glanced over her shoulder. Where was Di Giorgio when she needed him?

Vince parked the car a few minutes later. He got out, then opened her door for her. "Come on," he said, offering her his hand. "You'll like it."

He led her down a narrow path that gradually grew wider and then she saw it, a small pond surrounded by luminous white sand. The light of the moon cast silver shadows on the face of the water. Night-blooming flowers and tall, lacy ferns added a fairy-like touch.

"It's lovely," she murmured, her fears forgotten in the beauty that surrounded them.

"Yeah."

"How did you ever find it?"

"Just happened upon it one night. I've been waiting for someone to share it with."

Taking off his duster, he spread it on the ground for her to sit on, then sat on the grass beside her.

"It's so quiet here," Cara said. "So peaceful. It's like we're the only two people in the whole world."

"I'd like that." He doubted if she would, he thought with morbid humor, since she would be his only source of food.

"Vince, wouldn't you like to kiss me?"

"Is that a trick question?"

"Well, wouldn't you?"

"Is that an invitation?"

"If you want it to be."

Scooting closer, he drew her into his arms. He held her for a moment, one hand stroking the silk of her hair before he lowered his head and claimed her lips with his. She tasted of butter and salt, popcorn and lemonade—and life. It flowed through her veins, thick and rich and red, whetting his appetite, arousing his desire. He deepened the kiss, easing her down to the ground so that they were lying side by side. He draped his arm over her waist, holding her close, basking in her nearness. The heat of her body warmed his own, and he held her closer.

She moaned softly, her body pressing more intimately against his.

"Careful," he warned, and kissed her again. Her lips were incredibly soft and sweet.

She gasped when his tongue found her own, whether from passion or surprise, he didn't know, though he had a feeling no one had ever kissed her so deeply before. The fact that she had never been with another man tempted him beyond reason and yet it was the one thing that protected her. He had done a lot of vile things in the last year, but thus far, he hadn't defiled a virgin.

Cara whimpered softly. She was drowning, she thought, drowning in a sea of pleasure unlike anything she had ever known. Vince was kissing her, just kissing her, and yet she felt the heat of his kisses clear down to her toes. She was on fire and only he could put out the flame. She writhed against him, her hands clutching his back, kneading his shoulders. She wriggled underneath him, groaned at the welcome weight of his body on hers. Cara had little experience with boys, and less with men. In high school, she had been a nerd. She had never had a real boyfriend. The only kisses she had ever received were from playing kissing games at parties, but none of those kisses had been in the same universe as this one.

She slid her hands under his shirt, her fingers exploring his broad back, the indentation of his spine, the shape of his shoulder blades. She wanted to feel his skin against hers, to touch him and taste him. She was about to suggest he take off his shirt when he sat up.

"What's wrong?" she asked.

"Someone's here."

Cara glanced around, but she couldn't see anything in the dark. "How do you know?"

"I can feel it." He sniffed the air. "It's your watch dog, Di Giorgio."

"Di Giorgio!" She bolted upright, her cheeks burning with embarrassment and then horror as she realized that Di Giorgio would report everything to her parents.

Vince stood and then offered Cara his hand.

"Did he see us?" she asked anxiously.

"Not yet."

She breathed a sigh of relief, and then frowned. "How do you even know he's here?"

"I can hear him. He's right over there," Vince said, pointing.

"I don't hear anything."

"Come on, I'd better take you back to the library to get your car."

"I don't want to go home."

"And I don't want you to go," Vince said, wrapping his arm around her shoulders.

But it was probably for the best.

Chapter 8

Roshan made an effort to keep his temper in check as he stared at his daughter. She sat on the sofa, her hands clasped in her lap. As always, he was amazed to have her in his life. He had never expected to have a daughter, had resigned himself to being childless, and then she had come into his life, enriching it beyond measure. The thought of losing her was beyond bearing.

"What were you thinking?" he asked quietly. "Going off into the woods with some man you don't even know? Merciful heavens, Cara, don't you ever listen to the news? It seems like every other night there's a story about some girl who's disappeared!"

"I'm sure none of them had bodyguards, Daddy!"

"Di Giorgio said you were out of his sight for a short time. It only takes a minute to snuff out a life."

Cara stared at her father. His eyes had gone hard and flat, and he spoke with such conviction that she might have thought he had taken a life or two himself if she hadn't known better. "I'm sorry."

Taking a step forward, Roshan placed his hand on her shoulder. "I'm sorry, too, Princess. I don't mean to scold. I know you're a big girl now. But you're also a beautiful girl, and men have been taking advantage of beautiful young girls since time began."

"I don't mean to worry you, but, oh, Daddy, I like him so much!"

"Which one is this? The one who drives the BMW or the one who drives the Mustang? Or someone new?"

"The one who drives the Mustang, Dad. His name is Vince, and he owns a garage over on Seventh Street and . . ."

"And you can't think about anything but him."

Cara smiled up at her father. "Yes."

"Sounds a little like love to me, Princess," Roshan replied, and felt a sudden ache deep in his heart. This was the first time he'd seen that look in her eye or heard the excitement of first love in her voice. He had always known the day would come when another man would appear to take her away from him. Was this the man?

"Does it? Was that how it was for you with Mom? Did you know, the very first time you saw her, that she was the one?"

Roshan nodded. He had been on the verge of destroying himself when he fell in love with Brenna Flanagan's picture. His need to know more about her, to find out who she was and where she had lived and how she had died, had become his sole reason for survival. She had quite literally saved his life. Ah, Brenna, was there ever another woman like her? She had given him a reason to go on living. She had given him a daughter . . .

He stroked Cara's cheek. "Are we going to meet this young man?"

"Do you want to?"

What he wanted to do was send the man far away, erase him from Cara's mind. He wasn't ready for his daughter to leave home, didn't think he would ever be ready, but it was the way of the world and so, with a smile, he said, "I think so."

"When?"

"Preferably before the wedding," he said dryly.

"Oh, Daddy!" She gave him a playful punch on the arm. "We aren't getting married. I hardly know him. We're just . . . you know, friends. How did you and Mom meet?"

"The first time I saw your mother, she was dancing. I took one look and I was smitten . . ."

"Smitten! Oh, Daddy, how melodramatic."

"But true, nonetheless. I saw her and I knew I had to have her."

"Smitten." Cara shook her head. "I don't think I've ever heard anyone actually use that word. Did Mom feel the same about you?"

"Not at first, but I soon won her over."

"I'm not surprised."

"No?"

"Of course not. You're very sexy. For an old man," she added with a grin.

Old, he thought. She had no idea. "So, when do we get to meet this new man in your life?"

She started to say Sunday, then remembered that she had a date with Anton and no way to contact him so she could break it, although she might be able to get in touch with him by calling his mother's bookstore. She frowned thoughtfully. She had no way to get in touch with Vince, either, unless she went by the garage. "I'll talk to Vince and get back to you."

"All right." Leaning forward, he kissed her cheek. "Good night, Princess."

"Night, Dad."

Roshan blew out a sigh as his daughter left the room. If centuries of experience had taught him anything, it was that nothing stayed the same, but this was one change he wasn't looking forward to.

Chapter 9

Serafina sat on the floor in the back of her shop, opening boxes. Since she had discovered eBay, every day was like Christmas. It was amazing, all the weird and wondrous things you could find for sale there. Of course, her passion was books. The boxes she was opening now contained a collection of books she had purchased from a seller on eBay who claimed that the books had originally belonged to the seller's great-great-grandmother, who had been a practicing witch.

Serafina removed the books from the boxes reverently. One by one, she thumbed through them, thrilled with what she saw. The books were indeed old and rare, some so old they had been written in longhand.

One especially caught her eye. It was a book of ancient mystical blood rituals. There were spells for curing warts and insomnia and for healing a variety of illnesses, most of which no longer existed. There were love spells, of course. What witch hadn't been approached for a charm that would win the love of another? The last part of the book was dedicated to dark Magick.

Serafina hesitated to turn the page. She had been taught that witchcraft should only be used for good, but curiosity finally won out. She turned the pages, scanning them quickly, until she came to the last page.

The words seemed to blur before her eyes.

An Incantation to Raise the Dead

On All Hallow's Eve, between dusk and dawn,
The blood of kin must be drawn,
Nine drops, no more, no less,
The blood of kin you must bless.

To this the blood of love you add,
And the blood of an enemy, it must be had.
Seven drops of each, one by one,
Quickly now, it must be done.

Four drops of a maiden's blood,
Rosemary for remembrance,
An infant's blood, three drops for life anew.
A sprinkling of yarrow, a dash of rue.

Spread the blood upon the crypt,
When the moon commands the sky.
Call forth the dead, his name times three,
Doubt not, and he will come to thee.

A shiver ran down her spine as she read the spell a second time. All Hallow's Eve. Among witches and warlocks, it was considered the most magical night of the year, a night of power, when the veil that separated this world from the world of spirits was at its thinnest.

She read the poem again. It seemed much too easy and yet, if it was remotely possible, All Hallow's Eve was the perfect night for such a spell. In ancient times, it was the one night in the year when the dead could return to the land of the living. In Ireland, burial mounds were opened and torches lit so the dead could find their way, though all had to return to their rightful place at sunrise.

But if her incantation worked, Anthony would not have to return to the Otherworld. She closed her eyes, her mind filling with images of her beloved. Was it truly possible to raise the dead? To see him again! He would surely love her then!

The blood of kin. Anton, of course. The blood of an enemy. Roshan or his wife, either would do. The blood of a maiden? Roshan's daughter. An infant's blood, and rosemary. The blood of love would be her own blood, of course, freely given.

Hugging herself, she imagined how wonderful it would be to see Anthony again, to hear his voice, see his smile. And how wonderful for Anton to finally meet his father!

All Hallow's Eve. She had only a few months to plan and prepare. It seemed too long, and not long enough.

Chapter 10

Cara slept late Saturday morning, her dreams troubled. First she was dancing at The Nocturne with Anton, then she was making out with Vince while Anton and her father watched. In the distance, a woman danced naked under a full moon, and standing behind the woman was another man. She couldn't see his face but evil poured out of him like thick black smoke. It engulfed the woman, then snaked along the ground, licking at Anton's ankles. Terror held her in place as the smoke's cold black breath drew closer. She had to get away! If the smoke touched her, she would die! She tried to scream but no sound emerged from her throat. Eerie laughter rose from the midst of the smoke. She looked to her father for help but he seemed unaware of the danger. She had to get away! Heart pounding, she opened her mouth, terror releasing the scream that had been trapped in her throat . . .

And woke to the sound of her own screams ringing in her ears.

Sitting up, she glanced around, relieved to find herself in her own room, in her own bed. She was relieved that it had only been a nightmare, though it had been the most realistic nightmare she'd ever had. For some reason, a nightmare she'd had as a child popped into her mind. It was a dream she remembered clearly, even after all these years. In her dream, she had gone into her parents' bedroom early in the morning and climbed into bed between them. She had tried to awaken them, but they hadn't moved, hadn't been breathing. Terrified to think that they were dead, she had run back to her own room and pulled the covers over her head. When she told her father about it later, he had assured her that it had only been a dream, but for the longest time, she had been convinced it had actually happened.

But dreams were dreams and couldn't hurt you. Shaking off the last vestiges of her nightmare, she got out of bed and headed for the bathroom.

She felt better when she emerged from her shower fifteen minutes later, her hair freshly washed. She dried her hair, applied her makeup, pulled on a pair of jeans and a sweater. She stripped the sheets from her bed, carried them downstairs, and put them in the wash.

As usual, the house was clean and quiet. She went into the kitchen in search of food, but she wasn't really hungry, so she opted for tea and toast.

When she finished eating, she washed her dishes, then sat at the kitchen table, wondering what to do the rest of the day. Cara usually worked on Saturday, but the library was closed today while the floors were being refinished and wouldn't open again until Tuesday.

Maybe she would drive into town and take in an early movie, or maybe she would go shopping—not that she needed anything. She had enough clothes and shoes to outfit a dozen women. Still, she liked shopping . . . and one of her favorite stores was located on Seventh Street, only a few blocks from Vince's garage.

Happiness bubbled up inside her at the thought of seeing him again. Before she could talk herself out of it, Cara grabbed her keys and her handbag and hurried out the door.

Di Giorgio's car followed her down the driveway.

She had butterflies in her stomach when she pulled up in front of Vince's garage. It was a large corner building, with the entrance on Seventh Street. She sat there a moment, wondering if he would be happy to see her. Maybe he wouldn't like her dropping in unannounced when he was working. Well, there was only one way to find out.

Taking the keys from the ignition, she got out of the car. There was a side door that led to an office. The door was closed. She discovered it was locked when she tried to open it. Maybe he was in the garage.

She walked around the corner to where the service bays were, but this door was closed, too. Perhaps he didn't work on Saturdays, or maybe he was out picking up car parts or out to lunch.

Shoulders slumped in disappointment, she returned to her car. She waved at Di Giorgio as she slid behind the wheel, then drove to her favorite dress shop where she picked out a slinky black dress for her next date with Vince, whenever that might be, and a pretty pink silk dress to wear Sunday night.

She drove by the garage again when she finished shopping, but it was still locked up tight. Heaving a sigh of disappointment, she motioned for Di Giorgio to pull up beside her.

"I'm bored," she said. "Do you want to go to a movie?"

"Whatever you want, Miss DeLongpre."

"Okay, come on. I'll buy the popcorn."

It was dusk when Cara returned home. The sound of the upstairs shower told her that her parents were awake.

She tossed her handbag and packages on the sofa, then went into the kitchen. She had stopped at her favorite Italian restaurant on the way home. She didn't like eating out of the take-home containers, so she transferred the lasagna to a plate, along with a couple of bread sticks, grabbed a soda from the fridge, and sat down to eat.

As usual of late, her thoughts turned to Vince. She had driven by his garage again after the movie, but he hadn't been there.

She was rinsing off her dishes when her mother entered the kitchen.

"Hi, Mom."

"Hello, darling. How was your day?"

"It was okay. I went shopping and then Frank and I went to the movies."

"And what did you buy?"

"A couple of dresses. Wanna see?"

"Of course."

Going into the living room, Cara opened the boxes and held up each dress in turn. "What do you think?"

"I think that black one could get you into all kinds of trouble," Brenna said. She motioned for Cara to come and sit beside her. "Your father tells me you're in love."

"I might be."

"Does he make your heart sing? Do you think about him every minute of the day?"

Cara nodded.

"Dream of him at night?"

Cara nodded again, and then frowned, remembering the horrible dream she'd had the night before.

"I hope we get to meet him soon."

"Me, too."

"Be careful, sweetheart. Don't go too fast. Do you know what I mean?"

"Mom, I'm a big girl. I don't need a lecture on sex."

Brenna took Cara's hand in hers and gave it a squeeze. "I guess I should have given it to you sooner. You just grew up so fast." She shrugged. "I just don't want you to get hurt."

"I know." Cara kissed her mother on the cheek. "Thanks, Mom."

"Your father and I are going out for a walk," Brenna said. "We won't be long. Are you going out tonight?"

"I don't think so."

"All right, dear. We'll be back soon. Maybe we can play cards or something."

"Okay."

Brenna hugged her daughter, then left the room. Roshan was waiting for her by the front door.

Outside, Brenna and Roshan moved quickly and silently through the shadows. The downtown district was always a good place to hunt. As usual, they chose a young couple, took what they needed, and sent the pair on their way.

"Cara's growing up," Brenna remarked as they strolled back toward home.

"I think she's grown," Roshan said dryly.

"I guess I mean she's maturing, changing. I can feel her distancing herself from us. I don't like it."

Roshan put his arm around his wife's shoulders and gave her a squeeze. "I don't, either, but there's nothing we can do about it." He wasn't sure what he would do to the man she fell in love with. The thought of any man taking her away . . . He knew it was the natural way of things, for a young woman to marry and leave home. He just wasn't sure he could allow it.

"Do you think we've been good parents?" Brenna asked. "Did I make a mistake, bringing her home all those years ago?"

"Here now, stop that. We've raised a beautiful, well-adjusted daughter. She's smart and resourceful, and . . ."

"But she doesn't really have any friends except for Sarah Beth. A young girl should have friends."

"Maybe it's time we let her invite people to the house."

Brenna's eyes widened. "Do you think that's wise?"

"Our lair is secure. I don't think there's anything to fear."

"Maybe you're right. Maybe we've been overly protective of her for nothing." She smiled up at him. "I want to share every moment we can with her, while we can."

Cara was surprised by her parents' announcement. "But why the sudden change?" she asked, unable to believe what she was hearing.

"Your mother and I have decided we were being selfish, refusing to let you invite your friends over."

"That's great, Mom. Dad." She hugged them both. Of course, she didn't really have any friends her age except for Sarah Beth. Most of the friends she'd had in high school had moved away or she had lost touch with them. Still, it was nice to know she could bring company home if the occasion ever arose. Company like Vince . . .

They were about to sit down and play Canasta when the doorbell rang. Roshan looked at Cara. "Are you expecting someone?"

"No."

Looking thoughtful, he went to answer the door.

Vince rang the bell again, thinking this was probably the stupidest thing he had ever done, but he had been yearning to see Cara since he woke that evening and the yearning had only grown stronger.

He fought down a sudden sense of panic as the door opened.

The vampire who answered the door was tall and lean with powerful shoulders and long limbs. His hair was as black as the ace of spades, his eyes a bold midnight blue set beneath straight black brows. His skin was pale though not sickly looking—more like that of a healthy man who didn't spend a lot of time in the sun. Preternatural power rolled off him in waves. Coming here suddenly seemed like a really bad idea.

"Who are you?" the vampire asked. "What are you doing here?"

Vince squared his shoulders and thrust out his chin.

He had the feeling the man could squash him with a look. It wasn't a feeling he liked.

"I'm Vince," he said, his tone more belligerent than he had intended. "I came to see Cara."

"Is my daughter expecting you?"

"No." Damn, Vince thought, he'd been right. The vampire was her father.

Roshan glanced over his shoulder to find Cara standing behind him, her eyes wide. Roshan swore under his breath. Of all the bad luck! He had no sooner told the girl she could have guests than one came calling, and not just any guest, but a vampire! And not just any vampire, but the one whose presence he had sensed before, the one who had been in Cara's room. He looked at his daughter, his eyes narrowing. Was there more going on here than Cara had told him? Did she know Vince was Nosferatu?

"Roshan?" Brenna called, coming up behind him, "what's going . . ." She came to an abrupt halt, her gaze moving quickly between her husband and the young man standing on the doorstep. "What's going on?"

"Nothing," Roshan replied curtly. "Cara has a visitor."

"Mom, Dad, this is Vince Cordova," Cara said, smiling as she moved toward the door. "I told you about him."

"Oh, dear," Brenna murmured.

"Is something wrong?" Cara asked. She looked from her parents to Vince and back again. Tension crackled in the air. It crawled over her skin like the tickle of static electricity, though she could find no reason for it.

"Cara, I should like a few minutes alone with your young man," Roshan said, his gaze still resting on Vince's face. "We'll join you shortly."

"Dad . . ."

"Come, Cara," Brenna said, and taking her daughter by the hand, she led her into the other room.

Roshan stepped out onto the front porch and closed the door behind him. He was immediately struck by the power of the young man standing in front of him. Though the man was young in the life, he exuded the strength of a much older vampire. Such power could only be passed on by the ancient ones. "Who made you?"

"I don't remember her name. It was kind of hit-and-run, if you know what I mean?"

"Was it Mara?"

Vince frowned. The name sounded familiar, but so much of that night was hazy in his mind "It might have been," he allowed. "Does it matter?"

Mara, of course, Roshan thought. She was the oldest of their kind, a law unto herself. No one knew how old she was, when she had been made, or who had made her. There was speculation that she had been made in the valley of the Nile during the reign of Cleopatra. It was said that she was truly immortal, that she was impervious to blade or stake, and, perhaps most amazing of all, that the sun no longer had any power over her.

"What are you doing here, in my town?" Roshan asked.

"Your town?"

"My town."

Vince shrugged. "I was passing through, saw it, liked it. You got a problem with that?"

"As a rule, I don't allow other vampires to reside in my territory, especially disrespectful young punks who don't ask my permission to stay."

"Well, pardon me all to hell. I didn't know I had to ask."

"Mind your manners, whelp. You've been one of us less than a year. You still have a lot to learn."

"How do you know that?"

"I know a lot of things," Roshan retorted dryly. "I've been a vampire for over three hundred years."

"No shit."

"Have you no respect for your elders?"

Vince blew out a sigh. His mother would be ashamed

of him if she saw him now. He was a little ashamed himself. One thing was for certain, he wasn't making a good impression on Cara's father.

Meeting the other man's eyes, Vince muttered, "I'm sorry. Sir. I was out of line."

Roshan grunted softly. "What do you want with my daughter?"

"Not what you think."

"No?" Roshan's gaze burned into Vince's. "What were you doing in her room the other night?"

"Not what you're thinking!" Vince said emphatically.

Roshan's gaze bored into him, as if seeking the truth of his words.

"Dammit, we didn't do anything but talk."

"She doesn't know what you are, does she?" Roshan asked.

"No." Vince canted his head to one side. "She doesn't know what you are, either, does she?" He laughed softly. "I won't tell on you if you don't blow the whistle on me," he said, then frowned. "If you're over three hundred years old, she can't be your natural daughter." He still had a lot to learn about being a vampire, Vince mused, but if there was one thing he knew, it was that vampires couldn't create life.

"I want you to leave town," Roshan said. "Now. Tonight."

"And if I don't?" Vince lifted his chin and squared his shoulders, refusing to be cowed. He had come here to see Cara and, by damn, he was going to see her!

"I'll destroy you."

"Then do your worst, 'cause I'm not leaving. I'm in love with your daughter."

"And you're willing to die for her?"

"For her, with her, whatever."

In spite of himself, Roshan found himself admiring the young vampire's grit. "You'll bring her nothing but heartache."

"Shouldn't that be her decision?"

"If you hurt her . . ."

Vince held up his hands in a gesture of surrender. "I know, you'll destroy me."

"Without a qualm," Roshan said, though, if it came down to that, he wondered if he would emerge the victor. Though Cordova was young in the life, he exuded the power and arrogance of a much older vampire. Roshan held the younger man's gaze for stretched seconds and then, with a sigh of resignation, said, "Shall we go in?"

Cara was pacing the entry hall when her father entered the house. She felt relieved to see that her father hadn't scared Vince away. She couldn't keep her eyes off Vince as he walked toward her. He looked as handsome as sin in a pair of Levi's, a black T-shirt, and a dark sports jacket.

"We were about to play Canasta, Mr. Cordova," Brenna remarked. "Would you care to join us?"

"Sure. And it's Vince."

"Brenna," she said, smiling.

The atmosphere at the table was, to say the least, strained. At least it was between Cara's father and Vince. The tension was so thick between them, it was almost tangible. Cara had expected her father to be suspicious of any man she brought home, but this went way beyond that.

After a few hands, she asked Vince if he wanted a coke. When he declined, her father suggested a little red wine.

"Thanks," Vince said, "that sounds good."

"I'll have some, too," Brenna said with a smile. She turned to Vince. "So, tell us about yourself, won't you?"

"There's not much to tell," he replied good-naturedly.

"Have you been here long?"

"No."

"Where are you from originally?"

"Georgia."

"Ah, a southern boy," Brenna said, laughing softly.

"Yes, ma'am."

"Do you come from a large family?"

"I've got three brothers and a sister and about a dozen nieces and nephews."

"And a cat," Cara added.

Vince grinned at her. "And a cat."

"Your family sounds wonderful. I would have liked to have a large family," Brenna said wistfully. "But it never happened." She smiled at Cara. "I'm hoping for lots of grandchildren."

"Mom!"

"Cara tells me you're a mechanic," Roshan said, returning to the table with four glasses and a bottle of wine.

"That's right. You got a car that needs fixin'?"

"Not at the moment. How are things going?" After opening the bottle, Roshan filled a glass and handed it to Brenna.

"I'm doing all right," Vince said with a shrug.

"Are we going to play cards, or are you two going to give Vince the third degree all night?" Cara asked.

"You can hardly blame us for being curious," Brenna said. "After all, this is the first young man who's come calling."

"Mom!"

"Oh, I'm sorry, dear, was that a secret?"

Vince tried not to laugh, but he couldn't help it. The look of horror on Cara's face was priceless. He couldn't blame her parents for being curious about him. After all, he was dating their only daughter, and he was a vampire. He wasn't sure if that was a good thing in their eyes or not.

Roshan filled the other three wineglasses and resumed his seat.

Cara simply sat there, mortified by her mother's reference to grandchildren. What must Vince be thinking, and why had she ever thought having friends over would be a good idea?

At midnight, Vince took his leave.

Cara walked him to the door, then followed him outside. "I'm sorry about that," she said.

"Nothing to be sorry for. They're just looking out for you."

"I guess so."

Vince slid his arms around her waist and pulled her close. "I do think I deserve a reward, though."

"Do you?"

"Yes, ma'am. I was on my very best behavior all night long. I think at the very least I deserve a good-night kiss."

She swayed toward him. "Do you?" She was smiling now. She had never openly flirted with a man before, let alone one that was as handsome and sexy as Vince. It was a heady experience.

"Uh-huh. Do I need to ask daddy's permission?"

"No, silly, just kiss me."

Grinning, he lowered his head and claimed her lips with his. She tasted of sunshine and honey and warm summer days that were forever lost to him. She was love's first kiss and a baby's first cry, spring's first flower and presents on Christmas morning. He drew her closer, wanting to lose himself in her sweetness, to feel the heat of her skin against his own, to explore all the subtle curves and valleys of her body.

But this was not the time, and definitely not the place. Not with her father on the other side of the door.

Vince kissed her again, long and deep, savoring the taste of the wine on her lips before he moved away. "I'd better go. Can I see you tomorrow night?"

She started to say yes, and then remembered that Anton was coming to call. "I'm sorry, I've got a . . . a date."

"Ah."

"I'm sorry, I made it before we . . . a while ago."

"It's all right." He gave her a last, quick kiss. "I'll see you soon."

Chapter 11

Brenna sat in the window seat in the bedroom, brushing out her hair, her brow furrowed. "I didn't know there was another vampire in the city." She looked up at her husband. "You knew, didn't you? Why didn't you tell me?"

"There was nothing to tell. I sensed his presence once before." He didn't tell her he had sensed it here, in the house, in their daughter's bedroom.

"Do you think he means her harm?"

"No, I think he loves her."

"And she loves him," Brenna said. "You can tell that just by looking at her. Do you think she knows what he is?"

"No, I'm sure she doesn't."

"Maybe you should tell her, before things go too far. I don't want her to be hurt."

Roshan nodded. "You're probably right, but how do I tell her he's a vampire? And how would I explain how I know?" He shook his head. "Whoever thought parenting would be so complicated?"

"What if they decide to get married?"

Roshan swore softly. His little girl, married to a vampire? He didn't know of too many successful unions between vampires and mortals. In most cases, the differences between them drove them apart sooner or later. He raked a hand through his hair. Cara, married. Whether she married a vampire or a mortal, it meant losing her.

"I always wanted grandchildren," Brenna remarked. "Lots and lots of grandchildren. If she marries Vince . . ."

He nodded his understanding. If Cara married Vince, there would be no children, no grandchildren.

He looked at Brenna. Each year, she grew more precious, more beautiful in his sight. He hadn't missed the wistful note in her voice as she spoke of grandchildren. After all these years, was she having regrets for joining her life with his?

Brenna blew out a sigh. "Funny how our lives have changed so quickly in the last few days."

"And I'm afraid the end isn't in sight." Moving toward her, he drew her to her feet and into his arms. "Do you have regrets, Brenna?"

"What do you mean?"

"I watched you tonight, when you were asking Cordova about his family. I saw the yearning in your eyes when he talked about his family, and just now, when you spoke of grandchildren."

She didn't deny it.

"It made me think of something you said before I brought you across," Roshan went on. "You said being a vampire seemed like a lonely life. And then you said, 'What good is long life without love, without family, without children?'"

"But we have a child," she reminded him with a wry grin.

"Is she enough? Was I wrong to bring you across?"

Brenna stared into her husband's eyes. For the first time since he had brought her across, she let herself remember that night. At first, she had been horrified. She had screamed at him, then ran through house, destroying everything in sight—lamps, chairs, tables, dishes, glasses, she had smashed them all and reveled in the doing. Refusing to believe she was a vampire, she had taken a bite of chocolate pie, and been violently ill. She had begged him to destroy her, and when he refused, she had run away from him.

She ran tirelessly, amazed at her stamina. No wonder Anthony Loken had wanted the power of a vampire for himself! She felt as though she could run forever and never stop, never grow weary. Her body felt strong, yet lighter than air. Was that because she had shed her mortality, or because she had shed her soul?

The thought gave her pause and she slowed to a walk. Had she lost her soul? She considered that as she made her way across a bridge into a park. Why should she have lost her soul? She had done nothing wrong. She hadn't asked to be made a vampire; that decision had been made for her. She hadn't killed anyone. True, she had stolen a little blood, but surely she could be forgiven for that, if forgiveness was necessary . . .

She stopped beneath a weeping willow tree, lightly rolling one of the leaves between her thumb and forefinger, amazed at all the nuances in the texture of the leaf. How beautiful the tree was! She could hear the whisper of each leaf, hear the sap running through the branches, the creak of the wood as the tree swayed in the breeze. Everything was different when absorbed through her enhanced senses. No wonder Roshan didn't want to give it up. Except for the blood part, being a vampire seemed a wonderful thing.

She picked up her pace until she was running again. Never, in all her life, had she felt so wonderful, so free! Laughter bubbled up inside her. Why had she made such a fuss earlier? Would she truly rather be dead now? How awful it would be if she could never again catch the scent of rain in the air, or dance in the silvery light of a full moon. And what of Roshan? Would she be happy, even in heaven, if he were not there to share it with her?

She slowed as she reached the end of the park, her earlier en-

thusiasm waning. She would never have a child now. It was the only true regret she had. Of course, she thought, rationalizing, if he had let her die, she wouldn't have been able to have a child, either.

Roshan. She had spared a thought for little else since the first time she had seen him outside her cottage, and he was all she could think of now. His scent was in her clothes, in her hair. His voice was a welcome echo in her mind, his kisses a memory she would never forget. Roshan. He had told her, in word and deed, that he loved her. And she knew, without doubt, that she loved him. Perhaps she had loved him from the moment his eyes met hers.

Suddenly, she wanted nothing more than to be in his arms, to feel his lips on hers, to hear his voice whispering that he loved her.

Laughing out loud, she turned and ran toward Roshan. Toward home.

"No," she said, "you weren't wrong. I've never regretted a minute of our lives together." She caressed his cheek. "What's this all about? It's more than being worried about Cara."

He shrugged. "I just want you to be happy. Both of you."

"I am happy." She smiled up at him. "I can only think of one thing that would make me happier."

"Indeed?" He brushed a kiss across her cheek. "And what would that be?"

"Don't you know?"

"Maybe I just want to hear you say it."

"Maybe I'll just show you instead," she purred, and reached for his belt buckle.

Chapter 12

Cara slept late Sunday morning. After rising, she dressed, brushed her teeth, and went to church. Of course, going to church was something else her parents never did, not even at night, but Cara found comfort in the hymns and in the beauty of the stained-glass windows. She liked the ritual of it, the sense of communing with God, and the feeling of forgiveness that came with taking the sacrament.

After leaving the church, she took a walk through the park across the street. It was a beautiful day, bright and clear, with a sky so blue it almost hurt her eyes just to look at it. Taking off her shoes and stockings, she ran barefoot through the grass, and all the while she thought of Vince and the kisses they had shared on the front porch last night.

"Vince and Cara, sitting in a tree, k-i-s-s-i-n-g," she sang, then laughed out loud.

She felt as giddy as a schoolgirl with her first crush. Was this how her mother had felt about her father? She wished Sarah Beth was there. She needed someone to confide in, but Sarah Beth was gone for the weekend. In the past, Cara had always confided in her mother, but she couldn't bring herself to talk to Brenna about this.

When she came to a bench, Cara sat down and put her shoes and stockings back on. Reaching into her hand-bag, she pulled out a piece of chewing gum, then sat back and tried to decide what she would say when Anton came to call.

He appeared at seven sharp, with a heart-shaped box of candy in one hand and a bouquet of yellow roses in the other.

"Thank you," Cara murmured, accepting the gifts. "You shouldn't have."

"But I wanted to."

"Come in, won't you?" She stepped back so he could enter the foyer, then led the way into the living room, all the while wishing it was Vince walking beside her. "Mom, Dad, this is Anton. Anton, these are my parents, Mr. and Mrs. DeLongpre."

"Pleased to meet you," Anton said, nodding at her mother and father.

"I didn't catch your last name," Roshan said, shaking the young man's hand.

"Bouchard."

"It's nice to meet you, Mr. Bouchard," Brenna said. She looked up at her husband, a frown on her face.

"I'd love to stay and chat," Anton said, "But I made reservations at the Steak and Stein for seven-thirty."

"Of course," Cara said. She put the box of candy on the coffee table, then handed the flowers to her mother. "Mom, would you put these in water for me?" she asked, then glanced at Anton. "Just let me get my coat."

"What line of work are you in, Mr. Bouchard?" Brenna asked.

"My mother and I own a bookstore."

Warning bells went off inside Roshan's head. "Indeed? Would I know it?"

"I don't know, sir. It's called The Wiccan Heart."

"Witchcraft, then?"

"Yes, sir."

"And are you, yourself, a witch?"

"I dabble in the arts occasionally. Cara, are you ready to go?"

"Yes."

She handed Anton her coat, and he helped her on with it.

"It was a pleasure to meet you, sir," Anton said. "Mrs. DeLongpre."

Cara kissed her father's cheek and hugged her mother. "I won't be late."

Roshan stared after Anton Bouchard as he followed Cara out the door. Could it be?

He looked at Brenna and saw the same question in her eyes.

"Is it possible?" she asked.

"I don't know how it could be," Roshan muttered, "but he looks just like him."

"But he never married or had children, did he?"

"Not that I know of." Yet the resemblance between Anton Bouchard and Anthony Loken was chilling. It could have been coincidence, but Roshan had never believed in coincidence.

"I don't like this," Brenna said. "We shouldn't have let her go."

"She'll be all right. Di Giorgio won't let her out of his sight."

"Of course, Di Giorgio." Brenna smiled as she went into the kitchen for a vase. "How could I have forgotten about Di Giorgio?"

Anton glared at the burly bodyguard sitting near the front door of the restaurant. "Does he go everywhere with you?"

"Pretty much."

"Listen, I know this is none of my business, but have you ever thought about moving out? You know, getting a place of your own?"

"Well, sure, sometimes," Cara said defensively. And it was true. She had thought about it, but it seemed silly to move into a small apartment when she had the run of a huge house, and she was pretty sure that whether she lived at home or not, she would still have Di Giorgio to contend with. On the other hand, it would be fun to have a place of her own, to be independent. She thought about Vince. If she had a place of her own, they could be alone.

The thought made her smile. Alone with Vince. Talk about living on the edge! She couldn't think of anything more dangerous than being alone with Vince Cordova and his sexy smile. He had only to look at her and her insides melted like warm ice cream. And his voice; that deep, rich baritone that made her think of warm skin against cool sheets.

"Cara?"

She blinked at Anton. "Did you say something?"

"I asked if you were ready to order."

"Oh, sure. I'll have the shrimp and a house salad. And iced tea."

Anton ordered, then sat back, wondering how best to tell Cara that her parents were vampires. His mother was anxious to get Cara out of DeLongpre's house and out from under the vampire's immediate protection. Of course, telling her the truth about her mother and father didn't guarantee that she would move out, but the news was bound to come as a shock and maybe shake her faith in her parents. Even if she didn't move out, the fact that they had kept the truth from her might serve to drive a wedge between them. If that didn't work, well, he could always kidnap the little chit. Still, there was no need to worry about it yet. He had until All Hallow's Eve to come up with a way to separate Cara from her parents and her watchdog in a way that wouldn't arouse their suspicion or implicate him or his mother when Cara came up missing.

"You told me you weren't a witch," Cara said when the waitress moved away from the table.

"I beg your pardon?"

"The other night, I asked you if you were a witch, and you said no, but tonight you told my father you dabbled in witchcraft. Why did you lie to me?"

"Well, I didn't know you very well, and I was afraid it might scare you off," he lied smoothly.

"So, what kind of witchcraft do you practice?" Cara asked.

"Oh, just simple things. A woman came in last week. She was distraught because she'd lost her wedding ring and she didn't want to tell her husband. I helped her find it."

Cara nodded, wondering if he was telling her the truth this time, but it didn't matter. She had no intention of going out with him again.

"There's all kinds of Magick," Anton explained. "Herbal magick, candle magick, animal magick, and elemental magick. Some magick is done best during a particular phase of the moon. And there are love spells, of course."

"You mean you can make people fall in love?"

"Not exactly. But a sachet bag filled with rosemary, thyme, and sage is effective in attracting love. There are spells to attract money and spells to summon the spirits of the dead."

Cara shivered. "Have you ever done that? Summon the dead? It doesn't sound like a very good idea to me."

"No, I've never tried anything like that." Not yet, he thought. Alone in his room, he had tried several complicated spells, pleased when each had turned out perfectly. He definitely had the gift. One day, he hoped to be as powerful a warlock as his father had been, and if that meant dabbling in the Dark Arts, then so be it.

Dinner arrived and they spoke of trivial things. Later, after Anton paid the check, they left the restaurant.

"Where to now?" he asked. "Movies? A drive? A walk? Bowling?"

Cara glanced over her shoulder. Di Giorgio nodded at her from a discreet distance away.

"Or we could go dancing at The Nocturne," Anton suggested.

Butterflies fluttered in the pit of her stomach. Vince might be at The Nocturne.

"Well?" he asked, "what will it be?"

"Dancing sounds good," she said, especially if she found a way to dance with Vince.

She could scarcely contain her excitement as they made their way down the stairs to the club's entrance.

The dark, sensual beat of the music seemed to close around Cara as she followed Anton to a vacant table in the back. A man smiled at her, his hooded eyes dark with lust. She recoiled when she saw his fangs and then laughed self-consciously as she reminded herself that no matter how real they looked, they were fake.

She didn't know what it was that she found so appealing about this place. The people frightened her, the music made her think of dark, intimate acts.

She was disappointed when she didn't see Vince in the crowd.

Anton asked her to dance and even though she didn't want to be in his arms, she could hardly refuse, since she had been so enthusiastic about coming here.

The first song ended and the second one began. Anton was relating a story about something that had happened at the bookstore when one of the couples dancing nearby caught Cara's attention. Could it be? It was!

"What's wrong?" Anton asked.

"My parents are here!"

"What? Where?"

"Over there."

Roshan twirled her mother around just then and caught Cara staring.

"Well, hello," Brenna said, smiling. "What a nice surprise."

"I didn't know you two came here," Cara said.

"You seemed to like it, so we thought we'd give it a try," her father said. "We were just going to get a drink. Would you care to join us?"

Cara glanced at Anton. He was staring at her father through narrowed eyes, almost as if he hated him, yet that was ridiculous. The two had only met once before.

"Anton?"

With a shrug, he said, "It's up to you."

"Sure, we'd love to join you," Cara said, wondering at Anton's strange behavior.

Moments later, the four of them were seated at a large booth in the back.

"What are you drinking, Mom?" Cara asked when their drinks arrived. At home, her parents never indulged in anything stronger than a glass of red wine.

"It's a club specialty," her mother replied.

"It looks like a Bloody Mary," Anton remarked.

"It's very similar," her mother said.

They talked of the weather and the upcoming election. Roshan ordered another round of drinks, though both Brenna and Cara declined.

Her parents danced together again. Cara watched them, thinking how well they looked together. They moved effortlessly, almost as if they were floating. Her father, clad in his usual black attire, looked as though he belonged there. Without even trying, he looked more like a vampire than any of the wanna-be vampires with their long black cloaks and fake fangs. Her mother, clad in a flowing yellow and orange striped skirt and white blouse, looked like she should be dancing in a sunlit field of wildflowers.

At midnight, Cara asked Anton to take her home.

"So early? You're not going to turn into a pumpkin on me, are you?"

"No," Cara said, grinning. "I'm just tired."

"Very well." Rising, he bid a cool good night to her parents.

"We'll be along soon, Princess," Roshan said, giving his daughter a hug.

"All right. Night, Dad. Mom."

Cara stared into the darkness as Anton drove her home. She had so hoped to see Vince at the club. Of course, even if he had been there, she couldn't have spent any time with him, not when she was on a date with another man, but she was disappointed just the same.

Anton pulled up in front of the driveway and Di Giorgio pulled in behind him. A moment later, the gate opened and Anton drove up to the front of the house. He put the car in park, then turned to look at Cara.

"So tell me," he said, "how long have your parents been vampires?"

Chapter 13

Cara stared at Anton, unable to believe what she'd heard, and then she laughed. "Vampires!" she exclaimed. "What on earth are you talking about?"

"They were drinking Bloody Mariahs."

"So what?"

"It's not a mixed drink. It's blood."

"That's ridiculous!"

"Is it? You never see them during the day, do you?"

"No," she admitted, wondering how he knew about that, "but it's because they have an adverse physical reaction to sunlight."

"I'll just bet they do! Don't you find it the least bit strange that they both have it?"

"I don't know. I never gave it much thought." She had grown up knowing her mother and father were different and even though she'd had questions from time to time, she had accepted whatever they told her as the truth. After all, they were parents; she trusted them.

"So, they sleep all day and only go out at night. Have you ever seen them eat anything? Drink a cup of coffee or a glass of water?"

"They were drinking tonight," she reminded him.

"They were drinking blood. You don't find that odd?"

"You don't know that it was blood."

"Yes, I do. I ordered a Bloody Mariah once, just to see what it was."

"But . . . there's no such thing as vampires. They're just myths, like werewolves and fairies." Even as she protested, Cara found herself wondering if he could be right. It would explain so many things that seemed unnatural now that he had remarked on them, things she had blindly accepted. She shook her head. It couldn't be true. And yet, why would Anton make up such an outlandish story? What could he possibly hope to gain?

Anton placed his hand on her shoulder and gave it a squeeze. "I'm sorry, Cara, but I thought you ought to know. It isn't right for them to keep the truth from you." He gave her a sympathetic smile. "If you need anything, a shoulder to cry on, a place to stay, call me."

"Yes, I will, thank you," she said politely, her thoughts chasing themselves like a dog chasing its tail. "There's no need for you to walk me to the door. Di Giorgio's here."

Feeling numb, she got out of the car, walked up the steps, unlocked the door, went inside, and closed the door behind her.

She stood there in the dark a moment, and then laughed humorlessly. If what Anton had said was true, she had been in the dark her whole life.

What if it was true? What if her mother and father were vampires?

But they weren't her real parents. And if they were vampires, why would they want a human child? What did they intend to do with her?

She lifted a hand to her throat, then shook her head. If they meant to use her for food or some other nefarious scheme, wouldn't they have done so by now?

Even as she told herself it was impossible, some inner voice whispered that everything Anton had said was true. It explained so many things. It explained everything.

She ran up to her room, turning on lights as she went. She felt betrayed. Her parents had lied to her. Every answer they had ever given her to explain their strange lifestyle had been a lie. She blinked back her tears, saddened because she knew that she would never trust her mother or her father again.

Vampires! They drank blood from the living. They were dead but not dead. In movies, they were generally depicted as soulless monsters who killed indiscriminately to sustain their own existence, or else they were portrayed as humorous creatures, like George Hamilton in *Love at First Bite* or Leslie Nielsen in *Dracula, Dead and Loving It*. She suspected the truth was somewhere between the two extremes, but it didn't matter.

She couldn't stay here any longer; she couldn't face them, not now. For the first time in her life, she was afraid of her parents, afraid to be alone with them.

She pulled a suitcase from her closet and tossed in the contents from her dresser drawers. She filled her overnight case with the items from her bathroom, then grabbed her suitcases, her handbag, and her keys and ran out of the house.

She had to get away before they got home from The Nocturne. If it turned out that Anton had lied to her, that there really was a logical explanation for her parents' behavior and that they weren't vampires, well, then they could all have a good laugh about it later. But for now, she had to get away. She needed time alone, time to think, time to find out who she really was.

Roshan stood in the center of the living room. "She's not here."

"Maybe they went out for coffee," Brenna suggested hopefully.

"I don't think so." Roshan took the stairs to his daughter's bedroom two at a time. A single sweeping glance was all it took to tell him that she had packed her bags and left.

"But why?" Brenna asked when he told her the news. "Why would she leave? Where would she go?" Her eyes widened. "You don't think she ran off with Bouchard?"

Roshan snorted softly. "If she was going to run away with anyone, it would be Cordova."

"We've got to find her."

Roshan paced the floor in front of the hearth. Cara had seen them at the club. She had come home, packed her bags, and left. Why? There had to be a connection. What was he missing? And where would she go?

He opened his senses, hoping he could detect her whereabouts, but he had never taken his daughter's blood. The only way to find her would be to go outside and follow her scent.

He kissed Brenna on the cheek. "I'll be back."

"Wait! I'm going with you."

"No, you stay here in case she changes her mind and comes home."

"You don't think anything's happened to her, do you?" Brenna asked anxiously.

"No. I'm going out to see if Di Giorgio's home, then I'm going to go look for her."

"All right. Hurry!"

It took only moments for Roshan to reach the house Di Giorgio occupied at the rear of the property.

The bodyguard answered the door on the first knock. "Mr. DeLongpre," he said, his brows rising in alarm. "Is something wrong?"

Roshan came right to the point. "Cara's gone."

"What?"

"You heard me. She packed her bags and left."

Di Giorgio swore. "I . . . I don't know what to say. I watched her go into the house. Saw the lights come on downstairs and then in her room. I didn't hear her car leave, so I assumed she was in for the night, and I went to take a shower. It's my fault, and I have no excuse, sir."

"It's all right, Frank. I'm going out to look for her."

"Do you want me to go with you?"

"No. I'll call you if I need help."

"Very well, sir. Again, I'm sorry."

With a nod, Roshan vanished into the night.

It didn't take him long to find her scent. Though he was on foot and she was in her car, he had no trouble following her across the city to a hotel. He noted it was in a decent part of town.

Going inside, he stopped at the desk and asked what room his daughter was in.

"I'm sorry, sir, we don't have a listing for a Cara De-Longpre."

Roshan didn't argue. He left the hotel, dissolved into mist, and drifted up the stairs, his senses guiding him to Cara's room.

Taking on his own shape once again, he knocked on the door.

"Who's there?" Cara's voice, hesitant, suspicious.

"Your father."

He heard the click of the lock. A moment later, Cara stood in the doorway. A large silver crucifix dangled from a thick chain around her throat.

Roshan lifted one brow. Obviously, someone had already told her the truth. "May I come in?"

She stepped back, her fingers curling around the crucifix.

Roshan entered the room and closed the door behind him. The fear in his daughter's eyes cut him to his very soul. "Why have you done this?"

"You're a vampire, aren't you?"

He considered lying and dismissed the thought immediately. Right or wrong, he had been lying to her for years. It was time she knew the truth. "Yes." He gestured at the cross. "Do you really think you need that?"

"Better safe than sorry." She took a deep breath. "Is my . . . is Brenna one, too?"

"Yes."

Cara stared at him, tears welling in her eyes. He knew she had hoped he would deny it, that he could make everything right again.

"How did you find out?" he asked quietly.

"Anton told me. He said you were drinking blood at The Nocturne."

"And you believed him?"

"Where are my real parents? What happened to them? Did you . . . ?"

"I want you to stop this nonsense and come home with me, now. Your mother is worried."

"She isn't my mother. She isn't even human."

"Cara . . ."

"Where's my real mother?"

"I don't know. We never knew anything about her, except that she was a teenager in trouble. She needed a home for her baby, and your mother wanted a child. We helped bring you into the world late one night, and then we brought you home. You've been our daughter since that night."

"All this time, you never told me."

"Should we have told you the truth?" he asked quietly. "Would you have believed it?"

"I don't know. How long have you been a vampire?" Cara stared at the man who had raised her. He looked the same as always—tall and dark and very handsome. His eyes weren't blood red. She couldn't see any fangs. His fingernails weren't long. He didn't smell like death.

"Over three hundred years."

"Three hundred years." She shook her head in disbelief. "And my . . . and Brenna?"

"Twenty-two years, give or take a few months."

Cara's eyes widened as she realized that her mother must have become a vampire the same year she herself was born.

"Did you make my . . . Brenna, a vampire?"

"Yes."

"Did she ask you to?"

"No, but she was dying, and I couldn't let her go. I was willing to live with her hatred rather than risk losing her." He took a deep breath. "Please come home with me."

"No. I need some time alone to sort this out."

Roshan nodded. He could take her home by force, bend her will to his, but there was nothing to be gained by such high-handed tactics except her hatred.

"Be careful, Cara. Call us if you need us." He hesitated, debating the wisdom of what he was about to say, but she needed to be warned. "Cordova is one of us."

Her eyes widened. "I don't believe you!"

"It's true nonetheless."

"I suppose you're going to tell me that Anton is a vampire, too?"

"No, I'm not sure what he is, but I don't trust him."

"You're just saying all that to scare me so I'll come home."

"I just want you to be careful. If Cordova comes to call, he can't enter unless you invite him inside. He has the power to hypnotize you with a look. You need to be aware of the danger you're in. Stay away from The Nocturne."

Still clasping the crucifix in one hand, she looked up at him, her expression one of hurt confusion. It broke his heart.

"Are you sure you won't change your mind and come home where you belong?"

"I'm sure," she said, but she wasn't sure at all. She no longer knew who to trust or what to believe.

He took a step toward her. She recoiled from his touch. It hurt worse than anything he had ever known. "Good night, Princess."

The familiar endearment brought quick tears to her eyes. "Good night."

Cara watched her father leave the room, then she locked the door behind him.

He was a vampire. Her mother was a vampire. Vince was a vampire.

Had the world gone mad? How could she have lived with her parents for twenty-two years and never suspected? Now, looking back, it was so obvious. Why hadn't she seen it before? But, then, why would she? No one believed in vampires in this day and age. There were enough real monsters running around planting car bombs and molesting innocent children without looking for monsters of myth and legend.

She went to the window and looked out into the night, wondering what other monsters might be lurking in the shadows.

"Where is she?" Brenna asked anxiously. "What did she say? Is she coming home?"

"She's staying at a hotel over on Fourth Street. She said she needs time alone, to think."

"She knows, doesn't she? And now she hates us for lying to her?" Brenna paced the floor. "I knew we should have told her the truth years ago."

"We decided to wait, remember?"

"Yes, but now we've waited too long. What if she never comes back?"

Roshan drew his wife into his arms. "All we can do now is . . ." He started to say pray, but it had been years since he had done so. After all this time, he wasn't sure anyone would be listening. He blew out a breath. "She'll come around, in time."

Brenna looked up, her gaze searching his. "Are you sure of that?"

"Yes. She loves us. She knows deep inside that we love her. Once she gets over the shock, she'll realize nothing's really changed. In the meantime, Di Giorgio will be there. I got him a room at the hotel."

"I feel so helpless."

"I warned her to be careful, to stay away from The Nocturne. And I told her about Cordova."

"What did she say?!"

"She didn't believe me. I was afraid she wouldn't, but she had to be told. She needs to be aware of the danger she's in." Roshan rested his forehead against Brenna's. "There's something about Cordova . . ."

"What do you mean?"

"He's different."

Brenna tilted her head back so she could see her husband's face. "Different? What do you mean? Different how?"

"He told me Mara brought him across."

"Mara?" Brenna frowned. "Isn't she the ancient vampire you told me about?"

Roshan nodded.

"I always thought she was just a myth."

"No, she's real enough, though few of us have ever seen her. It's said that in all her long life, she has made only a handful of vampires. Her blood is strong, potent. I could sense it in Cordova. He could be a powerful enemy."

"Or a powerful friend."

Roshan grunted softly. "Mara has powers that no other vampires possess. I wonder how many of them she passed on to Cordova."

It was a question that troubled Roshan far into the night.

Chapter 14

Cara woke late Monday morning after a long and restless night. She had dreamed of vampires—vampires chasing her, catching her, ripping out her throat, and drinking her blood. Vampires with hideous red eyes and skin as pale as death, their skeletal hands like claws as they reached for her.

Banishing all thoughts of vampires from her mind, she went into the bathroom, brushed her teeth and her hair, pulled on a pair of jeans, boots, and a sweater, and left the hotel. The library was closed on Sundays and Mondays, and the day stretched before her.

She stopped at a nearby café for pancakes and lots of strong coffee, then drove to the garage where Vince worked. She had expected to find the place closed up tight, but the big doors were open.

After parking her car in front, she walked around the corner to the entrance of the garage. The doors were open, but there were no lights on inside. She found Vince in his office in the back of the building. Seated behind a battered oak desk with his feet propped up on one corner, he was talking on the phone. A large gray and white cat slept on top of a battered metal filing cabinet.

Relief flooded through Cara, leaving her feeling momentarily weak. The sun was high in the sky and Vince was up and awake. He couldn't be a vampire. Her father had been mistaken. She wondered what had made him think Vince was a vampire in the first place, then put the thought from her mind. She didn't know a lot about the Undead, but everybody knew they slept in their coffins during the day.

Vince smiled at her, then held up one finger, indicating he'd be done in a minute.

Cara glanced around the garage. There were three cars inside, all with their hoods up. A couple of big red metal tool chests stood against the wall to her left. Metal shelves lined the opposite wall. A wooden table was littered with tools and rags and greasy auto parts. It occurred to her that she had never seen her father putter around the house or work on his car or do any of the other mundane things most fathers did.

"Hey," Vince called as he hung up the receiver, "what brings you here?"

She smiled as he rounded the desk toward her, then shrugged. "It's my day off and I didn't have anything else to do."

"Well, I'm glad you came by."

"I guess you're busy?"

He nodded. "But never too busy for you."

She smiled, warmed by his words and the welcome in his eyes.

"Does your cat have a name?"

"I don't know. I just call him Cat."

"Not very imaginative of you."

He shrugged. "He's not really my cat. He just lives here. Can I get you something to drink?"

"What do you have?"

"Root beer, 7-Up, orange soda, Coke." He kept a Coke machine stocked for his clients.

"7-Up sounds good."

He got her a can from the machine, popped the top, and handed it to her. "So, how was your date with the stiff?"

She made a face at him. "It was all right. We went to dinner and then dancing at The Nocturne." She waited, hoping he would tell her what he had done last night. When he didn't, she said, "My parents showed up at the club."

He grunted softly. "Checking up on you?"

"I don't think so. They have Di Giorgio for that." She frowned, wondering if Di Giorgio would still be trailing her now that she had moved out of the house. She didn't remember seeing him this morning, but then, she hadn't been looking. She'd had thoughts only for Vince.

He leaned against a corner of his desk, waiting for her to go on.

Stalling, Cara sipped her drink, wondering if she should say anything. She wanted to talk to someone about her parents but she didn't think anyone would believe her.

"What is it, Cara?" Vince asked. "Is something wrong?"

"I moved out of my house last night."

"You did?" he asked, frowning. "Why?"

"I found out something about my parents that bothered me."

"Go on," he said, his expression suddenly guarded.

"Anton told me that my parents are . . . I didn't want to believe him, but I guess he was right." She looked up at him, her eyes shining with tears. "It's just so . . . so, I don't know. So unbelievable. I . . ."

"Go on, darlin'. What did he tell you about your parents?" Vince asked, though he had a pretty good idea about what she was going to say.

"He said they're vampires." She waited for him to laugh at her gullibility, to tell her she was crazy and that Anton had been making a bad joke. He did none of those things.

"What did your parents say?"

"My father told me it was true."

"And that's why you moved out?"

"Of course! Didn't you hear what I said? They're vampires!" She shuddered. "How can I stay there?"

"You've lived with them your whole life, Cara. Have they ever hurt you?"

"Well, no, but . . ."

"They obviously love you."

She stared up at him. "Why are you defending them? Don't you understand? They're not human!"

Vince blew out a sigh; then, knowing he was making a huge mistake, he took her into his arms.

Setting the soda can on the desk, Cara sagged against him, her cheek resting against his chest, her arms sliding around his waist. "My father said you were a vampire, too."

He went suddenly still. "Oh?"

"I don't know why he said that. I mean, it can't be true," she said with a forced laugh, "or you'd be sleeping in your coffin, so why would he say such a thing?"

"I don't know." Vince swore under his breath. Blast! What should he do now? Tell her the truth? Wait? Hope she never found out? "Cara . . ."

She looked up at him, her eyes wide. Innocent. Vulnerable.

He should tell her the truth, he thought, before it was too late, before things got out of hand. She'd hate him, sure, but better now than later. "Listen, Cara . . ."

"Hey, Cordova, my car ready yet?"

Vince put Cara away from him as the owner of the Dodge he had been working on earlier sauntered into the garage.

"Not quite, Murph," Vince said. "I need another thirty minutes or so."

Murph glanced at Cara, then looked at Vince and

grinned. "Yeah, I can see that. Mind if I grab a Coke while I wait?"

"No, help yourself." Vince took Cara's hand in his. "Why don't I pick you up tonight, say around eight? We can talk about it more then."

"All right. I'm staying at the hotel on Fourth Street. Room 302."

"Okay, I'll see you later."

He watched her walk away, wishing he knew what the hell he was going to tell her.

Chapter 15

Serafina knelt at Anthony's grave site. Even though his body wasn't there, she visited his grave each week to make sure it had fresh flowers. Sometimes, when the weather was nice, she pretended his body was buried there and she spent the afternoon by the grave, reading to him from a book of poetry; sometimes she told him about Anton and how proud of him she was.

"I'm sure he'll be as talented as you were." She caressed the headstone, her fingers tracing the letters of his name. "He's such a handsome young man, so like you in every way. You'll be so pleased when you see him. I've kept your lab just the way you left it. I'll be using it soon. Anton will have to help me subdue the vampire. I was going to use the woman's blood for the blood of an enemy, but I think Roshan's will be more effective. I'll probably have to kill him . . ."

She smiled. "Or maybe I'll let you do that. Would that please you?" she queried. Then, thinking about it, she frowned. "I think we might have to kill them all."

Dropping down on her knees, she pressed a kiss to the top of the headstone. "Rest well, my beloved, until next we meet."

Soon, she thought, soon the time would be right and they would be together forever, as they were meant to be.

Chapter 16

Cara stood in front of the bathroom mirror, examining her appearance with a critical eye. She wanted to look pretty for Vince. She had donned her favorite pair of slinky black slacks, a hot pink silk shirt, and a pair of black high-heeled sandals. She wore her hair loose, pulled away from her face with a pair of silver combs.

She had just put on her lipstick when she heard his knock at the door. What felt like a million butterflies immediately started doing somersaults in the pit of her stomach. He was here!

She took a slow, deep breath, and then another one before forcing herself to walk slowly to the door. She took another deep breath before she opened it. "Hi."

He whistled softly. "Hi, yourself. Wow, you look fantastic!"

"Thank you. Come on in."

When he stepped across the threshold, she felt a funny little tingle slip down her spine.

"So," he said, "where would you like to go tonight?"

"I don't know." She lowered her gaze. "Do we have to go somewhere?"

"Not if you don't want to."

"I could order something from room service and we could stay in and watch a movie."

"Sure, darlin', if that's what you want."

"Are you hungry?"

"You bet. You look good enough to eat."

She stared at him, wide-eyed, her cheeks almost as pink as her shirt. "Vince . . ."

He pulled her into his arms, his gaze capturing hers. "Do you want me to stop?"

"You haven't done anything yet," she said, her voice little more than a squeak.

"But I want to." His lips brushed her cheek, the tip of her nose, her eyelids. "I want to taste every inch of you, explore every curve."

She blinked up at him, her eyelids fluttering down as his mouth closed over hers. She was drowning in a haze of sensation. His mouth was everywhere, dropping feather-light kisses along both sides of her neck, nuzzling her breasts. His breath penetrated the thin silk of her shirt, heating her skin, melting her resistance. He kissed her again, long and deep, and when his tongue tangled with hers, she felt the electric heat of it sizzle all the way to the very center of her being.

Without knowing quite how they got there, she found herself lying on the sofa with Vince stretched out beside her, his mouth on hers, their bodies pressed intimately together from shoulder to thigh. His hand slid slowly, seductively, up and down her side, his thumb skimming the edge of her breast.

She moaned softly, thinking she had never known such pleasure, or such torment. She strained against him, her hips moving in the age-old dance of mating. Her body was on fire, screaming for relief.

"Cara, dammit . . ."

His breath whispered against her neck. She felt the heat of his tongue, the scrape of his teeth.

"Vince . . . please, Vince."

Her voice spurred him on, urging him to take what

she was offering, to satisfy her hunger and his own, even as the voice of his conscience warred within him. He closed his eyes, the scent of her need and her blood arousing him until it was almost painful.

It took every ounce of willpower he possessed to let her go. He took a deep breath, about to sit up and tell her they needed to take a walk and cool off, when her hand slid between their bodies, cupping his manhood, driving him over the edge.

Scooping her into his arms, he carried her into the bedroom and laid her on the bed.

She looked up at him, her eyes smoky with desire and a hint of uncertainty.

Vince swore softly. What the hell was he thinking? He had to tell her the truth, now. And when he did, she'd walk out of his life just like she'd walked away from her parents.

"Cara . . ."

"Make love to me, Vince."

"I don't think that's a good . . ."

"Don't think." She reached for his hand, drawing him down on the bed beside her. "Don't you want me?"

"Is that a trick question?" He had to keep things light between them before he did something they would both regret when it was over.

"Now you're making fun of me."

"No, darlin'. I just don't want to hurt you."

"I'm a big girl. I know what I'm doing." She ran her hands over his chest, up over his shoulders, down his arms.

"Have you ever been with a man before?"

"Of course."

He drew his fingertip along her cheek. "Now, why don't I believe you?"

"Come closer," she said, her hand sliding seductively over his belly, "and I'll prove it."

"Cara, we need to talk."

"Later," she said, and drawing his head down, she kissed him, and he was lost.

With a low groan, he pulled her into his arms and surrendered to the hunger burning through him.

Her skin was soft and smooth, warm with life, her lips sweeter than wine. His hand delved into the wealth of her hair, loving the way the strands curled around his fingers. He massaged her nape, her back, gentling her to his touch. She was passionate and pliable in his arms, willing to follow wherever he led. He caressed her until she writhed beneath him, as eager and anxious as he.

He basked in her touch as she explored his body in return. It took all his willpower to hold both his hunger and his desire in check until, with a soft whimper, she urged him to take her.

Murmuring her name, he lifted her hips to receive him, only then realizing that he had been right all along. She had never been intimate with a man. But by then, it was too late.

She fell asleep in his arms.

Feeling like the worst kind of heel, Vince stroked her hair while his nostrils filled with the scent of her blood, not just the blood he had tasted, but the virginal blood that stained the sheets, proving she had been a maiden.

He swore softly.

How could he have done such a despicable thing? Sure, he was a vampire, but he had always prided himself on remaining a gentleman. He didn't satisfy his thirst on the blood of innocents. He didn't vent his lust on virgins.

Tonight he had done both.

What was he to do with her now?

And what would Roshan do when he found out Vince had defiled his little girl? Vince swore softly. Whatever De-Longpre did to him would be no more than he deserved.

He was tempted to sneak out of the hotel and never see her again, but he couldn't bring himself to do such a cowardly thing. It was bad enough that he had defiled her.

Instead, he held her in his arms until he felt the approach of dawn, and then he kissed her cheek, pulled on his pants, and went home.

Cara woke with a smile on her face. For a moment, she lay there, her eyes closed, remembering the night past. Making love to Vince had been the most wonderful, incredible experience of her life. For a moment, she held the memory close, reliving every kiss, every caress, every word he had whispered in her ear, the way he had cried her name as his body melded with hers, the soul shattering ecstasy that had followed.

Vince. Feeling suddenly shy, she reached for him, only he wasn't there.

Opening her eyes, she sat up and glanced around the room. Then she saw the note on his pillow. Sitting up, she read it out loud.

"Cara, I had an early appointment and I didn't want to wake you. I'll meet you at the library at 9. Love, V."

She hugged the note to her breast and then, unbidden but inevitable, came the guilt. She had slept with a man she hardly knew. She told herself it didn't matter, that these days lots of people slept together when they weren't married or even engaged. No one even gave it a second thought. Couples lived together, slept together, and moved on. Movies and TV shows were all about sex. Advertisers used sex to sell everything from toothpaste to deodorant. And yet, deep inside, no matter how she tried to rationalize it, she knew what she had done was wrong.

With a sigh, she flopped down on her stomach. If her parents found out, they would be disappointed in her. She told herself she didn't care what they thought. They were vampires, after all. But she did care, far more than she wanted to.

Lying there in bed, she remembered all the good times she had shared with her parents. They had always made a big fuss over her birthdays, showering her with presents. Christmases had always been special. She smiled as she remembered how her father had always searched for the tallest tree, and how the three of them had always stayed up late to decorate it. She remembered laughter and presents and love. Lots of love. Her parents had taken her ice skating in the moonlight and for carriage rides in the park. They had arranged for her to take horseback riding lessons and ballet lessons. She remembered Easter egg hunts and enormous chocolate Valentines. She had never wanted for anything. Even now, she had a savings account with a balance of several thousand dollars that was hers to do with as she pleased.

She punched her fist into the pillow as the word *vampire* slithered through her mind. She told herself it didn't matter, but it did. She no longer knew how to relate to them. It was like suddenly finding out they were aliens or pod people. Their whole lifestyle was foreign to her.

Rising, she wandered into the living room. She didn't like staying in a hotel; she wasn't ready to go back home. But she could rent a house! Of course, it was the perfect solution.

Excited by the idea, she showered and dressed, grabbed a cup of coffee and a cinnamon roll at the hotel coffee shop, and then drove to the nearest real estate office. A glance in her rearview mirror told her that her watchdog was still watching—not that she was surprised. She was certain her father had informed Di Giorgio of her whereabouts the minute he got home.

However, she was too excited at the prospect of having a house of her own to be upset.

* * *

Vince spent the day alternately working on putting a new engine in an ancient Chevy and worrying about his date with Cara. Making love to her last night had changed everything.

He had never intended to fall in love, especially with a mortal female. He wasn't even sure when he had fallen in love with Cara DeLongpre. Sure, he had fallen in lust the moment he saw her in The Nocturne. What man wouldn't? But love? How the hell had that happened? He tried to tell himself he hadn't known her long enough to love her, but from that first night, he couldn't imagine his life without her.

Of course, he had never intended to make love to her, either. As good as it had been, he couldn't help feeling it had been a big mistake. Taking her blood had been an even bigger one, but, like taking her innocence, it couldn't be undone.

He muttered an oath as he scraped his hand on the engine block. He stared at the blood oozing from his knuckles, remembering how sweet Cara's had been, wondering if she remembered that, at the height of their lovemaking, he had tasted her.

When the phone rang, he figured it was the Chevy's owner calling to see if his car was ready. Instead, he heard Cara's voice, sweet and a little breathless.

"Hi," she said. "I hope you don't mind me calling you at work."

"Not at all." Lord, just hearing her voice made him hard. "You can call me anytime."

"Guess what I did this afternoon?"

"I can't imagine."

"I rented a house! Wait until you see it. I'm on my way to the store to buy dishes and stuff before I go to work. So, what are you doing?"

"Putting a new engine in an old Chevy."

"Oh."

He sat on a corner of the desk. "Why?"

"I thought . . . never mind."

"You thought what?"

"That maybe you'd go shopping with me. I could come by and pick you up."

Vince glanced outside. It wouldn't be dark for another couple of hours. "I'm afraid I can't leave right now, but we're still on for tonight, right? Nine o'clock?"

"Right." Though she tried to hide it, he heard the disappointment in her voice.

"I'm sorry, darlin'."

"It's okay, I understand. See ya later."

He swore softly as he hung up the receiver. Not that he particularly wanted to go shopping for dishes, but he hated to disappoint Cara. Still, it couldn't be helped.

At dusk, he took the Chevy for a test run. Twenty minutes later, the owner came to pick it up.

Vince closed up shop, took a shower, pulled on a pair of jeans and a black shirt, and combed his hair.

Leaving the garage, he prowled the streets, searching for prey. It didn't take him long. He fed quickly, then went to The Nocturne to pass a few hours until it was time to meet Cara.

It was with a mingled sense of anticipation and trepidation that he slid behind the wheel of the Mustang and drove to the library. Tonight. He would tell her the truth tonight.

Cara looked up when the library door opened. All night, she had been on pins and needles. Every time the door opened, she had hoped it would be Vince. She checked the time, thinking that the hours had never passed so slowly.

She was working in the stacks a few minutes before closing time when she sensed a presence behind her. Hoping it was Vince, she turned around, only to come face to face with Anton.

"Hi, sweet cakes," he said cheerfully.

"Hello."

"I haven't seen you for a while, so I thought I'd come by and make sure you're all right."

"I'm fine, thank you."

He canted his head to one side. "You're mad at me, aren't you?"

"Why should I be mad?" she retorted.

"Why, indeed?"

"You were right about my parents," she said. "I guess I can't be mad at you for that." *Even though you made me see my parents for what they truly are and ruined my life*, she thought bleakly.

"I'm sorry if I spoke out of turn," he said with an apologetic smile, "but I really thought you should know."

"And now I do. If you'll excuse me, I've got work to do."

"How about if I wait for you to get off? We could go out for a drink."

"No, thank you. I have a date."

"I see. How about tomorrow night?"

"I don't think so."

"So you are mad."

"No, I'm just not interested in seeing you anymore. I'm sorry."

"Because I told you about your parents?"

"Partly."

He lifted one brow. "Partly?"

"I really have to go, Anton."

He nodded, his eyes narrowing. He looked suddenly ominous, even dangerous. She told herself she was seeing things that weren't there, but she couldn't stifle the shiver of unease that ran down her spine. She watched him walk away and breathed a sigh of relief when he went out the door. Hopefully, she would never see him again.

"Is that him?" Sarah Beth asked, coming up behind her.

"Him?" Cara shelved the last book on the cart and started toward the front desk.

"The man who's had you tied in knots the last few days," Sarah Beth said, falling into step beside her.

"Oh, no."

"Good, cause I don't like his looks at all."

Before Cara could reply, the door opened again. This time she didn't have to look to know that Vince had arrived.

She ran a hand over her hair, took a deep breath, and turned to face him.

His megawatt smile made her heart skip a beat. "I guess I'm a little early."

"That's all right. Vince, this is my best friend, Sarah Beth. Bethy, this is Vince."

"Pleased to meet you, Sarah Beth," Vince said.

"It's nice to meet you, too," Sarah Beth replied airily. "Now I've got a face to go with the name."

Vince looked at Cara, one brow raised quizzically. "You been talking about me?"

She shrugged. "Maybe, a little."

"Only good things, I hope," he said with a teasing grin.

"Of course." Picking up the microphone on the desk, Cara made the announcement that the library would be closing in ten minutes.

"Run along, you two," Sarah Beth said, making a shooing motion with her hand. "Mary and I can lock up."

"Are you sure?" Cara asked.

"I'm sure," Sarah Beth said emphatically. "Now, go on, get!"

"So," Cara said as they left the library, "what shall we do tonight?"

"I thought you were fixin' to show me your new house."

"I'd like to."

"Then that's what we'll do." He walked her to her car, waited while she unlocked the door. "I'll follow you," he said.

"All right."

He closed her door, then walked to his own car. Di Giorgio pulled out of the lot behind him.

Vince tapped his hand on the steering wheel. Being alone with Cara seemed like a really bad idea, especially after last night. He told himself it couldn't happen again, but he doubted he had the willpower to leave her alone now that he knew what it was like to make love to her, to taste her sweetness. He had thought of little else all day. Time and again his mind had strayed toward last night. Mara might have been the most accomplished lover he had ever known, but she couldn't hold a candle to Cara's sweet innocence. His body had reacted every time he remembered how willingly Cara had given herself to him, how soft and supple her body had been, how her warmth had chased away the perpetual cold that was part of him now. All day, he had wanted nothing more than to make love to her again.

A short time later, she pulled up in front of a two-story house surrounded by a white picket fence. Rose bushes grew on both sides of the yard; flowers bloomed along the red brick walkway that led up to the house. A wicker rocking chair occupied one corner of the porch.

Vince swore softly as he parked his car behind hers. Talk about your vine-covered cottage! All that was missing was a cat sleeping on the rocker.

"What do you think?" Cara asked as he got out of the car.

"Looks nice."

"It is. I love it! Of course, it's not nearly as big or as nice as . . . never mind."

"That's okay. This place looks more like you than that old mansion."

"Do you really think so?"

He nodded.

She waved to Frank, then took Vince's hand in hers as they went up the walkway to the porch. She unlocked the front door, then waited for him to precede her.

"After you," he said.

Cara stepped inside, then glanced over her shoulder, frowning when she saw he was still standing out on the porch. "Aren't you coming in?"

"My mama always taught me to wait to be invited."

If Cordova comes to call, he can't enter unless you invite him inside. Her father's words rose in the back of her mind, but she dismissed them out of hand. She had seen Vince during the day, she had talked to him on the phone when the sun was high in the sky. He couldn't be a vampire. It had just been her father's way of trying to break them up.

"Okay," she said, flicking on the light switch, "you're invited. Come on in."

Vince crossed the threshold, his skin tingling as he did so. He wondered what it was about thresholds that had the power to repel him. If he ever saw Cara's father again, maybe he would ask him. Come to think of it, he still had a lot of unanswered questions about his new lifestyle.

"So, what do you think?" Cara asked as he looked around. "Most of the furniture came with the house. I really like the sofa, but I'm not sure I like the end tables or the . . ."

"It's real nice, darlin'," he said, and it was.

The walls were off-white, the floor was hardwood. A blue and white flowered sofa and matching love seat were arranged on opposite sides of a glass-topped coffee table. The end tables were a dark red oak, the lamps were wrought iron. An entertainment center took up most of one wall.

"Come on," she said, taking him by the hand, "I'll give you a tour."

He followed her into the kitchen, which was a sort of sage green with stainless steel appliances. A small round table held a vase of fresh flowers. In addition to the living room and kitchen, there was also a small guestroom, a bathroom, and a large linen closet on the first floor.

He followed Cara upstairs. There were two bedrooms here, each with their own bathroom. One bedroom was yellow; the other, larger room was a pale blue. She had taken the blue bedroom for herself.

Vince glanced at the bed. The spread was white. Several pillows in various shades of blue were scattered near the headboard. He swore softly as his mind immediately conjured an image of the two of them snuggling under the covers, their arms and legs intimately entwined.

He blew out a breath, banishing the images from his mind.

"I still need to buy a few things," Cara remarked.

"It's a nice place," Vince said. "It suits you."

"Thanks." She smiled, pleased. It was important to her that he liked the place, though she wasn't sure why. "Can I get you anything? Coffee? A cold drink?"

"No, I'm fine."

Still holding his hand, she led him back into the living room and sat down on the sofa. He dropped down beside her, every fiber of his being attuned to her presence—the scent of her hair and skin, the steady beat of her heart, the rhythm of her breathing, the warmth of her thigh brushing against his own. His body grew hard. His fangs ached.

He swore under his breath, quietly cursing himself for his lack of restraint last night, and for the hunger raging through him now. He had fed earlier and, for the first time, he had found little satisfaction in it. Having tasted Cara's sweetness, he was afraid he would never be satisfied with anything else.

"Do you want to watch some TV?" she asked.

He didn't miss the tremor in her voice. Was she as nervous as he was? Did her body ache for his touch the way his ached for hers? He should tell her the truth tonight. It was the right thing to do, but he couldn't bear to lose her, not now.

"Vince?"

"Sure, darlin', whatever you want to do is fine with me."

Picking up the remote, she turned on the TV, then turned it off again. "I'd rather talk, if that's all right with you."

"Something on your mind?"

"You," she replied candidly. "I really don't know very much about you."

He shrugged. "There isn't a whole hell of a lot to know."

"Tell me about your family. Are you close? Do you see them often?"

"Not as often as I'd like. I think I told you I've got three brothers and a sister."

"And a cat."

"Right."

"Are you the oldest? The youngest?"

"I'm the youngest son. My oldest brother, Ray, is a cop. He's married to an accountant and they've got three kids. My brother Frank is a fireman. He got married two years ago. Baby on the way. Joe is a paramedic. He's got four kids and another due any time now. My sister, Eve, got married last year. She's two years younger than I am."

"Are your parents still alive?"

"Yeah. My old man was a mechanic. My mother's a stay-at-home mom, although she's been talking about going to work since my dad retired," Vince said, grinning. "She said she understands now why so many older women go to work. She complains a lot about him being underfoot all day, but she doesn't mean it."

"It sounds like you have a wonderful family," Cara said wistfully. "I wish I had brothers and sisters."

"There were times when I wished I didn't," Vince remarked. Times like now, when he no longer fit into the family. "Have you talked to your folks lately?"

"No. I don't know what to say." She blinked back the hot tears that threatened to fall. "I'm not sure how I feel about them anymore. Why didn't they tell me the truth?"

"Probably because they were afraid you'd react just the way you did."

"They should have told me years ago."

"Would that have made it any easier to believe?"

"I don't know," she said miserably. "Maybe if they'd told me when I was a child, it would have been easier to accept." She shook her head. "Maybe not."

"They were probably afraid you'd tell someone when you were younger," Vince suggested. "It might have been a hard secret to keep."

"I guess so." She tried to imagine how she would have reacted if she had found out when she was eight or nine or fifteen. Would she even have believed it? As for keeping such a thing a secret, until she went to school, she'd had no one to tell.

"They've been good to you, Cara. They raised you the best they could. It's obvious that they love you. I think you're being too hard on them."

She rested her head on his shoulder. "Maybe."

"They're the only parents you've got," Vince said quietly. "You might want to remember that."

A tear slipped down her cheek. He was right, she thought. Vampires or not, they were the only family she had.

Chapter 17

Serafina stood by the table in Anthony's lab. She felt like shouting and wished Anton was there to share in her victory.

Bringing the dead back to life had sounded easy when she read the incantation in the book, but she had expected the actual execution of the spell to be far more complicated than it appeared on paper. With that in mind, she had found a spell for bringing animals back to life. She had practiced on a cat, a dog, a monkey, a sheep, a goat, and, lastly, a small ape she had stolen from a kid's petting zoo.

Restoring life to the dead had given her the most amazing sense of omnipotence, and reaffirmed her own powers, as well.

She could do this. She could bring her beloved back to life.

Anton walked through the house, wondering where his mother had gone. She had been away from home and the bookstore more and more of late. When he asked where she was spending her time, she just smiled and said she would tell him when the time was right. He wondered if she was having an affair. He wondered what she would say when he told her that he'd struck out with Cara. Not that he cared. True, her rejection had stung his pride, but that was all. He'd never wanted to date her in the first place. She was too blond and far too innocent for his taste. He preferred women with dark hair and dusky skin, women who knew the score and were willing to play the game according to his rules. As for his mother's plans for revenge, well, he'd worry about that when the time came.

After grabbing a beer from the fridge, he went down to the basement. Lately, he had become more and more fascinated with his father's journals and diaries. His father had made a note of the date he had met Brenna Flanagan, and of the subsequent times he had met her either at Myra's bookshop or at The Nocturne. The name Roshan DeLongpre was also mentioned, as was a young vampire named Jimmy Dugan. His father had used Dugan's blood in some of his experiments. All experiments with Dugan's blood had failed.

His father had taken copious notes on his research. He had listed the people he had tested, among them a young man named Roger West. Anton studied the various compounds and ingredients his father had used, and the reaction of each subject to each new injection. His father had noted that Roger West had rejected the vampire's blood and that he had died a violent death, his body slowly shriveling up until, at the end, he had looked like a human dried apple.

Anton read the entries with cool detachment. His father's anger and frustration as each new attempt failed came through loud and clear. Anton didn't make any judgments about whether what his father had been doing was right or wrong; instead, he studied his father's notes and tried to figure out where his father's formula had gone wrong.

An elixir with the power to grant eternal life. Anton smiled, thinking of the possibilities, the fame and fortune that would come to a man who could provide mankind with such a wondrous gift.

Chapter 18

The vampire stood on the sidewalk in front of the house with the white picket fence. She didn't have to be inside to know what was happening. Her preternatural senses were so keen, she could almost picture the couple inside. The woman was mortal, young, and in love. The man was the vampire's own fledgling. She had brought him across exactly a year ago. In all her long existence, she had only bestowed the Dark Gift on five other men. She had made them, used them, and forgotten them.

But this last one, Vince, there was something about him, something that kept him alive in her memory, and so she had decided to come and see how he was getting along in his new life.

Her mind connected with his. *Come to me.* It was not a request, but a command, one he could not ignore.

Smiling, she faded into the shadows and waited.

Come to me.

Vince frowned as a familiar voice whispered through the corridors of his mind. It was a voice he would never forget, one he was compelled to obey.

Cara frowned when he eased out of her embrace and rose from the sofa. "Where are you going?"

"I've got to go."

"Why? It's early."

"It's after midnight." He tried to fight the compulsion to leave, but it was useless. Leaning down, he kissed her. "I've got a customer bringing a car in early in the morning. I'll see you tomorrow night, okay?"

She looked up at him, her expression worried. "Is something wrong?"

"No, darlin'."

"You're sure?"

"I'm sure." He kissed her again. "Good night."

It was all he could do to keep from running out of the house toward the vampire who waited for him—the vampire who had changed his life forever.

Once outside, he stood on the sidewalk and then, as if guided by an invisible hand, he walked down the street until he came to a small park.

The vampire was waiting for him on a park bench. She smiled as he approached.

"Vincent. How well you look."

"What do you want?" She was even more beautiful than he remembered. Her skin was like smooth porcelain; her hair was thick and black and fell to her hips in rippling waves. Her eyes were an amazing shade of green. Clad in a pair of skin-tight black pants and a wine-red sweater that outlined every curve, she looked sexy as hell.

"Is that any way to speak to me?" She spoke like a queen questioning a commoner and as she did so, he felt her power roll over him, sizzling through his veins like an electric shock. The hair prickled along his arms.

"I'm sorry." His tone was curt.

"Come, sit beside me."

He hesitated only a moment, certain that any refusal would only cause him more pain.

"So tell me," she said, "how are you getting on?"

"What do you care? You made me and dumped me."

"Mind your tongue!"

He bit back the sharp retort that rose in his mind.

She dragged her fingernails down his arm, leaving tiny furrows of blood behind. Her touch made him shiver. "I've thought of you often this past year."

"I've thought of you, too," he muttered darkly.

"I'm sure you have."

Her gaze bored into him. He had the distinct impression that she could see into his very soul, that she knew everything he had said and done in the past year, every thought that had crossed his mind, then and now.

Her fingers kneaded his biceps. "Is there anything you would like to ask me?"

"Your name, for a start."

She laughed softly. "You may call me Mara."

"I thought vampires had to sleep during the day. Why doesn't the sun render me powerless?"

"My blood is very old and very powerful," she explained. "The sun no longer has any effect on me, and since my blood now runs in your veins, you are able to be active during the day. In a year or two, the sun will have no power over you at all."

Vince felt a rush of excitement. If what she said was true, someday in the near future he would be able to return to his family and resume his old lifestyle. "What is it about thresholds? What power do they hold?"

She shrugged. "They have a built-in power all their own. Every home that has not been defiled is protected by that innate magic."

"Defiled how?"

"Homes where there has been foul play, murder, incest, or any kind of depravity. Such acts destroy the threshold, rendering it powerless."

Vince nodded. It made sense in an otherworldly sort of way. "How long have you been a vampire?"

"I was made when Cleopatra ruled Egypt." Seeing his frown, she added, "Sometime in 51 BC."

Vince swore in astonishment. These days, most people lived to be seventy-five or eighty. A few lived to be over a hundred. But to live for thousands of years . . . he shook his head. It was incredible. "Is the vampire who made you still living?"

"No."

"Am I the only vampire you've made?"

"No. There were five before you."

"Are they still alive?"

She made a vague gesture with her hand. "I don't know. I don't care."

"Then what are you doing here? I mean, if you didn't give a damn about them . . ."

She laughed softly. "Why do I care about you?"

"Yeah."

"I don't know. That's why I came." She frowned thoughtfully. "The woman inside. Cara. What is she to you?"

"How do you know her name?"

"I read it in her mind. She's in love with you. Are you in love with her?"

"Why ask? Can't you just read my thoughts?"

"If I wish, but conversation is more stimulating."

"Yes," he said. "I love her. Have you ever been in love?"

"Many times," she replied, her expression wistful. "But it never lasts. Mortals are such fragile creatures, and they live such a short time."

"The ones you made, were you in love with them?"

"No."

"Why did you bring them across?"

She shrugged. "It's been so long, I don't recall. Curiosity, I suppose. Or maybe boredom."

"Is that why you brought me across?" he asked bitterly. "Because you were bored?"

She laughed again, the sound soft and musical, like the chiming of silver bells on a summer day. "I'm afraid so."

Vince muttered an oath.

"You're not happy with your new state of being?"

Vince frowned into the distance. Was he happy as a vampire? There were things about his new lifestyle that he liked, but until she had told him he would soon be able to go out in the sun, he would have said that, all things considered, he would rather be mortal.

Out of curiosity, he asked, "Can you undo what you've done?"

"No. Only death can free you." She studied him dispassionately for a moment. "Would you like me to release you?"

"You'd destroy me?" he exclaimed with a snap of his fingers. "Just like that?"

"If you wish."

"Damn, woman, you're one heartless . . ." He let the thought die, unfinished, at the warning look in her eyes.

"I don't want you to be unhappy," she said. "I'm not sure why. Come, spend the night with me."

"Is that a command?"

"Are you refusing me?" She looked suddenly like a child whose stocking was empty on Christmas morning.

"I'm sorry, but . . ."

"Your little mortal wouldn't like it." She finished his thought for him as she caressed his cheek. "Perhaps it was that streak of honor that first attracted me to you. Ah, well, I'll see you again," she said, and vanished from his sight.

Vince shook his head. If there was one thing he didn't need, it was another woman in his life.

* * *

Mara watched her fledgling get into his sleek black car and drive away. Sometimes she longed for the old days. Life had been simpler then, slower. There had been a charm and beauty to life in the long ago time that was missing today. She had seen so many changes in the eons since she had been made. Occasionally, when the rush and noise of the world grew too great, she sought shelter in the arms of the earth. There, lost in the quiet darkness, she sometimes slept for hundreds of years. Each time, she emerged regenerated, only to find a new world awaiting her.

So many changes. Kingdoms rose and fell. New discoveries were made in the earth and in the heavens. There were always wars in distant lands. Cures were found for old diseases while new ailments were constantly being discovered. Earthquakes, tidal waves, tornadoes, and floods reminded humanity of how frail and precarious their existence was. Airplanes flew higher, cars went faster. Mankind was constantly inventing new and better ways to destroy itself. Sometimes she wondered how mortals slept at night when their lives were in constant peril.

She shook her head. The only constant was change.

Her fledgling had changed, as well. Until Vince, she had not made a new vampire in over a thousand years. She was surprised at how powerful he had become in such a short time. Did he have any idea of just how invincible he was?

She thought of the young female inside the house and experienced a rush of unexpected jealousy. For a moment, she toyed with the idea of destroying the female. It would be all too easy. She could do it from here with no more than a thought, but to what end? Mortals lived such a short time, there was little satisfaction in depriving them of the few years they had.

Perhaps hunting for prey would dispel her melancholia. It had been years since she had needed to feed, but she was suddenly overcome with the urge to hunt, to hold a mortal in thrall, to feel the rapid beating of a fearful heart, to savor the warm sweet taste of life's elixir.

Leaving that part of the city, she sought a place to hunt. Though she had no fear of recriminations, old habits died hard. It had ever been her wont to find her prey among the poor and downtrodden. Should she decide to drain her victims dry, there would be no one to mourn their passing, no one to comment on their absence.

She had just turned down a seedy looking street when she realized there was another vampire nearby.

Curious, she sought him out. He was young in the life, compared to her; but then, compared to her, they were all little more than fledglings.

He came to an abrupt halt when he saw her, his eyes narrowing as he recognized her for what she was.

Mara plucked his name from his mind. "Roshan De-Longpre," she murmured. "I bid you good evening."

He bowed from the waist. "I'm afraid you have me at a disadvantage, madam."

His voice was deep and rich, his manner respectful yet wary. She liked him immediately. "I am Mara."

Though he tried to hide it, his surprise was evident in the widening of his eyes and the sharp intake of his breath. "Like all of our kind, I have heard of you."

"Oh?" She took a step closer, noting his finely chiseled features, the strength of his jaw, the spread of his shoulders. "And what have you heard?"

"That you are truly immortal, and that the sun no longer holds any power over you." His gaze moved over her in frank admiration. "And that you are the most beautiful of women."

She smiled, pleased by the compliment and his obvious sincerity. "I take it you are the master of the city." She had known it wasn't Vincent. He was too young in the life and too new to the area.

"I am."

"I am surprised you allow another into your domain."

"You speak of Cordova?"

She nodded.

"He is my daughter's friend."

Ah, she thought, the woman in the house. Cara. "How is it that you have a child?"

"We adopted her when she was an infant."

Mara digested that for a moment. "What was it like, raising a human child?"

"It was . . ." He searched for the right word. "Interesting."

She smiled, thinking that *interesting* was probably an understatement. "How did she feel, having vampires for parents?"

"Until recently, she didn't know. She was understandably upset when she found out."

"Yet she is in love with a vampire."

"She doesn't believe he's one of us."

"It should be . . . interesting . . . when she finds out the truth," Mara remarked with a faint smile. "Come, hunt with me."

"It would be my pleasure."

"And mine," she said, linking her arm with his. "I have not hunted with a companion in many years." She threw back her head and took a deep breath. "Do you smell it?" she asked, and he heard the underlying note of excitement in her voice, saw it in the predatory gleam in her extraordinary green eyes.

Roshan nodded. The scent of prey was in the air.

Mara was a skilled and ruthless hunter, but then, that was to be expected, Roshan thought with a wry grin, seeing as how she'd had thousands of years to perfect her skill.

She called her desired prey to her with a look, and because she was in the mood to hunt, she took only a taste from each of her chosen victims before offering them to Roshan.

There was nothing like it, he thought, the thrill of the hunt, the surge of power as you held your prey in your grasp, the thick, rich taste of their life's blood sliding over your tongue, the way it filled you with warmth and strength, the exhilarating sense of being invincible. In the last few years, he had hunted only when necessary and taken only what he needed to survive. But tonight, tonight they drank from dozens until even his prodigious thirst was quenched.

And then, to his surprise, Mara drew him into her arms. "Shh," she whispered, "don't be afraid. I want only a taste."

He would have refused, but he found himself powerless to resist. He stared into her eyes, eyes as deep and green as the Nile, sighed as her fangs pierced the skin of his neck just below his left ear. It had been a long time since anyone had drunk from him. He had forgotten what it was like, the heat of it, the sensual pleasure that bordered on ecstasy. And yet, even as he reveled in it, he felt the sharp prick of his conscience, certain that Brenna would not approve.

Mara licked the wound in his neck, then swept her hair aside, offering Roshan her throat. A thrill of anticipation ran down his spine. To drink from Mara was akin to drinking from the wellspring of eternal life.

With a shake of his head, he backed away from her. "No, I can't."

"Of course you can."

He shook his head again. It was bad enough that he had let her drink from him. To drink from her would be like betraying Brenna.

"Do not be so quick to refuse," Mara said. "I'm offering you more than you know."

"I don't understand."

"As you yourself said, the sun no longer has any power over me."

"You mean . . . ?"

"Exactly. Once you have drunk from me, you will no longer be under its spell. You may even find that, after a year or so, you can walk in its light."

He pondered that a moment—to walk in the sun's light again, to feel its warmth on his face. Was it truly possible? "Why are you offering this to me?"

She lifted one slim shoulder and let it fall. "Consider it a gift in appreciation for your company this night."

"If my wife drinks from me, will she be affected the same way?"

"I should think so, though it may take longer."

It would be a miracle to walk in the light of day again, to no longer be rendered helpless each dawn. Surely Brenna would understand! He knew how much she missed the brisk days of autumn and the warm halcyon days of summer.

Mara was watching him, waiting for his decision. Taking a deep breath, he reached for her.

She closed her eyes as he lowered his head. Her skin was smooth, cool to the touch. Her blood was like liquid fire on his tongue. He felt the power of it sing through every fiber and cell of his being. More, he thought, he wanted more. He wanted it all.

Enough!

Her voice rang out in his mind and he drew back, unable to resist her command.

"Forgive me," he murmured, horrified by what he had so desperately longed to do.

"There is nothing to forgive," she said, and he saw the understanding in her eyes.

"Thank you," he replied fervently, and then asked, "What of Vince? Is he able to walk in the sun's light?"

"Not yet, but soon. The sun does not render him powerless, though he must remain indoors, and at some point during the day he must rest. But as he grows older and stronger, the sun will have less power over him."

In a courtly gesture, Roshan took Mara's hand in his. He bowed over it, then kissed the back of her hand. "Again, my thanks."

"Take care of yourself, Roshan DeLongpre. There is evil in this city."

He frowned. "What do you mean?"

"Can't you feel it?"

"Not as strongly as my wife. Do you know who or what it is?"

"No, only that it is nearby and growing stronger." She smiled at him, her green eyes glowing, and then she vanished from his sight.

He stood there for a long while, reliving all that had happened, all that Mara had told him, and then he went home, eager to tell Brenna of the night's events.

Brenna looked up from the book she was reading when Roshan entered the room. "What took you so long?"

"You won't believe this," he said, dropping down on the sofa beside her. "I ran into Mara."

"She's here, in the city?"

He nodded. "She asked me to go hunting with her."

"Oh?"

Roshan grinned. There was no mistaking the edge in his wife's voice or the jealousy in her eyes. "How could I refuse? But, Brenna, listen, she took my blood . . ."

"What?" Her eyes narrowed ominously.

"Hush, love, and listen . . ."

Brenna sprang to her feet. Hands fisted on her hips, she stared down at him. "How could you let her do that?"

"I didn't *let* her," he said curtly. "She wanted it and she took it." He took a deep breath. "Brenna, listen to me. She took my blood and she gave me hers." Even now, he couldn't believe it. "I can feel it inside me. Brenna, you can't imagine the power!"

"You drank from her?" she asked, her voice little more than a whisper. Between vampires, the sharing of blood was akin to making love.

"Brenna." Rising, he drew her into his arms. "Listen to me. She said the sun will no longer have any power over me and that I won't be rendered helpless during the day. That in a year or two it won't have any power over me at all. Do you know what that means?"

She stood stiff and unmoving in his arms, her eyes swimming with tears. "You betrayed me."

"Brenna, I did it for you. She said if I give you my blood, the day will come when you, too, will be able to walk in the sunlight. Think of it, love. You won't be trapped in the darkness anymore."

Brenna blinked at him, her brow furrowed. "I don't believe you."

"It's true. Read my mind if you don't believe me. You'll see that it's true." He caressed her cheek. "Think of it, love, to be able to walk in the sun again." He drew her down on the sofa once more and turned his head to the side. "Drink, love."

She hesitated a moment before she licked his skin, and then her fangs pierced his flesh. His blood was warm as it flowed over her tongue. She had tasted him before, but it was different now. She felt a sudden rush of power flood her being, felt her senses expand as never before.

Lifting her head, she gazed into her husband's eyes. And even though she knew it was only her imagination, she saw the sun shining there.

Chapter 19

Cara slept late the following morning. Rising, she made her bed, showered and dressed, and then went downstairs where she had a bowl of cereal and a glass of orange juice for breakfast.

And all the while, she thought about Vince. Last night, he had dried her tears, and while he comforted her, one thing had led to another and they had made love, and it had been even more wonderful than the first time.

Smiling with the memory, she did a load of wash, dusted and vacuumed, took the clothes out of the dryer, folded them, and put them away. She had a tuna salad sandwich and a soda for lunch and before she knew it, it was time to get ready for work.

Leaving the house, she drove to her parents' home, aware that Di Giorgio was right behind her. She wondered where he was staying now and when he slept, since he was always there, no matter what time she went out.

She pulled up to the curb across the street from her parents' residence and put the car in park. Sitting there, she stared at the house she had once called home. She had been happy there, she thought. Although birthdays and holidays had been far from ordinary, her parents had done their best to make them happy occasions. She had never wanted for food or clothing or shelter. Or love.

She remembered when they told her she had been adopted. She had been eight at the time. She recalled listening carefully as Brenna explained that she couldn't have children and how badly she had longed for a child of her own, and how, out of all the children in the world, they had chosen Cara to be their daughter. Of course, she knew now that she hadn't been chosen out of all the children in the world. Her parents had taken her home because her birth mother hadn't wanted her. But that didn't change the fact that her parents had loved her unconditionally every day of her life.

Tears stung her eyes as she pulled away from the curb.

She tried to hold onto her anger and her sense of betrayal as she drove to the library, but it was no use. The truth was, she still loved her parents in spite of everything, and that just left her feeling more confused than ever.

She had a sudden urge to see Vince, but a glance at her watch showed her she couldn't swing by the garage and still make it to work on time.

With a sigh of regret, she drove to the library. Sarah Beth pulled in right behind her.

"I so didn't want to come to work today," Sarah Beth said as she got out of her car. She placed her hand over her swollen abdomen. "I can't believe I have another two months to go. I feel like I'm ready to explode."

"You look like it, too," Cara said with a grin. "Are you sure you don't have triplets in there?"

"Bite your tongue! I don't know how I let Dean talk me into this baby. I don't even like kids!"

"Well, it's too late to change your mind now." Cara opened the door for Sarah Beth and followed her inside. "Why don't you take it easy today? Maybe go through the young-adult database and make sure it's up to date? You can do that sitting down."

"You're a good friend," Sarah Beth said. "So, tell me, how are things with you and the hunk?"

"Very well, thank you," Cara replied. She knew she was blushing but she couldn't help it.

She hoped Bethy wouldn't notice, but of course she did.

"Anything you want to tell me?" Sarah Beth asked.

"No." Cara dropped her handbag into the bottom drawer of her desk and switched on her computer.

Sarah Beth smiled a knowing smile. "You don't have to say a word. It wasn't so long ago that I had that same dreamy look in my eyes."

Cara picked up her mail. "I'm sure I don't know what you mean."

"I'm sure you do."

Cara made a shooing motion with her hand. "Run along, Mrs. Coleman, I have work to do. And so do you."

"Have it your way," Sarah Beth said, laughing. "I'll see you later."

Cara read her mail and sent the necessary replies, then spent an hour reading the latest book reviews and announcements of upcoming books. She shook her head, thinking it was a good thing she worked in a library because she would never be able to afford to buy all the books she wanted to read. She filled out a purchase order for new books, answered several phone calls, and it was time for dinner.

She usually ate with Sarah Beth but Dean had the night off and he came by to take Sarah Beth out.

Leaving the library, Cara got into her car and drove to Vince's garage, deciding she would rather see him than have dinner.

He was under a car when she got there.

"Hey, Cara," he called, "what are you doing here this time of night?"

"How did you know it was me?"

"I'd know you in the dark with my eyes closed."

She found the thought thrilling and a little frightening.

He slid out from under the car and nimbly gained his feet. "What brings you here?"

"I just wanted to see you. Do you mind?"

"Of course not." He pulled a rag from his back pocket and wiped the grease from his hands. "How long can you stay?"

"Not long. I only get forty-five minutes for dinner."

"Did you eat already?"

"No, I decided to come here instead."

He drew her into his arms and gave her a hug.

"Is that the best you can do?" she asked with mock disappointment.

"You know better than that, darlin'," he said with a roguish grin.

"Show me."

His kiss was like silken fire and lightning, sending heat shooting through every fiber of her being. She pressed herself against him, wanting more.

"Here, now," he said, "what do you think you're doing?"

"Nothing," she said innocently.

"Nothing?" He drew her body tight against his, letting her feel his arousal.

She smiled at him, a decidedly sexy, wanton smile.

"You keep looking at me like that and I'm going to take you upstairs and have my wicked way with you."

"Really?"

"Really."

"Better hurry," she said, "I have to be back at work in half an hour."

He didn't waste any time. He closed the garage, swung her into his arms, and carried her swiftly up the stairs. His hands made quick work of undressing her and then he shed his own clothing. Naked, he fell back on the bed, carrying her with him, his hands and his mouth doing wonderfully erotic things, arousing her until she couldn't think straight, couldn't think of anything but him. She moved her hands over his body, loving the feel of his skin beneath her fingertips, the texture of his hair, the way his body quivered beneath hers. She explored him in a way she never had before, touching, tasting, learning what made him moan with pleasure. She was surprised to find that he was ticklish, and she filed that away for future use.

Time lost all meaning. She didn't care if she ever went back to work; she didn't want to be anywhere but where she was, in Vince's arms, in Vince's bed.

Completion, when it came, was like Christmas and the Fourth of July all rolled into one.

Sated, she collapsed on top of him, her head pillowed in the hollow of his shoulder, her heart beating in time to his. Gradually, her breathing returned to normal. She shivered as the sweat cooled on her skin.

"Here." Vince pulled a blanket over the two of them. "Better?"

"Hmm."

He massaged the back of her neck, his fingers delving into her hair. "Are you sure you have to go back to work?"

"I don't want to."

"I don't want you to."

She smiled against his neck. "I wonder what time is it."

"Six twenty-five."

Cara opened her eyes and glanced at her watch. It was exactly six twenty-five. She raised herself on her elbows and stared down at him. "How did you know that?" There was no clock in the room; he wasn't wearing a watch.

He shrugged. "A good guess."

She frowned, but there was no time to argue. She had

to be back at work in fifteen minutes. "Can I use your shower?"

"Only if I can share it with you."

The thought of showering with Vince made her blush from head to toe even as it made her smile with anticipation.

She experienced a twinge of embarrassment as she followed him into the bathroom. She wasn't accustomed to such intimacies.

He turned on the water, adjusted it, stepped into the shower stall, and offered her his hand.

"I've never done this before," Cara said, closing the door behind her.

"You've never showered before?" he asked with a wry grin.

"No, silly," she replied, punching him on the arm. "I've never showered with anyone before." She felt her blush deepen. "Lately, I've been doing a lot of things I've never done before."

Vince grunted softly. "I've got no objection, as long as you do them all with me." He handed her the soap. "Next time, we'll wash each other."

"Why not this time?"

"It's okay with me," he said, "but you won't make it back to work on time if we do."

Feeling as though she had swallowed a piece of the sun, Cara washed quickly and stepped out of the shower. Moments later, she was dressed and ready to go when Vince came out of the bathroom wearing nothing but a towel wrapped around his lean waist. She eyed him hungrily, admiring the width of his shoulders, his muscular chest and biceps, the way the water glistened in his long black hair, and she wanted him all over again.

His knowing grin brought a quick flush to her cheeks.

"You'd better get out of here while you can," he said, drawing her into his arms.

She nodded. "Will I see you later?"

"You bet." He kissed her, hard and quick, then gave her a playful swat on her rump. "I'll meet you at nine at the library. Now, go on, get out of here before I change my mind."

Smiling, she grabbed her handbag and her car keys and left the garage. On the way back to work, she pulled a candy bar from her purse. It wasn't exactly a well-balanced meal, but she wouldn't have traded her time with Vince for a seven-course dinner.

She had only been back at work for a few minutes when Sarah Beth breezed into her office. "Hey, I was wondering . . ." She stared at Cara, her eyes wide.

"Wondering what?" Cara asked.

"If I didn't know better, I'd say you just crawled out of a warm bed."

Cara felt a rush of heat flood her cheeks. "I'm sure I don't know what you're talking about."

"Uh-huh." Sarah Beth sat in the chair beside Cara's desk. "Had a little quickie, did we?"

"Bethy!" Cara glanced at her open door. "Do you mind?"

"My dear, I think you do protest too much. And judging by that glow in your eyes, it must have been fantastic."

"It was," Cara said softly.

Leaning forward, Sarah Beth gave Cara a quick hug. "I'm happy for you, Cara. Really! I was beginning to think you were going to be an old maid."

Cara blew out a sigh. "I just met the man, Bethy. It's too early to be thinking about marriage." And far too early to be sleeping with him. Cara shook her head. She must be out of her mind. She had only known Vince Cordova for a few days and not only was she already sleeping with him but she was eagerly looking forward to the next time they could make love. She had never, ever done anything like this before. She'd never even been tempted. But then, she had never known anyone like Vince before, never felt anything like this before, either. She told herself that no matter how it ended, she wouldn't be sorry, but she couldn't completely still the small, insistent voice of her conscience that whispered what she was doing was wrong.

"So," she said, shaking off her troubling thoughts, "what can I do for you?"

"What?" Sarah Beth blinked at her, and then laughed. "I forgot what I came in here for."

"Well, come back when you think of it, or give me a call. I need to tackle this pile of paperwork. Weren't computers supposed to put an end to all this? Honestly, where does it all come from?"

"Gremlins," Sarah Beth said, rising. "See ya later."

The rest of the day passed quickly. As usual, toward nine o'clock, Cara found herself glancing repeatedly at her watch, willing the minutes to go faster.

She was shutting down her computer when a tingling down her spine told her Vince was near. Leaving her desk, she went to her office door and there he was, striding toward her. Lordy, she thought, the man had to be the sexiest thing on two legs. She loved the way he moved, fluid and self-confident, like some big jungle cat that knew he was the king of the beasts. There were only a few women in the library, but they all turned to stare at him as he passed by. And then he was there, in her doorway, a slow smile spreading over his handsome face—a smile that said he was remembering their earlier lovemaking and was looking forward to more of the same.

"Hey, darlin'," he drawled.

"Hey, yourself." She knew she was blushing again, but she couldn't help it.

Closing the distance between them, he drew her into his arms and kissed her.

"Vince!"

"Sorry, I couldn't wait."

She scooped up her purse in one hand and caught his arm with the other. "Come on, let's go."

"Goodnight, Cara," Sarah Beth said with a wink. "Have fun."

Cheeks burning, Cara hurried out the door.

"What was that all about?" Vince asked.

"Nothing."

"Nothing?" He opened the car door for her and closed it behind her. "Sounded like something to me," he said, sliding behind the wheel of the Mustang.

"Oh, she thinks she's so smart!"

Vince laughed. "I guess the jig is up, huh?"

"It's not funny. I mean, if she can tell just by looking at me . . ." Cara shook her head.

"Are you ashamed of what we did?"

"No, but, well . . ." She looked at him, her expression troubled. "Is it that obvious? Can everyone tell?"

"I don't think so, but I've got to say, you do have a certain glow in your eyes . . ."

"That's what Bethy said!"

"Yeah?" Taking her hand in his, he gave it a squeeze. "All I can say is that I'm glad I was the one who put it there."

"Me, too. Where are we going?"

"I don't know." He slid a glance in her direction. "Where would you like to go?"

"I don't know." She wanted to go to his place, but she wanted Vince to be the one to suggest it. She was so new to this, so uncertain. Maybe it hadn't been as wonderful for him as it had been for her. Maybe it hadn't meant as much to him.

All her doubts were swept away when he turned down Seventh Street. Moments later, he pulled into the driveway, unlocked the iron security gate, and drove into the garage.

Butterflies erupted in her stomach as he closed the

door behind them, cocooning them in darkness. She stayed where she was until he opened the car door and reached for her hand.

"Okay?" he asked.

She nodded, then realized he probably couldn't see her in the dark. Or maybe he could, she thought, when he lifted her into his arms and carried her across the floor and up the stairs to his apartment.

Inside, he turned on the lights; then, letting her body slide against his, he slowly lowered her feet to the floor.

Cara smiled inwardly as her body brushed intimately against his. He wanted her, there could be no doubt of that.

He proved it by swinging her up into his arms and carrying her to bed.

Chapter 20

Anton was about to leave the house late Wednesday night when his mother came home.

"Anton! Where are you going?"

"I thought I'd go hang out at The Nocturne for a while. Where've you been? You're never here anymore."

"I've been at your father's laboratory."

"The lab? What were you doing there?"

Taking his arm, Serafina led him back into the house and into the living room. Sitting on the sofa, she pulled him down beside her.

"I've been practicing a spell I found in an old book."

"What kind of spell?"

Serafina plucked at the hem of her skirt, suddenly reluctant to tell her son what she had been doing.

"Mother? What kind of spell?"

"Bringing dead animals back to life."

Anton frowned. "Why would you want to do that?"

Turning toward Anton, she took his hands in hers. "I bought some old books on witchcraft from someone on eBay." Her voice trembled with excitement. "There's a spell in one of them, a spell for bringing the dead back to life."

Anton's frown deepened. "Dead animals?"

"Dead people. Your father, Anton, I've found a way to bring him back."

Anton stared at his mother. She was out of her mind, he thought. She had grieved for his father so hard and for so long, it had driven her over the edge.

"Even if such a spell worked," he said quietly, "I doubt if it would work on someone who's been dead as long as my father."

"There was no time limit," she said. "It will work, I know it will."

"What's the spell?"

Serafina had read it so often, she could recite it from memory. "On All Hallow's Eve, between dusk and dawn, the blood of kin must be drawn, nine drops, no more, no less, the blood of kin you must bless. To this the blood of love you add, and the blood of an enemy, it must be had. Seven drops of each, one by one, quickly now, it must be done. Four drops of a maiden's blood, rosemary for remembrance, an infant's blood, three drops for life anew. A sprinkling of yarrow, a dash of rue. Spread the blood upon the crypt, when the moon commands the sky. Call forth the dead, his name times three. Doubt not, and he will come to thee."

Anton swore under his breath. She really was crazy. The blood of kin. No doubt she intended to use his own blood, Anton thought. The blood of an enemy. Probably that of the vampire, DeLongpre. And the blood of a maiden? Cara's.

"Was this the revenge you had planned all along?" he asked.

"No, but this is better. Don't you see? I'll bring your father back and he can exact his own vengeance." She clasped her hands to her breasts, her expression one of pure bliss. "And we'll be a family. Think of it, Anton, the three of together at last."

"There's no way to know if it will work," Anton said. "No way to practice it before we try it on my father."

"It will work," she said again, and there was no doubt in her voice. "I know it will."

Anton stared at his mother. She sounded so certain. "You didn't . . . ?" He shook his head. Surely she hadn't tried that silly incantation on anything besides animals; and if she had, he didn't want to know.

She's crazy, he thought again. Yet even as he worried that his mother was losing her mind, he found himself wondering if the incantation would, indeed, work.

Chapter 21

It was after midnight when Vince drove Cara back to the library to get her car.

"I wish I didn't have to go home," she said as he handed her out of the Mustang.

"Me, too." He drew her into his arms for one more kiss.

Cara waited for Vince to ask her to move in with him, thought about asking him to move in with her, and decided neither option was a good idea, at least not now. Things were already moving too fast.

"I should go," she said reluctantly.

"In a minute." He backed her up against the side of the car and kissed her again, his body leaning into hers. They had made love only a short time ago and he was already wanting her again. He'd become addicted to her, he thought, hopelessly, helplessly addicted to the sound of her voice, the warmth of her smile, the touch of her hand. Damn! He had it bad.

Vince kissed her again, and then again. He would have kissed her one more time if he hadn't suddenly become aware of being watched. Lifting his head, he scanned the darkness, then swore softly. It was only Di Giorgio, discreetly watching them from the shadows.

"You'd better go," Vince said.

"I thought . . . what happened?"

"Di Giorgio's keeping an eye on us. Kind of ruins the moment, don't you think?"

Cara blew out a sigh. "I thought he'd stop following me when I moved out of the house."

"Well, I'm kind of glad he's there," Vince said, opening her car door for her. "Gives me one less thing to worry about."

"Do you worry about me?" she asked.

"You bet." Bending down, he kissed her cheek. "I'll see you tomorrow."

"I can't wait."

"Me, either."

"Good night, Vince."

"Night, darlin'."

He watched her pull out of the parking lot, watched Di Giorgio pull out behind her. Out of habit, he glanced at the sky, judging the time. There were still hours until dawn.

He was about to get into his car and drive home when he decided to take a walk instead.

The streets were dark and quiet at this time of night. Walking with preternatural speed, he soon reached the outskirts of the city. He continued on, enjoying the solitude and the beauty of the moonlit countryside.

He was about to turn back when the scent of blood filled his nostrils. Unable to resist, he followed the scent to what looked like an abandoned brick building. The windows were boarded up on the inside and barred on the outside.

Vince frowned. The scent of blood was strong here and seemed to be coming from inside. He took a deep breath, only then realizing that the blood was animal, not human.

Grunting softly, he walked around the perimeter. Save for the smell of blood, there was no sign that anyone had been there recently, not that it mattered to him one way or the other. Still, it was curious.

Returning to the library parking lot, he got into his car and drove to The Nocturne. He felt Mara's presence as soon as he crossed the threshold. Amazingly, no one else seemed aware of the preternatural power that surrounded her.

Her voice whispered inside his mind. *Come,* she said, *join me.*

It was not a command this time, but an invitation.

He found her sitting at a small table in the rear, a Bloody Mariah in one hand. A second drink sat, untouched, on the table.

She smiled as he approached, then indicated he should take the chair across from her. "That drink is for you."

Vince arched one brow. "How did you know I'd be here?"

She smiled a mysterious smile. "Did you think coming here was your own idea?" Her voice was low, almost hypnotic.

"You mean it wasn't?"

"No. I was feeling lonely."

"So you planted the thought of coming here in my mind?"

She nodded, not the least bit guilty for tampering with his thoughts. "The nights can sometimes be long."

"Too long," he agreed. "And it must be worse for you. Tell me, what's it like to exist for so many years? Do you ever tire of it? Ever grow bored with your existence?"

"Now and then."

"How do you handle it?"

"There are ways to refresh yourself. The best way is to rest in the earth."

"You mean, like burrow into the ground and sleep there?"

"Yes."

"What about the bugs and the worms? Don't they . . ."

"They will not come near you."

The idea of burying himself in the earth should have been repulsive; instead, he found it strangely appealing. He glanced at the glass in his hand. He should have found drinking blood repulsive, too, but he didn't. Funny, how one's perspective changed when one became a vampire.

Vince was about to remark on it to Mara when he saw Anton saunter into the club as if he owned the place. Vince grinned inwardly. Talk about repulsive. He didn't know what it was, but there was something about the man that made his skin crawl.

"Evil," Mara said quietly.

"What?"

"That man is evil."

Vince followed Mara's gaze and saw that she was staring at Anton Bouchard.

Anton nodded at several women as he made his way to the bar. He hadn't seen Cara DeLongpre lately, but courting her was no longer necessary. His mother had other plans for DeLongpre's daughter now.

He was halfway across the room when he saw Vince Cordova sitting at a small table with a remarkably beautiful woman.

Anton snorted softly. Looked like Miss Cara Aideen DeLongpre had better find herself a new squeeze. Anton smiled at the pretty redhead waiting for him at the bar. He hadn't wasted any time in finding someone to take Cara's place. Her name was Stephanie and he had met her at The Nocturne last week. She was a looker, she was, with curly red hair, dusky skin, and dark brown eyes.

She smiled as he sat down beside her. Unlike Cara, Steph wasn't interested in anything but having a good time. They'd had a hell of a good time last night, he thought as he kissed her cheek, and unless he missed his guess, they would be having another good time tonight.

Chapter 22

Cara sat in the middle of her living-room floor, sorting
through cardboard ghosts, black cats, orange pumpkins,
scary witches, and the other holiday decorations spread out
around her. It would be Halloween soon. She had always
helped her mom decorate the house on October first,
and she was determined to carry on the tradition now
that she had a place of her own, even though she missed
the old, familiar decorations she had grown up with.

When she had lived with her parents, Halloween had
been her favorite holiday. She had loved going trick-or-
treating with her mom and dad when she was a little girl,
seeing the looks on the faces of the other trick-or-treaters
when they saw her mom and dad in their costumes . . .

Of course, she realized now that her father's costume
hadn't been a costume at all, and hard on the heels of that
thought came the astonishing realization that her mother's
witch costume hadn't been a costume either . . . Funny,
she'd never thought of that before. Cara shook her head.
It was hard enough to imagine her mother as a vampire,
but a vampire *and* a witch? No way! And yet, why was that
any harder to believe than anything else?

Remembering days past filled Cara with bittersweet

memories. Even when she had grown too old to go out trick-or-treating, it had been fun to stay home and hand out candy and see the costumes the neighborhood kids wore.

Rising, she began to decorate the house, but it wasn't with the sense of fun and enthusiasm she had experienced when she decorated her parents' home. Shaking off her gloom, she put a pair of Halloween candles on the mantel, along with a ceramic pumpkin and a couple of witches.

"Witches," she muttered darkly. "Maybe I'll dress up as a vampire witch this Halloween!"

By the time she finished decorating the house, both inside and out, it was two-thirty and she had to hurry to get ready for work.

She was about to leave the house when the phone rang.

Her spirits picked up when she heard Vince's voice on the other end of the line.

"Hey, darlin'."

"Hi." The sound of his voice filled her with a warm glow. "How are you?"

"Same as always. Just thought I'd call and see what you were doing."

"I was just about to leave for work." Smiling, she toyed with the phone cord. "I guess you're working."

"Oh, yeah, got three cars in here today, and four more coming in tomorrow morning."

"Oh." She bit down on her lip, wondering if he was calling to say he was going to be too busy to see her tonight.

"Hey, you all right? You sound a little glum all of a sudden."

"No, I'm fine."

"You sure?"

She forced a note of cheerfulness into her voice. "Of course. Why wouldn't I be?"

"I don't know, you tell me."

"Vince, I'm fine, honest."

"All right. Listen, I've got to go. I just wanted to hear your voice."

"You did?"

"Yeah. I'll see you later, okay?"

"It's more than okay. Vince?"

"Yeah?"

"I'm so glad you called."

"Me, too. Later darlin'."

"Bye."

Smiling, she hung up the receiver. He had called just to hear her voice. He really was the sweetest thing. Last night, after they had made love, her stomach had growled rather loudly, reminding her that, since breakfast, she hadn't eaten anything but a candy bar. Vince had insisted on ordering a pizza and green salad for her. He hadn't eaten anything, saying he had already had dinner, but he shared a bottle of wine with her. Wine and candlelight and Vince, who could ask for more?

"Time sure goes by fast," Sarah Beth said as she helped Cara hang a ghost and pumpkin mobile in the children's reading room. "I can't believe it's almost Halloween."

"I know," Cara said. "Seems like the holidays come faster every year. It's just a hop, skip, and a jump until Christmas."

Sarah Beth groaned. "Don't remind me. We're spending Christmas with Dean's family this year."

"It's only one day," Cara said.

"I know, but his mother hates me."

Cara patted Sarah Beth's tummy. "She'll change her tune once the baby's born, wait and see."

"Maybe," Sarah Beth said dolefully. "So, on a happier note, how are things with you and the hunk?"

Just the thought of Vince made Cara's stomach flutter with excitement. "Things are wonderful."

"Sounds like love," Sarah Beth mused.

"Is it possible to fall in love so fast? I mean, I've known him such a short time."

"Cara, time has nothing to do with it. Hearts don't have calendars."

"Then I guess I love him," she said with a happy sigh. "Just thinking about him makes me smile, and when we're together . . . oh, Bethy, I've never felt like this before. It scares me."

"Just relax and enjoy the ride, sweetie."

They placed a Halloween display on the front desk, taped cardboard cutouts of laughing ghosts, grinning vampires, scowling witches, and howling black cats wherever there was space.

After they decorated the library, Sarah Beth went to do some work at her desk and Cara went into the children's section and set up a display of books with Halloween themes.

When she finished setting up the book display, it was time for her dinner break.

She was definitely hungry, she thought with a sigh, but not for food.

Vince sensed Cara's nearness long before she entered the garage. By the time she arrived, he had washed his hands and face and combed his hair. He waited for her just inside the door.

He breathed in her scent as she stepped out of the car,

let it permeate every fiber of his being. How had he ever existed without this woman in his life?

Her smile settled deep in his heart and made him think of things he had thought forever lost to him, things like a real home and a woman of his own.

She walked straight into his arms as if she had always belonged there. "Hi."

"Hi, darlin'."

Her eyelids fluttered down as she lifted her face for his kiss.

But a kiss wasn't enough, would never be enough again.

Holding her close with one arm, he pulled down the security door, his need for her building with every breath.

"I don't think we're gonna make it upstairs," he muttered, his voice gruff.

"I don't care."

"Damn." He glanced around, seeking a place where he could lay her down. Grabbing an old blanket, he spread it on the floor, gently lowered her onto it, and followed her down.

She was as needy and greedy as he. Their clothing disappeared as if by magic and then she was in his arms, her heat warming him, chasing away the inner chill that had become a part of him with Mara's bite.

He kissed her deeply, almost desperately, his hands delving into her hair, massaging her scalp.

She moaned softly, her body arching beneath his in silent invitation.

"Cara." Knowing he had no right, he took her anyway, unable to resist the siren call of her sweetness or the sense of homecoming that engulfed him whenever she was in his arms.

Time slowed. The rest of the world faded away until there was nothing but the two of them reaching for that one moment when two bodies, two hearts, and two souls became one. It was, quite simply, magical, and over too soon.

Vince blew out a deep breath, and then he kissed her eyelids, her cheeks, the tip of her nose, and her chin.

"We've got to stop meeting like this," she said with a grin.

"We do?"

She nodded. "I don't know about you, but I think this cement is awfully hard, blanket or no blanket. From now on, let's do it in a bed. Yours or mine, I don't care."

Relief washed through him. For a moment, he had been afraid she was telling him good-bye.

She laughed softly. "And preferably someplace where your cat can't watch us."

"What?"

She pointed toward her feet. Following her gaze, he saw Cat sitting at the edge of the blanket, watching them through unblinking yellow eyes.

Muttering, "Darn cat," Vince sat up and drew Cara up beside him. His hand slid aimlessly up and down her back. He loved the silky feel of her hair, the heat of her skin, the musky scent of her.

She looked up at him, her head canted to one side. "Can I ask you something?"

"Sure, darlin'."

"Have you ever heard of a vampire who was also a witch?"

He frowned. "No. Why? Have you?"

She hesitated a moment, then blurted, "I think my mother is a witch."

"A witch *and* a vampire." He whistled softly. "That's a hell of a combination."

"It's not funny!"

"Am I laughing? What makes you think she's a witch?"

Cara shrugged. "I'm probably just being silly, but every

year for Halloween my father dressed in black and wore a long black cloak and my mother dressed as a witch . . ." She shook her head. "Never mind, it sounds silly."

"But you think it's true."

She nodded. "How could I have been so blind for so many years? When I look back at my childhood, there were signs everywhere."

"But you weren't looking for them," Vince pointed out.

"I know. The worst thing is, I miss them both."

"Of course you do, darlin'. I think you should go and see them."

"I wouldn't know what to say."

"I doubt if words will be necessary."

"But I like living on my own and I know they'll want me to move back home."

"You won't know that until you talk to them." He gazed into the distance. "Don't cut yourself off from your family if you don't have to."

"Maybe you're right."

"I know I am."

"Will you go with me?"

"No, darlin'. I think this is something you have to do on your own." Coward that he was, he didn't want to be there if her parents convinced her that he was a vampire, didn't want to see the hurt or the sense of betrayal in her eyes when she discovered the truth. And she would, sooner or later, he thought ruefully. He couldn't hide his true nature from her forever. Guilt assailed him. He never should have let things go this far; he never should have made love to her, or let himself care.

But it was too late now.

Back at the library, Vince's words kept running through Cara's mind. *Don't cut yourself off from your family if you don't have to.* For the first time, it occurred to her that her parents had all the time in the world. Being mortal, she didn't have that luxury. Did she want to waste even one more day being angry with the two people who loved her more than anyone else—two people that she loved in spite of everything?

Her decision made, she called Vince and told him she was going to visit her parents after work.

"You're doing the right thing, darlin'," he said.

She clung to that thought as she pulled out of the library parking lot later that night. Nearing her parents' home, she was overcome with second thoughts and drove on by. What if Vince was wrong? What if it wasn't as easy as he seemed to think it would be? She drove aimlessly for almost an hour; then, muttering, "this is ridiculous!" she drove back to her parents' house.

It was with a sense of trepidation that she climbed the stairs and rang the bell.

A moment later, her father stood in the doorway. She had rarely seen him at a loss for words, but for a moment, he just stood there, staring at her.

"Hi, Dad."

"Cara!" He swept her into his arms and held her tight.

"Roshan, who's at the . . . ?"

The sound of her mother's voice brought tears to Cara's eyes. Then her mother was hugging her, too, and Cara realized that Vince had been right again. There was no need for words, no need to apologize or explain.

"So, tell us," her mother said a short time later when they were all seated in the living room. "How have you been? What have you been doing? What's your new house like? Do you need anything?"

Warmth and belonging flooded Cara's being. "I'm sure Di Giorgio has kept you up to date," she said, but there was no censure in her voice. "Mostly, I've been working and decorating my place. I'd love for you and Dad to come and see it sometime."

"Just name the day and we'll be there."

"How about Monday night?"

Brenna glanced at her husband, who nodded. "Shall we say ten o'clock?"

"Perfect," Cara said.

"Di Giorgio tells us you're spending a lot of time with Cordova," her father said, his tone carefully neutral.

"Yes."

"Is he the reason you're here?"

"What do you mean?" Cara frowned. They couldn't possibly know that Vince was the one who had convinced her to come here, could they?

"I thought maybe the fact that you're dating a vampire had made you see your mother and me in a different light."

"He's not a vampire," Cara said emphatically. "He can't be. I've seen him during the day, working at his garage."

Her mother and father exchanged glances but said nothing.

Cara took a deep breath. "Do you sleep in coffins?" The very idea creeped her out.

"No, dear," her mother said. "We sleep in a king-size bed."

"But you drink blood?"

"Yes."

"And you're a witch, aren't you?"

Brenna's eyes widened in surprise. "Who told you that?"

"No one. But it's true, isn't it?"

Needing support, Brenna reached for her husband's hand. "Yes."

"Maybe I'd better tell you the whole story," her father said. "It will save a lot of time and questions."

Cara listened, fascinated by the tale her father told

her. She had thought that after learning her father and mother were vampires, nothing else could surprise her. She had been wrong. Her father was over three hundred years old. He had traveled back in time to save her mother from being burned at the stake by an angry mob. Later, both of her parents had been part of a horrible experiment conducted by a warlock. When her mother was close to death, her father had turned her into a vampire because he couldn't bear the thought of going on without her. Then one night they had found a teenage girl giving birth in an alley . . .

It was a remarkable story. Had she heard it from anyone but her father, had she not been the baby born in that alley, she would never have believed a word of it.

"I don't suppose you'd consider coming back home?" Brenna asked hesitantly.

Cara shook her head. "I don't think so." Seeing the hurt and disappointment in her mother's eyes, Cara said quickly, "It's not because of you or because of what you are, Mom, it's just that I really like having my own place."

"Because of Vince," her father said.

"Partly," Cara admitted. "But that's not the only reason. It's not that I don't love the two of you, it's just that, living here, I still feel like your little girl, and I'm not a little girl any longer."

"You'll always be our little girl," her father said.

"Even when I'm old and gray and you're not?" Cara laughed softly but without humor. "In a few years, people will think the two of you are *my* children."

"Cara, sweetheart . . ."

"It's all right, Mom. It just takes a little getting used to, you know?"

Brenna nodded, her eyes filling with tears. Cara had never seen her mother cry before and couldn't help noticing that her mother's tears were red. Roshan quickly handed his wife a handkerchief.

"I'd better go," Cara said, rising.

"We'll see you Monday night, Princess."

"Right." She hugged her father and her mother, kissed their cheeks. Had their skin always been so cool? "See you then."

Leaving the house, she felt as if she were leaving the weight of the world behind. She could hardly wait to see Vince so she could tell him that he had been right.

She drove quickly to the garage, only to find that it was locked up tight. No lights shone in any of the windows, upstairs or down. She glanced at her watch. It was only eleven-thirty. Surely he wasn't in bed already?

With a sigh of disappointment, she started to leave, then decided to wait a few minutes in hopes that he would return.

She turned off the headlights. Switching off the engine, she left the radio on, then leaned back in her seat. She closed her eyes and her mind immediately filled with images of Vince bending over her, his dark eyes filled with desire. Images turned to vivid memories—the feel of his hands sliding over her bare skin, the taste of him, the sheer pleasure of his body melding with hers, his tongue dueling with hers, the husky sound of his voice as he whispered love words in her ear . . .

She spoke his name when the car door opened, a smile of welcome curving her lips as she opened her eyes and looked up.

Only it wasn't Vince looking back at her.

Chapter 23

Cara stared at the man leering down at her through the window. He had spiked blond hair and a skull tattooed on one cheek. Four other, equally rough-looking young men stood behind him. Feeling like a rabbit caught in a trap, she stared back at them. Her first thought was that she was in big trouble, but then she remembered Di Giorgio. For a moment, the thought of her bodyguard comforted her—but only for a moment. Di Giorgio was good, but was he good enough to take on five men in their prime?

Even as the thought crossed her mind, Frank was there, gun in hand, demanding that the hoodlums move away from the car.

What happened next happened so fast, it was nothing but a blur. The five men all whirled around to face Di Giorgio. Moonlight and streetlights glinted on the guns and knives that appeared as if by magic in their hands.

She screamed as a hail of gunfire punctuated the quiet of the night.

One of the men fell back against the car, then slid to the ground. A second man collapsed on top of him. A third staggered away into the night, a dark stain spreading across the back of his shirt.

Another gunshot shattered the stillness of the night. Cara screamed Di Giorgio's name as he stumbled backward, fell, and lay still.

The two remaining thugs were turning back toward her when a feral growl rose out of the darkness.

Cara peered out the window, but clouds had drifted across the moon and she couldn't see anything clearly. Determined to defend herself or die trying, she opened the door and snatched up a gun one of the hoodlums had dropped, then closed the car door and locked it. She had never held a gun in her life or imagined herself in a situation where she would have to use one.

She looked out the window again, wondering what had happened to the remaining two men and if Di Giorgio was still alive. The street was eerily quiet and empty.

She had to get out of there, she thought frantically, but she couldn't just drive off and leave Frank lying in the street. What to do, what to do? Go, she thought. Getting out of the car would be foolish when there were still three men out there somewhere in the dark. Once she was safely away, she could call 911.

She was fumbling with her car keys when a face appeared at the window.

A scream rose in her throat as she raised the gun, her finger curling around the trigger.

"Cara!"

Vince's voice.

With a cry of relief, she dropped the gun on the passenger seat, opened the door, and practically fell into his arms.

"Are you all right?" His gaze moved over her. "Cara?"

"I'm . . . I'm fine. Di Giorgio . . ."

"He's badly hurt. Open the back door. We need to get him to a doctor, pronto!"

She did as she was told, unable to stop the convulsive tremors that shook her from head to foot.

Vince settled Di Giorgio on the back seat, took one look at Cara's pale face, and said, "I'll drive."

She didn't argue. She put the gun on the floor and scrambled into the passenger seat. "What about the men that Di Giorgio shot? Are they dead?"

"The two in the street are dead," Vince said flatly.

Cara glanced out the back window. "Three of them got away. I think one of them was wounded. Shouldn't we call the police?"

"They didn't get away."

Cara stared at him. "But . . ."

"They're all dead," he said, and his voice was as cold and implacable as death itself.

Sinking back into the seat, Cara wrapped her arms around her middle, colder than she had ever been in her whole life. She wanted to ask how the men had died, but she was suddenly afraid of the answer.

When they reached the hospital, Di Giorgio was put on a stretcher and whisked away into surgery, leaving Cara to answer questions and fill out forms, only she lacked the information necessary. She realized then that, except for his name, she knew very little about the man who had watched over her for almost half of her life.

After saying, "I don't know," for the fifth time, she asked to use the phone and called her father.

"We'll be there in five minutes," Roshan said, and hung up.

They made it in four.

Leaving Brenna and Cara to take care of the paperwork, Roshan took Vince aside.

"What happened?" he asked curtly.

Vince shrugged. "I'm not sure. When I got home, I saw Cara's car parked out front. Di Giorgio and five thugs were shooting it out. He got two of them. I got the other three."

"Where are the bodies?"

"In the dumpster behind my garage. I'll dispose of them when I get home."

Roshan nodded, his admiration and respect for the younger vampire growing in spite of himself. "I owe you a debt for rescuing my daughter and saving Di Giorgio's life."

Vince shook his head. "You don't owe me anything."

"Nevertheless, if you ever need anything, you have only to ask. In the meantime, you might want to go home and change your clothes."

Frowning, Vince glanced down, surprised to see his shirtfront was splattered with blood—his own blood. He grunted softly. He'd been shot and hadn't even realized it. Lifting his shirt, he saw that the wound was already healing. Even as he watched, all sign of the injury disappeared. He stared at it in astonishment. He knew he healed quickly. He often got minor scrapes and cuts at work, but having a gunshot heal in minutes was nothing short of miraculous.

He looked up as Cara appeared at his side. Her eyes widened when, for the first time, she noticed the blood on his shirt.

"You're hurt!" she exclaimed.

"No." He removed his shirt and tossed it in a nearby trash container. "It isn't my blood." He didn't like lying to her, but there was no other way to explain it. She would never believe he had been shot and healed in the same night. He could hardly believe it himself.

She stared up at him, her eyes wide, her face almost as white as the walls. "I think I'm going to . . ."

"Faint," he finished for her, and caught her in his arms as she pitched forward.

"I'm going to go check on Di Giorgio," Roshan said. "I trust you'll look after Cara until I return?"

Vince nodded. Cradling Cara against his chest, he sat down on a puke green plastic chair. Ordinarily, he wouldn't have cared if Di Giorgio lived or died, but the bodyguard had been wounded trying to protect Cara, and for that, Vince owed the man a life debt. As for the five thugs, Vince didn't know who they were or what their intentions toward Cara had been. They might have intended to do nothing more than rob her or steal her car, but it didn't matter. They had accosted her, frightened her, and for that, he had killed the surviving three men.

But first, he had drained them dry.

When Cara opened her eyes again, she found herself staring up at Vince. For a moment, she couldn't remember where she was or what had happened, and then it all came back in a rush. The five men staring down at her. Di Giorgio coming to her defense, being shot . . .

"Is he dead?"

"He's gonna be fine," Vince said, smiling. Di Giorgio would, in fact, be more than fine since Roshan had gone into the man's room and given him a bit of his blood.

"I feel so silly," Cara said. "I've never fainted before."

"What the devil were you doing sitting out in front of my place so late at night?"

"I wanted to see you."

"Dammit, girl, you could have been killed."

"But it's a nice part of town. I didn't think . . ."

"The world's a different place late at night, darlin'. People might tell you not to be afraid of the dark, that there's nothing in the dark that isn't there in the light, but it's just not true." He stroked her hair, slid his knuckles down her cheek. "Promise me you won't ever pull a fool stunt like that again."

"I promise."

"What did you want to see me about?"

She shrugged. It didn't seem important now, not with Di Giorgio in intensive care.

"Cara?"

"I just wanted to tell you that I took your advice and went to see my parents . . . and you were right . . . and . . ." Tears welled in her eyes. "He could have been killed and it would have been all my fault."

"Shh. He's out of danger. Your parents are with him now."

She rested her head against his shoulder, thinking what a comfort he was.

A short time later, her parents joined them.

"Is it true?" Cara asked anxiously. "Is Frank going to be all right?"

Her mother nodded. "He'll be home in a few days."

"I have to go see him. I have to tell him how sorry I am . . . for everything."

"It will have to wait until tomorrow," her father said. "He's sleeping now."

"And you should be sleeping, too," Brenna said.

"But . . ."

"Your mother's right," Vince said. "You've had a rough night."

"We'll take you home," Roshan said.

"I'll take her home," Vince said.

A muscle worked in Roshan's jaw. Hands clenched, he took a step forward, only to be stayed by Brenna's hand on his arm.

"Call us tomorrow night, dear," Brenna said.

"I will."

Rising, with Cara still cradled to his chest, Vince followed her parents out of the hospital.

"I don't like it," Roshan said, watching Vince pull out of the parking lot. "I don't like it one damn bit."

"Unfortunately, she's old enough to do as she pleases," Brenna said.

"Maybe you could put a spell on him," Roshan muttered. "Turn him into a lizard or a toad."

Brenna laughed softly. "It's too late for that. She loves him."

"And what happens when she finally realizes what he is?"

"Who can say? Either it won't matter, or it'll break her heart. All we can do is be there for her when the time comes."

Roshan shook his head. Women! Old or young, there was no understanding any of them. "Come on, wife," he said, slipping his arm around her waist. "Let's go home."

Vince refused to let Cara walk. When they reached her house, he carried her inside, undressed her, and put her to bed. He gave her a glass of warm milk to relax her, then sat beside her, her hand lightly clasped in his.

He glanced at the curtained window, sensing the approach of dawn. Soon he would have to either leave or risk spending the day in her house.

She made the decision for him.

"Stay the night with me," she said. "I don't want to be alone."

"Sure, darlin'." He brushed a kiss across her brow. "But I'll have to leave early."

"I don't care."

Sitting on the edge of the bed, he removed his boots and socks, stood to remove his jeans, and then crawled in beside her. It was only a few hours until dawn, but he cherished every minute he could spend with her.

She snuggled against him, her head resting on his shoulder, one arm curved over his waist.

Her eyelids fluttered down, and she was asleep.

Vince slipped his arm around her. It scared him to think how close he had come to losing her. Had he arrived a few minutes later, there was no telling what might have happened.

He wrapped a lock of her hair around his hand, inhaling the flowery aroma, along with the scent of her skin. Her blood. It called to him, warm and sweet. For the first time, he thought about bringing her across. He wouldn't have to worry about losing her then.

He stared up at the ceiling. Because Mara had made him, he could move about during the day. Would his blood have the same effect on Cara, or would she have to get it directly from Mara?

His gaze caressed the face of the woman sleeping beside him. She was beautiful now; as a vampire, she would be radiant.

Even as he let himself imagine what it would be like if she joined him, he knew she wouldn't agree. Her parents were vampires. She'd had time to accept the idea, had made peace with them, but she had never mentioned accepting the Dark Gift for herself; never, as far as he knew, had she even wondered what it would be like. Indeed, though she had accepted that her parents were vampires, she was still repelled by the whole idea.

What would she say, what would she do when she learned the truth about him? Should he leave her now, go without a word before she found out? Would it be kinder in the long run to let her think he had only been toying with her affections or tell her the truth?

He blew out a heavy sigh. Either way, she was bound to hate him.

Chapter 24

She was dreaming and she knew she was dreaming, but she couldn't stop, couldn't wake up. The men who had accosted her were dead and yet, in her dream, they surrounded her, their eyes filled with menace as their hands reached for her. They dragged her out of her car and threw her on the ground. One held a knife at her throat while another bent over her, his foul breath making her sick to her stomach. He was lowering himself onto her when a large black wolf appeared out of nowhere. With a low growl, the wolf attacked the men, ripping out their throats, lapping at their blood . . .

She woke with a scream on her lips, her body bathed in perspiration.

"Cara, shh, it's all right, I'm here."

She blinked at the man beside her, her heart pounding like a wild thing. For a moment, one strange moment, she thought she was staring at the wolf from her nightmare.

"Vince!" With a cry, she flung herself into his arms.

"It's all right, darlin'. It was just a bad dream."

She nodded, her arms tight around him. "But it was so real."

He brushed her hair away from her face and then lightly stroked her back. "I'm here."

She looked up at him, her beautiful blue eyes wide and scared. "Don't leave me, Vince. Promise me you'll never leave me."

"I'll always be here, darlin'," he promised. "For as long as you want me around."

She kissed his cheek, and then she smiled. "Then you'll always be here."

Vince was gone when Cara woke in the morning. Sitting up, she pressed the pillow he had used to her face and sighed as she breathed in his now-familiar scent. She had it bad, she thought. Really bad, when just the thought of him brought a smile to her face and caused her heart to pound as if she'd just run a marathon.

Last night he had promised he would never leave her . . . happiness welled inside her, and then she was overcome with a wave of guilt. What right did she have to be so happy when Di Giorgio was lying in the hospital in intensive care?

Rising, she took a quick shower, dressed, had breakfast, and drove to the hospital. When she reached intensive care, the nurse advised her that Frank had been moved to a private room on the second floor.

Cara thanked the nurse and took the elevator down to the second floor. She found Di Giorgio sitting up in bed reading the newspaper. Bouquets of flowers and baskets of fruit occupied every inch of available space.

He looked up when she entered the room. "Miss DeLongpre."

Cara shook her head. "Honestly, Frank," she said as she drew a chair closer to the bed, "don't you think it's time you called me Cara?"

"I'm surprised you're speaking to me at all," he muttered bleakly.

"What are you talking about?"

"I failed you." He shook his head, his eyes filled with self-condemnation. "The first time you really needed me, and I failed you. Maybe it's time I retired."

"You didn't fail me. I'd probably be dead now if it wasn't for you."

He snorted softly. "And I'd be dead if it wasn't for who-ever, or whatever, jumped those hoods."

Cara frowned. What did he mean, "whatever"? "It was Vince," she said.

"If you say so."

"What are you talking about? I saw him."

"If you say so. Whatever I saw had eyes as red as hell-fire. And it growled." He shook his head. "I could have imagined it, I guess."

"You must have," Cara said, but even as she spoke the words, she remembered standing on the balcony of her bedroom and seeing a pair of red eyes staring up at her from the yard below. "I'm so sorry this happened."

"I'm sorry I let you down."

Cara shook her head. The man had been shot while protecting her and he felt he had failed. "If you hadn't been there, it would have been a lot worse. Now, stop blaming yourself and just get better."

A smile tugged at the corner of his mouth. "Yes, ma'am."

"Do you need anything, Frank?"

"Are you kidding? Your father's taking good care of me. I told him I was well enough to go home, but he told me to stay put for a day or two. Not only that, but he's having all my meals catered so I don't have to eat hospital food." He snorted softly. "I get new flowers or a fruit basket every hour. I've had so many, the nurses are giving them to other patients. In addition to all that, your father gave me a raise."

Cara smiled, pleased that Frank was being well taken care of. She had come to the hospital expecting to find him at death's door; instead, he looked as strong and fit as ever.

Rising, she took his hand and gave it a squeeze. "If there's anything I can do for you, let me know."

He nodded. "Thanks for coming."

"I'm sure my folks will be by later tonight," she said, and wondered if Frank knew that his employers were vampires.

Di Giorgio nodded. "You be careful out there."

"I will."

After pulling out of the hospital parking lot, Cara glanced in her rearview mirror. For the first time in years, Di Giorgio wasn't behind her. It seemed odd not to have him following her. For years, she had thought it was foolish of her parents to insist she have a bodyguard. Now that he was gone, she felt suddenly vulnerable—and guilty. Frank Di Giorgio was in the hospital and it was all her fault.

At home again, she called a florist, and even though Frank didn't need any more flowers, she ordered a bouquet to be sent to his room. And then, knowing he had a sweet tooth, she called the best candy store in the city and asked them to send him a two-pound box of assorted chocolates. It wasn't much, but it made her feel better.

After kicking off her shoes, she opened a couple of windows, then took the trash outside and dumped it in the barrel, only to hurry back inside when she heard the phone ringing.

She grabbed the receiver, hoping it was Vince, felt her heart skip a beat when she heard his voice.

"Hey, darlin', where've you been? I've been calling you all morning."

"Oh, I went over to the hospital to see Frank."

"How's he doing?"

"He looks fine. He's in a private room."

"How are you?"

"I'm okay."

"You sure?"

"Yes." She smiled into the receiver. "Will I see you later?"

"You bet."

She heard the sound of a horn honking in the background.

"Blast, I've got to go," Vince said. "I've got a customer. I'll see you soon."

"All right. Bye."

"Bye, darlin'."

Sarah Beth's eyes widened in horror when Cara told her what had happened the night before.

"You could have been killed! Or worse! Are you all right?" Sarah Beth's narrow-eyed gaze moved over Cara from top to bottom. "You must have been terrified!" she exclaimed.

"That doesn't even come close to describing it."

"That's some bodyguard you've got. You could have been killed."

"Bethy, he got shot twice trying to save me. He could have been killed, too, you know. Both of us might have been killed if Vince hadn't come home when he did."

Sarah Beth sighed. "Who says there are no more knights in shining armor?"

Cara shook her head. "Honestly, Bethy, you find romance in everything."

"You mean to tell me you aren't impressed with the man? He shows up out of nowhere to save you in the nick of time, just like the Seventh Cavalry."

Cara laughed. "Make up your mind, girlfriend. Is he a chivalrous knight or a brave soldier?"

"I think he's both, don't you?"

"Yes," Cara admitted, "I do." A dark, violent part of her wished she had seen him fighting off the thugs who had accosted her, but it had been too dark to see anything clearly. She suddenly remembered that Frank had told her he heard a growl. Now that she thought about it, she was sure she had heard one, too. Probably just a dog.

Sarah Beth hugged her. "I'm just glad you're all right. Listen, why don't you and Mr. Macho come over Monday night? We could have dinner and go to a movie."

"I'd love to, but my folks are coming over."

"Well, how about next Monday?"

"I'll have to ask Vince," Cara said, and even as she said the words, he was striding through the library doors, as big as you please. He smiled when he saw her.

Dressed in black jeans, a white T-shirt, and a black jacket, he didn't look much like a knight or a soldier, but he looked sexy as all get-out as he walked toward her.

"What are you doing here so early?" she asked. "It's not even six."

"I couldn't wait until later," he said. "I had to see for myself that you're all right."

"A true knight," Sarah Beth murmured for Cara's ears alone. Walking toward the door, she said, "Behave yourselves, you two."

"What fun is that?" Vince said, drawing Cara into his arms.

"Vince," Cara admonished. "The door."

He kicked it shut with his heel. "Can I kiss you now?"

"Hmm, please."

His kiss was slow and wickedly sensual. Lowering his head, he nuzzled her neck. "I've been missing you all day."

"Me, too, you."

"Good." He captured her lips with his own, his tongue delving into her mouth.

Desire shot through Cara with the intensity of a lightning bolt, stealing her breath and her thoughts, leaving her aware of nothing but his body pressed intimately against hers, the seduction of his mouth on hers, the strength of his arms, and the evidence of his arousal.

She didn't know how many times the phone rang before it penetrated the haze of passion that engulfed her.

Grabbing the receiver, she managed a raspy, "Miss DeLongpre, can I help you?" She listened to the voice on the other end, made what she hoped were the proper responses, and said good-bye.

When she hung up the receiver, she couldn't remember who she'd been talking to or what the man had wanted.

"One more kiss," Vince said, pulling her into his embrace again, "and then I'd better go."

"Do you have to?" She had visions of herself locking her office door and making love to Vince on top of her desk, or maybe on the floor . . .

The gleam in his eyes told her he knew what she was thinking. "You've still got three hours of work ahead of you," he reminded her, "and I've got a few things at the shop to finish up." He kissed the tip of her nose. "I'll see you at nine. Don't go outside until I get here."

"Yes, master! Oh, wait, Sarah Beth wants us to come over for dinner a week from Monday and then go to a movie. Can you make it?"

"I'll have to see what's on my calendar and let you know, okay?"

"Okay."

And so saying, he kissed her again, hard and quick, and then he was gone, leaving her to stare after him, her fingertips pressed to her lips, his taste still on her tongue.

Oh, yes, she thought again. She had it bad.

Vince was as good as his word. He arrived at the library at nine sharp. Cara bid a quick good-bye to Sarah Beth, grabbed her handbag, and hurried outside, eager to be alone with Vince.

"Do you want to go out?" he asked.

"No, let's go home. Did you check your calendar?"

"No, I forgot." He hated lying to her again, but dinner with her friend just wasn't in the cards. "So, your place or mine?"

"Mine," she said. "I don't have a nosey cat. Besides, I want to change into something more comfortable."

"Like nothing at all?" he asked with a wicked grin.

She batted her eyelashes at him. "Maybe, maybe not. Guess you'll just have to wait and see."

"I'm game," he said, "but 'nothing at all' has my vote."

"Men!" she muttered, her tone indicating she had tons of experience on the subject though she really had very little. "Oh, Vince, maybe we should swing by the hospital and see how Frank's doing."

"Whatever you want, darlin'," Vince said.

"You're going to spoil me, you know," Cara said, unlocking her car door.

"That's my plan."

"The hospital first, then," she said.

With a nod, he closed her door, then went to his own car.

When they arrived at the hospital, they learned that Frank had signed himself out earlier that day.

"I guess he's feeling better," Cara said as they walked back to the parking lot.

Vince grunted softly, wondering what kind of effect Roshan's blood would have on the bodyguard. It wouldn't make him a vampire, but it might increase his strength and his longevity.

He followed Cara home and pulled into the driveway after her, only then realizing that she already had company. Her mother and father were waiting for them on the front porch. As usual, her father was attired in black from head to foot. Her mother wore a gauzy white blouse, a colorful skirt, and suede boots. A necklace of amber and jet circled her throat.

Cara felt a twinge of unease as she climbed the stairs. "Mom, Dad, is something wrong?"

"No, dear," her mother said, smiling. "We were just worried about you, that's all."

"I'm fine."

"I can see that," Brenna said, "but after last night . . . we just wanted to make sure you were okay."

"Oh." Cara glanced at Vince, then unlocked the front door and stepped inside. Vince followed her.

Roshan and Brenna remained on the porch.

When Cara realized her parents were still outside, she turned back toward the door. "Aren't you two coming in?"

"We can't enter without an invitation," her father said. "Remember?"

"Oh, right," she said, recalling that vampires needed an invitation. "So, you really can't come in unless I invite you?"

Her father nodded. "Exactly."

Cara grinned, thinking how odd that was. "What happens if you try?"

"The threshold repels us."

"I don't believe it."

"Would you like a demonstration?"

"Sure."

Cara stepped back and her father moved forward. As soon as he reached the threshold and tried to cross, it was like he ran into an invisible barrier.

"Are you doing that on purpose?" she asked.

"No."

"Amazing. Well, come on in, both of you."

Although he was standing a few feet behind Cara, Vince felt the ripple of preternatural power as her mother and father crossed the threshold into the house. He glanced at Cara, but she seemed unaware of it. It was probably a good thing, he mused. If she didn't sense her father's power, then she probably hadn't sensed his, either, though her father's power was so strong, Vince wondered how she could remain oblivious. But then, most mortals were completely ignorant of the supernatural world.

Cara smiled at her parents. "Do you need an invitation to sit down, too?" she asked, thinking Sarah Beth would never believe any of this. Not that she would ever tell her!

"No, dear," Brenna said, taking a seat on the sofa, "but it is good manners."

Roshan sat on the sofa beside his wife. Cara sat beside her father, leaving Vince to take the chair.

"Is there anything else I need to know about your . . . uh, lifestyle?" Cara asked. She frowned, thinking about all the old vampire movies she had seen. Her parents didn't seem anything like the ravening monsters portrayed on film.

Her mother and father exchanged glances. Cara wondered if they were communicating with each other somehow, saying things only they could hear. She had a feeling they were deciding how much to tell her and how much to keep secret.

After a moment, her father said, "Most of what people believe about vampires is false. The truths are that silver burns our skin, we can pass unnoticed among humans if we wish, we are capable of changing our shapes, and we cast no reflection in a mirror."

Cara stared at her father. Funny she'd never noticed that the only mirrors in her parents home had been the ones in her own room. Now that she thought of it, she realized that the drapes had always been drawn across the windows, as well. Her mother loved jewelry, but none of it was silver.

Cara glanced at Vince. Did he find this conversation as bizarre as she did? He smiled at her, his expression impassive.

She took a deep breath. She didn't want to talk about vampires anymore, so, to change the subject, she said, "We went to the hospital to see Frank, but they said he'd gone home."

Her mother and father exchanged looks again. It was obvious they understood why she had changed the subject.

"Frank's resting comfortably," her father said. "He asked me to thank you for the flowers and the candy, and to tell you that he would be back on the job on Monday."

Now you see why we wanted you to have a bodyguard. Though her father didn't say the words aloud, Cara could almost hear them hanging, unspoken, in the air.

"I'm glad he's going to be all right," she said, "though I can't understand how he could recover so quickly."

Vince glanced at Roshan, but said nothing.

"Some people have remarkable recuperative powers," Brenna said to fill the silence. She glanced around. "I love what you've done with your new place. It suits you."

Cara smiled, thinking Vince had said the same thing. "Would you like to see the rest? It's not very big, but I like it."

"Of course," Brenna said. "Are you coming, Roshan?"

"In a minute, love." He waited until his wife and daughter had left the room, then focused his attention on the other man. "Just how serious are you about my daughter?"

Chapter 25

Vince stared at Cara's father. It was all he could do to keep from laughing. They were vampires, both of them, yet DeLongpre glared at him like a character out of a gothic novel, asking the hero about his intentions—except that Vince was no hero, and he had no right to court DeLongpre's daughter. Other than the sizzling physical attraction between them, they had nothing in common and no hope for a future together. He knew it, and so did DeLongpre.

Vince blew out a deep breath. "I love her."

"Does she know what you are?"

"Only what you told her."

"Except that she didn't believe me."

Vince shrugged. "Is that my fault?"

"Your whole relationship is built on a lie."

"I know that. Don't you think I know that? I want to tell her, but . . ."

"You're afraid you'll lose her."

"Yeah."

"And you can't exist without her."

Vince nodded. "Why do I get the feeling you've been down this road yourself?"

"I loved Brenna the moment I saw her, but I never

pretended to be anything other than what I am. If you love Cara, you owe her the truth before things go any further."

Vince swore softly.

DeLongpre's eyes burned into him. "You know I'm right, don't you?"

"Yeah."

"So you'll tell her?"

"When the time is right."

Anger rolled off the other vampire. "And just when will that be?"

"How the hell should I know? I don't like . . ." Vince cut his words off in midsentence as Cara and her mother reentered the room.

"What don't you like?" Cara asked, sitting beside her father.

"The way the playoffs are going," Vince lied smoothly. "My team's losing."

Brenna looked at Vince sharply as she sat down, her expression telling him she had heard the entire conversation between Vince and her husband, and that she agreed with Roshan.

Cara glanced at her father and then at Vince. "All right, what's going on? What aren't you telling me?"

Vince shook his head. "Nothing, darlin'."

"We should go," DeLongpre said, rising. "We didn't mean to intrude."

"You're not intruding," Cara said. "You're my parents. You're welcome here anytime."

"Thanks, sweetie," Brenna said, also rising, "but I think your father's right. We just wanted to come by and make sure you were okay, and you are, so we'll see you Monday night, all right?" She took her husband by the hand. "Come on, Roshan, I think we've interrupted their date long enough."

Cara walked her parents to the door and kissed them good night. She watched them walk down the path and disappear into the darkness, then closed the door behind them. "All right," she said, returning to the living room where Vince waited, "what's going on?"

"Nothing, darlin'. Your father just wanted to know what my intentions are."

"Your intentions toward what . . . oh!" Embarrassment flooded her cheeks. "You don't mean he was asking about your intentions toward me?" She pressed her hands to her cheeks. "How could he?"

"He's just worried about you," Vince said, drawing her down onto his lap. "Nothing for you to be upset about."

She glared at him. "You can't be serious! He's always trying to . . . to . . ."

"To what?"

"Run my life!" She wriggled off Vince's lap, too upset to sit still. "Honestly, I'm twenty-two years old and they treat me like I'm two! Do you realize this is the first time in my life that I haven't had a bodyguard parked outside my door? Of course, all that will change on Monday."

"I think you're forgetting something here," Vince said mildly. "That bodyguard saved your life."

"You saved my life. And his!"

"Hold on now. He was in action before I got there."

"Now you're taking their side? I don't believe it!"

Rising, Vince pulled Cara into his arms. "Calm down, darlin'. They just worry about you, that's all. You can't blame them, you know. They can't be there for you during the day. It's only natural that they'd take steps to protect you."

She looked up at him curiously. "You accepted the fact that my parents are vampires mighty quick, didn't you?" she asked, frowning. "I remember when I told you, you didn't even seem surprised."

"Didn't I?"

"No. Why weren't you?"

Vince cleared his throat. "You seemed so convinced,

I thought it would just make it worse if I doubted you, that's all."

She regarded him for several moments. "Why did my dad think you were a vampire?"

"I don't know. Maybe he saw me at The Nocturne."

Cara shook her head. "No, I don't think so. I mean, if that was true, wouldn't he think all the people at The Nocturne were vampires?"

"I don't know, darlin'." He caressed the last word, hoping to divert her thoughts to something else, something more intimate.

"You wear a lot of black, just like my dad," she remarked, her brow furrowed. "And I've never seen you eat."

Vince swore silently. She was getting close to the truth. Too close. He tightened his arm around her waist, drawing her body up against his. "Speaking of eating," he murmured, "you're looking mighty tasty."

"Not now, Vince."

"No?" Lowering his head, he kissed her, long and slow and deep, until she sagged against him, breathless. Her hands slid under his shirt, her nails lightly raking his back.

She didn't protest when he swung her into his arms and carried her into the bedroom. Knowing it might be for the last time, he made love to her tenderly, drawing out each touch, each caress, pleasuring her until he ached inside, until, with a low growl, he buried himself deep within her.

Later, on his way home, Vince cursed himself for his cowardice. He should have told her the truth. Hell, if he had just let her keep talking, she would have figured it out for herself. Instead, he'd kissed her until she was hungry for his touch.

It had been a despicable thing to do, and he had no excuse except that he loved her and couldn't bear the idea of existing without her. He knew he would have to let her go sooner or later, but, dammit, he didn't have to like it.

Every time he saw her, he told himself it would be the last time, even though he knew it was a lie.

And yet, how much longer could he go on deceiving her now that she was asking questions? And what was he going to do about going to Sarah Beth's house? He couldn't very well go to the woman's house for dinner and then not eat!

Damn! He hadn't eaten solid food in a year. He supposed he could plant the suggestion in their minds that he had eaten dinner with them, but he hated to deceive Cara and her friends that way. He swore a vile oath. Letting her believe he was human was a far bigger deception.

Disgusted with himself and his own company, he drove on past his place and headed for The Nocturne.

Late as it was, the club was in full swing. Vince took a seat at the end of the bar, his gaze sweeping the couples on the dance floor. As usual, most everyone in the place, including himself, was wearing black.

The thought made him frown. He hadn't started wearing black until he'd been made, and then it seemed like the most natural thing in the world. He supposed he gravitated toward it unconsciously. He was a creature of the night now. How better to blend into the darkness that was so much a part of him than to dress in black? He wondered if it would throw Cara off the scent if he started wearing brighter colors again.

He glanced at the woman beside him. She was eating a chili cheeseburger and fries. Curious to see what would happen if he ate solid food, Vince ordered a hamburger, even though the smell of cooked meat made his stomach churn.

When his order arrived, he stared at it for several moments before taking a bite. It seemed odd to be chewing solid food. He swallowed quickly and knew he'd made a huge mistake.

Bolting out the club's back door, he ducked into the bushes. The burger tasted far worse coming back up than it had going down.

He was wiping his mouth when he heard the sound of merry laughter behind him. Turning slowly, he came face to face with Mara.

She shook her head in astonishment. "What are you doing? Have you learned nothing since I brought you across?"

Vince shrugged sheepishly. "I had to try."

"Whatever for? I know you don't have any desire for food."

"I've been invited to dinner."

"Ah. I take it you still haven't told your little mortal what you are."

He shook his head. "No, but she's starting to get suspicious."

"You can't hide the truth forever," Mara said, slipping her arm through his. "Come, I know just the thing to take that awful taste out of your mouth."

Chapter 26

Serafina stood in the doorway of the room in the basement of the laboratory, admiring her handiwork. Everything was as ready as she could make it.

Anthony's crypt rested in the corner.

Two metal operating tables stood in the center of the
room. One had been refitted with solid silver restraints to
hold the vampire, restraints far stronger than the ones
Anthony had once used. As much as she loved Anthony, she
didn't intend to underestimate DeLongpre's strength the
way her beloved had. She had bought a portable crib to
hold the infant until she needed it, prepared a second table
with leather restraints to hold DeLongpre's daughter, and
obtained the necessary equipment to draw blood.

She had considered many ways to wreak vengeance
against Roshan DeLongpre, but using DeLongpre's
blood and that of his daughter to resurrect her beloved
was far superior to any of the others. Letting Anthony
destroy DeLongpre once and for all would be the coup
de grâce. As for DeLongpre's daughter, once Serafina
was through with her, Anton could decide whether the
chit should live or die.

Even though she had kept all of Anthony's old shoes and
clothes, Serafina had bought him a whole new wardrobe,

including underwear, socks, and handkerchiefs. He had always been a little vain, and she didn't want him to appear in public in clothes that had been out of style for over twenty years.

She had purchased his favorite blend of coffee, as well as his favorite wine and whiskey. When the day for his return grew closer, she would stock her pantry with his favorite foods. She made a mental note to pick up a bottle of his favorite cologne, a new toothbrush, a new wallet, a new comb, and a razor.

She smiled, thinking how wonderful it had been to shop for him, to fill her dresser drawers with his things.

She had bought new sheets and pillows for her bed, wanting everything to be perfect for their new life together.

She ran her hand over the metal table. If only there was a way to test the spell before she tried it on her beloved.

If only she could make the days and hours pass more quickly!

If only her beloved were there beside her.

"Soon." The word had become her mantra. "Soon."

Chapter 27

The next two weeks passed quickly. Cara saw Vince every night after work and sometimes during her break, and the more she saw him, the more she loved him. He was kind, patient, and fun to be with. And their love-making . . . each time seemed better than the last. Sometimes they made slow, sweet love in her bed, sometimes on the floor of the living room in front of the fire, sometimes in the bathtub, and once in the kitchen on the table.

The Monday night her parents had come to visit, they had hinted several times that she should move back home, but Cara refused to consider it. Now that she'd had a taste of living on her own, there was no way she was moving back in with Mom and Dad.

She continued buying odds and ends for her house— a full-length mirror for the bathroom door, a lacy fern in an earthenware pot, a painting for over the fireplace, a new lamp for the living room.

Frank had fully recovered. There were still times when she felt a twinge of resentment when she looked in her rearview mirror and saw his Lexus trailing a short distance behind her, but for the most part, she found his presence vastly reassuring.

Now it was Monday night and she and Vince were going to Sarah Beth's house for dinner and then to a movie. She was surprised at how excited she was to be going to Bethy's for dinner, or maybe it was Vince who had unleashed the butterflies in her stomach. Or maybe it was just the fact that it was the first time she and Vince would be going to visit one of her friends as a couple.

"Whatever," she muttered as she finished applying her makeup, put on her shoes, and went into the living room to wait for Vince.

She was looking out the window, wondering where he was, when the phone rang. Lifting the receiver, she said "hello."

"Hey, darlin'."

"Vince, where are you?"

"I'm sorry, but I'm running late. I had to go into the city to buy some parts and I got hung up in traffic. Why don't you go on to dinner and I'll meet you there."

"Are you sure? Maybe we should just go next week."

"No, that wouldn't be fair to Sarah Beth. You go on and I'll get there as soon as I can."

"All right. Hurry."

Vince hung up, stung by the disappointment he heard in Cara's voice, but there was no help for it. It was still daylight; there was no way he could leave the garage until the sun went down.

After closing and locking the security door, he went upstairs to take a shower and get dressed. Cat trailed after him. Vince knew it was his imagination, but he would have sworn Cat's eyes were filled with accusation.

"I know," Vince said irritably. "I've got to end it. And I will, but she wants me to be with her on Halloween. It's her favorite holiday, you know. When it's over, I'll either tell her the truth or I'll just leave a note and get out of her life forever, okay?"

Cat stared up at him through unblinking yellow eyes.

"I promise, all right?"

With a twitch of his tail, Cat jumped up on the bed and began his daily ablutions.

Muttering an oath, Vince went into the bathroom and closed the door.

Cara had just finished helping Sarah Beth clear the dining room table when she heard the doorbell and then the sound of Vince's voice as he introduced himself to Sarah Beth's husband, Dean.

Smiling, she hurried into the living room. "You made it!"

He kissed her on the cheek. "Sorry I'm late."

"Would you care for something to drink?" Dean asked. "A coke, a beer?"

Vince shook his head. "Nothing, thanks." He glanced around the room, noting the large beveled mirror over the fireplace. Two dark green sofas faced each other in front of the hearth. A rectangular glass-topped coffee table stood between the sofas. A floor-to-ceiling shelf held a hodgepodge of books, knickknacks, and framed photographs.

"Hi, Vince," Sarah Beth said, entering the room. "Please, sit down and make yourself comfortable. We've got half an hour or so before the movie starts."

Mindful of the mirror, Vince walked behind the sofa and then sat down, grateful that the mirror was high enough that it didn't reflect the furniture in front of it. Cara sat beside him. Sarah Beth and her husband made themselves comfortable on the other couch.

"So, Vince," Dean said, "Beth tells me you're a mechanic."

Vince nodded.

"I've got an antique T-bird out in the garage that I've been wanting to restore."

"What year is it?"

Dean laughed. "You know, I'm not sure. It belonged to my grandfather."

"Does it still run?"

"Barely."

"Well, bring it on by," Vince said, "and I'll take a look at it."

"Great."

"Don't get too excited. I can't guarantee I'll be able to find parts for it."

"I hope you can't," Sarah Beth said. "That old thing's been taking up space in the garage for three years. If he'd get rid of it, I could park my car in there."

Dean shook his head. "Women."

Sarah Beth made a face at him, then punched him in the arm. "Be nice. We have company." She smiled at Vince and Cara. "So, what movie do you two want to see?"

"It doesn't matter to me," Cara said.

"How about you, Vince?" Sarah Beth asked.

"Whatever you guys want is fine with me."

"No one asked me," Dean said, "but I'd like to see that new horror flick."

"Okay by me," Vince said. "Ladies?"

"It's not all blood and gore is it?" Sarah Beth asked.

"I don't think so, honey."

When Cara and Sarah Beth both agreed, Dean checked his watch. "We'd better go. It starts in fifteen minutes."

The horror flick turned out to be a love story, of sorts, about a female vampire in love with a werewolf and the problems they had to overcome. It wasn't filled with blood and gore, as Sarah Beth feared, but Vince was pretty sure Cara would have objected to coming if she had known what it was about.

He watched it with a sense of wry amusement. He didn't know anything about werewolves, assuming they existed at all, but whoever had written the script didn't know a thing about vampires.

It was still early when the movie was over. Sarah Beth suggested they go out for coffee and dessert. While Vince was trying to think of a good excuse, Cara came to his rescue.

Slipping her arm through his, she smiled at Sarah Beth. "Not tonight, Bethy."

"Gonna have your dessert elsewhere?" Sarah Beth asked with a knowing grin.

"Beth," Dean admonished, "mind your own business."

Thirty minutes later, Vince and Cara were cuddling on her sofa in front of a cozy fire.

"I guess the movie was a bad choice," Vince remarked, stroking her cheek.

"Well, it's certainly not one I would have picked, but it did have a happy ending, of sorts, if you don't mind being a vampire."

Vince grunted softly. In the movie, the werewolf had found a cure for his ailment, the vampire had brought him across, and they had walked off into the darkness, apparently to live happily ever after by night.

"Your parents seem pretty happy," Vince remarked.

"As happy as you can be living as a vampire, I guess," Cara allowed.

"Maybe it's not as bad as you think."

She looked up at him, her brow furrowed. "Not bad? Why would anyone want to be a vampire?"

He shrugged. "Maybe they don't always have a choice."

"Well, if you were given the choice, what would you do?"

"I'd choose to live." He didn't have to think about it; he'd made that choice a year ago. "What about you?" he asked. "What if you had to decide between living as a vampire or dying?"

"I'd rather die," she said emphatically.

"Are you sure?"

"Of course. At least I think I am." She thought about her mother and father and what she knew of their life together. Vince was right. They seemed perfectly happy the way they were. She had never heard them fight and rarely heard them disagree. It was obvious that they were still madly in love. Her father brought her mother lingerie on Valentine's Day, flowers on Mother's Day and jewelry for Christmas. They seemed to share practically everything and, perhaps most important of all, they would be together forever.

She thought about Vince and how few were the years they would have together compared to the hundreds of years her parents could expect to share, and suddenly being a vampire didn't seem like such a terrible thing, if the one you loved was a vampire, too.

It was a thought that haunted and intrigued her long after she had bid Vince good night.

It was midnight on the night before Halloween. Cara was walking home when, all of a sudden, she was in her parents' living room. She glanced around, shocked by the changes that had been made. The walls were papered in dark red, the furniture was black leather, the carpet was white.

Thinking she was in the wrong house, she turned toward the door, only the door was gone. She ran around the room, looking for a window, only there were no windows. Tears of fear and frustration filled her eyes when she realized there was no way out. She was running her hands over the walls, vainly searching for an exit, when her father suddenly appeared behind her.

"It's time," he said.

She whirled around. "Time?" she asked breathlessly. "Time for what?"

He held out his hand. "To join us. Come."

She backed away, her heart pounding in terror when she realized there was no place to hide. With a growl, he was upon her, dragging her toward the sofa.

She shoved her hands against his chest, trying to push him away, all the while pleading, "No, please!"

"There's no use resisting." He smiled, showing his fangs, and suddenly it was Vince staring down at her.

"No!" She screamed the word as he forced her head back, exposing her throat. Her nails were puny weapons against his much greater strength. There was a sharp stab of pain as he pierced her flesh. Fear was overcome by weakness as the world went from gray to black to nothing at all . . .

She woke covered in perspiration, her heart pounding, the blankets on the floor and her legs tangled in the sheets.

She was trembling and she couldn't stop. It had seemed so real. Afraid of what she might find, she lifted her hand and touched her neck and then, to make sure, she went into the bathroom and turned on the light. She turned her head from side to side, but she didn't see any telltale bite marks.

She breathed a sigh of relief. A nightmare. Of course, it had only been a nightmare. It wasn't surprising, she thought, considering the movie she had seen earlier that night and what she had recently discovered about her parents.

Cara was getting ready to go to work the next day when Vince called, "just to say hello."

They had been chatting for a few minutes when he said, "All right, darlin', tell me what's wrong."

"What makes you think there's anything wrong?" she asked.

"I can hear it in your voice. Are you mad at me because I missed dinner last night?"

"Of course not. Don't be silly."

"Then what is it?"

She hesitated a moment, then said, "It's nothing, really. Just a bad dream that I had."

"Wanna talk about it?"

"I don't know. It was nothing, really, but, well, in my dream, I went to visit my parents. I was in their house and suddenly it didn't look like their house anymore. The walls were red and all the doors and windows were gone. I was looking for a way out when my father suddenly appeared behind me and told me it was time, and when I asked time for what, he smiled a horrible smile and I saw his fangs. 'Time to join us,' he said, and he dragged me toward the sofa and then . . . this is so silly."

"Go on. What happened next?"

A nervous laugh escaped her throat. "All of a sudden it wasn't my father bending over me."

Vince held his breath as he waited for her to go on. Somehow, he wasn't surprised when she said, "It was you."

Chapter 28

Muttering an oath, Vince said, "Hey, darlin', don't let it worry you. It was only a bad dream."

"I know, but it seemed so real."

"You know how nightmares are," he said. "Your dad told you I was a vampire and your subconscious remembered it, that's all."

"I guess you're right."

"I'll see you later, okay?"

"Sure. Maybe we can go look for Halloween costumes."

"Costumes?" Vince exclaimed. "For who?"

"For us. We need to shop early, before the good ones are all gone."

"Wait a minute. What do I need a costume for?"

"To hand out candy on Halloween, of course."

"You wear a costume for that? I don't believe it."

"It's tradition," she said. "Mom and Dad always . . . I just thought . . ."

"Hey, if you want to dress up, we'll dress up. What are you going to be?"

"I've always been a witch."

"I'll bet you make a pretty one, too. So, what do you want me to be?"

"Whatever you want."

Vince grunted softly. One thing was for certain, he wouldn't be dressing as a vampire!

He met Cara at her house when she got off work later that night. Together, they drove to a costume shop that stayed open late during the week. Di Giorgio followed them at a discreet distance.

Upon entering the shop, Vince realized he never should have come. There were full-length mirrors at intervals throughout the store. It took some fancy footwork on his part to avoid them. Fortunately, Cara was too engrossed in looking at costumes to notice.

Vince pulled a pale blue princess costume from one of the racks. "I like this one," he said, holding it out to her.

"Oh, it is pretty," Cara said.

"I know you've always been a witch for Halloween," he said, "but if you were a princess, I could be a knight."

Cara grinned, remembering how Sarah Beth had called Vince her knight in shining armor. "Okay, I'll go try it on. Why don't you look for a knight costume?"

"Will do."

He kissed her on her way, then wandered through the shop until he found what he was looking for.

A short time later, Cara emerged from the dressing room. "What do you think?" she asked, twirling in front of him.

Vince whistled softly. "You look beautiful, darlin'." The dress was the exact blue of her eyes. The low-cut, fitted bodice displayed a generous expanse of creamy flesh and showed off her delectable curves.

"Thank you. Did you find a costume?"

He nodded.

Cara looked at it and frowned. "A *black* knight?" She shook her head. "I should have known."

"You ready to go?" he asked.

"Aren't you going to try that on?"

"Not now. Come on, let's get out of here."

"Where to now?" she asked when they left the shop.

"I should probably take you home," he said. "It's late."

"It's not that late," she said, pouting prettily.

"It won't hurt you to get to bed at a decent hour," he said. "I've been keeping you up pretty late the last few weeks."

She smiled at him. "I'm not complaining, am I?"

He slipped his arm around her waist and gave her a squeeze. "See that you don't."

When they reached her house, he walked her to the door. "Sweet dreams, darlin'."

"Are you sure you don't want to come in for a little while?"

"Not tonight." As much as he wanted to be with her, he hadn't yet fed and didn't trust himself to make love to her when the hunger burned within him. Drawing her into his arms, he kissed her, savoring her sweetness, yearning to carry her to bed and satisfy all of his cravings.

Summoning all the willpower he possessed, Vince put her away from him. Another kiss like that and he wouldn't be responsible for what happened next.

"I'll see you tomorrow night," he said and hurried down the stairs toward his car. He could feel Cara's gaze on his back as he opened the door and slid behind the wheel. Rolling down the window, he waved to her as he pulled away from the curb.

What would she think if she knew where he was going and why? Silly question, he thought. She had made her views on vampires quite clear. He felt an unwanted twinge of guilt for leaving her, yet staying would have been a very bad idea.

Lashed by his hunger, he sped toward The Nocturne. It had become one of his favorite haunts, a place where he could sit and contemplate his future, order a drink, or find prey. Tonight, he didn't want a glass of lukewarm blood and he didn't want to think about the future. He wanted to hunt—to find a pretty woman, take her in his arms, and satisfy his hellish thirst.

Arriving at The Nocturne, he parked in the lot, nodded to the man at the door, and went inside.

It was like coming home—the dim lights, the flickering candles, the scent of heated bodies and beating hearts.

He sought out a table in the back of the room, wishing that he could drown the voice of his conscience in a bottle of whiskey, but those days were gone. Unfortunately, there was no forgetfulness in a Bloody Mariah.

Perhaps it would be best for all concerned if he simply left town. No tearful good-byes. No explanations. Just pack up and go. Sure, Cara was bound to be hurt. No doubt she would believe he had just pretended he cared for her so he could get her in the sack; still, in the long run, maybe that would be kinder than telling her he loved her but that they couldn't have a future together.

Or he could simply tell her that he was a vampire. One thing was certain. No matter what he told her, he was going to have to leave town. He couldn't stay here. He didn't have the willpower to be in the same city and not seek her out.

But did he have the willpower to leave?

Cara sat curled up in a corner of the sofa, the book in her lap forgotten. She had gone to bed two hours ago, only to lie awake, wondering why Vince had seemed so distant and why he had left so early. Rising, she had tried to read, but the words made no sense. All she could think about was Vince. Had he tired of her? Was he seeing someone else? It was hard to believe he could be seeing another woman so late at night, but not impossible. The hours the two of them kept were proof of that.

Something was wrong. She knew it, but what? She couldn't put her finger on anything specific, and yet he seemed to be withdrawing from her in a way she didn't understand.

She told herself she was just imagining it, that everything was all right, but deep inside, she knew he was keeping something from her. She just hoped it wasn't anything as horrible as the secret her parents had kept for so long. She blinked back the tears that threatened to fall. The only thing she could think of that would be as devastating as learning that her parents were vampires was discovering that Vince was seeing someone else.

Going into the kitchen, she fixed a cup of hot chocolate, hoping it would help her sleep.

It didn't.

Later, lying in bed, she stared up at the ceiling, silent tears dripping down her cheeks.

Sitting in the dark at The Nocturne, Vince was all too aware of Cara's pain, and equally aware that he was the cause of it. With every fiber of his being, he yearned to go to her, to draw her into his embrace and wipe away her tears.

Instead, he went home to pack.

Cara rose early after a restless night. She took a quick shower, dressed, drank a glass of grapefruit juice, and drove to Vince's garage, determined to find out what was wrong and make it right.

Getting out of her car, she stared in disbelief at the hand-printed sign on the door.

BUILDING FOR RENT

Cara went cold all over. Going around to the office, she peered through the window. There were no cars inside waiting to be repaired, and no sign of Vince's car, either.

Pulling her cell phone from her purse, she dialed the number of the garage, felt her heart somersault at the sound of his voice.

"Hi, this is Vince. I've closed the garage and left town. If this is Phil, you can pick your car up at the Shell station across the street. If you're a customer with a car that needs repairs, try Don's Auto Shop on Fourth Street." There was a slight pause, then, in a softer tone, "If this is Cara, I'm sorry."

She stared at the phone, unable to believe he had left town, left her, without a word of explanation.

When Cara went to work, Sarah Beth took one look at her face and knew something terrible had happened.

"What is it?" She followed Cara into her office and closed the door. "For goodness' sake, girl, you're as pale as a ghost. What's wrong? Did someone die?"

Cara shook her head. "It's Vince."

"What happened? Did you two have a fight?"

"He's gone."

"Gone? Gone where?"

"I don't know. He left town."

"Just like that?"

Cara nodded, unable to speak past the lump rising in her throat.

"Oh, honey, I'm so sorry. Is there anything I can do?"

With a shake of her head, Cara sniffed back the tears that were waiting to fall. She had to pull herself together, had to believe he would call and explain. She clung to that thought like a lifeline.

"Cara . . ."

She took a deep, calming breath. "I'm fine, Bethy. I'd just like to be alone."

"Sure, hon. I'm here if you need me."

"I know. Thanks."

Cara waited until Sarah Beth left, then, needing to be busy, she reached for the stack of mail on her desk.

He didn't call that day or the next. By the end of the week, she had resigned herself to the fact that he was never going to call. By the middle of the following week, she was convinced she had gotten exactly what she deserved. She had met a stranger in a bar and had impulsively and foolishly believed everything he told her. She had taken him into her house, into her heart, and into her bed. And what did she have to show for it? Nothing but an empty bed and a broken heart. She pressed a hand to her stomach as a new thought occurred to her. Good Lord, what if she was pregnant?

She fretted over the possibility for the next three days and then resolutely put it from her mind. It was almost Halloween, her favorite holiday, and she wasn't going to let him spoil it for her.

Chapter 29

Serafina glanced at the clock on the wall, counting the hours until dusk. Everything was in readiness. A baby rested in the crib downstairs, drugged to insure it would sleep through the night. She had the necessary herbs: rosemary, yarrow, and meadow rue. Even now, Anton was on his way to pick up DeLongpre's daughter. As soon as the girl was safely in the lab, Anton would deliver a message to DeLongpre. Serafina had no doubt the vampire would do as he was told when he realized his daughter's life depended on his compliance.

It was All Hallow's Eve.

Soon had finally come.

Tonight, she would be with her beloved.

Chapter 30

Anton pulled into the parking lot behind the library just as the sun went down. Instead of parking in one of the spaces for patrons, he parked close to the back door. He sat there for a moment, wondering at the wisdom of what he was doing. Did he really believe his mother could raise his father from the dead? True, he had seen his mother perform some remarkable incantations in the last few weeks, but raising the dead? Still, the need to avenge his father's death, a need his mother had drummed into him every day of his life for as long as he could remember, burned strong within him. What did it matter if she killed a vampire? DeLongpre was already dead. They would return the baby to its parents in a few hours. And Cara . . . he felt a twinge of regret at the thought of her demise, but it was quickly swept away in the embarrassment of her choosing Vince over himself. Foolish girl. She would reap the consequences of that foolish decision tonight.

Getting out of the car, he looked around for her bodyguard's Lexus. He had followed Cara and her bodyguard for the last week, getting to know their routine. The bodyguard always followed her inside, stayed for an hour or two, then left the library to stretch his legs.

Anton whistled softly as he walked toward the bodyguard's car. Getting Cara to the lab would be relatively easy, but first he had to fix it so her bodyguard couldn't follow. Pulling a knife from his pocket, he slashed all four tires on the Lexus.

Still whistling softly, he slid the knife into his pocket, then walked around the building to the entrance.

Cara was at the front desk helping an elderly woman fill out a form for a library card when she saw Anton walking toward her. She couldn't help wondering what he was doing there, since it had been weeks since she had seen him.

"Just sign here, Mrs. Green," Cara said, handing the woman a pen.

Anton rested one elbow on the edge of the counter. "Hey, sweet cakes, long time no see."

Cara nodded at him. Taking the pen from Mrs. Green, she handed the woman a temporary card. "You can use this tonight. You should receive your card in a couple of days."

"Thank you, dear," Mrs. Green said. She looked from Cara to Anton and smiled, then walked slowly toward the back of the library.

Cara looked at Anton. "What brings you here?"

"Just stopped by to say hello and see how you were doing."

"I'm fine, thank you."

"How about going out for a cup of coffee?"

"I don't think so."

He leaned forward and lowered his voice. "I really need to talk to you."

"What about?"

"Your father."

"My father! What about him?"

Anton glanced around, as if he was afraid of being over-heard. "I don't think this is the place to discuss it, do you?"

Cara tapped the pen on the counter. He was right, of

course. This wasn't the place to discuss anything that had to do with her parents. She glanced around. The library was empty save for Sarah Beth, Mary, Mrs. Green, an elderly man reading a newspaper, and Frank, who was sitting at a nearby table working on a crossword puzzle. Still, she wouldn't want anyone to overhear her having a conversation that included vampires.

"Let me tell Bethy that I'm stepping out for a moment," Cara said, dropping the pen in a drawer. "I'll be right back."

Cara took Sarah Beth aside and told her she was going outside for a few minutes.

Sarah Beth glanced at Anton, who was leaning casually against the front desk. "Is everything all right?"

"I don't know," Cara said. "He said something was wrong with my father, but . . ." She shook her head. "I can't imagine what it could be, or why Anton would know something I don't."

"I hope your father's okay," Sarah Beth said sympathetically.

"I'm sure he is. I won't be gone long."

She nodded at Frank as she walked by his table, then headed toward the rear of the library. Ever the gentleman, Anton held the door for her, then followed her outside. She noticed his car was parked near the back door instead of in the lot.

"So," she said, turning to face him, "what's all this about my father?"

"Let's talk in the car."

She shook her head. No way was she getting into the car with him. She didn't trust him any farther than she could throw him! "We can talk here."

"No," Anton said curtly, "I'm afraid we can't." And so saying, he grabbed her by the arm, opened the passenger-side door, and thrust her inside, slamming the door behind her.

Alarmed, Cara tried to open the door, only it was

locked and wouldn't budge. Before she could do anything else, Anton slid behind the wheel and sped out of the parking lot.

"Anton, what are you doing?"

"All in good time."

"Let me out of here, now!"

"Just sit tight, sweet cakes. It'll all be clear soon enough."

Overcome by a sudden nameless fear, Cara glanced out the back window, hoping to see Frank's car behind them, only there was no sign of him, and as they reached the outskirts of town, there was no sign of anyone at all.

"What's going on, Anton? Where are you taking me?"

"To see your father, of course."

Cara looked out the window. There was nothing to see but a few old houses and soon even they were gone. "What would my father be doing out here?"

"He's not here yet." Anton looked over at her. "But he will be."

"I don't understand."

"All in good time," Anton murmured. "All in good time."

Cara stared out the window, chilled from the inside out. Where was he taking her? And why? And what did her father have to do with it? She bit down on her lower lip as her father's voice rose in her mind. *"I'm a wealthy man,"* he had once told her, *"and I have many enemies. Frank is there to make sure that no harm comes to you."*

Only Frank wasn't there.

Vince sat at his usual table in the rear corner of The Nocturne. Time and again he stared at his watch, as if glowering at it could make the hands move faster or the hours pass more quickly. He had left town almost two weeks ago, fully intending never to return, determined to put Cara out of his mind forever. It sounded simple enough. It turned out to be impossible. She filled his every waking moment. He missed her voice and the sound of her laughter. His body ached for her touch. He missed her in his arms, and in his bed.

Remembering Mara's advice, he had burrowed deep into the ground, seeking oblivion, but the memory of Cara's sweetness had followed him even there. Right or wrong, he had to see her again. He would tell her the truth and live with the consequences. Even if she rejected him, at least he would see her one more time. He felt like the worst kind of coward for leaving town without telling her good-bye, but when it came right down to it, he just hadn't had the nerve to face her, couldn't bear to see the hurt and disillusionment in her eyes and know he had put it there.

He glanced at his watch again, an oath escaping his lips. Would nine o'clock never come? He thought of storming into the library and confronting her there, but that would never do. If she denounced him in public, it would be embarrassing for both of them. If she accepted him for what he was, that would be embarrassing, too, because no matter where they were, as soon as she said she was his, he intended to drag her into his arms and make love to her until they were both exhausted.

Would nine o'clock never come?

Cara's heart lodged in her throat when Anton pulled up in front of what looked like an old abandoned building. She knew, in the deepest part of her being, that if she entered the place she would never leave it alive.

Grabbing the door handle, she shook it fiercely, willing it to open, and when that failed, she tried to roll down the window in hopes of climbing out, but to no avail.

Anton's laughter, cold and brittle, like the sound of

dead leaves striking a tombstone, filled the confines of the car. "What's the matter, sweet cakes?"

"Please." She forced the word through lips gone dry. "Please let me go."

"No can do." His hand closed over her forearm, dragging her across the console and out the driver-side door.

"My father's not in danger, is he?"

"Not yet, but he will be." Anton unlocked the door to the old building and dragged her inside.

She tried to wrest her arm from his grasp and when that failed, she pummeled his chest with her fists, then kicked him in the shin.

"Stop that!" he growled.

"Let me go!"

He slapped her across the face, hard enough to make her ears ring. "I said stop it!"

"Anton, is that you?"

Glancing over her shoulder at the sound of a feminine voice, Cara saw a middle-aged woman, clad in a long black dress and white apron, ascend the stairs. She was of medium height, with dark brown hair tied at her nape. Her skin was pale and clear; her eyes were gray. A hint of madness lurked in their depths.

The woman's gaze, sharp as a dagger, raked over Cara. "You must be DeLongpre's brat."

"Who are you?" Cara asked.

"Serafina. Has your father never mentioned me?"

"Not that I recall."

"Perhaps I'll tell you the story while we wait."

"Wait for what?"

"Your father's arrival, of course. Didn't Anton tell you? Bring her down, Anton. Everything is ready."

Knowing it was useless, Cara continued to struggle as Anton dragged her down a flight of stairs, through a laboratory, down another flight of stairs, and into a large, windowless room. Two metal tables stood side by side in the middle of the floor. One was fitted with thick silver

restraints, the other with leather straps. A stone crypt occupied one corner; a table covered with a black cloth
stood beside it. Two dozen black candles provided light.

In spite of Cara's frantic struggles, Anton lifted her
onto one of the tables. He held her immobile while the
woman strapped her wrists and ankles to the table.

Cara tugged against the restraints, her heart pounding so loudly in her ears that she couldn't hear anything
else. "Please." She glanced at Anton and the woman.
"Please, don't do this."

"It's time," the woman said.

Anton nodded. "I'll be back soon, Mother."

Cara stared after him. Where was he going? Surely not
to confront her father. No sane man would rile a vampire. And yet, her father was her only hope.

Wringing her hands, the woman paced between the
metal tables. "It will all be over soon," she said.

"Why?" Cara asked, choking back a sob. "Why are you
doing this?"

Serafina stopped pacing and glared at Cara, her eyes
blazing with hatred. "Why? You ask me why? Your father
killed the man I love, that's why!" She walked to the
crypt and knelt beside it. "My Anthony." Her hand caressed the cold stone. "Soon, my love, soon we'll be together." Rising, she came to stand beside Cara once
again. "Tonight I will bring my Anthony back," she said,
the madness in her eyes growing brighter, "and tomorrow he will be mine again."

Smiling, Serafina walked to the covered table and drew
back the cloth, revealing a silver bowl, a black-handled
silver dagger, and several small jars.

Cara stared at the dagger and hoped that her death
would be quick.

Anton was surprised to find the gate leading to DeLongpre's house standing open. But then, maybe DeLongpre

was expecting him. No doubt the bodyguard had already informed the vampire that Cara was missing.

Lights shone in all the downstairs windows. The front door opened even before Anton was out of the car and Roshan DeLongpre stood silhouetted in the doorway.

Anton slipped his hands into his coat pockets. The left one held a bottle of holy water, the right one contained a string of garlic. A sharp wooden stake rested against the small of his back; he wore a silver crucifix on a thick silver chain. It felt heavy around his neck.

DeLongpre moved to the end of the porch. "Bouchard, what are you doing here?"

"I have a message concerning your daughter."

The vampire was down the stairs in the blink of an eye. He towered over Anton, his dark eyes blazing. "You know where Cara is?"

"I do."

"Tell me now."

"All in good time."

Roshan's eyes narrowed ominously. "What's going on? What kind of game are you playing?"

"No games."

"Tell me what you want."

"Back off," Anton said, "or you'll never see her alive again."

"Roshan?"

"Stay in the house, Brenna," DeLongpre said curtly. "I'll take care of this." His eyes burned into Anton's. "What do you want?"

"This is how it's going to be," Anton said, pleased that his voice betrayed none of the fear that trembled just below the surface of his calm exterior. "You will get in the back of my car. You'll find a pair of handcuffs there. You will put them on. You will put the hood over your face. You will not try any of your mind games on me, nor will you offer any resistance when we reach our destination. Is that clear?"

"Where is my daughter?"

"With my mother. Cara's life depends on your obedience."

"And who is your mother?"

"You might remember her. Serafina Bouchard. You might also remember my father," Anton said. "Anthony Loken."

Roshan nodded as everything became suddenly clear. He was aware of Brenna listening at the door, sensed her frustration because he had sent her inside. Glaring at Anton, he considered his options. He could easily overpower Bouchard and search his mind for Cara's whereabouts, but to do so might put Cara's life in danger. Then there was the witch, Serafina, to contend with. She was a far greater threat than her son.

"So, vampire," Anton said impatiently, "what do you say?"

"You've given me little choice," Roshan said. Better to play along for now. He would deal with Anton when Cara was out of danger.

"Exactly. Get in the car."

Anton remained out of reach, his hand curled around the bottle of holy water, while the vampire did as he'd been told. Only when the hood and the silver-plated handcuffs were in place did Anton get behind the wheel. Feeling a bit weak with relief that everything had gone as planned, he slid the key into the ignition and headed for the lab.

Roshan sat back, his eyes closed beneath the mask. His skin burned like hellfire where the handcuffs touched his skin. It was a pain he had suffered in the past at the hands of Anton's father. The mask, too, had been lined with a sheet of fine silver, burning his face even as it prevented him from seeing through the material.

He swore softly, his rage growing with each passing mile. No matter what happened this night, whether Cara

was hurt or not, Bouchard and the witch would die for
what they had done.

Roshan? Brenna's voice sounded in his mind. *What
should I do?*

*Nothing at the moment, love. Keep Di Giorgio with you when
he gets home.*

You're in pain. I can feel it.

*He's handcuffed me with silver to restrain me. I think we're
going out to Loken's old lab.*

I should be with you.

No.

You'll call me if you need me?

He smiled in spite of the pain in his wrists. *Who else
would I call?*

I love you. Be careful.

A short time later, the car rolled to a stop. The engine
stilled. The door beside Roshan opened, admitting a
draft of cool air.

"We're here," Anton said. "Get out."

Moving blindly, Roshan did as he was told. He felt
Anton's hand close over his arm, guiding him toward
the lab. There was the sound of a key turning in the lock.
Roshan followed Anton until the threshold's power
stopped him.

"Oh, I forgot," Anton said, his voice thick with con-
tempt, "come in."

Roshan crossed the threshold. Feeling like a lamb
being led to the slaughter, he followed Anton down two
flights of stairs. A door opened and he caught his daughter's scent.

"Cara?"

"Daddy!"

"Shut up, both of you!" Anton said brusquely. He
shoved Roshan backward. "Climb up on that table."

Revulsion swept through Roshan as he did as he was
told. He remembered all too clearly the last time he had
been in this place. He flinched as someone carelessly cut

away his shirt, slicing into his flesh as well. The silver blade seared his skin, as did the heavy silver strap they laid across his chest to secure him to the table. Silver manacles were clamped around his ankles; the hand-cuffs were removed and replaced by silver shackles. A thick silver strap was fastened across his neck so that he couldn't raise his head.

They were taking no chances this time, he thought. He could already feel the heavy silver leeching his strength, weakening his powers, leaving him blind and helpless.

"Get the baby." Serafina's voice, filled with barely sup-pressed excitement. "It's upstairs, in the lab."

A baby! Roshan shuddered to think what they would do with the child, but it was the fate of his own child that filled him with despair. "Bouchard?"

"He's not here," Serafina said.

"I came without a fight, now let my daughter go."

"All in good time," the witch said. "We are not through with her yet."

"What are you going to do to her?"

"Take a little blood."

Roshan swore a vile oath. "Don't tell me you're pursu-ing Loken's foolish dream of immortality!"

"No." She laughed maniacally. "Something better than that."

He strained against the bonds that held him, wincing as the silver shackles cut deeper into his flesh. "Damn you!"

He heard the sound of Anton's footsteps coming down the stairs, a baby's sleepy whimper, caught the odor of sulfur as someone lit a match.

Roshan tensed as hands took hold of his arm.

"Keep him steady," Serafina said.

He felt a sharp jab as she plunged a needle into his arm, smelled his own blood as it filled the syringe.

"Now the girl, and then the baby," Serafina said.

Roshan heard Cara gasp as Serafina drew her blood.

The baby made no sound at all. He wondered if it was still alive.

"Take the brat back to the lab," Serafina said.

He listened to the sound of Anton's footsteps walking away, heard the woman muttering to herself as she paced the floor. A short time later, he heard Anton return.

Roshan tugged against his bonds again, but the silver was already doing its work, sapping his physical strength, weakening his preternatural powers, burning his skin everywhere it touched. If only he could see what was happening!

As if in answer to his unspoken wish, Anton removed the hood.

Roshan glanced to his right where Cara was bound to a metal table. Blood dripped from her arm. The scent of it enflamed his preternatural senses even as it stirred his hunger.

He turned his head to the left and Anton and Serafina came into view. For the first time, he saw the stone crypt in the corner.

Was it for his daughter, he wondered bleakly, or for himself?

Chapter 31

Vince glanced at his watch for the tenth time in as many minutes. Eight-thirty. He swore under his breath, wondering if the damn thing had stopped.

He stared into his empty glass, thinking he hadn't been this nervous about seeing a girl since he was sixteen years old and had a crush on Amy Broderson.

He thought about Cara and realized he didn't have the vaguest idea of what he was going to say when he saw her again. He supposed groveling would be in order. And confession. It was supposed to be good for the soul, though he wasn't sure he possessed one anymore.

So, what should he say to her? *Cara, I'm sorry I left without saying good-bye. I was a fool. I love you. And oh, by the way, your dad was right. I'm a vampire.*

Blowing out a sigh, he leaned back in his seat and closed his eyes. Soon after leaving town, he had gone home to visit his family. He hadn't seen his folks in over a year, and he'd wondered if they would notice the change in him. He'd shown up on a Sunday evening, making sure he arrived well after dinner and dessert. Even then, his mother had offered him cake and coffee, which he had politely refused, insisting he'd stopped for dinner on the road.

It had been good to see his folks again, to feel the love of his mom and dad, his sister and his brothers and sisters-in-law, to play with his nieces and nephews, and to catch up on their lives. His sister, Eve, was pregnant with twins. Once he'd gotten caught up on what they'd been doing, they wanted to hear about him, curious to know how he was doing, and if he had met anyone.

He had found himself telling his family about Cara and, with every word, he realized he didn't want to exist without her, that he loved her with every fiber of his being, and that he wanted nothing more than to share the rest of her life, however long or short that might be. It wouldn't be easy. She would age, sicken, and die. But that was the way of the mortal world and he couldn't change it.

His mother had been excited at his news, eager to see her youngest son marry and settle down, eager for more grandchildren. He had teased her, asking if ten grandkids weren't enough, and she had replied that, "you could never have too many grandchildren."

Now, sitting in a darkened nightclub, Vince felt a twinge of regret that he would never have a child of his own, never know what it was like to hold a son or a daughter in his arms. It was something he hadn't considered when he chose the life of a vampire. Of course, fatherhood would also have been out of the question if he had chosen death instead of life when Mara offered him the choice, so maybe it was a moot point and not worth thinking about.

Had Cara missed him as much as he had missed her? Was she angry because he'd been too gutless to tell her good-bye in person? Would she forgive him? Would she even see him?

He shook off his doubts. If she truly loved him, she would at least give him a chance to explain. He held that thought close as he glanced at his watch one more time.

It was eight forty-five.

Chapter 32

Cara glanced at her father for reassurance, though she found little to reassure her. The smell of his singed flesh filled the confines of the room. The skin at his wrists was raw and bright red, as was the skin at his neck, ankles, and chest. His face was also badly burned. Though his expression remained impassive, she knew he must be in agony.

She tugged on the leather straps that bound her hands and feet. She had to get free, had to help him. She had always thought her father was indomitable. Since learning he was a vampire, she had assumed he was indestructible. It was frightening to see him subdued and helpless. If he couldn't fight Serafina, what hope did she have of getting away from the woman?

A movement at the other end of the table drew Cara's gaze. There was a sudden hush as Serafina lit a long white candle and placed it in a holder in the center of the cloth-covered table beside the crypt. Shaking out the match, Serafina turned toward Anton, who held out his left arm. She filled a syringe with his blood and emptied it into a small glass vial. Next, she drew blood from her own arm and put it into another vial. In all, there were five vials on the table, along with three jars and a silver bowl. Serafina smiled at her son, and then she began to chant softly.

"On All Hallow's Eve, between dusk and dawn, the blood of kin must be drawn." She picked up an eye-dropper and dipped it into one of the vials. "Nine drops, no more, no less, the blood of kin you must bless."

She made a pagan sign over the eye-dropper, then slowly added nine drops of Anton's blood to the silver bowl.

"To this the blood of love you add, and the blood of an enemy, it must be had. Seven drops of each, one by one, quickly now, it must be done."

Once again, she added blood to the bowl, seven drops of her own blood, seven drops of Roshan's.

"Five drops of a maiden's blood," she intoned, and added five drops of Cara's blood to the bowl. "Rosemary for remembrance." She sprinkled rosemary into the dish. "An infant's blood, three drops for life anew." More blood was added to the bowl. "A sprinkling of yarrow, a dash of rue."

Serafina added the remaining ingredients, then stirred them together with a silver spoon. "Spread the blood upon the crypt, when the moon commands the sky." Serafina knelt beside the crypt, her expression rapt as she poured the contents of the bowl onto the crypt and then smeared the bloody mixture over the top with her bare hands. When that was done, she nodded at Anton, who pushed the top of the stone crypt aside. It fell to the floor with a resounding crash, revealing the casket within.

"Call forth the dead, his name times three. Doubt not, and he will come to thee." Serafina stood, her arms lifted over her head, blood dripping from her fingertips. "Anthony!" she cried. "Anthony! Anthony!"

Cara felt a shiver run down her spine as Serafina's voice echoed off the walls. She felt the hair raise along the back of her neck and along her arms as a strange current ran through the room. She glanced at her father. Judging by his expression and the way he jerked weakly against his restraints, she guessed that he, too, had sensed the otherworldly power vibrating through the night.

Serafina continued to stare at the coffin, as if she could will her beloved to rise.

Anton frowned at her. "Maybe you did it wrong."

"No!" Serafina exclaimed. "I did everything I was supposed to do." With her bare hands, she ripped the lid off the coffin. A horrible smell rose in the air. "Anthony, come to me!"

A low hum vibrated through the air and then, to Cara's horror, the body inside the coffin moved.

"Yes!" Serafina's voice was filled with exultation. "Yes, my love, come to me!"

And Anthony Loken rose from the coffin.

Cara stared at the thing that had once been Anthony Loken. His eyes glowed a dull red, his skin was pale; in some places, it had rotted away.

Anton stared at his father in horror. "Something's gone wrong!"

Serafina whirled around, her eyes wild. She held up her hand, fingers spread wide. "The blood of kin," she said, folding one finger down. "The blood of love." She folded another finger down. "The blood of an enemy. A maiden's blood." She stabbed her forefinger in Cara's direction. "Are you a virgin?"

Cara stared at the woman, wondering which would serve her better, the truth or a lie?

The witch turned on her son. "Did you touch her?"

"No, I swear it."

Once again, Serafina directed her attention to Cara. "Whore! Your blood was not pure! See what you've done!" She turned toward the thing that had been Anthony.

The creature stood in front of the coffin, unmoving except for his eyes, which were filled with confusion.

"Mother, you've got to put him back," Anton said. "You haven't raised my father. You've raised a monster!"

The thing that had been Anthony Loken turned its head and stared at Anton. "Son?" His voice was rusty with disuse.

"Yes," Serafina said, her smile radiant. "Our son."

"Liar!" Loken roared.

"It's true, my love." Apparently unaware of any danger, Serafina moved toward Anthony, one hand outstretched, a smile of welcome on her face. "Anthony, my beloved, come to me."

Teeth bared, he reached for her. There was a sharp crack as he broke her neck, and then he tossed her aside.

Anton took one look at his mother's broken body and ran out the door and up the stairs.

Fear congealed deep in Cara's belly as Anthony Loken moved woodenly toward her. She screamed as he drew near, went weak with relief when he lumbered past her toward the stairway.

Vince's head snapped up as Cara's voice rang out in his mind. He had no sense of where she was, only that she was terrified.

With preternatural speed, he left The Nocturne. Where was she? He knew Mara could find anyone at any time, but he hadn't yet perfected that part of his vampiric nature.

However, some things came easy. A thought took him to the library. Sarah Beth told him that Cara had gone outside with Anton a little after six o'clock and hadn't returned.

"I went outside at six-thirty and she was gone, though her car's still here, and so is her bodyguard's. I called her cell phone a few times, but she's not answering." Sarah Beth shook her head. "I've spent the last half hour wondering if I should call the police. Do you think I should call them?"

"No," Vince said curtly. He didn't want anyone to get hold of Anton before he did. Keeping a tight rein on his anger, he headed for Cara's house, telling himself all the while that there was nothing to worry about. She had dated Anton before; perhaps she was dating him again. He didn't believe it for a minute, but he clung to the thought in an effort to stave off an ever-increasing sense of dread.

He knew her house was empty even before he rang the bell. Something was definitely wrong. He could feel it in his gut. Fighting down a growing sense of panic, he headed for DeLongpre's house. He needed help, and he couldn't think of anyone more qualified than her father.

Brenna met him at the door. "Roshan, did you . . . Vince! What are you doing here?"

"I'm looking for Cara. Do you know where she is?"

"No, and it's driving me crazy with worry. Roshan left here hours ago with Anton Bouchard."

"Bouchard!" Damn, what was Anton up to? Nothing good, that was for sure.

"Yes, I wanted to go with them, but Roshan told me to stay here. I overheard Anton telling Roshan that his mother had Cara."

"Do you know where they might have gone?"

"I have a feeling they've gone to that abandoned laboratory outside of town. I was just about to go out there."

"I'll go with you."

"I sent Frank to check it out. He's probably there by now."

"Let's go."

It was strange, traveling at preternatural speed with another vampire. He had never done it before. They passed through the night like shadows, invisible to human eyes.

It was a peculiar sensation. Like everything else in his new lifestyle, it had taken some practice to master, and some getting used to. He wondered how long it would take for things like shape shifting and dissolving into mist to become second nature.

They reached the lab in a matter of moments. One of DeLongpre's cars was parked off the road, screened by a section of dense brush. Di Giorgio was waiting for them by the car. He carried a sawed-off shotgun. It looked very much at home in the crook of his arm.

"Have you seen anything?" Brenna asked anxiously.

"No. I circled the building. The only entrance is the front door, and it's locked."

"Come on," Brenna said. "Roshan's in trouble."

Frank went first, followed by Brenna and Vince. Vince nodded in grim satisfaction as a blast of the shotgun shattered the lock. So much for the element of surprise, he mused as he followed the bodyguard and Cara's mother down a flight of stairs, wondering, as he did so, why the threshold had no power to stop him. Perhaps it only worked on homes, he thought, and then he smelled blood and he knew the answer. Violence had been done here, shattering the threshold's protective power.

They paused in the first room before moving through it to another flight of stairs.

Again, Di Giorgio went first, his shotgun at the ready.

A cry of horror escaped Brenna's lips when she entered the room at the bottom of the stairs.

Coming up behind her, Vince swore a vile oath. The last vestiges of black magick hung heavy in the air, along with the scent of blood, death, and decay.

He stared at the woman sprawled facedown on the floor. It was obvious, from the angle of her neck, that she was dead.

He swept past Brenna to Cara. After freeing her from the restraints, he drew her into his arms. "Are you all right?"

She nodded. "My dad . . ."

Vince glanced at the vampire. Roshan's eyes were closed, his skin the color of old parchment.

Brenna reached for one of the straps holding her husband down only to let out a harsh cry of pain as the silver burned her hand. "Frank! Do something!"

Setting the shotgun aside, Di Giorgio quickly removed the silver manacles that bound DeLongpre to the table.

"Roshan!" Brenna placed her hand on his shoulder. "Roshan, can you hear me?"

Cara went to stand beside her mother. "What's wrong with him?" she asked, her voice thick with unshed tears. "He can't be dead!"

"It's the silver," Brenna explained. "It's like poison to us. We've got to get him off that table. Frank . . ."

"I'll take him," Vince said. "Di Giorgio, you go on ahead, make sure the coast is clear."

With a curt nod, Di Giorgio scooped up the shotgun and moved toward the stairs. Brenna and Cara followed him. Both women glanced repeatedly over their shoulders to make sure Vince was right behind them.

When they reached the top of the stairs, Cara came to an abrupt halt. "Wait. The baby . . ."

"What baby?" Brenna asked.

"There's a baby in the lab. We can't just leave it."

"Who does it belong to?" Brenna asked.

"I don't know, but we can't leave it here." Turning on her heel, Cara ran to the lab and scooped the baby from the crib. Still drugged, it lay in her arms like a rag doll. Crooning softly, Cara rejoined the others. "Poor little thing," she murmured.

Vince stared at her. She made a pretty picture, standing there with the infant cradled in her arms. For a moment, he imagined she was his wife and that the baby was his. The impossibility of such a thing filled him with a nameless anger.

"What the hell are you going to do with it?" he asked gruffly.

"After we get my father home, I'll take the baby to the police and say that I found it. I'm sure the parents must be frantic."

"What if it's an orphan?" Brenna wondered aloud.

"I don't know," Cara said. "We'll cross that bridge when we come to it."

Vince grunted softly as he followed her outside. He hadn't missed the wistful note in Brenna's voice. He couldn't help wondering if she was thinking about adopting another baby or, in this case, stealing one. But it wasn't his concern.

He settled Roshan in the back seat of Frank Di Giorgio's car. Brenna refused to be separated from her husband. Climbing into the back seat, she cradled his head in her lap. Cara got into the front seat with the baby, and Vince squeezed in beside her.

"Someone should burn that horrible place down," Brenna muttered.

"Maybe someone will," Di Giorgio remarked.

Seeing the expression on the bodyguard's face, Vince was pretty sure that the lab would be nothing but a pile of rubble come morning.

They traveled in silence for a while and then Cara looked up at Vince. "Where did you go?" she asked. "Why did you leave like that, without even telling me good-bye."

Mindful of the others in the car, he said, "I had to leave town suddenly."

"So suddenly you couldn't take five minutes to call me?"

"I couldn't get to a phone." Another lie, he thought ruefully. When would it end?

"So, when did you get back in town?"

"Late last night."

"Oh. Where are you staying?"

"I'm back at the garage," he said, grinning. "The owner made me sign a one-year lease this time."

Before she could ask any more questions, the car careened around a corner and rattled over a rut in the road. A short time later, Di Giorgio pulled up in front of DeLongpre's house.

Holding the baby in one arm, Cara ran to open the front door. Di Giorgio went back to close and lock the gate while Vince carried DeLongpre into the house. Brenna hovered at his side.

"Upstairs," Brenna directed, running ahead.

With a nod, Vince carried the unconscious vampire up the stairs and into the bedroom where Brenna waited. She had turned down the covers on the bed and Vince settled the vampire on the mattress.

Cara stood in the doorway, her face pale. "Will he be all right?"

"He'll be fine," Brenna said, stroking his hair. "He just needs rest."

And blood, Vince thought. He looked across the bed at Brenna and knew she was thinking the same thing.

"Cara," Brenna said quietly, "send Frank up here, then wait for me downstairs."

"Why? What can he do?"

Brenna blew out a sigh. "Your father needs blood right away."

"Frank knows what you are?"

"Of course."

Cara glanced at her father, then took a deep breath. "If he needs blood, he can have mine."

"No, Cara."

"Why not?"

"Because he wouldn't want you to see this part of our existence."

"I don't care. He's my father and he needs help. I've

given blood before . . ." She laughed humorlessly. "Recently, in fact."

"But not like this."

Cara laid the baby on the love seat by the fireplace then looked at her mother. "We're wasting time. Tell me what to do."

Brenna's shoulders slumped in defeat. Every moment she wasted arguing was one more moment of suffering for Roshan.

"Come, child," she said, "sit here, beside him."

Now that she'd gotten her way, Cara began to have doubts, but she thrust them aside. All her life, her father had cared for her, loved her, and protected her as best he could. She wasn't going to turn her back on him now, when he needed her.

"Are you sure you want to do this?" Brenna asked. "It's going to hurt."

"I'm sure," Cara said, though her voice quivered noticeably.

Brenna looked over at Vince. "I need your help."

"You've got it."

"Stand here and hold Cara's other hand."

Vince did as she asked, effectively blocking Cara's view of what was about to happen. Taking a deep breath, Brenna used her thumbnail to make an incision in Cara's wrist.

Blood flowed in the wake of the cut.

Lifting Cara's arm, Brenna held it to Roshan's lips. "Drink, love," she commanded softly.

A shudder ran through the vampire's body as he grasped his daughter's arm with both hands, his mouth closing over the wound.

Vince understood why Brenna didn't offer her husband her own blood. It was a rare thing for one vampire to drink the blood of another, but in this instance, he heartily wished that Brenna had refused Cara's offer.

The scent of her blood teased his nostrils, tempting him to push Roshan aside and lift her arm to his own lips.

Cara stared into Vince's eyes, unable to believe what was happening, wondering if now she, too, would become a vampire. As repulsive as the idea was, it seemed a small price to pay to save her father's life.

After what seemed like a very long time but was only a few moments, Brenna drew Cara's arm away. She ran her tongue over the wound and it immediately stopped bleeding.

Vince lifted Cara to her feet and put his arms around her. "Are you all right?"

Cara nodded, her gaze on her father. He looked a little better, she thought, not quite so pale.

And then, to her surprise, her mother made a gash in her own wrist and held it to her father's lips. Only for a moment, but the transformation was amazing.

The lines of pain that had been etched deep into his face disappeared as if by magic. The color returned to his cheeks. Even the raw places where the silver had touched his skin didn't look as red and angry as before.

Opening his eyes, Roshan saw Brenna hovering over him. "Cara?"

"She's here," Brenna said, taking his hand in hers.

"Hi, Dad," Cara said, moving closer to the bed. "How do you feel?"

Roshan stared at his daughter, an expression of horror crossing his face. "Why?" He looked at Brenna. "Why did you let her do it?"

"You needed blood," Brenna said, squeezing his hand.

"You should have asked Di Giorgio."

"I wanted to," Brenna said, "but Cara insisted."

Roshan looked at his daughter. He could feel her blood flowing through his veins; he had but to wish it to read her thoughts. "I never wanted you to see, to know . . ."

"It's all right," Cara said, forcing a smile.

"No." He closed his eyes, as if he could shut it from his mind. "No, it's not."

Still holding Roshan's hand, Brenna looked at her daughter. "What happened back there?"

"Anton's mother used our blood to raise a man from the dead," Cara said. She folded her arms across her chest, as if she had a sudden chill. "Only something went wrong." She shivered, remembering the crazed look in the witch's eyes. "Anton ran out of the lab and the thing went after him." She shivered again. "I thought it was coming after me."

"What of the witch?" Roshan asked.

"Serafina's dead," Brenna said without regret.

"If her incantation didn't raise Anton's father, what did it raise?" Cara asked.

"A zombie, I would imagine," Brenna replied. "If it finds Anton . . ."

The unfinished sentence hung in the air. There was no telling what would happen to Anton if the creature Serafina had raised found him, Cara thought. The creature hadn't seemed to believe Serafina's claim that Anton was his son, or had that enraged "No!" been a horrified response to finding himself resurrected in such a ghastly form? Did he even know who he was, or was he simply a shell of a man without a mind, without a soul?

Cara couldn't help feeling a twinge of guilt. If she had been a virgin, would Anthony Loken have risen whole and healthy from the grave?

"Let's go downstairs," Brenna said. "Roshan needs to rest."

"And I need to take the baby to the police," Cara said, lifting the infant into her arms.

"Speaking of the police," Vince said, "shouldn't we be reporting the fact that Anton kidnapped Cara?"

"No," Roshan said, his voice gruff but firm. "No police."

"Why the hell not?" Vince asked, but even as he spoke the words, he knew the answer. The last thing DeLongpre wanted was a bunch of cops coming around asking questions.

"We'll take care of this ourselves," Roshan said.

"What about the baby?" Cara asked. She stroked the infant's downy cheek with her finger. "Poor little thing. We've got to get him back to his parents as soon as we can."

Roshan was silent a moment, then sighed heavily. "You're right. Go."

"I'll go with her," Vince said.

"Take Frank, too," Brenna said, following the two of them down the stairs.

"Maybe he should stay here, with you," Cara suggested.

Brenna shook her head. "Don't worry about me. I can take care of things here. Frank . . ."

She frowned. "Where is he?"

"I don't know," Cara said, cuddling the baby. "Maybe he went to his place."

"It's not like him to just take off without telling anyone," Brenna said, frowning.

"We'll go by his house," Cara said. "Be sure to lock the door behind us."

Brenna looked at her daughter and smiled. "Anyone who comes here tonight will get more trouble than he's looking for."

Chapter 33

When he reached home, Anton drove into the garage and hit the control to close the garage door. Breathing heavily, he sat there for several minutes, his forehead resting on the steering wheel while he relived the horror of the last half hour. For a moment, he had been certain his mother's incantation had worked. She had actually raised his father's body from the crypt, only the creature that had risen from the coffin wasn't his father at all, but some mindless zombie.

Anton had bolted out of the laboratory with the creature right on his heels. Who'd have thought that something so decayed could move so fast? If his car door had been locked, he would have been a goner. As it was, he had managed to get behind the wheel and lock the door scant moments ahead of the creature. He had started the car and taken off in a cloud of dust and gravel. Just thinking about it was enough to give him the shakes.

He cursed viciously, damning Cara DeLongpre and her whole wretched family. It was all the girl's fault. She was supposed to be a maiden. How could they have made such a mistake? Anton would have bet his last dollar that she had never been with a man, but if that was true, his father would be here now and his mother would still be alive.

Getting out of the car, he went into the house through the door that connected the garage to the kitchen; then, his mind in turmoil, he moved from room to room, making sure that all the doors and windows were closed and locked.

What would he do if DeLongpre went to the police and reported that he had kidnapped Cara? He told himself there was nothing to worry about, that the vampire wouldn't want to get the police involved, but what if he was wrong? Cara had nothing to fear from the police. And what about the baby? They couldn't arrest him for taking the kid, although he thought they might be able to hold him as an accessory. Perhaps he could somehow cast all the blame on his mother . . . But it wasn't the police or what they could do to him that worried him. It was the vampire, DeLongpre.

Damn! Maybe he should just pack up and leave town tonight! Tempting as the thought was, he knew he couldn't go off and leave his mother's body lying in the basement of the lab like so much refuse, and yet he recoiled from the thought of going back.

Guilt roared through him as he recalled the cowardly way he had bolted out of the building, leaving his mother behind. What if she wasn't dead after all? He salved his conscience by telling himself it was the only option he'd had. After all, what else could he have done? Staying would have been akin to committing suicide. This whole catastrophe was Cara's fault. If she had been pure, the incantation would have worked and his father would be here now. Instead, his mother was dead and there was a zombie running loose in the city.

Going into the kitchen, Anton took a bottle of Irish whiskey from the cupboard and poured himself a stiff drink. Like it or not, he had to go back and get his mother's body. He owed her that much, though he had no idea how he would explain her death.

And what of the creature? What if it killed someone else?

Anton took another drink to fortify his nerves. The easiest thing to do would be to bury her body where it wouldn't be found and then leave town, but he couldn't do that, not until he'd found a way to undo what his mother had done. But first, he had to get his mother's body out of the lab.

He refilled his glass, drained it in a single long swallow, and left the house. Climbing into the car, he locked the door before driving out of the garage, his gaze darting from right to left before he pulled out of the driveway.

He kept one eye on the rearview mirror as he drove toward the lab, ever mindful that the creature was still out there somewhere.

He saw the smoke first, great plumes of dark gray smoke drifting skyward on the rising wind. The wail of a siren screamed in the distance.

Muttering an oath, Anton drove around the corner, then hit the brakes, hard.

His father's laboratory was engulfed in flames.

Chapter 34

Cara was quiet on the way home from the police station. She had told the sergeant in charge that she and Vince had been out for a walk when they heard a baby crying in the park and that they had found the infant wrapped in a blanket on a bench. The police had asked numerous questions, but no matter what the question, Cara had given them the same answer: "I don't know."

The sergeant had asked them to wait while he made a phone call, and ten minutes later, a man and a woman, both clad in pajamas, bathrobes, and slippers, ran into the station. They had taken one look at the baby and dissolved in tears of joy. They had showered Cara and Vince with hugs and fervent words of thanks. They had offered them a reward, which Cara refused.

Finally, after more questions, the police had decided Cara and Vince didn't have anything to do with the kidnapping and, after taking their names, addresses, and phone numbers, had let them go.

Though she knew it was foolish, Cara felt bereft, her arms empty as she left the police station. She had held the baby only a short time, but holding the infant had made her yearn for a child of her own, a little girl with Vince's black hair and deep brown eyes.

"You're awfully quiet," Vince remarked as he braked for a stoplight. "Are you worried about your father?"

"Not really. He's a vampire, after all," she said with a forced laugh. "I'm sure he'll be all right."

Vince glanced out the window. It had been a long night; it would be dawn soon. "What's bothering you then?"

"You'll think it's silly."

"Maybe, but tell me anyway."

"Holding that baby suddenly made me want one of my own." She looked up at him. "Do you like kids?"

"Sure. I always wanted a big family."

"Wanted?"

Thinking quickly, he said, "I'm not sure big families are practical these days."

"Maybe not."

Cara snuggled against Vince, her head resting on his shoulder. Frank hadn't been at his house, so they had taken one of her father's cars and driven to the police station without him. With a sigh, she closed her eyes. It had been a long, nerve-racking night. Replaying everything in her mind, she knew she was lucky to be alive.

"Where do you think Anton went?" she asked.

"I don't know."

"And that creature . . ." She sat up, her adrenaline flowing. "It's out there somewhere."

Vince put his arm around her and drew her against him once again. "Don't worry about it now. That thing has no reason to come after you."

"But . . ."

"Shh, darlin', you're safe here with me," he said, though he, too, had been wondering where the creature had gone and what it might do. Did it have any memory of its former life? Would it go through the city, wreaking havoc, like the zombies in horror movies? How long would the incantation last? A day? A week? Would the enchantment dissipate on its own, or would it have to be broken, and if so, how?

He was still pondering those things when he pulled up in front of DeLongpre's house. The place was dark save for a light in one of the windows downstairs.

Brenna opened the passenger-side door almost before the car came to a stop. "Is everything all right?"

"Yes, although for a while I thought we were going to be spending the night in jail," Cara muttered. "Honestly, do I look like a kidnapper to you?"

"Of course not," Brenna said, smothering a grin.

"How's Dad?" Cara asked, following her mother into the house.

"Resting. He'll be fine in a few days."

"Can I see him?"

"He's not here."

Cara's eyes widened. "Where is he?"

"He's resting where he won't be disturbed."

"But . . ."

"No more questions tonight, dear," Brenna said. "You need to get some rest. Frank's in the kitchen. He'll be staying in the house tonight."

"Where was he?" Cara asked. "We went by his place, but he wasn't there."

"He was out taking care of a few loose ends," Brenna said, her eyes twinkling. "Vince, you're welcome to stay, too, if you like."

"Thank you, but I'd best be getting home."

Cara squeezed his hand. "I wish you'd stay."

"I've got a few things to do, but I'll see you tomorrow. Promise me you won't go anywhere alone."

"Promise me you'll still be here tomorrow."

"I promise. Now you."

"Don't worry, I won't go anywhere."

"That's my girl," he said with a wink. He looked at Brenna. "If there's anything I can do . . ."

"Could I see you for a moment, alone?" Brenna asked.

"Sure." He followed Brenna outside and waited while she closed the door. "Is something wrong?"

"Have you told Cara the truth yet?"

"I've been meaning to, but . . ." Vince shrugged. "I'm afraid I'll lose her."

"The longer you put if off, the harder it will be," Brenna said. "Believe me, I know."

"I'm surprised you haven't told her."

"Her father already did," Brenna reminded him, "but she didn't believe it. Maybe she just doesn't want to believe it."

Unable to think of a suitable reply, he remained silent.

Brenna regarded him curiously for a moment. "You're different from the rest of us, aren't you? Roshan says it's because Mara brought you across. He said you aren't trapped by the Dark Sleep, and you don't seem over-whelmed by the need for blood, the way most new vam-pires are."

Vince shrugged. "Sometimes I don't feel like a vampire, either, but I'm vampire enough to know I can't live with my family and expect them not to notice the changes in me."

"I want you to promise me that you'll tell Cara the truth before things go any further between you," Brenna said, and then paused, her eyes narrowing. "Things have already gone too far, haven't they?"

"You'll have to ask Cara about that," Vince said.

Brenna shook her head. "You're going to break her heart; you know that, don't you?" She blew out a sigh. "At least you can't get her pregnant." Squaring her shoulders, she took a deep, calming breath. "I want to thank you for your help tonight, and . . ."

She turned as the door opened and Cara stepped out on the porch. "What's going on out here?" she asked, looking from Vince to her mother.

"Nothing, dear, I was just thanking Vince for his help."

"And you had to come out here for that?"

"Didn't anyone ever tell you what happened to the curious cat?" Vince asked, tweaking her nose. "Anyway, it's late and I should go."

Drawing Cara into his arms, he kissed her; mindful that her mother was watching, he didn't make the kiss as long or as deep as he would have liked.

"Sweet dreams, darlin'." He gave her a quick hug and a wink before letting her go.

With a nod in Brenna's direction, Vince descended the porch stairs.

He paused a moment, and then he walked the perimeter of the grounds before settling down in the shadows to keep watch until the sun came up.

The creature wandered aimlessly through the night, its mind as dark as the sky overhead. Now and then it saw something that looked fleetingly familiar, but before he could make sense of it, the memory was gone.

Keeping to the shadows, the creature lumbered up one street and down another until it came to a large house located on a hill. A high wrought-iron fence surrounded the yard. No lights shone in the windows.

The creature stood there for a long time. There was something oddly familiar about the house, something that drew it up the hill, through the gate, and up the stairs to the front porch.

Chapter 35

Cara slept late Sunday morning, but that was only to be expected, she thought, after the horrors of the night before.

Rising, she pulled on a fluffy pink robe, stepped into a pair of furry pink slippers, and opened the French doors that led to the balcony, only then realizing that it was raining. She stood there for a few minutes, listening to the rain and the thunder, watching as lightning streaked across the lowering sky. She had always loved storms and loved the rain, as long as she didn't have to drive in it.

After closing the doors, she left her bedroom, glad that she didn't have to go to work. In the hallway, she paused outside her parents' room. Remembering her mother's words the night before, she wondered where her father had gone to rest where he wouldn't be disturbed. Was it somewhere in the house? Had her mother gone to join him there?

She reached for the door, her hand closing around the knob; then, with a shake of her head, she went downstairs. She had never violated her parents' privacy; she wouldn't start now.

She found Di Giorgio in the kitchen, the Sunday

paper spread out on the table. He looked up when Cara entered the room.

"Morning, Miss DeLongpre."

"Good morning, Frank. Have you been awake all night?"

"I caught a few winks on the sofa."

"Oh, I was just going to make some breakfast. Would you like . . ." Her voice trailed off when she happened to glance at the morning headline.

FIRE DESTROYS ABANDONED BUILDING
BODY OF UNIDENTIFIED WOMAN FOUND INSIDE
FOUL PLAY SUSPECTED

Leaning over Frank's shoulder, she quickly read the story, which stated that the fire department suspected arson and the police department suspected murder. At present, the police had no leads and no suspects.

Cara stared at Frank, her mother's words echoing in her mind: *Someone should burn that horrible place down,* Brenna had said. And Frank had replied, *Maybe someone will.*

"You did it, didn't you?" Cara said. "You burned down the lab."

Di Giorgio looked up at her, his face impassive. "Who, me?"

"Yes, you."

Di Giorgio tapped on the newspaper. "No leads," he said with a sly grin. "No suspects."

Cara shook her head. She should be appalled by what he had done but all she felt was relief that she would never see that lab again, coupled with a faint sense of sadness for Anton. His mother had died a horrible death, her body burned beyond recognition in the fire. Of course, Cara thought, there was no one to blame for Serafina's death except Serafina. For a moment, the horror of all that had happened flashed through her mind: the mind-numbing fear of being strapped to a metal table, her concern for her father, the sharp prick of the needle as Serafina drew her blood, the icy terror that had chilled her to the marrow of her bones when Anthony Loken's body rose from the coffin . . .

She shook off the memories. What was done was done, and she was glad the building was gone. She hoped the city would level whatever was left of it.

"So, Frank, would you like something to eat?"

"Sure."

"French toast and bacon okay?"

"Anything you want to fix is fine with me." He reached for the coffee cup on the table. "You got any plans for today?"

"Not really." Opening the refrigerator, Cara took out a carton of eggs and the bacon and placed them on the counter, then she pulled a frying pan from the cupboard. "Although I might go out later and see if Vince is home."

"I'll be driving you anywhere you want to go today."

Out of habit, she started to insist she didn't need a babysitter, but the words died unspoken. After last night, she was lucky to have Frank around. In fact, she wasn't sure she ever wanted to go anywhere alone again.

After breakfast, she went upstairs to shower and dress, and then Di Giorgio drove her over to Vince's garage, but the place was locked up tight.

Disappointed, she asked Frank to take her back to her parents' house. After walking her to the door and seeing her safely inside, he told her he was going to his place for a quick shower and a change of clothes.

"Don't be running off without me," he warned. "Your folks will have my hide if anything happens to you."

"Don't worry," Cara said, "I'm not going anywhere."

Anton woke with a start. Disoriented for a moment, he glanced at his surroundings, relieved to find that he was at home. Apparently, he had fallen asleep on the sofa.

Sitting up, he ran a hand through his hair. He'd had the most horrible nightmare. He shuddered at the memory. His father had been terrorizing the city and his mother's burned body had been at his father's side. It had been like every horrible zombie movie he had ever seen. The two of them had had him backed into a corner, their skeletal hands reaching for his throat, when he woke up.

Rising, he went into the bathroom to splash cold water on his face. Leaving the bathroom, he paused outside his mother's bedroom. She had never let him into her room, insisting she liked her privacy. Well, she wasn't there to stop him now. It took only a moment to force the lock.

Stepping inside, he hit the light switch, then glanced around, wondering what she'd had to hide. He saw nothing out of the ordinary: a double bed with a flowered comforter, a pair of nightstands, a lamp with a fancy shade, a six-drawer dresser littered with yellowed newspaper clippings. He wondered how many times she had read the story about his father's death.

Moving farther into the room, he went to her closet and opened the door. Her dresses took up one side; the other was filled with men's clothing—all new, with the price tags still in place.

Going into his mother's bathroom, he opened the medicine cabinet, where he found an assortment of men's toiletries.

Regret burned deep in his soul. His mother had been certain her incantation would work. And it would have, he thought, his anger rising, except for DeLongpre's daughter. But for her, his father and mother might be here with him now.

Anton clenched his hands at his sides as he remembered how it had been, growing up without a father, listening to other guys talk about playing football with their dads and going camping and hunting and fishing. Their fathers had taught them how to drive and mow the yard and bait a hook. Their dads were there to cheer them on at Little League games. Other boys had fathers they could talk to about things that a guy couldn't discuss with his mother.

Anton sighed. He had never had a father, and now his mother was gone, too, and it was all that tramp Cara De-Longpre's fault.

Going back into his mother's bedroom, he stood there a moment and then, not certain why, he went to his mother's dresser and opened the drawers one by one. The right side was filled with his mother's underthings. The left side held neatly folded T-shirts, shorts, and handkerchiefs intended for his father. It occurred to Anton that it all belonged to him now: the house, the cars, and the contents of the house. He picked up one of the T-shirts, then rummaged through the others, noting that there were a variety of colors—red, navy, green, and black. Under the last shirt he found a wand wrapped in a sheet of tissue paper.

It wasn't his mother's, and it wasn't his.

Curious, Anton picked it up and felt a faint vibration of latent power flow from the wood up his arm. He ran his fingertips over the satin finish, knowing it must have belonged to his father.

Taking the wand with him, he left his mother's room. Now that Cara's parents knew who he was, it was unlikely that he would ever be able to get close to her again.

Frowning thoughtfully, Anton ran his thumb over the wand. If he could find a way to control the creature, he might be able to avenge his mother's death before sending the creature back where it belonged.

Going down to the basement, he began rummaging through his mother's spell books, searching for an incantation that would enable him to control the creature inhabiting his father's body.

* * *

Vince woke late in the afternoon to find Cat sitting on his chest. "What do you want?" he muttered irritably. "Go on, get out of here."

Cat yawned, displaying sharp white teeth, then, tail sticking straight up in the air, he padded to the edge of the mattress where he sat down and began washing his face.

With a shake of his head, Vince sat up. He had kept watch outside the DeLongpre's house last night until the rising of the sun had forced him to seek shelter.

As always, his first waking thought was for Cara. Drawing on his preternatural power, he concentrated on her and after a moment, as if there was a tangible link between them, he knew she was at home and that she was thinking of him.

Vince smiled, pleased that he had apparently mastered a new vampire skill. If it wasn't just a fluke, it meant that he would always be able to find her. Thinking of what Brenna had said to him the night before, he decided maybe that wasn't such a good thing after all. If he was going to sever his ties with Cara, it would be better if the break was clean and permanent.

Damn! How was he going to tell her the truth after all this time? Would she hate him for waiting so long, or simply for being what he was? And yet, why should she hate him? She loved her parents. He tried to tell himself there was no difference, but, of course, there was.

For a man who had resigned himself to spending the rest of his existence alone, he had fallen hard and fast. Damn and double damn. He never should have come back here. Nothing had changed. He couldn't just walk out on her without a word this time, not when he had promised her that he would see her today, even though that would probably be easier on both of them. He would see her tonight, he thought, and then he would never see her again. He shook his head, thinking he had promised himself the same thing only a short time ago.

He swore softly, remembering how Cara had looked

with that baby in her arms, the light in her eyes when she had talked about having a big family. Leaving her again would be like ripping the heart from his chest, but he loved her too much to ask her to give up a normal life and the family she longed for and deserved.

Cara stood in front of the bathroom mirror, brushing her hair. She had spent the day cleaning house, not that there was much to clean. Her parents were very tidy people. Still, dusting, vacuuming, mopping the floors, and washing her few dishes had kept her busy. Changing the sheets on her bed had made her think of Vince. It seemed like years since they had last made love. She had clutched her pillow to her chest, closed her eyes, and imagined that he was there with her, that his hands were caressing her, that his mouth was hungrily kissing her, that he was lowering her to the mattress, his body covering hers . . .

In the midst of her daydream, he had called to say hello. Hearing his voice had put a smile on her face, a glow in her heart, and a flush of embarrassment on her cheeks. Thank goodness he couldn't read her mind! She smiled at the memory as she pulled the brush through her hair.

"My, my, what put that smile on your face?"

Cara turned to see her mother standing in the doorway. "Mom! You startled me."

"I'm sorry, dear. You're not planning to go out, are you?"

Cara nodded. "Vince called a little while ago. He's picking me up in twenty minutes."

"Do you think that's a good idea?"

"I'm just going over to Vince's for a few hours."

"Why don't the two of you stay here?"

Cara turned back to the mirror, a faint blush warming her cheeks. How could she tell her mother she wanted to be alone with Vince, that she wanted to curl up in his arms and stay there forever?

But no words were necessary. "I see," Brenna said quietly.

"Have you heard from Dad?" Cara asked, hoping to change the subject.

"No, but he's fine."

"How do you know?"

"I just do. Cara, please don't go out tonight."

"Mom, I'll be fine. Frank will . . ."

"Frank was there when Anton kidnapped you, remember?"

"Are you saying you think I'm in danger with Vince?"

"No, of course not. Do I need to remind you that that creature is still out there, and so is Anton? Both of them are dangerous."

Cara bit down on the inside corner of her lower lip. Her mother was right, of course. As much as she wanted to be alone with Vince, going out suddenly seemed foolish.

"I'll stay in my room if you and Vince want some time alone," Brenna offered, thinking it might be wise for her to be nearby. If Vince chose tonight to tell Cara the truth, her daughter might need consoling later.

Cara blew out a sigh. "All right, we'll stay here."

"You promise?"

"I promise, Mom."

Relieved, Brenna gave her daughter a hug. "Call me if you need me," she said, and left the room.

Cara stared after her mother. What an odd thing to say, she thought, and then forgot all about it when she heard the doorbell ring.

Hurrying down the stairs, Cara looked through the peephole before opening the door, felt her heart somersault inside her breast when she saw Vince standing on the porch.

"Hi," she said breathlessly.

"Hi yourself. Are you ready?"

"I'm afraid I can't go. I promised my mom I'd stay in tonight."

"Oh? Why's that?"

She looked at him as if he wasn't too bright. "Hello? That creature is still out there, you know, and Mom seems to think Anton might be a threat, too."

Vince followed Cara into the living room, admiring the sway of her hips and the way the lamplight shone in the wealth of her hair.

"She's probably right." He suspected the real reason Brenna wanted Cara to stay home was to keep the two of them from "going any further."

Cara sat on the sofa, then looked up at him expectantly.

He sat beside her, drawn by her warmth, the glow in her eyes, the seductive smile playing over her lips. Did she have any idea how beautiful she was, or how hard it was for him to resist her? Even now, it was all he could do to keep from dragging her into his arms, brushing her hair away from her neck, and tasting the sweetness pulsing through her veins. She attracted him on so many levels—her beauty, her intelligence, her ready smile. With her, he felt whole, complete. Loved. He closed his eyes. How could he leave her? Even if he lived as long as Mara, he knew he would never again find anyone like Cara.

"Vince? Is something wrong?"

He opened his eyes to find her staring at him, her brow furrowed with concern.

"No, darlin'. How could anything be wrong when I'm here with you?"

She batted her eyelashes at him. "Why, sir," she said in a mock Southern accent, "you do say the sweetest things."

"And you, miss, are the most enchanting female I've ever known."

His voice moved over her like a velvet caress. "Vince . . ."

"Come here, darlin'."

She scooted closer, her eyelids fluttering down as his

mouth found hers. In moments, she was lying on her side on the sofa, his body aligned with hers, their legs entwined. He kissed her as if he could never get enough, as if he needed her as much as the air he breathed, as if his very survival depended on her. It was a heady sensation.

His hands caressed her with tender urgency and she drew him closer, reveling in the feel of his body pressed against hers. Heat unfurled deep within her, spreading outward, warming her, arousing her until the rest of the world fell away and there was only this man, this moment.

She murmured his name, begging him to carry her upstairs, to make love to her all through the night.

"Ah, darlin'," he replied, his voice ragged, "I'd like nothing better."

"Then what's stopping you?"

"We're not alone," he reminded her.

"Then let's go to your place."

"I thought you promised your mother you'd stay here?"

"I did, but . . ." She pressed her face against his chest. "I want you so much."

It was tempting, but he wasn't about to put her life at risk. He wasn't afraid of Anton. He could destroy the weasel with a look, but he wasn't so sure about the creature inhabiting Anthony Loken's body. Vince blew out a sigh. Against mortals, he was nearly invincible. Against a creature raised from the dead . . . he didn't know, and he didn't intend to find out, not if it put Cara's life at risk.

She stared up at him, her lips swollen from his kisses, her breathing uneven. He could smell himself on her, smell her need, her desire.

"Please, Vince?"

Damn! How could he refuse her when he wanted her as much as she wanted him?

For a moment, he was tempted to pull her into his arms and carry her to his place, creature or no creature. After all, though she didn't know it, this was to be their last night together. Coward that he was, this time he was going to kiss her good-bye and walk out of her life for-ever. For a moment, his yearning warred with his good sense. In the end, his good sense won out. Leaving Cara again was going to be the hardest thing he had ever done, but she had no place in his world. He couldn't be certain that he would always be in control of his hunger or his lust, and if anything happened to her because of him, because of what he was . . .

Muttering an oath, Vince sat up, his body aching with need. Keeping a tight rein on his desire, he took Cara into his arms again. With his fingertips, he stroked the soft curve of her cheek, the wealth of her hair, the sweet temptation of her lower lip.

"You know that I love you, don't you?" he murmured. "You do?"

"More than I've ever loved anyone, or anything."

"Oh, Vince . . . I love you, too!"

"I know." He rained kisses on her cheeks, the tip of her nose, her forehead, the tempting swath of warm skin be-neath her ear. The hunger rose within him, whispering for him to take her now, take it all, even as his desire urged him to bury himself in her sweetness one last time.

"Vince, let's go upstairs . . ."

Ah, love, he thought, *if only I dared.* But as much as he wanted her, needed her, he couldn't take her here, under her father's roof. He couldn't make love to her knowing he intended to leave her once again with no ex-planation, only this time it would be for good.

He kissed her and caressed her until her eyelids grew heavy.

"Go to bed, darlin'," he said, lifting her to her feet.

"I don't want you to go," she murmured drowsily.

"And I don't want to go," he said, "but it's late and you're half asleep."

"No, I'm not," she protested, smothering a yawn.

Vince laughed softly. "Go to bed, darlin', and dream of me."

With a sleepy sigh, she lifted her face for one more kiss.

"Good night, my love," he whispered, though it wasn't good night, but good-bye. He held her close, knowing it was for the last time, and then he let her go.

He walked out of the house, a great emptiness in his chest where his heart had been.

Sliding behind the wheel of the Mustang, he backed out of the driveway, then headed for a deserted stretch of highway. Putting the pedal to the metal, he pushed the car as fast as it would go. He was doing the right thing and he knew it, but dammit, why did it have to be so hard and hurt so damn much? She was the best thing that had ever happened to him. He slammed his fist against the steering wheel. He had lost his humanity; he shouldn't have to lose the only woman he had ever loved, or would ever love, as well.

Of course, he wasn't leaving town just yet. He would hang around until the creature was no longer a threat to Cara's safety, but he wouldn't see or speak to Cara again. It was for her own good, he told himself, and for his, as well.

But he didn't have to like it.

Chapter 36

The creature stirred with the coming of night. Disoriented and confused, it wandered through the house,
oblivious to the foul stench rising from the bodies piled
in a careless heap in a corner of the living room floor.

Anton woke with a start. He had spent most of the last
twelve hours searching for an enchantment that would
allow him to summon and then control the creature his
mother had raised. Rubbing his eyes, he stared at the
book on the floor in front of him. If he remembered
right, there had been an incantation on one of the pages
that had sounded promising, but he had fallen asleep
before he finished reading it.

Picking up the book, he thumbed through the pages
again. Where was it? Ah! There it was.

Following the directions, he fashioned an altar from
an old wooden crate and placed a photograph of his
father on it, along with his father's wand and a cloak he
found in his mother's closet.

Next, he found a box of salt and drew a summoning
circle on the floor; then, using his own wand, he wove a
strong protective spell around the circle. He added

lavender, cinnamon, and wormwood to the center, as well as a sliver of wood shaved from his father's wand.

When that was done, he took a piece of chalk and drew a second protective circle on the floor a few feet away from the first.

Then, taking a deep breath, he picked up a small silver bell and spoke the necessary words.

"Wandering spirit, blood of my blood, come to me now as this bell I ring, come to me now as this bell I ring, come to me now as this bell I ring."

He waited, listening.

When nothing happened, he repeated the charm again, and then again.

In the dark house on the hill, the creature that inhabited Anthony Loken's body paused in its restless wandering. Lifting its head, it turned this way and that and then it left the house, following an invocation only it could hear.

It was coming! Anton felt the creature's nearness in the very marrow of his bones. In his hand, the wand began to vibrate.

Filled with excitement and trepidation, Anton stepped into the protective circle he had drawn, his gaze riveted on the basement door.

He heard the front door open upstairs. Footsteps moved across the floor, down the stairs, and then the creature was there, walking toward him. As soon as it stepped into the center of the summoning circle, Anton spoke the words to close the circle and bind the incantation.

The creature stood there, arms hanging at its sides, soulless eyes staring at him, waiting.

Feeling weak, Anton could only stare back. The

zombie was here, called at his command. But would it do his bidding?

"Raise your right hand."

The creature stared at him a moment, then, slowly, raised its right hand.

Damn! A thrill of power ran through Anton. "Lower your hand."

Again, the creature obeyed.

Mindful of the creature watching his every move, Anton fought down a rush of exultant laughter. The creature was his to command at his will.

At last, he had the means to avenge the deaths of his mother and father.

Revenge would be his at last.

Chapter 37

Frank Di Giorgio was waiting for Cara when she entered the kitchen the following morning.

"I'll be driving you wherever you want to go again today," he said.

Cara nodded. She didn't have to ask why. The creature was still out there somewhere. She hoped it had left town, then felt guilty for doing so. Who knew what havoc it might cause in another city? Then again, maybe they were all worrying for nothing. For all they knew, it might be harmless now that Serafina was dead.

Cara fixed breakfast for herself and Frank, put the dishes in the dishwasher, left a quick note for her mother, and grabbed her handbag.

Di Giorgio followed her outside and held the door to the Lexus open for her. "Where to?" he asked.

"Vince's."

Cara stared out the window as Di Giorgio pulled out of the driveway. She had spent a sleepless night tossing and turning as she replayed Vince's leave-taking in her mind, unable to shake the feeling that he hadn't been saying good night but good-bye. She told herself she was wrong, that he wouldn't walk out of her life like that again, but she didn't believe it. She was certain he was hiding something from her, but what?

She was out of the car before it came to a full stop, a surge of relief sweeping through her when she saw that the security door was open. He was still here! Chiding herself for her foolish fears, she hurried inside, only to come to an abrupt halt when she saw that his car was gone. Then she noticed that his big red toolbox was also missing, and that Cat wasn't curled up on a corner of the desk.

"Can I help you, miss?"

Cara stared at the man walking toward her. He wore a pair of overalls and carried a paintbrush in one hand. "Who are you?"

"Max Felton; I own this building."

"I'm looking for Vince Cordova," she said, a sinking feeling in the pit of her stomach.

"Vince, yeah. He called me late last night and said he was moving out and he wouldn't be back." The man shook his head. "I got here around seven this morning and he was already gone. He must have taken off in the middle of the night."

"Do you know where he went?"

"Sorry, I sure don't."

She swallowed the lump rising in her throat. "Did he leave any messages for anyone?"

"Not that I know of."

"Thank you." Feeling as though her heart was breaking, she walked back to the car.

Di Giorgio was there to open the door for her. "Where to now?"

"Just take me home. My home," she clarified.

With a nod, Di Giorgio closed the door.

Cara stared out the window, scarcely aware of anything around her. He was really gone this time, with no good-bye and no hope of her ever seeing him again. This time it was final; she felt it in the deepest part of her being.

A short time later, Di Giorgio pulled up in front of her

place. Opening the door, he handed her out of the car and followed her up the walkway and into the house. He went from room to room, making sure everything was as it should be.

"I'll be right outside if you need me," he said.

Cara nodded. She felt suddenly old and dried up, as if all the life had been sucked out of her body.

Frank patted her shoulder, his eyes filled with compassion. "I'm sorry," he said quietly.

She nodded again, too numb to speak. All she could think of was that Vince had left her. Again. Only this time it was for good. She moved woodenly through the house, watering her wilted plants, dusting the furniture, vacuuming the carpets, and all the while, the words, "he's gone, he's gone," repeated themselves in her mind over and over again.

After putting the vacuum away, she went into the bedroom and sat down on the edge of the bed. She stared at the floor, more unhappy than she had ever been in her life, hardly aware of the tears that trickled down her cheeks.

Vince was gone and nothing else mattered.

Frank Di Giorgio stretched his arms over his head, then checked his watch. It was a quarter past three. Cara had been inside for almost four hours. He wondered what she was doing in there now. The last time he had looked in on her, she had been vacuuming; that had been almost an hour ago. She was a sweet thing. Too bad life had handed her such a raw deal. Of course, there were those who would think she had it pretty easy. She lived in a big house, she had lots of money, and enough clothes for a passel of females. Still, it couldn't be easy, having vampires for parents.

Rising, he stretched the kinks from his back and

shoulders, then decided to take a turn around the yard to stretch his legs.

He paused when he reached her bedroom window. Moving closer, he listened but heard nothing. Maybe she was asleep.

He had just reached the corner of the house when the short hairs prickled along the back of his neck. Drawing his gun, he spun around, his finger on the trigger.

For a split second, Frank and the creature stared at each other, and then Frank pulled the trigger. The bullet struck the creature in the heart, but it had no visible effect. Frank fired again and yet again.

He was about to pull the trigger a fourth time when Anton stepped out from behind the creature and, with a flick of his wand, sent the gun flying out of Di Giorgio's hand.

With a guttural cry, Frank lunged toward Anton.

And then everything went black.

She was dreaming. Vince had come for her and he was carrying her away. Smiling, she tried to wrap her arms around his neck, only her arms wouldn't move. Frowning, she tried again, but to no avail.

Opening her eyes, she saw the creature staring down at her.

Cara screamed and screamed again, trying to wake herself up.

And then, to her horror, she realized she wasn't asleep.

She closed her eyes and opened them again, but the creature was still there, staring down at her, its eyes empty of feeling, of life. There were three neat holes in its white shirt. It took her a moment to realize they were bullet holes. A living man would have been bleeding or dead, but the creature wasn't alive, nor was it Undead, like her parents. It was . . . she didn't know what it was.

Anton stood beside the thing that had been his father, his face impassive as he watched her.

She tried to move, only then realizing that she was in what looked like a basement and that she was lying on the floor, her hands and feet bound behind her.

"I'm sorry it had to come to this," Anton said.

"Wh . . . what do you mean?" She hated the quiver in her voice, the way her body shook with fear.

"I promised my mother I would avenge my father's death, and now I must avenge her, as well, thanks to you."

"Where are we?"

"My father's house."

"Where are the people who lived here?" she asked, certain she wasn't going to like the answer.

He glanced toward the far corner.

Cara followed his gaze, her stomach churning when she realized that what looked like a pile of smelly clothing covered by a sheet was in reality the house's former occupants. "You killed them?"

"No, I'm afraid the creature did that." He smiled. "It seems fitting, don't you think? My father died here, at your father's hands, and now you'll die here, at my father's hands." He laughed softly, maniacally. "It's perfect, don't you think?"

She was cold, so cold, and it had nothing to do with the cement floor beneath her. She was going to die, here, in this place, and there was no one to save her this time, no one who even knew where she was. "Please . . ."

"I'll be back when it's over."

"Anton! Please! Wait! Please, don't do this!"

But it was too late. He was gone and she was alone with a monster.

Vince prowled the confines of the room he had rented, his agitation growing with every passing minute as he waited for darkness to shroud the land. Cat sat on the windowsill, regarding him through unblinking yellow eyes.

For the last hour, Vince had tried to summon Cara's image and come up empty. The fact that he couldn't find her, couldn't sense her, filled him with quiet terror. Did it mean she was too far away? Unconscious? Or . . . he refused to consider the possibility that something had happened to her. And yet what other reason could there be?

It was not yet sunset when Vince left the house. The last rays of the sun singed his skin, but he paid no heed to the pain as he traveled with preternatural speed toward the De-Longpre's house.

Brenna answered the door, her welcoming smile fading when she saw the stark expression on his face. "Vince, is something wrong?"

"Where's Cara?"

"I don't know. I thought she was with you."

"Me? No. What gave you that idea?"

"She left me a note saying she was going to see you."

"How long ago was that?"

"I don't know. I just found it a few minutes ago."

Vince muttered an oath. Why was it that every time he left the girl, she got into trouble?

"She must be all right," Brenna said. "I mean, Frank's with her. If something was wrong, he would have called unless . . ."

"Unless he couldn't," Vince said flatly.

"We've got to find her," Brenna said.

"Let's go," Vince said. "We'll start at the garage."

It took them only moments to travel across town and ascertain that Cara wasn't there. The garage was closed; there was no sign of Di Giorgio or Cara, no sign that there had been foul play.

"Maybe she's gone to her house," Brenna suggested.

A thought took them there. "She's here!" Brenna said. "Look, there's Frank's car."

Brenna ran up the stairs and into the house, with Vince on her heels.

"Cara?" Brenna called. "Cara, where are you?"

A quick search of the house turned up nothing, but she had been there. Vince was certain of it. Where could she be? Cursing softly, he went out the back door.

He found Di Giorgio's body wedged in a corner behind the shed and the back fence. The man's neck was broken.

Coming up behind Vince, Brenna murmured, "Oh, no." A single blood-red tear slid down her cheek. "Poor Frank." She clenched her hands at her sides. "I wish Roshan was here."

"Where is he?"

"Gone to ground," she said.

Vince nodded. It was what he had expected. "What do you want me to do with the body?"

Brenna shook her head. "I don't know. We should probably report this to the police."

"Later," Vince said tersely. Di Giorgio was dead. Nothing could be done for him now. "Let's take him inside," he said, picking up the body. "You can worry about notifying the police after we find Cara."

Brenna followed him into the house. While she went looking for something to cover Frank, Vince carried the body into the laundry room and laid it on the floor.

"Where do we look now?" Brenna asked, covering Di Giorgio with a sheet.

"Damned if I know." Vince closed his eyes, his preternatural senses expanding, searching. *Cara? Cara, dammit, darlin', where are you?*

He was about to admit defeat when his blood stirred and he felt the latent connection between himself and Cara shimmer to life.

Brenna laid her hand on his arm. "Vince, what is it?"

"Wait!" He gathered his power around him and felt the connection grow stronger as every fiber of his being reached out to Cara.

"Vince, we're wasting time."

"Come on," he said, and headed for the door.

"Where are we going?" Brenna asked, hurrying after him.

"I don't know, but Cara's there."

So saying, he set off down the street, not stopping until he came to a house set on a hill.

"There," he said. "Cara's in there."

Brenna felt a chill skitter down her spine as she stared up at the house that had once belonged to Anthony Loken, the inside of which she had hoped never to see again. A quick mélange of images flashed through her mind: Anthony Loken standing over her, a demonic smile on his face as he cut a gash in her arm, his eyes glittering with madness as he and Myra watched the wound heal; the look of surprise on Myra's face when Loken killed her; the sight of Myra's body sprawled on the floor like a pile of dirty laundry. So much misery and death, Brenna thought, and all because Anthony Loken had thought he'd created an elixir that would allow him to live forever and he didn't want to share it.

"I'm going in," Vince said.

"And I'm coming with you."

With a nod, Vince moved toward the fence. He took hold of two of the iron bars, widening the space between them. He ducked inside, with Brenna on his heels. Moments later, they reached the front door.

Brenna glanced around. There were a couple of old newspapers scattered on the front porch.

The door was locked, of course. Vince swore impatiently. The lock was no problem, but the threshold was. He glanced over his shoulder at Brenna. "Now what?"

"I've been here before," she said. "Maybe I don't need an invitation."

Then again, maybe she did, since the house had changed owners. Still, it wouldn't hurt to try. A bit of vampire magic unlocked the door. It swung open on well-oiled hinges. "There's something dead in there," Vince muttered.

Brenna nodded. "And it's been dead for a day or so. Come on."

She crossed the threshold without any trouble. Whatever power it had once held had been negated; by what, she didn't know.

Vince followed her inside, surprised that he felt no shimmer of power as he entered the house. Inside, the stench of death was stronger.

Vince moved through the dark house, as unerring as a cat, the scent of Cara's blood like a road map to his vampire senses.

The trail led to a door which led to a set of steps. Wary now, Vince moved silently down the stairway into the basement. Something unnatural stirred in the air, a left-over vestige of magical power.

He moved deeper into the basement, a low growl rising in his throat as he rounded a collection of old furniture and boxes and came face to face with the creature, but it was Cara who held his attention. She was huddled on the cement floor at the creature's feet, her eyes wide with fear as she stared up at it. Oblivious to anything else, it reached for Cara's neck, its hand closing around her throat.

With a wild cry, Vince launched himself at the husk that had been Anthony Loken and the two of them crashed to the floor.

Brenna hurried to Cara's side. "Are you all right?"

Cara nodded, thinking she had never been so glad to see anyone in her whole life. Her mother untied her wrists and she groaned softly as blood rushed into her hands. Brenna made short work of the rope that bound Cara's ankles, then effortlessly lifted Cara to her feet.

"Vince," Cara murmured, horrified to see him locked in a deadly embrace with the creature. "We've got to do something!" She took a step forward, her own safety forgotten in fear for Vince's life. No mortal man could over-power that thing!

Brenna grabbed her daughter's arm. "No."

"Let me go!" Cara struggled to free herself. She couldn't stand by and watch him die. She just couldn't!

"You will not interfere," Brenna said, exerting her pre-ternatural powers on her daughter for the first time. "You will do exactly as I tell you. Do you understand?"

Cara nodded, confused by her sudden lack of willpower. She wanted to go to Vince, to help him fight the creature, but she couldn't move; she could only stand there, watch-ing helplessly as he drove his fist into the creature's face and body, seemingly with no effect at all.

She screamed when the creature picked up a crowbar and brought it crashing down on Vince's back. She sobbed when Vince fell to the floor, certain that his back had been broken, only to watch in disbelief as he rolled nimbly to his feet and launched himself at the creature again.

Deciding that the battle had gone on long enough, Brenna pulled her lipstick from her skirt pocket and quickly drew a summoning circle on the floor. She didn't know what kind of spell Anton had cast on the creature; all she could do was hope that her magic was stronger than his. Using an incantation she had learned as a child, she summoned the creature to the circle.

As she spoke the words, "So say I, so mote it be," the creature slowly turned away from Vince. Moving wood-enly, it stepped into the circle, then stood motionless, its empty eyes focused on Brenna.

"What the hell," Vince murmured.

"I haven't practiced my witchcraft in years," Brenna said, smiling. "I'm glad it still works."

"Yeah, me, too." Vince looked at Cara, who stood there as motionless as the zombie. "What did you do to her?"

Brenna shrugged. "It was the only way to keep her

from joining the fight." With a snap of her fingers, she released Cara from her spell.

"Vince!" Cara ran to him, her hands lightly exploring his back. "Are you all right?"

"I'm fine."

"But he hit you with a crowbar!"

Vince shrugged. "It was just a glancing blow. I'm fine." He studied the creature through narrowed eyes. "What are we going to do about that?"

"I'm going to send it back where it came from," Brenna said, "and then we'll get out of here."

"You're not going anywhere."

Cara shuddered as Anton stepped into view, a gun in his hand.

"Well, now," Anton drawled. "Isn't this cozy?"

Vince took a step forward, his anger rising as he came face to face with the man responsible for putting Cara's life in danger.

Anton leveled the gun at Cara's head, his finger curled around the trigger. "I wouldn't," he warned. "Not unless you want her dead."

Vince froze. "So," he asked, his voice like ice, "where do we go from here?"

"First, you back off," Anton said, gesturing with the gun. "And you . . ." He glanced at Brenna. "You release my father."

"He's not your father," Brenna said. "Send him back to wherever your mother summoned him from."

"Not yet."

"You can't kill me," Brenna said in a reasonable tone. "So send the creature back where it belongs and let us go."

Anton shook his head. "What do you take me for, a fool?"

Vince took another step forward. "Dammit . . ."

"Back off," Anton said, cocking the pistol. "I'll kill her, I swear I will."

Vince glared at Anton. He was certain he could disarm Bouchard before the bastard could fire the gun and yet, what if he was wrong? He looked at Brenna, who shook her head, silently urging him to wait.

"You can't win, Anton" Brenna said quietly. "No matter what you do, you'll have to face me."

"And me." Roshan DeLongpre materialized in a shimmer of silver motes beside Brenna, his face taut with barely suppressed rage. "Put the gun down, Bouchard."

Anton's face paled as he stared at DeLongpre. The vampire's face, only half-healed from the effects of the silver, was terrible to behold, but far worse was the look of retribution in the vampire's eyes.

Anton looked into those eyes and knew he was a dead man. He looked at the thing that had been his father and knew he would find no help there.

"Let her go," Roshan said.

Anton took a step backward, and then, shouting, "I'll have my revenge," he pointed the gun at Cara's back, his finger tightening around the trigger.

Vince threw himself between Anton and Cara a heartbeat before Anton fired the gun, once, twice, three times.

Vince felt the bullets rip through flesh, piercing his heart and lungs. The impact drove him back against the wall. Momentarily stunned, he slid to the floor.

In the sudden silence that followed, Anton turned and bolted up the stairs.

Roshan glanced at Brenna, then went up the stairs after Bouchard.

"Vince! No, no! Vince!" Running toward him, Cara dropped down on her knees at his side, tears streaming down her cheeks as she stared at the dark red blood oozing from his chest. She eased his shirt over his head, her stomach roiling as she stared at the ragged holes in his flesh. Cradling his head to her breast, she rocked back and forth. He was dying and it was all her fault! But maybe he didn't have to die.

Cara looked up at her mother, grateful for the first time in her life that her mother wasn't like other mothers. "Mom, please," she begged. "Do something!"

"I am," Brenna said, lifting her wand. "I'm sending this creature back where it belongs."

Cara stared at her mother in disbelief. How could her mother think about that creature when Vince was dying, perhaps dead already?

She looked down at him, her eyes widening with shock when she saw him looking back at her.

"Are you all right?" he asked, sitting up.

"I'm . . . you were . . ." She glanced at his chest. The ugly holes were growing smaller, the flesh knitting together, until only smooth skin remained. "How . . . ?" She looked up at her mother, then back at Vince. "My father was right. You're one of them, aren't you?"

Vince nodded. "I wanted to tell you, but . . ."

Pushing herself away from him, she stood, one hand braced against the wall.

There was a whoosh of supernatural power as Brenna sent the creature back where it belonged.

Cara glanced at the place where the creature had stood, looked at her mother, and then stared at Vince. Zombies and witches and vampires, oh my. She wondered where her father had gone, but at the moment, it didn't seem to matter. She had to get out of here, she thought desperately, she had to go someplace where she could be alone to sort out her thoughts.

Vince reached out to her, but she brushed his hand away. She wasn't ready to deal with him yet, wasn't sure she ever wanted to see him again.

She took a step and then, feeling suddenly light-headed, she dropped to her knees, felt herself spiraling down, down, into oblivion.

Chapter 38

Cara woke in her bed in her parents' house with no memory of how she had gotten there. The sun was shining through the windows and she was alone in her room. For a moment, her mind was mercifully blank and then, like the ocean at high tide, it all came flooding back—Anton and the creature, her mother and Vince coming to the rescue, Vince getting shot . . .

Vince. Her father had been right. Vince was a vampire . . . vampire . . . vampire.

The word echoed and re-echoed in her mind. Vampire.

She told herself it didn't matter, that it wasn't important. Her parents were vampires and she still loved them. She stared out the window, reliving the moments in the basement last night, recalling the sharp report of the gunshots, the acrid stink of gunpowder, the sickly sweet scent of blood. Vince's blood. Vampire blood, oozing from the wounds in his chest. She recalled, all too vividly, the coolness of his skin, the sticky wetness of his blood on her hands, her certainty that he was dead, and then the miracle of watching his torn flesh heal right before her eyes.

Vampire.

Undead.

She had always imagined she and her husband shar-

ing intimate, candlelit dinners at home, dining out in
nice restaurants on birthdays or anniversaries. Did she
want to spend the rest of her life eating her meals alone?

How would she feel in ten years or twenty, when she
showed the signs of aging and he didn't? Did she want to
live with a man who would look forever young, a man
who couldn't go outside during the day?

Did she love him enough to accept him as he really
was? Did she want to spend the rest of her life with a man
who wasn't a man at all?

Did she want to spend the rest of her life without him?

She felt betrayed because he hadn't been honest with
her. Neither had her parents, she thought ruefully. She
could understand her parents' reluctance to tell her the
truth. She could understand Vince's, too, but the fact remained that, right or wrong, good reasons or not, the
people she loved most in the world had all lied to her.
It was worse with Vince, though. He had let her fall in
love with him when she didn't really know who, or what,
he was.

With a sigh, she realized that the signs had been there
all the time, but she had refused to see them—arriving
late at Sarah Beth's so he wouldn't have to explain why
he didn't eat dinner, never leaving the garage when the
sun was up, always leaving her house before dawn. She
had never seen him eat or drink anything except that
glass of wine at her parents' house and a Bloody Mariah.
She frowned thoughtfully, wondering why he could
drink wine and nothing else.

Where was he now? Where was her dad? He had left
the basement last night in pursuit of Anton, and she
hadn't seen him since.

She glanced at the clock. It was time to get ready for
work. For the first time, the thought held no appeal.

She got ready anyway, thinking that going to work
would help keep her mind off Vince.

With a start, she realized she hadn't seen or heard

from Frank since the day he had driven her to her house. Had he been hurt? Was he in the hospital again?

Ashamed for not thinking about him sooner, she hurried out to his house in the back and knocked on the door. There was no answer. Biting down on her lower lip, she turned the knob, somewhat surprised when the door opened.

She had never been inside his house before. It was small and surprisingly neat for a man who lived alone. The furniture was sparse but of good quality. A number of photographs sat on the mantel. She moved closer for a better look. The first depicted a young couple holding a little boy. There were three other photos of the same couple. The boy was older in each picture; in the last one, it was easy to see that the boy was Frank. There were several photos of a beautiful young woman. Was it Frank's sister, or was the woman the reason he had never married?

Cara blinked back tears when she looked at the last two photos. One was a picture of herself sitting on a pony when she was about five or six, the other was her graduation picture.

"Oh, Frank," she murmured, thinking that he had devoted most of his life to protecting her. She wished she knew where he was, wished she could crawl into her father's lap and let him make everything right again, the way he had when she was a child. So much had happened that she didn't know about and didn't understand. Where was Anton? Was he still a threat? Where was her father?

Where was Vince? She told herself she didn't care, that she never wanted to see him again, but in the far reaches of her heart and soul, she was afraid it was a lie.

Wiping away her tears, she left Frank's house and went to get ready for work.

Vince prowled the confines of his hotel room, his mind in turmoil. He had planned to leave town, to leave Cara when he was certain she was out of danger, and now that she knew what he was, leaving seemed like the wisest thing to do, and yet he couldn't go, not until he had seen her one more time. Not until she told him, in her own words, that she never wanted to see him again. Until then, he clung to the faint hope that she would understand, that she would find it in her heart to forgive him for withholding the truth for so long.

Raking a hand through his hair, he dropped down on the sofa, one hand idly scratching Cat's ears. He wondered if DeLongpre had found Anton, and if so, what he had done to the bastard, and if DeLongpre had gone to the police to report Di Giorgio's death, and what story he had concocted. He was pretty sure no mention had been made of witchcraft or zombies rising from the dead.

He didn't really care about any of that, though. All he wanted was for the sun to go down so he could see Cara. Only then would he know if the rest of his existence was going to be worth living.

The minute Cara walked into the library, Sarah Beth hurried to meet her. "What is it?" she asked. "What's wrong?"

"Am I that transparent?" Cara asked.

"Girl, you look like you just lost your best friend."

"Well, I didn't," Cara said, forcing a smile, "since you're still here."

"You know what I mean. What's happened? It's not your parents?"

Cara shook her head. "No."

"It's Vince!" Sarah Beth exclaimed. "Oh, no, don't tell me you broke up!"

"I really don't want to talk about it, Bethy."

"All right," Sarah Beth said, giving her a quick hug, "but I'm here if you need me."

Cara nodded. Walking into her office, she wished it was that easy, wished she could pour out her heart to Sarah Beth, tell her everything, but she couldn't, of course. Who would believe that her parents were vampires, that she had fallen in love with a vampire, or that some crazy witch had raised a zombie? It all sounded like some horrid nightmare, which was exactly what it was, she thought, only she wasn't dreaming.

Sitting at her desk, she switched on her computer, then sat staring at the blank screen.

She didn't know how she got through the day, but suddenly it was nine o'clock and time to go home. Whose home, she thought, her own or that of her parents?

She said good-bye to Mary and Sarah Beth, turned out the lights, and went out the back door, only to come to an abrupt halt when she saw Vince standing beside her car. Her first impulse was to run to him. Instead, she crossed her arms over her chest and waited.

"Cara, we need to talk."

She shook her head. "No. Not now. I need time to think."

He took a step toward her and she backed away, blinking back the tears that burned her eyes.

"Cara, I know you're angry . . ."

"Please, Vince, just go away."

He stared at her, a muscle throbbing in his jaw. "All right, if that's what you want."

She nodded, unable to speak past the lump in her throat.

With a nod, he turned and vanished from her sight.

Cara stared after him; then, with a shake of her head, she went home.

She met her parents at the door. "Where are you going?" she asked.

"We were just coming to look for you," her father said.

"Oh. I thought I'd stay here tonight, if that's okay?"

"You're always welcome here," Brenna said, kissing Cara's cheek. "You know that."

Moving into the living room, Cara sat on the sofa between her parents. Looking at her father, she asked, "Where's Frank? I went by his house earlier, but he wasn't there."

Roshan slipped his arm around her shoulders. "He's dead, Princess."

So much death, she thought, and then felt a bubble of hysterical laughter build inside her. Everyone she had ever cared for was dead in one way or another. She sniffed back her tears. "Where . . . what have you done with him?"

"I buried him in a corner of the backyard, beneath the old elm tree."

"The backyard? Why?"

"It was easier than trying to explain what had happened to him."

"And Anton, what happened to him?"

"I don't know. I couldn't find him."

"But . . . how could he get away from you?"

"I'm not the only one with supernatural powers, you know. Anton's a warlock, and a pretty powerful one."

The thought that Anton was still out there somewhere should have frightened her, but she was too numb to care.

"Don't worry about him now," Roshan said. "Besides, if he's got any sense at all, he's left town."

"Cara?" Brenna laid her hand on her daughter's arm. "It's okay to cry."

Cara looked at her father, at the love and compassion in her mother's eyes, and burst into tears.

Vince prowled the deepest, darkest part of the city, his thoughts as bleak as his surroundings. He had been afraid of what she would say, hadn't been surprised that she didn't want to see him again, and he still hadn't been prepared for the pain her words caused him. He told himself that, with time, she would change her mind, but he didn't believe it. He told himself it was his fault, that he should have told her the truth before they made love, but he was convinced the outcome would have been the same. At least he had known what it was like to have her love for a short time, and yet even that failed to comfort him. Having loved and lost, he couldn't help thinking it was better not to know what you were missing.

Cara passed the next three weeks in a kind of haze. She ate very little, slept even less, and forced herself to go to work, but her heart was empty, her emotions numb. She saw the concern in the eyes of her parents and Sarah Beth and assured them she was fine.

Every day, she told herself she would move back to her own house, that she would put Vince Cordova out of her mind, that she would forget the horror of that awful Halloween night.

But she couldn't forget Vince.

One morning in late November, she woke up feeling nauseated. Bending over the toilet, she thought how unfair it was that she should catch the flu now. Didn't she have enough misery in her life?

She was nauseous for several days, and then it passed.

At the end of November, Cara and Mary gave Sarah Beth a baby shower. Cara couldn't help feeling an unwanted twinge of jealousy as she sat in Sarah Beth's living room, watching her best friend ooh and ahh over baby blankets and dresses and tiny little booties. She wondered if Sarah Beth knew how lucky she was. She had a husband who loved her and a baby on the way. Her life was normal, ordinary, unlike Cara's, which had lately been filled with vampires, witches, and zombies.

Later, after everyone else had gone home, Sarah Beth and Cara sat in the living room, drinking coffee and nibbling on leftover cake.

"Cara, please tell me what's wrong."

"I don't know what you mean."

"I watched you tonight. You were smiling on the outside, but I saw tears in your eyes. I know you're unhappy because of Vince but . . . is that all it is? You can tell me anything, you know that."

"I wish I could tell you," Cara said. "I do, but I can't."

"I can't imagine what could be so awful that you can't talk about it."

"Bethy, if I told you . . ." Cara shook her head. How could she tell Sarah Beth that her parents were vampires, that Vince was a vampire? What if Sarah Beth didn't believe her or laughed at her? Worse, what if she believed it and accidentally told someone else? Cara wasn't sure how people would react to knowing that there were vampires running around. In movies, vampires were feared, hated and hunted. She had a feeling that if people discovered vampires were fact and not fiction, they would react with fear and loathing. For the first time, she wondered how many other vampires were out there. Her parents and Vince made three. Whoever had made her father and Vince made four and five.

"Cara?"

"I'm sorry, Bethy, it's a secret and I can't break it."

Taking Cara's hand, Sarah Beth said, "All right, hon, I understand. I just wish I could help."

Cara nodded. "Me, too."

Brenna watched Cara slowly climb the stairs to her bedroom. Gone was the bright-eyed young woman who had filled their house with joy, and in her place stood a listless girl with pale cheeks.

"Roshan, what are we going to do about Cara?"

He shook his head. "There's nothing to be done, love. She has to work her way through this. No one can do it for her."

"But it breaks my heart to see her looking like that. There must be something we can do to cheer her up."

"Short of kidnapping Vince and bringing him here, I can't think of anything."

"Let's do it then," Brenna said, her eyes alight.

"Brenna, be serious."

"I am!"

"If she wanted him, don't you think he'd be here? It's obvious that she can't accept what he is . . ."

"But she accepts us," Brenna remarked.

"Like it or not, we're her parents. She didn't have a choice in the matter. But she has a choice with Vince, and she's made it. Bringing him here would only make it worse."

"I don't think so. She still loves him, she's just hurt and confused."

"Maybe, maybe not, but it has to be her decision, not ours. Besides, I'm not so sure I want her to be married to a vampire."

She pinched his arm. "Have you forgotten that I'm married to a vampire?"

"No, love, but you're not mortal."

"Maybe Vince could bring her across," Brenna said. "Think how wonderful that would be! The four of us, all together."

With a sigh, Roshan put his arm around his wife and drew her against his side. "That would have to be Cara's decision, too, love."

Brenna grunted softly. "I liked it better when she had to do as she was told."

Roshan nodded. "Life was certainly easier then," he agreed. "But, like it or not, children grow up."

"Maybe we should have brought her across when she was a little girl," Brenna muttered.

"Maybe next time," he said with a laugh. "Come on, love, let's go for a walk."

From the shadows across the street, Vince watched Roshan and Brenna leave the house. When he was certain they were out of sight, he took a deep breath, then ran across the street and knocked on the door before he lost his nerve. He knew Cara didn't want to see him, but he had to see her one last time.

He shook his head. It seemed he was always leaving town, but this time he was going and he was going for good. It was just too damn painful to be in the same city, to know she was near, and not see her.

He knocked again, wondering if she had gone to bed, wondering if he shouldn't just forget the whole thing.

Then it was too late. The door opened and Cara stood there clad in a long pink bathrobe, her hair falling over her shoulders like liquid gold.

She stood there blinking at him. Her cheeks were pale and her eyes were red, as if she had been crying. "What are you doing here?"

"I came to say good-bye."

"You're leaving? Again?"

"I think it's for the best," he said. "Don't you?"

She didn't say anything; just stared at him, a single tear slipping down her cheek.

Vince caught it on the tip of his finger and carried it to his lips. "Be happy, darlin'," he murmured, and walked down the stairs.

"Vince, wait. I . . ."

He turned to face her. "What?"

She didn't say anything; she just stood there, looking at him.

"I'm sorry I lied to you," he said fervently. "Your father warned me that I'd break your heart. If I did, I'm sorry. I wanted to tell you the truth, but I was afraid I'd lose you." He shook his head ruefully. "I lost you anyway, didn't I? But I'll always love you."

"Will you kiss me good-bye?"

With a nod, he climbed the stairs, his gaze moving over her face, committing it to memory. As if he'd ever forget. He stroked her cheek with his knuckles, then bent his head and kissed her.

"Good-bye, darlin'."

"Don't go." Tears streamed down her cheeks. "I don't want to live without you. I love you."

"Cara!" He swept her into his arms, felt his own eyes burn with tears as he held her close. Holding her, inhaling the fragrance of her hair, was like coming home after a long absence. "Darlin'."

"I missed you." She murmured the words against his chest. "I missed you so much. Every day, every night." She looked up at him. "Promise me you'll never leave me, no matter what. Even if I tell you to go, promise me that you won't."

"I'll never leave you again, I swear it on all that I hold dear."

"And you'll still love me, even when I'm . . . I'm old and you're . . . you're not."

He stroked her hair. "Even then."

"You're crying." Lifting her hand, she captured one of his tears. It shimmered red in the porch light. Frowning, she looked up at him. "It's blood."

He nodded, wondering if she was already having second thoughts.

And then she licked it from her finger. "Come on," she said, "let's go inside."

He followed her into the house and sat beside her on the sofa. He ached with the need to hold her, to bury himself in her softness and partake of her sweetness, but he was all too aware that Roshan and Brenna could return at any minute.

A wave of his hand brought the fire in the hearth to life.

Again, Cara stared at him, her eyes wide with wonder.

"I guess your folks never used any of their vampire powers in your presence," Vince remarked.

She shook her head. "I guess I've got a lot to learn."

"That makes two of us."

"What do you mean?"

"I've only been a vampire for a year."

"Oh. How did it happen?"

Vince frowned, wondering what she'd say if he told her about Mara. Skirting the issue, he said, "The usual way. A vampire took my blood, then I drank hers."

"Hers?"

He laughed softly. "You're not jealous of a vampire, are you?"

"Did you love her?"

"Love her? I hated her for a while."

"And now?"

He shrugged. "Once you get used to it, being a vampire isn't so bad."

"What did your parents say when you told them?"

"They don't know."

"Why didn't you tell them?"

"For the same reason you can't tell anyone. Mortals are distrustful of anything they don't understand, suspicious of anyone that's different." His gaze bored into hers. "You haven't told anyone, have you?"

"No. I guess you drink . . . blood."

He nodded. "Are you all right with that?"

"Well, I'd be lying if I said it didn't bother me . . ."

"Can you live with it?"

"I'll get used to it, I guess. Do you sleep in a casket?"

"No. I tried it once, but . . ." He shook his head. "I couldn't sleep."

"I saw you during the day. How is that possible?"

"I've got Mara to thank for that. She's the oldest living vampire. Apparently her blood is really powerful and some of that power was transferred to me."

"It all seems so impossible."

"Yeah, that's what I thought." He took a deep breath, afraid to ask the next question, but it was one they had to discuss. "What about children, darlin'? You know I can't have any. I saw the way you looked at that baby in Loken's lab, your sadness when you had to give it back . . . I know how important having a family is to you."

She was silent for several moments.

Vince cursed inwardly. He should have known that his inability to father a child would be the deal breaker.

Cara looked up at him. "My parents adopted me. I guess we could adopt a baby, or maybe have artificial insemination. That way the child would be half ours. Could you live with that?"

"Anything you want is all right with me." Leaning closer, he brushed his lips over hers. "I love you, Cara. Will you marry me? Share my life with me? I know it's a lot to ask, but . . ."

Murmuring, "yes, oh, yes," she wrapped her arms around his neck and kissed him.

She was still kissing him when a deep voice said, "Looks like you were worried for nothing, wife."

Glancing over her shoulder, Cara saw her mother and father standing in the doorway.

Cara bounded to her feet, smiling from ear to ear. "Mom! Dad! Guess what? Vince just asked me to marry him! Isn't that wonderful?"

"Wonderful," Brenna murmured. She opened her arms and Cara ran to her.

"I guess this calls for a drink," Roshan said.

Brenna hugged Cara. "So, when's the big day?"

"I don't know," Cara said, looking at Vince. "We didn't get that far."

"Whenever she wants is fine with me," Vince said.

While Brenna and Cara huddled on the sofa, already deep into wedding plans, Roshan handed Vince a glass of wine.

"I know you probably don't approve," Vince said, "but I can't live without her."

Roshan swirled the wine in his glass, thinking that the day he had dreaded had come. "I know you're what Cara wants," he said quietly, "so that makes it all right with me, but if you ever tire of her, don't just leave her. You bring her back here to me. She's my little girl, and I'll always love her."

"I'll never leave her. You have my word on that."

"I always wanted a son," Roshan said. "Just remember, if you hurt her . . ."

"I know," Vince said, grinning broadly. "You'll destroy me."

"Without a qualm," Roshan replied, lifting his glass. "Welcome to the family."

Chapter 39

"Will I see you tomorrow night?" Cara wound her arms around Vince's neck. It was after three AM and they were standing on the front porch saying good night.

"What do you think?"

"I don't think I can wait that long to see you again."

"Then come by the garage in the morning."

"You're working there again?"

"Yeah," Vince said, grinning. "Looks like it's for good this time."

"I'll be there bright and early," she said, and then frowned. "How early is too early?"

Reaching into his pocket, he withdrew a key and handed it to her. "Come on by anytime," he said. "If I'm still in bed, well . . . you can just crawl in beside me."

"But I thought . . . I mean, won't you be . . . umm, sleeping the sleep of the dead?"

Vince laughed. "Believe me, darlin', if you're nearby, I'll know it."

Yawning, Cara slipped the key into her pocket. It had been a long night. "I don't know how early it will be," she said, smothering another yawn, "but I'll be there."

He nuzzled her neck, just behind her ear. "I love you."

"I love you, too," she murmured, and then frowned. "You're not going to want to drink my blood, are you?"

"I hate to tell you this, darlin', but I've wanted to do that since the night we met."

"Oh." The thought should have been repulsive; instead, she found it oddly intriguing.

"I tasted you once."

Her eyes grew wide. "What? You did?" She lifted a hand to her neck. "When?"

"The first time we made love."

"I don't remember that part."

"I only took a little taste, darlin', just enough to satisfy my curiosity."

"Your curiosity about what?"

He ran his fingertips up and down her neck, traced the outline of her ear and her cheek. "How you'd taste."

"Doesn't everyone taste the same?" She couldn't believe they were standing on her front porch having this conversation.

"No."

"I didn't know blood came in flavors," she muttered.

"I've never tasted anything as sweet as you, darlin'." Resting his forehead against hers, he inhaled deeply, drawing in the scent of her hair, her skin, her life's essence. "You've spoiled me for everyone else."

She was flattered, and then wondered why. It wasn't as if he was complimenting her on a new hairstyle or a new dress or the color of her eyes. He was saying he liked the taste of her blood!

"Guess I shouldn't have said that," Vince drawled.

Cara lifted one shoulder and let it fall. "No one's ever complimented me on my blood before," she said, laugher evident in her tone. "I'm not sure what to say."

"You don't have to say anything, except that you still love me." He canted his head to one side. "You do, don't you?"

Standing on her tiptoes, she laced her hands behind his neck and kissed him, long and slow. "What do you think?"

"I think I loved you the first time I saw you at The Nocturne," he replied. "And I'll love you for as long as you live."

"I love you, too. Please don't be angry if sometimes I seem . . ."

"Disgusted by what I am?"

"No, not that!" She pressed her fingertips to his lips. "It's just all so new. You, my parents . . . sometimes I feel like I'm the one who's different."

She thought about those words as she drifted off to sleep and wondered what they would mean to any child they might bring into their home. She thought about her own childhood and how strange it had been. Of course, her son or daughter wouldn't have two parents who were vampires, or a father who was only there at night. Vince could be active during the daytime, and Cara would be there to take their child to school and go to conferences and school plays and award ceremonies. She could attend graduations and birthday parties and piano recitals. Her child's life would be normal, or as close to normal as Cara could make it. If Vince was willing, they might even adopt more than one . . .

It was her last thought before sleep claimed her.

Cara and Vince decided to be married as soon as possible. Cara and Brenna spent every evening for the next week shopping for wedding dresses. Cara didn't know how she would ever decide on a gown, since she loved every one she tried on, whether it was short and sexy or long and elegant. It was the same with veils. She liked the shoulder-length ones; she liked the long ones.

Now, standing in front of a three-way mirror clad in a froth of white lace, she glanced at her mother. "I love this one, too! I'll just have to ask Vince which dress he likes the best."

"Don't you know that's bad luck, for the groom to see the bride in her wedding dress before the wedding?"

"You don't believe that, do you?" Cara asked, surprised that a woman who was a witch and a vampire would believe some silly superstition; then again, maybe her mother believed it because she *was* a witch and a vampire!

Brenna grinned. "Why take chances?"

With a sigh, Cara went into the dressing room to change into her own clothes. She absolutely loved trying on wedding gowns, but sooner or later, she was going to have to pick one. Or maybe not, she thought with a grin. She loved shopping with her mother. When they weren't looking at wedding gowns, they were buying things for Cara's house—new sheets for the bed, a picture for above the fireplace, a scratching post for Cat, and a new screen for the fireplace. Brenna bought Cara a sheer black nightgown for her wedding night, a pair of matching slippers, and several sets of sexy underwear in a variety of colors.

In addition to buying things for the wedding and the wedding night, Cara and Brenna shopped for Christmas presents for their husbands. Cara loved walking through the mall, looking at all the decorations and listening to the Christmas carols. She and Vince had spent the night before putting up Christmas lights and looking for a tree. Cara had always loved the Christmas season, but never more than this year, when Vince was there to share it with her.

Cara and her mother were leaving the mall Tuesday night after yet another shopping spree when Cara had the feeling that they were being followed. Frowning, she glanced over her shoulder to see two gray-clad women walking along the street behind her and her mother. A chill ran down Cara's spine as she recalled the two women she had seen in Serafina's book shop. She told herself she was being silly. These weren't even the same women she had seen.

"Something wrong, dear?" Brenna asked. "You look as white as a ghost."

Cara looked at her mother. "What?"

"I asked you if something was wrong."

Cara shook her head, then glanced over her shoulder again. There was no sign of the two gray-clad women. Nevertheless, she was glad when they reached her car.

Vince was waiting for her when she and her mother got home. One look at him and she forgot everything else.

"So, how did the shopping go?" he asked. "Did you find a dress yet?"

"Dozens of them!" she replied.

He shook his head. "What's the problem?"

"She can't make up her mind," Brenna said.

"She never could," Roshan said, smiling fondly at his daughter. "Remember how long it took her to decide on a car?"

"Weeks," Brenna said.

Vince groaned as he drew Cara into his arms. "At this rate, we'll never get married," he muttered, then frowned at her. "You're not getting cold feet, are you?"

"Of course not. But the dresses are all beautiful."

"And she looks beautiful in them," Brenna said.

"I'm sure she does," Vince agreed. "How about if I pick one out?"

"Don't you know it's bad luck for the groom to see the bride in her gown before the wedding?" Cara asked, winking at her mother.

Vince shrugged. "I won't see you in it, I'll just pick it out." He nuzzled her neck. "I'm getting tired of living alone."

"All right, I'll pick one out tomorrow, I promise."

"Good."

"So, where are we going to be married?" Cara asked. "I guess a church is out of the question."

"A church is fine with me," Vince said.

"Really? I didn't think vampires and churches went together."

"I know the perfect place!" Brenna exclaimed. She looked at Roshan. "Do you think you could get Father Lanzoni to perform the ceremony?"

"I'm sure I could," Roshan said, "but it's not for us to decide."

"What church?" Cara asked. "And who's Father Lanzoni?"

"Father Lanzoni is a vampire," Roshan answered. "He was a priest before he was turned."

"Is he still a priest?" Vince asked.

"I've never asked him," Roshan said. "The church is located in a secluded place. It's where Brenna and I were married." He smiled fondly at his wife. "Of course, we're not sure it was legal."

Cara looked at Vince. "What do you think?"

"It's all right with me. As far as I'm concerned, you became my wife the first time we made love."

Cara's cheeks bloomed with color. "Vince!"

"He's not telling us anything we didn't already know," Brenna said with a laugh. "You can't hide something like that."

"So, we're agreed then?" Vince asked.

"I think it sounds wonderful." Cara glanced at her parents and then at Vince. "It seems so romantic, to get married in the same place as my parents. Oh! What about your parents? Your family? Are you going to invite them?"

"I thought I would. We need to set a date."

"How about two weeks from Saturday?" Cara suggested. "That'll give you time to rent a tux and give your parents time to make arrangements for a place to stay while they're in town." She kissed him on the cheek. "And we'll be married for Christmas."

"Works for me," Vince said.

Roshan and Brenna nodded.

Cara looked up at Vince, a dreamy smile on her face. "Two weeks," she murmured. "I can't wait."

Vince called his parents the following night to tell them the good news. As he'd expected, his mother was eager to meet Cara and thrilled that he was finally settling down. His father, ever the practical one, asked if he'd gotten Cara in trouble and that's why they were getting married in such a rush. With complete confidence, Vince assured his dad that wasn't the case. When he called his brothers and his sister, they all congratulated him and promised they would be there. One and all, they were a little surprised to learn that the wedding was at night. Vince used the same excuse that Roshan had used with Cara and explained that her parents were allergic to the sun.

After telling his sister good-bye, Vince rubbed the bridge of his nose, wondering if inviting his family had been such a good idea. They would expect a get-together after the wedding, dinner and cake and champagne.

Vince glanced at his watch. He'd worry about his folks later. Right now, it was time to meet Cara at the library.

Cara glanced at her watch, willing the hands to move more quickly. It was eight-thirty and there were only a handful of people in the library. She glanced at the table across the room, her stomach clenching at the sight of the two gray-robed women who sat there, each quietly reading a book. They never looked at her and seemed totally oblivious of her presence, and yet she couldn't shake the feeling that they were watching her every move. Even when she couldn't see anyone, she often had the feeling she was being watched, followed. No wonder she often felt nauseated in the morning. Paranoia and her upcoming wedding had her stomach tied in knots.

It was playing havoc with her menstrual cycle, too. She hadn't had a period in over a month.

She told herself to stop worrying. Serafina was gone. The creature she had raised no longer existed. Anton had disappeared. Her parents and Vince had searched the city, but Anton was nowhere to be found. There was nothing to fear. Vince would protect her.

The ladies in gray left the library at eight fifty-five. Vince arrived at the stroke of nine. "Hey, beautiful, you ready to go?"

They drove to what had become "their spot," that quiet, fairy-like place beside the lake. Vince spread a blanket on the ground and they lay side by side, looking up at the stars.

"Three more days," Cara said. "Three more days and we'll be together forever."

"Forever," Vince murmured. Rising on his elbow, he gazed down at her. She was the best thing that had ever happened to him, beautiful, forgiving, understanding, and kindhearted. He couldn't bear the thought of losing her after fifty or sixty years when he might exist for hundreds or a thousand. What would he do without her?

She smiled up at him, one hand caressing his cheek. "What are you thinking about?"

"How much I love you."

"No more than I love you."

"Wanna bet?"

She laughed softly, the sound the sweetest music he had ever heard.

"Cara . . ."

"What?" She frowned at his serious expression. "Is something wrong?"

"I don't want to lose you, ever."

"I know." She drew his head down and kissed him. "I don't want to lose you, either."

"There's a way to keep that from happening."

"You mean by me becoming a vampire, don't you?"

He nodded. "Have you ever thought about it? Wondered what it would be like?"

"Thought about becoming one?" She shuddered. "No. Of course I've wondered what it's like, I mean, how could I not, since I seem to be surrounded by them."

"It's not so bad." He stroked her cheek. "Think what it would mean. Centuries together instead of a few short years. You'd never age. We could see the world together."

"I know what it would mean, and I don't want it." Her gaze searched his. "You won't ever force it on me, will you, the way my father did my mother?"

"No."

"You promise?"

He hesitated a moment, then sighed. "I promise."

"It doesn't change anything between us, does it?"

"No, darlin'. Nothing could change that."

Drawing her into his arms, he kissed her, all the while thinking, hoping, that the day would come when she would change her mind, when they could truly be as one.

Vince's family, all seventeen of them, arrived the afternoon before the wedding. Since he couldn't travel from his place to hers while the sun was up, Vince had spent the previous night at Cara's house. He had been a little uneasy at doing so. Since becoming a vampire, he had always slept alone, aware of the fact that, when the Dark Sleep overtook him, he was vulnerable. He had also been a little apprehensive about how Cara would react, but reasoned it was better to find out now than after they were married.

When he asked her that morning what it had been like, sleeping with a vampire, she had shrugged.

"Come on," he said. "Tell me. Did I look dead?" He'd always wondered about that, since he'd never seen a vampire at rest and couldn't watch himself sleeping.

"You didn't look dead, but it was kind of spooky," she

admitted. "Once I tried to wake you up, but I couldn't."
She canted her head to one side. "What if someone finds
you when you're asleep? I mean, you're helpless."

"Not exactly. I can sense when there's someone nearby
who means to do me harm."

"Then why didn't you wake up?"

"Probably because I'm not afraid of you."

Now, as they got ready to meet his parents, he didn't
know which of them was more nervous. He told Cara
not to worry, certain that his family would love everything about her. As for himself, he couldn't stop pacing
the floor. How would he explain the fact that he didn't
eat or that he only drank wine?

A knock at the door told him that the time for worrying was past. They were here.

Cara smiled as Vince introduced his parents, his brothers and sister, and their spouses and children, certain she
would never remember all their names. His parents
seemed truly glad to meet her, his brothers and sister
made her feel as if she was already part of the family.

Vince watched Cara as she cuddled first Joe's baby
daughter and then Frank's son. Feeling his gaze, Cara
looked up at him and smiled. Looking at her, Vince
knew he'd cut off his right arm to be able to father a
child, to see her hold a baby of their own in her arms.
Regret rose up within him, making him wonder again if
she would be better off without him. She was such a
warmhearted, generous soul, filled with enough love for
a husband and a dozen children—children he could
never give her.

"Isn't he darling?" Cara asked, coming to stand beside
him. She took a deep breath. "Babies always smell so
good!"

Vince nodded.

"Do you want to hold him?"

"Sure." Taking the baby from Cara, Vince smiled

down at his nephew. "Hi, Donny," he murmured. "I'm your Uncle Vince."

Cara glanced around her house, which was overflowing with people. "You have a wonderful family."

"Yeah." Vince frowned as the scent of urine reached his nostrils. "I think we'd better find Rose. I think Donny needs a diaper change."

A short time later, Roshan and Brenna arrived. After piling into a number of cars, they drove to the restaurant for dinner.

Seated at a large table in one of the banquet rooms, Vince and Roshan exchanged glances after everyone had ordered.

"I'll take care of it," Roshan said, and Vince felt a sudden surge of preternatural power flow through the air.

Vince glanced around the table, noting that everyone seemed to be having a good time. Brenna and his mother were laughing together like they were old friends and, thanks to Roshan, no one seemed to notice that the vampires at the table never ate a bite.

It was late when the party broke up. Finally, after a half an hour of hugs and good nights, Vince and Cara were alone.

"Do you think they liked me?" she asked as they drove back to her house.

Vince reached over and gave her hand a squeeze. "They loved you. And even if they didn't, I love you, and that's what counts."

Cara laughed softly. "I guess that's true."

Pulling up in front of her house, he draped his arm across the back of her seat. "Cara."

"What?"

"Are you sure this is what you want?"

"What do you mean? You haven't changed your mind, have you?"

"No, I just want to make sure you know what you're getting into, and that you won't be sorry later."

"What brought this on?" she asked. "Haven't we been through all this before?"

"I know, but I watched you tonight with the kids, and . . . I just don't want you to be sorry a few years down the road."

Taking hold of his hand, she drew his arm down around her shoulders. "I won't be sorry. I love you as you are, now and for always. I told you before, we can always adopt a baby, and if you're not comfortable with that, then . . ."

"Dammit, Cara, I don't want you making sacrifices on my account."

"Well, get used to it, because I'm not going anywhere."

"I'm marrying a tough chick, huh?"

"Darn right, mister," she said, punching him in the ribs, "and don't you forget it!"

As her father had said, the church was located in a secluded glade well off the main highway. Surrounded by tall trees and shrubs, the building looked like it had been transplanted from some medieval setting. Moonlight danced across the stained-glass windows. The air was filled with the fragrant scent of evergreens; night birds called to each other; crickets played a serenade. An owl hooted softly in the distance.

As Cara crossed the threshold with her father, she could easily imagine knights and their ladies passing through the carved oak doors.

The priest was waiting for them in the vestibule, along with Sarah Beth, who had agreed to be Cara's matron of honor. Vince had asked his oldest brother to stand up with him.

"Father Lanzoni," Roshan said, "it's good to see you again."

"And you, my friend," the priest replied. "And this must be your daughter. She is lovely."

Cara felt herself blushing as she murmured, "Thank you, Father."

While Roshan and the priest spoke, Cara hugged Sarah Beth, who looked very pretty in a tea-length peach silk dress and matching heels.

"You look radiant, Cara," Sarah Beth said. "Are you nervous?"

"A little."

Sarah Beth laughed. "I know, I was, too, but you'll forget all that when you see Vince. Mary and a couple of the part-time ladies from the library are here." Sarah Beth glanced around. "This is a beautiful place. However did you find it?"

"My parents were married here," Cara said.

"Oh," Sarah Beth exclaimed, "that's so romantic!"

"Are we ready?" the priest asked. "The groom is waiting."

Cara smiled. "Very ready."

With a nod, the priest went to take his place at the altar.

Cara peered through the doors that led into the chapel, noting that the pews and the altar were carved from oak; the carpet was a deep blue. Vince's family had already arrived. His sister-in-law, Patti Jean, sat at the organ, playing softly. Candlelight filled the chapel with a warm golden glow, lighting the faces of the wooden statues, but Cara had eyes only for Vince. She had always thought him the most handsome of men, but tonight, clad in a tux, his hair neatly combed, he was the most gorgeous thing she had ever seen, as he stood at the altar, waiting for her. The priest stood beside Vince. He was of medium height with wavy black hair going gray at the temples.

Patti Jean began the wedding march and Sarah Beth started down the aisle. Everyone rose as Cara and her father appeared in the doorway.

Cara winked at her mother, smiled at Mary and at Sarah Beth's husband, and then, with butterflies in her stomach, she met Vince's gaze and felt her heart swell at the love she saw in his beautiful dark eyes.

"Who giveth this woman to be married to this man?"

"Her mother and I do," Roshan said. Lifting Cara's hand to his lips, he kissed it; then, after placing her hand in Vince's, he stepped back to sit beside Brenna.

"We are gathered here this evening to join Cara Aideen DeLongpre and Vincent Cordova in the bonds of holy wedlock, an honorable institution ordained of God for the blessing of His children. There is no secret to a happy marriage," the priest said, glancing from Cara to Vince. "You have only to remember to put your loved one first and yourself second, to treat your spouse as you wish to be treated, and to remember how much you love one another on this day. Remember these things, and you will have a life of peace and happiness for as long as God grants you breath.

"I will say the words that bind you together, but the true marriage between the two of you must take place within your hearts.

"Cara, do you promise to love and cherish Vincent, here present, for as long as you shall live?"

Cara squeezed Vince's hand. "I do."

"Vincent, do you promise to love and cherish Cara, here present, for as long as you both shall live?"

Vince took a deep breath. "I do."

"Then, by the power vested in me, I pronounce you husband and wife. You may kiss your bride."

Vince lifted Cara's veil. For a moment, he simply looked at her, wanting to remember how she looked on this night, the glow in her eyes, the rapid beating of her heart as she waited for his first kiss as her husband. Murmuring, "I love you," he drew her into his arms and kissed her.

He might have kissed her for an hour or two if he hadn't become aware of the quiet cheers and chuckles of his family.

Cara's cheeks were flushed when he released her.

"And now, at last," the priest said, a smile in his voice, "I give you Mr. and Mrs. Vincent Cordova."

Cara turned to face Vince's family, relieved to see that everyone was smiling. A faint movement at the back of the chapel drew her eye; she felt her insides turn cold as two gray-clad women slipped out the door.

Cara tugged on Vince's arm as he walked her down the aisle. "Did you see them?"

"See who, darlin'?"

"Two women in gray robes. They just went out the door."

"I didn't notice. Are they friends of yours?"

"No. I don't know who they are."

Vince escorted Cara to the limo waiting outside the church, helped her inside, and drew her into his arms. "Why did seeing those women upset you so? Maybe they were nuns."

Cara shook her head. "No. I've seen others dressed like that. The first time was in Serafina's bookstore, and then again the other night, when I was at the mall, and now here." She clutched Vince's hand. "I don't like this."

Vince wrapped his arms around her. "Take it easy, darlin', no one's ever going to hurt you again."

"I'm frightened." She glanced out the rear window. "Anton is still out there somewhere."

"Don't think about that now." He kissed her cheek, wondering if he should find her another bodyguard.

Cara shook off her fears as they turned off the highway. This was her wedding night and she wasn't going to let Anton or anyone else ruin it for her.

A short time later, they arrived at her parents' house, where cake and champagne were waiting.

Cara was overwhelmed by the love she felt from Vince's family, from Sarah Beth and Mary, and from her own parents, of course. Because Vince's family lived so far away, Cara decided to open their wedding presents that night. She sat on the floor, her gown spread around her, while Vince handed her their gifts. They were the usual gifts friends and family give to newlyweds: a toaster, pots and pans, a set of silverware, linens for the bed and for the table, a cookie jar, bath towels and kitchen towels, glassware, and a set of dishes. Later, her father took her and Vince aside and gave them a check for a hundred thousand dollars "to buy whatever else the two of you might need," he said, "or to put a down payment on a little house of your own."

"Dad, this is way too much," Cara said.

"I told you I was a rich man," her father reminded her.

"I know, but . . ." She looked at Vince.

"She's right," Vince said. "It's way too much."

Roshan grunted softly. "What else am I going to do with my money? If I were a mortal man, I'd leave it in my will, but since I'm hoping to hang around for a good long while, I want Cara to have it now."

Cara threw her arms around her father. "Thank you, Dad!"

Vince added his thanks to Cara's, then the two of them went to mingle with their guests. Later, they cut the cake. Vince offered Cara a bite, choked back a gag when she fed him a small piece, which he didn't swallow. When no one was looking, he spit it into his handkerchief.

While the caterer served the cake, Vince and Cara enjoyed their first dance as man and wife.

"Are you having a good time?" he asked.

"Yes! This is the happiest night of my life."

"Mine, too." Pulling her close, he rained kisses on her cheeks, her eyelids, and the tip of her nose. "I love you, wife."

"And I love you, husband."

His hands slid slowly up and down her back, drawing her body closer to his, letting her feel how much he loved her, wanted her, needed her.

Cara blew out a long shuddering sigh as her body responded to his. "Later," she whispered.

"Not too much later," he said with a growl.

As much as he wanted to spend what time he could

with his family, he wanted to be alone with Cara more, so after they listened to toasts from their parents and Vince's brothers, Vince took Cara by the hand and they slipped out the back door when no one was looking, then ran around to the front of the house where the limo waited.

Vince opened the back door for Cara, then climbed in beside her. As soon as he closed the door, he drew her into his arms. "Hey, Mrs. Cordova."

"Hey, yourself, Mr. Cordova." She glanced out the window as the limo pulled away from the house. "Does the driver know where to go?"

"Yeah, I told him before we left the church."

With a little sigh of contentment, Cara snuggled against her husband. Husband. The word made her smile.

"Did I tell you how beautiful you look tonight?" Vince asked.

"No. Do you like my dress?"

"It's beautiful, too, and you make it more so." Indeed, he had never seen her looking lovelier than she had when walking down the aisle. Her gown was long and simple, with a round neck, long, fitted sleeves, and a slim skirt that showed off her figure perfectly, but it was the look of love in her eyes, the shy smile that was just for him, that had gone straight to his heart.

"We never talked about going anywhere for a honeymoon," he said. "Is there anywhere you want to go?"

"Just to bed," she murmured, lifting her face for his kiss. "With you."

Chapter 40

When they reached Cara's house, Vince paid the limo driver, then lifted his bride into his arms and carried her up the walkway. The door opened at his command and a fire sprang to life in the hearth.

Cara's breath whispered against his neck as she murmured, "Oh, my."

"Better than witchcraft," Vince said, smiling down at her.

She nodded. "It's a little scary, finding out all the supernatural things you can do."

"There's nothing for you to be afraid of," he murmured. "Nothing at all."

He carried her into the bedroom and eased her to the floor. Someone, Brenna he supposed, had been to the house earlier. The new sheets Cara had bought were on the bed, the covers already turned down. A bottle of red wine and two glasses waited for them on the bedside table. A crystal vase held a bouquet of long-stemmed white roses; a basket of fruit sat on the dresser.

He saw it all in a glance, but it was Cara who held his gaze. How was it possible for her to grow more lovely every time he looked at her? He removed her veil and tossed it over a chair, then drew her into his arms, one hand reaching behind her to unfasten her gown. She stepped out of it and he tossed it aside as well, then he took a step back so he could look at her.

Cara blushed beneath his heated gaze. True, they had made love before, but he had never looked at her quite like this, and they hadn't been married at the time. For some reason, it made her suddenly shy to stand there wearing nothing but her bra, panty hose, and heels.

Vince whistled softly. "You're the prettiest, sexiest thing I've ever seen."

"And you," she said, "are overdressed."

"Well, if you don't like it, you know what to do."

He didn't have to tell her twice. In minutes, his coat, cummerbund, tie, shirt, and trousers were on the floor, leaving him attired in a T-shirt, briefs, and his shoes and socks.

Vince looked down at himself and grimaced. "I look pretty silly."

"Well, the shoes have to go," she said.

"Right." Sitting on the edge of the bed, he removed his shoes and socks. "Come here."

She moved toward him and he removed her heels, then slowly peeled off her panty hose. Her bra came next, then his T-shirt.

Cara watched him, her body trembling with anticipation as he tossed his briefs aside, then drew her down on the bed beside him, their bodies fitting together perfectly, like two halves of a whole.

She felt like purring as his callused hands moved over her willing flesh, stroking, teasing, arousing her until she thought she'd go mad with wanting him. She slid her hands over his shoulders and down his arms, loving the way his muscles quivered at her touch. It was a heady sensation, knowing that her touch aroused him as much as his aroused her.

Raking her nails down his back, she murmured, "Now, Vince!" She sighed with pleasure as he rose over her, his body melding with hers, easing into a slow, steady rhythm that made her cry out, her hands clutching his shoulders, her body arching beneath him, until that one beautiful moment when she couldn't tell where he ended and she began. It was like flying through a rainbow, drowning in waves of ecstasy . . .

As from far away, she heard Vince's voice, filled with soft entreaty. "Let me taste you."

For a moment, she didn't know what he meant, and then she felt his tongue lave the side of her neck.

"Please?" His voice was rough, filled with longing.

"I'm afraid."

"I won't hurt you, I swear it."

She loved him with all her heart, how could she refuse him anything? How could she agree?

"Never mind," he said quietly.

Guilt washed over her. "It's all right."

"Are you sure, darlin'?" His breath was warm against her neck. She could feel the tension in his body, hear the need in his voice.

"I'm sure," she said, and closed her eyes.

He kissed her, long and slow, his hand gliding up and down her thigh, gentling her, she thought. She stilled as his tongue warmed the skin below her ear, felt a tiny prick as his fangs pierced her flesh. She had expected to feel horror and revulsion; instead, she felt only a kind of sensual pleasure that was over too soon.

"Did I hurt you?" he asked.

Cara's eyelids fluttered open. "No," she murmured. "It felt wonderful. Can we do it again?"

Clad in a pair of jeans, Vince sat on the porch stairs, gazing up at the stars. He had left his bride asleep in her bed after making love to her one more time. Never in his life had he felt so at peace. Cara was his for as long as she lived. Perhaps, in time, he would be able to convince her to accept the Dark Gift. He could think of nothing better than spending the rest of his existence, however long that might be, with her at his side. He would spend this night here, with his bride, though it made him uneasy. He didn't like being vulnerable while he slept and there was no way to secure her house against intruders. Starting next week, he would take his rest at the garage until they found a house of their own, and then he would take the necessary precautions to protect his new lair.

A stir in the air brought his senses to immediate alert. A moment later, Mara materialized at his side. Moonlight haloed her long black hair; her full-length gown, also black, outlined every curve. Once, he had thought her the most beautiful woman he had ever seen, but that had been before Cara entered his life.

"Good evening," she murmured.

"Hey."

"Lovely night for a hunt, don't you think?"

"Not tonight."

"No?"

Vince shook his head.

"Why is that?" Sitting down, Mara spread her skirts around her, like the petals of an ebony rose. "Your little mortal is asleep. She won't even know you're gone."

"It's my wedding night," Vince said with a smile. "How would it look if I went off with another woman?"

"You married her?" Mara exclaimed.

"Yep."

"Unless you bring her across, she'll just die and leave you."

"Is that why you never married?" Vince asked. "Because he'd leave you?"

She sighed softly. "I lied to you before. I did marry once, many years ago. I knew I would regret it, but I loved him and he refused to bed me without the blessing of the church." She laughed softly. "Truly, a man unique among men."

"Were you happy together?"

"Yes, for many years, until he began to grow old and I did not, until he began to hate me. The older he got, the stronger his hatred became, until it soured everything between us."

"What happened to him?"

"One night, as I held him in my arms, he drove a knife into my heart. Had it been a silver blade, I wouldn't be here now. When he realized he hadn't killed me, he ran out of the house. A passing carriage struck him and killed him instantly."

"I'm sorry, Mara."

"As I said, it was a long time ago." She looked at him, her eyes filled with pain. "You'd think it would have stopped hurting by now."

Uncertain of how she would react, Vince slipped his arm around her shoulders and drew her close. She stiffened in his embrace, and then she relaxed. It took him a moment to realize she was crying. Two large teardrops slid down her cheeks like crimson rain. Vince captured them on the tip of his finger and carried them to his mouth. It was like tasting liquid fire.

Turning her head, Mara kissed him on the cheek. "I hope you will be happy," she said, and vanished from his sight.

No sooner had she gone than he heard the door open behind him and Cara stepped out onto the porch. "Vince?"

"I'm here, darlin'."

"I thought I heard voices."

Rising, he kissed her on the cheek. "There's no one here but me," he said, and taking her by the hand, he led her inside and locked the door behind him.

The next week was the most wonderful of Cara's life. She took a week off from work and Vince closed his shop. They stayed up late and slept late. He reached for her when he woke up and they made love late in the morning.

He read the paper while she ate breakfast and then they made love again; she went shopping or cleaned house or took a nap while he took his rest. At night, they went to the movies or for walks, stayed home and watched TV, or just went to bed early. She never tired of touching him, watching him, or being near him.

They spent Christmas Eve with her parents. Cara ate dinner before leaving the house. They spent a pleasant few hours with her mom and dad. After they opened their presents, they shared their favorite Christmas memories.

Later, back at home, Vince and Cara sat in front of the fireplace, sharing a glass of red wine while they admired the lights on the tree. Christmas carols played softly in the background.

They spent Christmas morning in bed, making love. Later, while Cara made herself something to eat, Vince called his folks to wish them a merry Christmas.

Cara was putting the dishes in the dishwasher when Vince came up behind her. "Close your eyes," he said.

"Why?"

"Just do it, darlin'," he said, and when her eyes were closed, he slipped a gold bracelet onto her wrist. "Okay, you can open them now."

"Oh, Vince," she cried, "it's lovely!"

"Just a little something I thought you might like. Merry Christmas, darlin'."

"Merry Christmas."

"Don't I get a kiss?" he asked.

"Oh, yes!"

It was the best kind of kiss, one that led them back into the bedroom, and back to bed.

Life would have been perfect, Cara thought a few days later, except for her constant bouts of nausea in the morning. She didn't mention it to Vince or her parents, didn't want to think what it might mean. Had Vince been mortal, she would have thought she was pregnant, but such a thing was impossible. She couldn't help thinking of all the horrible possibilities, all of them fatal, but if she was dying, she didn't want to know.

She managed to hide her illness from Vince until he rose unusually early one morning and caught her vomiting in the bathroom.

He quickly wet a cloth and handed it to her, his brow furrowed with concern. "What's wrong?"

"Oh, nothing," she lied as she wiped her mouth.

"Did you eat something that didn't agree with you?"

She shrugged. "Maybe, I don't know. I'm fine now."

Lifting her to her feet, he gazed into her eyes. "Has this happened before?"

Her gaze slid away from his. "No."

"Cara, don't lie to me."

She looked up at him, her eyes welling with tears. "Every morning this past week. Oh, Vince, I'm so afraid!"

"Shh, there's nothing to be afraid of," he said, drawing her into his arms. "It's probably just the flu or a bug of some kind."

She sniffed. "But I don't feel like I've got the flu. I don't have a fever . . ."

"Have you called the doctor?"

"No."

"Why not?"

"I'm afraid of doctors. They never give you anything but bad news."

"Well, we're calling one now."

She tried to change his mind, but he was adamant, and because she refused to call, he made the appointment for her.

"Four o'clock tomorrow," he told her, "and I don't want any excuses. It's Monday, and you don't have to go to work." He took her chin in his hand. "And don't think about missing it. If I have to, I'll make the appointment for later in the day and I'll take you myself."

"You can't go out during the day," she retorted, "and they close at five, so you can't make me go."

"Then I'll just have to suffer the consequences, won't I?"

The thought of Vince going outdoors when the sun was up was enough to insure that she would keep her appointment.

The next day, at five after four, Cara pulled into the parking lot at her doctor's office. She was sitting in the car, gathering her courage, when she happened to look in the rearview mirror. A cold chill ran down her spine when she saw a car pass slowly behind her, a car driven by a woman that looked vaguely familiar. It took Cara a moment to place her and when she did, she jumped out of the car and ran into the doctor's office. The driver had been one of the gray-clad women she had seen before.

"Miss, are you all right?"

Cara looked up to find the receptionist staring at her. "What?"

"Are you all right? You look like you're going to faint."

"No, I'm fine." She took the papers the receptionist handed her, willed her hand to stop shaking as she filled out the necessary forms. In spite of her promise to Vince, she was sorely tempted to leave without seeing the doctor, and only the thought of the pain he would endure if he carried out his threat to bring her here himself kept her from running out of the building—that and the fear that someone might be waiting for her in the parking lot.

Fifteen minuets later, she was wearing a paper gown and seated on an examining table. A nurse recorded her weight and took her blood pressure, and then the doctor came in. He looked at her chart, listened to her symptoms, and concluded that she was pregnant.

Cara shook her head. "I can't be."

"You're a married woman," the doctor said, referring to her chart. "Is your husband impotent?"

"No," Cara said quickly, and felt her cheeks burn at her enthusiastic reply.

"Then I assume you have relations with your husband?"

"Yes, but . . ."

He asked her a few more questions, like the date of her last period and other intimate details, and then he examined her.

Forty minutes later, Cara left the office, wondering how she was going to tell Vince he was going to be a father and wondering how she would ever convince him that the baby was his.

Chapter 41

Cara drove home in a daze, everything else forgotten but her unexpected news. What was she going to tell Vince?, How could she possibly be pregnant when her husband was a vampire?

She was relieved to find he wasn't home when she got there. In the last few days, he had started going to the garage before the sun came up so he wouldn't be trapped in the house during the day. Sitting on the sofa, she placed her hands on her stomach. She couldn't think about fixing dinner, she couldn't think about anything but the new life growing within her. She was pregnant. With child. Gestating. She wanted to call her parents. She wanted to call Sarah Beth. She wanted to tell the world, but first she had to tell Vince.

Sitting on the sofa, she hugged herself, unable to stop smiling. She was going to have a baby, a little boy with Vince's black hair and dark eyes.

Her smile faded when she heard Vince's key in the lock.

"Hey, wife," he said, kissing her on the cheek. "I expected you to call me when you got home from the doctor. What did he say?"

"I'm perfectly healthy," she said slowly. "For a woman who's pregnant."

Vince stared at her, his eyes narrowing. "Pregnant? That's impossible. There must be some mistake."

"That's what I said, so they ran the tests twice."

A muscle throbbed in his cheek. "So, who's the father?"

Even though Cara had expected just such a reaction, the words hit her like a blow. How could he believe she had been unfaithful to him? How could he not, when everyone knew vampires couldn't create life?

Still, she couldn't help being hurt by his immediate assumption that she had betrayed him. She blinked rapidly. She didn't want him to see her cry or know how badly his words had hurt.

"Dammit, Cara, answer me!"

"You, you big jerk, you're the father!"

"That's impossible and we both know it."

"Well, it's true whether you believe it or not," she said, and, bursting into tears, she ran out of the room.

Vince swore softly. He couldn't be the father. It was impossible. And yet, in spite of his implied accusation, he knew that she hadn't been intimate with any other man. But . . . how could it be true? The doctor had to be mistaken.

He swore again, cursing himself for making her cry. Taking a deep breath, he went to their bedroom and knocked on the door.

"Cara?"

"Go away."

He turned the handle, scowling when he realized she had locked the door. Well, she had a lot to learn about living with a vampire, he thought ruefully. The door opened at the touch of his hand.

Cara looked up, her eyes red and swollen. "That's not fair," she sniffed.

Crossing the floor, he sat on the edge of the bed and drew her into his arms. "I'm sorry, darlin', but . . ." He shook his head.

"I know, I didn't believe him either, not at first." She placed her hand on her stomach. "But somehow, on the way home, I knew it was true." She sniffed again. "And I knew you wouldn't believe me." She looked up at him, her eyes wet with tears. "You don't really think that I . . ."

He placed his hand over her mouth. "No, I don't think that." He kissed her lightly. "I'm sorry. Can you forgive me for being a jerk?"

"I guess so. Being a man, you probably can't help it."

"Hey."

She smiled at him through her tears. "How do you think it happened?"

Vince grunted softly. "The usual way, I imagine."

"You know what I mean. I thought vampires couldn't make babies."

"Yeah, that's what I thought, too. Have you told your folks?"

"No, I wanted to tell you first." She smiled shyly. "Isn't it wonderful?"

"Darlin', nothing could make me happier than having a baby with you." But even as he said the words, he couldn't help wondering what kind of baby it would be.

"A baby." Cara said with a sigh. "Our baby." She looked up at him. "It's like a dream come true."

"It's more like a miracle." Using his fingertips, he wiped the tears from her eyes. "Come on, let's go tell your folks the good news."

Roshan and Brenna looked as stunned as Vince felt when Cara told them the news later that night. Once their initial shock wore off, they bombarded Vince and Cara with congratulations and questions. Vince accepted the hugs and handshakes; as for answers, he didn't have any.

Later, sitting in the living room, Roshan proposed a

toast, and then, after having giving it some thought, he said, "I've never heard of a vampire who could reproduce, but Cara's pregnant, so it must be possible. I think it's a combination of two things: Mara's ancient blood and the fact that Vince has been a vampire for such a short time. I would imagine that, as he grows older in the life, his power to reproduce will gradually disappear."

Vince nodded. It was as good an explanation as any, but only led to more questions.

Cara voiced one first. "What about the baby? Will it be half vampire? Is such a thing even possible?"

Roshan shook his head. "I'm afraid we'll just have to wait and see."

Cara nodded, but Vince saw the worry in her eyes.

"This is such wonderful news!" Brenna exclaimed. "Cara, I'm so happy for you. And for me," she admitted with a smile. "I never thought we'd have grandchildren. Are you hoping for a boy or a girl?"

"It doesn't matter," Cara replied, "as long as it's healthy."

"Of course, that's the important thing," Brenna agreed.

Cara stared out the window as Vince drove them home. Her initial joy at the thought of having a baby had paled as thoughts of having a child that was half vampire filled her mind. Would she have a baby who couldn't go outside during the day or that needed blood to survive? Would she give birth to some kind of inhuman monster?

"We should start looking for a new house," Vince suggested as he pulled into the driveway. "One with a big back yard."

Cara nodded, only half listening to what he was saying. Would the doctors discover there was something abnormal about her baby before it was born?

"Cara?" He turned off the ignition and killed the lights. "Do you want to talk about it?"

She turned to face him, tears shining in her eyes. "What have we done?"

"What do you mean?"

She placed her hands over her womb. "I'm afraid."

"I know, darlin'." If he had known she would become pregnant, he never would have made love to her. The worst part of it was, there was no precedent; he had no idea if the baby would be normal or if she would be able to carry it to full term. Damn! He took a deep breath. "Do you want to abort it?"

She looked at him, her eyes wide. "No!" She shook her head. "How could I kill our baby? How can you even suggest such a thing?" She stared at him. "Is that what you want?"

He shook his head. "I just want you to be happy."

"I am happy," she murmured, "I'm just afraid for our child, afraid it won't be normal . . ."

Getting out of the car, he went around to open the door for Cara. Lifting her into his arms, he kicked the door shut with his heel and carried her up the walkway and into the house.

"What are you doing?" she asked.

He locked the door behind them. "Taking you to bed."

"Oh."

In their bedroom, he stood her on her feet, his eyes gazing deeply into hers as he summoned his power.

"From now on, you won't be afraid," he said, his voice low. "You won't be sick in the morning and you won't worry about the baby, do you understand?"

She nodded, her gaze trapped by his.

"Good." He kissed the tip of her nose and then slowly undressed her, his hands gliding over her skin, lingering on her stomach as he tried to imagine his child growing inside. He still couldn't believe it.

He carried her to the bed and laid her on it, then

stripped off his own clothes and sat on the mattress beside her.

"Turn over," he said, and when she was lying comfortably on her stomach, he massaged her back and shoulders, easing away the last of her tension, until her even breathing told him she was asleep.

He sat there for a long time, trying to sort out his feelings about being a father. Under any other circumstances, he would have been ecstatic. Before he became a vampire, he had dreamed of having a large family. That dream had died when Mara brought him across. Now, there was a very real possibility that his dream would turn out to be a nightmare. Whatever the product of their union, he was strong enough to handle it, but what about Cara? If the baby was abnormal or deformed, how would she feel about it? About him? Would she blame him? Would she hate him for not telling her what he was or for not using protection when they made love? Could he blame her if she did?

He swore softly. He hadn't prayed since Mara turned him, but he prayed now, prayed that his child would be born normal and healthy, not only for the baby's sake but for Cara's.

"If someone has to be punished for what I've done," he murmured, "then let it be me."

Blowing out a sigh, he stretched out beside Cara and drew her into his arms.

His last thought before sleep claimed him was that it was going to be a long seven months.

Chapter 42

Anton Bouchard invited the two gray-clad women into his house, bid them make themselves comfortable, and offered them refreshment. He had only recently returned to town, having decided that a lengthy vacation would be good for his health. He had spent the last several months enjoying la dolce vita. During his absence, he had enlisted two of the witches from his mother's coven to keep an eye the DeLongpre-Cordova families.

Now he was back and eager to hear of any developments that had taken place while he was away. Enough time had passed that DeLongpre had probably forgotten him, Anton thought, but he would never forget them—not the vampire who had killed his father so many years ago, and not the people responsible for ruining his mother's plans so that, instead of raising his father, she had raised a monster.

He listened carefully as Estelle, the older of the two witches, brought him up to date, ending with the news that Cara Cordova was pregnant.

Anton stared at her. "Pregnant!" That was something he hadn't counted on. "Are you sure?"

The witch delved into one of her voluminous pockets and withdrew Cara's medical records. "She's due any day now."

Anton read the report, then, muttering a vile oath, he wadded the paper up and threw it across the room. As much as he wanted revenge, he wasn't sure he could destroy Cara while she was pregnant. Of course, he could take the baby from her. There were spells that required the blood of an unborn child . . .

He shook the thought from his mind. He would not go down that path. His parents had both dabbled in Dark Magick, and both had met untimely ends.

Not that he was above using a little Dark Magick now and then. In the months he had been away, he had sought out the world's most knowledgeable wizards. He had practiced his craft until he was certain that he was more powerful than DeLongpre or his witch wife. Now, certain that he was invincible, he had returned to exact vengeance on those who had killed his mother and destroyed his father. He would make no mistakes this time. It no longer mattered if Roshan and the others knew who it was who killed them, or if he saw their faces as they died. It was regrettable that Cara was pregnant, but that was her misfortune, not his. He had only to wait until they were all together and then he would have his revenge. A spell he had learned in Italy, a fire, and all those who had harmed his family would at last meet their doom.

Chapter 43

Cara sat in front of the fireplace, rocking softly, one hand resting lightly on her swollen abdomen. She could scarcely believe that the baby she had never expected to have was due any day. The time had flown by. Of course, they had been busy. They had spent two months looking for a house before they found the perfect place. Cara had walked in the front door, took one look around, and said, "this is it."

Like her parents' house, this one was located on a large piece of property at the end of a quiet street. There were, in fact, only three other houses on the block, all separated by brick walls. The house had three bedrooms, two bathrooms, a fair-sized living room, and a large family room. Vince had taken a look at the large kitchen and dining room, then looked at her and grinned. Even though he hadn't said anything, she knew he was thinking that it was a waste of space, but Cara had plans for the dining room, thinking it would make a wonderful playroom. It would make it easy for her to keep an eye on their baby while she was cooking or doing dishes.

Her parents had helped her and Vince move in. No doubt their new neighbors had thought it strange that they moved in at night, but it didn't matter. She was too happy at the idea of having a house all her own to worry about it.

As soon as they were settled, Vince had taken every possible precaution to protect their home from intruders. It still amazed her that he held such power and that he could surround their house with wards to repel anyone who might do them harm.

Three weeks ago, Sarah Beth had given Cara a baby shower—at night, of course, so Brenna could attend.

Two weeks ago, Cara had quit her job so she could stay home with the baby.

Last week, she had put the finishing touches on the nursery. It had become her favorite room in the house, with its cheerful yellow walls and white curtains. The crib was set up, diaper service had been ordered, and all was in readiness. She could hardly wait to hold her child in her arms.

Every day, presents for the baby arrived from one set of grandparents or the other, ranging from the practical to the comical—a stroller, blankets, a football in case it was a boy, a rag doll in case it was a girl. Her father's latest gift had been a fat, stuffed vampire, complete with long black cloak and tiny white fangs. Cara had put it in the crib, thinking that her child was going to know the truth about its father as soon as it was old enough to understand!

She smiled as she felt the baby kick. At her last visit, her doctor had assured her that everything was fine. The baby was growing as it should, the head was in position, and he expected her to go into labor within the next day or two, three at the most.

A rush of anticipation made her heart skip a beat when she heard Vince's key in the front door. Married seven months and as big as a house with her first child, and she still felt a warm thrill of excitement every time she saw him.

"Hey, darlin'." Leaning down, he kissed her, then placed his hand on her abdomen. "How's our baby doin' tonight?"

"I think he's playing leapfrog. Here," she said, moving his hand a little lower, "feel that?"

"Does it hurt?"

"No, it feels wonderful." She loved being pregnant, loved the thought of Vince's child growing inside her.

Vince grinned. "With a kick like that, he's bound to be a soccer player, or maybe a punter."

"It might be a girl, you know."

Vince shrugged as he sat on the sofa beside her. "Well, girls play soccer, too. I don't know about pro ball, though."

Cara laughed. "The baby's not even born yet and you've already got him, or her, playing soccer."

"I don't care what he does for a living," Vince said, nuzzling her neck. "I just wish he'd get born so I could have my wife back."

The doctor had warned her not to have intimate relations with Vince during the last few weeks of her pregnancy. It wasn't easy on her, either. They'd been married such a short time, sexual intimacy was still new. Not that they didn't spend hours cuddling and caressing each other, she thought, smiling.

"Did you take your vitamins today?" he asked. "Drink lots of milk?"

Cara blew out a sigh of exasperation. "Honestly, you're worse than my mother!"

"Hey, I just want to make sure that you and the baby are both healthy. After all, we may never have another one."

"I know. And yes, I took my vitamins and drank my milk like a good girl." She didn't tell him it was chocolate milk.

"I'm going upstairs to take a quick shower," Vince said, "and then I'll come down and rub your back. How's that sound?"

"Heavenly."

He kissed the tip of her nose, then went upstairs.

Reaching for the remote, Cara turned on the TV. She was truly blessed, she thought, smiling. Vince treated her like a queen. When she'd had a craving for watermelon in the middle of the night, he had gone to the store to buy her one. As her pregnancy advanced, he refused to let her do anything too strenuous. He rubbed her back and her feet every night. He mopped the floors, dusted the furniture, vacuumed the rugs, scoured the toilets, and took out the trash—and he brought her flowers or candy at least once a week.

Sometimes, when she thought about it, it made her laugh out loud. After all, vampires were supposed to be ravenous, bloodthirsty monsters, not housekeepers!

She glanced up when she heard the shower come on, her mind immediately filling with an image of Vince all soapy and sudsy. Thinking how lucky she was to have him, she pushed herself off the sofa and waddled into the kitchen for a can of soda.

She was filling a glass with ice when her water broke. Startled, she dropped the tumbler. For a moment, she stared at the ice cubes and shards of green glass scattered in the puddle on the floor, and then she gasped.

She was in labor. The baby was coming.

Upstairs, Vince turned off the shower. Though he had never mentioned it to Cara, he grew more nervous about the baby with each passing day. Sometimes he wished he could hypnotize himself the way he had Cara! He had talked with Roshan and Brenna privately only to find out that they were both just as worried as he was. What if the child was abnormal? What if it needed blood instead of mother's milk? What if it was some kind of freak? He could just imagine Cara's horror, the doctor's shock, and the media circus that would ensue. And the child, it would be subjected to endless tests, ridicule . . .

Shaking his morbid thoughts from his mind, he slipped into a pair of jeans and a T-shirt and went downstairs.

"Cara?"

"In here."

He found her sitting on the kitchen floor, one hand pressed against the small of her back. Water, ice, and shards of glass littered the floor around her.

"What happened?" he asked, skirting the mess.

"My water broke." She groaned softly. "The baby's coming."

Bending down, he lifted her into his arms and carried her into the living room. Cradling her to his chest, he picked up the phone and called the doctor, and then her parents.

Next, he carried her upstairs to put on some dry clothes. He handed her the bag she had packed for the hospital and then, not trusting himself to drive, he took her in his arms and transported the two of them to the hospital.

Minutes later, she was on her way to the maternity ward and he was pacing the floor, waiting for them to assign her to a room so he could join her there.

Roshan and Brenna arrived just as the nurse came to tell him what room Cara was in.

"How is she?" Roshan asked.

"I don't know. I'm on my way up there now."

Roshan nodded. "You two go on. Brenna, let me know how it goes?"

With a nod, she and Vince took the elevator up to the third floor.

Cara smiled at them when they entered.

"How are you, sweetheart?" Brenna asked, taking Cara's hand in hers.

"I'm good."

Standing on the other side of the bed, Vince brushed a lock of hair from her brow. "You're going to be fine, remember? Nothing to be afraid of."

"I remember. It's a nice room, isn't it?"

Vince glanced around. In addition to the bed, there was a sofa, a table, a couple of chairs, and a TV. Except for the bed, it didn't look anything like a hospital room.

A short time later, a nurse came in to check on Cara. When she finished, she patted Cara's hand, then smiled reassuringly at Vince and Brenna. "It won't be long now."

To Vince, it seemed like an eternity. Watching Cara, feeling her pain, he would have given anything to be able to endure it for her.

At one point, when he didn't think he could stand watching her any longer, he started to leave the room, only to have the nurse stop him.

"Your wife can't leave," the nurse said sternly, "and neither can you."

With a nod, Vince returned to Cara's side. He rubbed her back and held her hand, and when he couldn't stand to watch her suffer anymore, he cupped her face in his hands and gazed deep into her eyes.

"Look at me," he said. "Only me. You don't feel the pain anymore, just a little pressure, but it's not bad. Look at me, darlin', that's it. This will all be over soon and we'll have a beautiful baby."

Half an hour later, the doctor came in and delivered the baby. Watching Cara expel the child from her womb, Vince knew it was the most amazing thing he had ever seen. His heart swelled with an emotion he had never felt before as he listened to his child's first lusty cry. To his ears, it was the most beautiful music in the world.

"It's a fine, healthy boy," the doctor said. He looked at Vince. "Would you like to cut the cord?"

"Sure."

When it was done, the nurse wrapped the baby in a

blanket and took it aside to clean it up. Relieved, Vince smiled at Brenna. The baby looked and acted like any normal child, although it was quite small.

Vince was watching the nurse weigh his son when a gasp from Cara sent him hurrying back to her side. "What is it?" he asked anxiously.

"I don't know," she said, panting.

"Oh, lordy," the doctor said, reaching for a fresh pair of gloves, "here comes another one!"

Vince sat on the sofa in Cara's room, his stocking feet propped on the coffee table. Cara was sleeping soundly. He still couldn't believe she had delivered identical twin boys. Like Vince, Roshan had been in shock. With a baby in each arm, Brenna had been in seventh heaven. Cara was simply exhausted.

Roshan and Brenna had gone home several hours ago, but Vince was spending the night, at least until dawn.

Rising, he walked quietly to where his children lay sleeping peacefully in their little beds, distinguishable only by the blue and white ribbons on their tiny wrists. Because he and Cara hadn't yet come up with names they liked, the infants were known as Baby A and Baby B.

During Cara's pregnancy, they had spent hours trying to come up with names they both liked, but to no avail. Inevitably, they had ended up laughing over suggestions like Archibald and Throckmorton. They would have to come up with something soon, Vince thought with a wry grin, and then shook his head. Twins. He still couldn't believe it.

They'd have to buy another crib, more diapers, more clothes. They needed to hire a nanny or a housekeeper to help Cara during the day. He figured Brenna would be there most every night, at least for a while. As for himself, Vince shook his head. He was going to have to leave the house just before dawn to get to the garage and wouldn't be able to return home until after dark.

He glanced out the window as his hunger made itself known. It had been several days since he had fed. As much as he hated to leave Cara, he had learned through experience that it was best to feed when the need arose—best for him, and definitely best for those who crossed his path.

As he was leaving the hospital, he thought he saw two women clad in long gray cloaks on the sidewalk, but when he turned for a second look, they were gone.

Chapter 44

Vince was on his way back to the hospital when Mara appeared at his side. "I've come to say good-bye," she said, slipping her arm through his.

"You're leaving?"

"Yes, I find this little town extremely boring, don't you?"

Grunting softly, Vince thought about the family waiting for him in the hospital and shook his head. "Not anymore. So, where are you going?"

"I'm not sure. Italy, perhaps. I haven't been there in the last thirty or forty years. Why don't you come with me?"

He laughed softly. "Italy sounds mighty tempting, but I'm afraid I can't leave right now."

"Of course, I forgot, you're tied to that mortal now."

"More than you know," he said, grinning. "I'm a father."

Mara came to an abrupt halt, her eyes wide with disbelief as she looked up at him. "What did you say?"

"I'm a father."

"That's impossible."

"Yeah, that's what everybody keeps telling me."

"Where is it? I want to see it."

"Them," Vince said. "Not it."

She blinked at him in disbelief. "Them? As in, more than one?"

"Yep. I've got twin boys. Come on, I'll prove it to you."

Cara was still sleeping soundly when Vince and Mara entered her room.

Mara immediately went to where the babies lay sleeping, her expression softening as she gazed at the two infants. "How can this be?"

"Beats the hell out of me," Vince said. "Near as I can figure, it was a combination of you being so old in the life and me being so young."

She mulled that over a bit and then nodded. "I suppose that could explain it, but . . ." She shook her head. "No one will believe this."

"Since you're partly responsible, how would you like to be their godmother?"

Mara gaped at him. "Me? A godmother?" A slow smile spread over her face. "I'd like that very much. What are their names?"

"They don't have any."

"Why not?"

Vince shrugged. "Cara and I can't find any that we agree on."

Mara studied the babies for a moment; then, lifting her hand, she placed her finger on the forehead of Vince's firstborn son. "This one shall be called Raphael," she said. "And this one," she said, touching the other baby's brow, "will be Rane."

Vince nodded, wondering how he would explain what had just happened to Cara and how they would change the babies names without hurting Mara's feelings if Cara didn't like them.

He was still wondering about that when Mara picked

up Raphael. Before he realized what she meant to do, she scored the pad of the baby's thumb with her finger-nail, and licked the single drop of blood that oozed from the tiny cut.

"What the hell do you think you're doing?" Vince demanded.

"I'm bonding with my godson," she said.

Vince stared at her, his eyes narrowed.

"This way, I'll always know where he is," she explained, kissing the top of the baby's head, "and how he is."

Vince watched as she gently put the baby back in his bed, then picked up Rane. Watching Mara lick his son's blood, he decided this was something Cara didn't need to know about.

Mara smiled as she kissed Rane's cheek, then put him back to bed. "I guess I won't be leaving town after all," she said, "at least not for fifteen or twenty years."

She kissed each baby again and then, with a wave of her hand, she was gone.

Vince stared after her, wondering how he would tell Cara that her children's godmother was a vampire. And then he grinned. Another vampire in the family shouldn't come as much of a shock.

Chapter 45

Cara went home two days later, and the babies went home two days after that.

Cara still couldn't believe that Vince had let a vampire she had never met name their children. She might have argued about it, only the names Mara had chosen seemed perfect.

The reality of being a mother didn't quite measure up to the way Cara had imagined it. She wasn't prepared for mountains of dirty diapers and T-shirts stained with spit-up milk, or for colicky babies who cried for hours no matter how you tried to comfort them.

At times, she felt totally inadequate as a mother. Perhaps if she'd had younger brothers or sisters, she would have known what to expect. One thing for certain, she gained a new respect for her own mother. It was Brenna who did the first diaper change after they brought the babies home from the hospital, Brenna who rocked one baby while Cara nursed the other, and Brenna who helped her interview nannies.

The nanny they all agreed on was named Mrs. McPike. She was a middle-aged woman who had raised nine children of her own, and who agreed to come Monday through Friday and to do light housekeeping, as well as help with the babies.

After a week of motherhood, Cara wondered if she was going to survive.

After two weeks, she was certain she would never again have any time to herself. It seemed as though she spent all her time with one baby or another at her breast. Fortunately, she had plenty of milk. She was certain there were cows with less!

After three weeks, she felt as if she had been a mother all her life.

During this time, Vince was her rock. He held her when she needed holding, listened to her secret fears, rubbed her back, ran errands in the middle of the night, changed diapers when necessary, brought her flowers for no reason at all, and assured her that things would get better when the babies were a little older.

"How do you know?" she asked. "You've never had kids before."

"Ah, but I have nieces and nephews, and I babysat for all of them," he said with a wink. "You're doing a great job."

She basked in his praise.

As he said, the time came when the babies ate less and finally slept through the night.

Cara spent hours on the phone with Bethy, exchanging recipes and bragging about how smart their children were.

Roshan and Brenna came to visit several times a week, but tonight, Cara had wanted to get out of the house and they had gone to visit her parents.

About nine o'clock, the babies fell asleep on her parents' bed.

"Honestly," Brenna said, glancing from one sleeping child to the other, "they just get more beautiful all the time."

"More handsome," Roshan said. "Boys are handsome."

"Ordinary boys are handsome," Brenna said. "Our boys are beautiful. Come now, let's let them sleep," she said. "They'll be awake again soon enough."

Downstairs, Roshan picked up the remote and turned on the TV. He was flipping through the channels when the image of a vampire appeared on the screen.

"Not that old thing," Cara said.

"What's the matter?" Vince asked, tweaking her nose. "Don't you like vampires?"

"Not old black-and-white ones. That movie's older than dirt."

"But always good for a laugh," her father said.

Resigned, Cara settled back on the sofa. She laughed in spite of herself as her father and Vince made jokes about the campy settings and the stilted dialogue. She was about to go into the kitchen for a soda when her parents and Vince went suddenly still.

"What is it?" Cara asked. "Are the babies crying?"

Vince looked at Roshan. "Do you feel that?"

Roshan nodded.

"I do, too," Brenna said. "There's black Magick in the air."

Vince went to the door, but when he turned the knob, nothing happened.

"What's going on?" Cara looked at her father, then at Vince, and felt their tension communicate itself to her.

She watched in growing horror as Vince and her father went from room to room, trying all the windows and doors.

"They won't open," Vince said, his voice hard and flat. "None of them."

"It's a spell of some kind, meant to seal us in," Brenna said. "I can almost taste it."

Cara started to ask who would do such a thing, but she knew.

They all knew.

"Why would Anton want to seal us inside?" Cara asked.

"I don't understand . . ." She broke off as the smell of smoke teased her nostrils, shrieked when the carpet beneath her feet burst into flame.

"My babies!" she cried, and ran up the stairs to her parents' room, her heart pounding. The house was on fire and there was no way out!

Vince looked at Roshan and Brenna and knew they were thinking the same thing. One sure way to destroy the Undead was by fire, and this was no ordinary fire. As he followed Brenna and Roshan upstairs, he noticed that the fire didn't touch the walls; only the contents inside the house were burning. Pausing on the landing, he watched the sofa explode into flames. Thick smoke rose in the air, and with it the stink of brimstone. Anton had summoned hellfire.

He thought of Cara and his sons. If he couldn't find a way to get them out of here, they would soon suffocate, which might be a blessing, he thought morbidly, and wondered if the smoke would render him unconscious, as well, or if all the vampires in the house would be cognizant when the flames found them.

In minutes, the living room was a sheet of flames.

"We're running out of time," Roshan said. "Brenna, can't you counteract the spell?"

"Maybe, if I knew what kind of spell it was."

Vince muttered an oath. Dissolving into mist, he floated up the fireplace chimney, thinking perhaps they could get out that way. No such luck. Bouchard, the bastard, had thought of everything.

Materializing again, Vince paced the floor, his mind racing. There had to be a way out!

The smoke was getting thicker now. The floor beneath his feet grew hot, hotter.

Roshan picked up a chair and threw it against the window. The window shook but didn't break.

"Let's try ramming it together," Vince said. "On three. One, two, three!"

Together, Vince and Roshan slammed their shoulders against the window. Again, nothing happened.

Vince swore softly. For the first time since becoming a vampire, he felt totally helpless. He looked at Cara and his children. Would the smoke render his family unconscious before the flames reached them? He knew the end would be quick for himself and Cara's parents. The flames would destroy them in an instant. But Cara, and his sons . . . In his mind's eye, he saw them in flames, heard their anguished screams as the fire licked their skin, their hair.

He looked at Roshan and knew that his father-in-law was thinking the same thing.

"Do what you have to do," Roshan said quietly; and then, squaring his shoulders, Roshan went to Brenna. Murmuring, "I'm afraid I won't be able to save you from the flames this time," he drew her into his embrace.

She looked up at him, her expression serene, her eyes filled with love. "We've had a good life together. I have no regrets."

Vince returned to Cara's side. She stood in a corner away from the door and the windows, a crying infant cradled in each arm.

She looked up at him, her face pale and scared. "What are we going to do?"

"I won't let you suffer," he said. "I won't let the flames take you or our sons."

She stared at him, her eyes growing wide as she understood what he was saying, and she nodded.

Wrapping his arms around his wife and children, he murmured, "Whatever happens, remember that I will always love you, whether in this life or the next."

* * *

Anton stood across the street. He stared unblinking at the DeLongpre house, his whole being focused on maintaining the spell that would destroy the people who had killed his father and his mother.

It was Dark Magick at its most powerful. If only his mother could see him now, he thought. She would be so proud of him. Only a few wizards in all the world had mastered hellfire, and now he was one of them.

Sweat beaded his brow and dripped down his back. Only a few more minutes and it would be over. His parents would be avenged. He could get on with his life.

No smoke escaped the house to alert the neighbors. Even if someone called the fire department, it wouldn't matter. They couldn't get in. No one could get in—and no one could get out.

Only a few more minutes and the whole inside of the house would be in flames. When that happened, the house would explode.

Only a few more minutes.

He heard a noise to his right, felt his concentration waver as it came again.

He blinked when a woman stepped in front of him.

"Nice night for a fire," she said. "Too bad I didn't bring any marshmallows."

When she smiled, her fangs were very white.

He didn't have time to scream as she sank them into his throat.

His spell died with him.

The fires went out as quickly as they had started. Cara clutched her babies closer. Had she imagined the whole awful incident?

She looked up at Vince. "What happened?"

"I don't know," he said, "but I think maybe the cavalry is here."

She stared at him askance as he took Raphael from her arms and then followed Roshan and Brenna out of the bedroom. They stopped on the landing.

The staircase was gone. Nothing remained of the first floor but the walls, the fireplace, and the foundation.

Brenna took Rane, Roshan took Raphael, Vince swung Cara into his arms, and they all floated down to the first floor. The cement was surprisingly cool beneath their feet.

Moments later, the front door opened seemingly of its own accord.

Cara stared at the woman who entered the house. She knew, somehow, that it was the vampire who had named her children. Vince confirmed it when he greeted the woman.

"Thanks, Mara," he said fervently. "I thought we were goners."

"I couldn't let anything happen to my godsons, now could I?"

"No," Vince said, remembering how she had tasted the blood of his sons so she would know where and how they were. "I guess not."

"I brought you a present," she said. "I left it in the back yard. You might want to dispose of it before anyone sees it."

Roshan stepped forward and bowed over Mara's hand. "If there's ever anything we can do for you . . ."

Mara dismissed his thanks with a wave of her hand. "Just take good care of my boys," she said, her gaze lingering on Vince's face. "All of them."

Gliding across the room, she kissed each baby in turn, and then she smiled at Vince. "I'll be around," she said, and vanished from sight.

Cara looked at Vince. "How did she know we were in trouble?"

"I'll explain it to you later," he promised.

"Mom, Dad, I'm so sorry about your house," Cara said. "You can stay with us while you rebuild."

"I don't think we will rebuild," her father said. "We've stayed here too long as it is. We should have moved a long time ago."

"Move?" Cara exclaimed. "You're going to move?"

"Not far," Roshan assured her. "Just to the next town, where no one knows us."

"But what about this house?"

"We'll tear it down and sell the land."

Cara shook her head. "But where will you spend the day tomorrow?"

"Don't worry about us," Brenna said with a wink. "We'll find a place. Here, take Rane."

Cara took Rane from her mother and Vince took Raphael from Roshan. "But . . ." Cara shook her head. Everything was happening so fast!

"Ready, love?" Roshan asked, taking Brenna by the hand.

"Ready." Brenna smiled at her daughter. "Don't worry about us," she repeated. "We'll see you tomorrow night."

Cara nodded as she watched her parents dissolve into mist and drift away. There were some things she didn't think she would ever get used to.

"I still don't understand how Mara knew we were in trouble," Cara remarked.

"Like I said, I'll explain it all to you later," Vince said. "But for now, let's go home."

Epilogue

Two years later

Cara sat in front of the fireplace, watching her sons roll around on the floor like two feisty puppies. Much had happened since the night of the fire. Vince had disposed of Anton's body. The insurance company had been reluctant to pay her parents' claim since they could find no cause for the fire but, in the end, they had come through.

Her father had razed what was left of the house and her parents had moved in with her and Vince until they had found a new home.

She often found herself watching her boys, looking for signs that they had inherited a lust for blood from their father, but as near as she could tell, they were just normal kids. She held her breath each time she took them to the doctor, fearing their pediatrician would find something wrong, but thus far, he had found nothing out of the ordinary.

Now, watching her sons play, she found herself yearning for another baby. Because they didn't know if she could get pregnant again or not, they had been using a contraceptive.

But not tonight, she thought.

She put the boys to bed early, showered, and shaved her legs.

When Vince came home from work, she met him at the door wearing a smile and a whisper of black silk.

He whistled softly, then swung her into his arms and carried her up the stairs where he fulfilled her every desire.

Here's an excerpt from
Amanda Ashley's next novel,
HIS DARK EMBRACE,
available from Zebra Books in February 2008.

Shannah had followed him every night for the last four months. At first, she hadn't been sure why, other than the fact that she was dying and out of a job and had nothing better to do.

She remembered the first time she had seen him. She had been sitting by the back window in the Potpourri Café across the street from the town's only movie theater. She had been sipping a cup of hot chocolate when she had seen him emerge from the theater. It had been in October, near Halloween, and the theater had been running classic vampire movies all month, showing a different movie each night of the week. The old Bela Lugosi version of *Dracula* had been playing that night.

The stranger had been wearing a long black duster over snug black jeans and a black T-shirt. With his long black hair, her first thought was that he could have been a vampire himself except that his skin was a dusky brown instead of deathly pale. A wannabe vampire, obviously. She knew there was a whole cult of them in the city, men and women who frequented Goth clubs. They wore black clothes and capes. Some of them wore fake fangs and pretended to drink blood. She had heard of some who didn't pretend, but actually drank blood. Others role-played on the Internet in vampire and Goth chat rooms.

Shannah had been sitting by the window in that same café when she saw the stranger the second time. He hadn't been coming out of the movie theater that night, merely strolling down the street, his hands thrust into the pockets of his jeans, which were black again. During the next few weeks, she saw him walking down the same street at about the same time almost every night, which she supposed wasn't really all that strange. After all, she went to the same café and sat at the same booth in the back at about the same time every night.

One evening, simply for something to do, she left the café and followed him, curious to see where he went. She followed him the next night, and the next. And suddenly it was a habit, a way to spend the long, lonely nights when she couldn't sleep. Sometimes he merely walked through the park across from City Hall. Sometimes he sat on one of the benches, as unmoving and silent as the bronze statue of the town's founding father that was located near the center of the park.

While following the man in the long black duster, she learned that he went to the movies every Wednesday evening and always sat in the last row. He wandered through the mall on Friday nights. He spent Saturday nights in the local pub, invariably sitting in the shadows in the far corner. He always ordered a glass of red wine, which he never finished. Other than the wine, she never saw him eat or drink anything. He never bought popcorn or candy at the movies. He never bought a soda or a cup of coffee or a hot dog in the mall.

When she followed him home, she learned that he lived in an old but elegant two-story house at the edge of town. The house had bars on the windows and a security screen door, and was surrounded by a block wall that must have been twelve feet high, complete with an impressive wrought iron gate. She wondered what he was hiding in there and spent untold hours pondering who and what he might be. A drug lord? An arms dealer? Some sort of international spy? A reclusive millionaire? A serial killer? A mad scientist? A terrorist? Her imagination knew no bounds.

The holidays came and went. He didn't go to visit family for Thanksgiving, and no one came to visit him. As far as she could see, he didn't celebrate Christmas. No tinsel-laden tree appeared in the large front window. No colorful lights adorned his house. He didn't go out to celebrate the new year. But then, neither did she. As far as she knew, he didn't buy flowers or candy on Valentine's Day, nor did he go to visit a lady friend. He was a handsome man—tall, dark, and handsome—which begged the questions, why wasn't he married, or at least dating? Perhaps he was in mourning. Perhaps that was why he always wore black. Then again, maybe he wore it because it looked so good on him.

She camped out in the woods across from his house three or four times a week, weather permitting, but she never saw him emerge during the day. He took a daily newspaper, but he never picked it up until after the sun went down. The same with his mail. He never had any visitors. He never had pizza delivered. No repairmen ever came to call.

She wasn't sure when she started to think he really was some kind of vampire, but the more she thought about it, the more convinced she became. He only came out at night. He lived alone. He didn't eat. He always wore black. He never had any visitors. She never saw him with anyone else because . . .

He was a vampire.

Vampires lived forever and were supposed to be able to pass immortality on to others.

Ergo, he was the only one who could help her.

All she needed now was the courage to approach him. But how? And when? And what would she say?

It was the first of March when she finally worked up enough courage to put intention into action. Tomorrow night, she decided resolutely. She would ask him tomorrow night.

But, just in case he refused her or she changed her mind at the last minute, she armed herself with a small bottle of holy water stolen from the Catholic Church on the corner of Main Street, wondering, briefly, if stolen holy water would retain its effectiveness. She found a small gold crucifix and chain that had belonged to her favorite aunt. She fashioned a wooden stake out of the handle of an old broom. She filled the pockets of her coat and jeans with cloves of garlic.

That should do it, she thought, patting her coat pocket. If he was agreeable, by this time tomorrow night she would be Undead. If he decided to make a meal of her instead of transforming her, she would just be dead a few weeks earlier than the doctors had predicted.

If you loved this Amanda Ashley book,
then you won't want to miss any of
her other fabulous vampire stories
from Zebra Books!
Following is a sneak peak . . .

DEAD SEXY

The city is in a panic. In the still of the night,
a viscious killer is leaving a trail of
mutilated bodies drained of blood.
A chilling M.O. that puts ex–vampire hunter
Reagan Delaney on the case,
her gun clip packed with silver bullets,
her instincts edgy.

But the victims are both human and Undead,
and the clues are as confusing as the
vampire who may her best ally—she hopes . . .

They called it You Bet Your Life Park, because that's what you were doing if you lingered inside the park after sundown, betting your life that you'd get out again. It had been a nice quiet neighborhood once upon a time, and it still was, during the day. Modern, high-rise condos enclosed the park on three sides. Visitors to the city often remarked on the fact that most of the buildings didn't have any windows. A large outdoor pool was located in the middle of the park. The local kids went swimming there in the summertime. There was also a pizza parlor, a video game arcade, and a couple of small stores that sold groceries, ice, and gas to those who had need of such things.

Large signs were posted at regular intervals throughout the park warning visitors to vacate the premises well before sunset. Smart people paid attention to the signs. Dumb ones were rarely heard from again, because the condos and apartments that encompassed You Bet Your Life Park were a sanctuary for the Undead. A supernaturally charged force field surrounded the outer perimeter of the apartment complex and the park, thereby preventing the vampires from leaving the area and wandering through the city.

Regan Delaney didn't have any idea how the force field worked or what it was made of. All she knew was that it kept the vamps inside but had no negative effect on humans. It was against the law to destroy vampires these days, unless you found one outside the park, but the force field made that impossible. Any vampire who wished to leave the park and move to a protected area in another part of the country had to apply for a permit and be transported, by day, by a company equipped to handle that kind of thing. What Regan found the hardest to accept was that vampires were now considered an endangered species, like tigers, elephants, and marine turtles, and as such, they had to be protected from human predators. The very thought was ludicrous!

It hadn't always been so, of course. In her grandfather's day, vampires had been looked upon as vermin, the scum of the earth. Bounties had been placed on them and they had been hunted ruthlessly. Many of the known vampires had been destroyed. Then, about five years ago, the bleeding hearts had started crying about how sad it was to kill all those poor misunderstood creatures of the night. After all, the bleeding hearts argued, even vampires had rights. Besides, they were also human beings and deserved to be treated with respect. To Regan's astonishment, sympathy for the vampires had grown and vampires had been given immunity, of a sort, and put into protective custody in places like You Bet Your Life Park. And since the Undead could no longer hunt in the city, the law had decided to put the vampires to good use. For a brief period of time, criminals sentenced to death had been given to the vampires.

The thought still made Regan cringe. Though she had no love for murderers, rapists, or child molesters, she couldn't, in good conscience, condone throwing them to the vamps. She didn't have to worry for long. In less than a year, the same bleeding-heart liberals who had felt sorry for the poor, misunderstood vampires began feeling sorry for the poor unfortunate criminals who had become their prey, and so a new law had been passed and criminals were again disposed of more humanely, by lethal injection.

Unfortunately, the new law had left the Undead with no ready food supply. In order to appease their hunger and keep them from killing each other, blood banks had agreed to donate whole blood to the vampire community until synthetic plasma could be developed. In a few months, Locke Pharmaceuticals invented something called Synthetic Type O that was reported to taste and smell the same as the real thing. A variety of blood types soon followed, though Type O remained the most popular.

Taking a deep breath, Regan shook off thoughts of the past and stared at the lifeless body sprawled at her feet. Apparently, one of the vampires had tired of surviving on Synthetic Type O. She felt a wave of pity for the dead man. In life, he had been a middle-aged man with sandy brown hair and a trim mustache. He might even have been handsome. Now his face was set in a rictus of horror. His heart, throat, and liver had been savagely ripped away, and there wasn't enough blood left in his body to fill an eyedropper. The corpse had been found under a bush by a couple who had been leaving the Park just before sunset. From the looks of it, the victim had been killed the night before.

"Hey, Reggie."

Regan looked away from the body and into the deep gray eyes of Sergeant Michael Flynn. Flynn was a good cop, honest, hardworking, and straightforward, a rarity in this day and age. He was a handsome man in his mid-thirties, with a shock of dark red hair and a dimple in his left cheek. She had gone out on a number of dates with Mike in the last few months. He was fun to be with and she enjoyed his company. She knew Mike was eager to take their relationship to the next level, but she wasn't ready for that, not yet. She cared for him. She admired him. She loved him, but she wasn't in love with him. It was because he was the best friend she had in the city that she didn't want to complicate their friendship, or worse, jeopardize it, by going to bed with him. She had seen it happen all too often, a perfectly good friendship ruined when two people decided to sleep together.

"So," Flynn said, "definitely a vampire kill, right?"

"Looks that way," Regan agreed, but she wasn't sure. She had seen vampire kills before. The complete lack of blood pointed to a vampire, but the fact that the victim's heart, throat, and liver had been ripped out disturbed her. She had never known a vampire to take anything but blood from its prey.

"So, you about through here?" Flynn asked.

"What? Oh, sure." She wasn't a cop and she had no real authority on the scene, but in the past, whenever the department received a call about a suspected vampire killing, they had asked her to come out and take a look. She had been a vampire hunter in those days, and a darn good one, but that had been back in the good old days, before vampires became "protected" and put her out of a job. Fortunately, she had a tidy little inheritance from her grandfather, though it wouldn't last much longer if she didn't find another job soon.

"I'll call you next week," Flynn said with a wink.

Regan nodded, then moved away from the scene so the forensic boys could get to work. It gave her an edgy feeling, being in the park after the sun went down, though she supposed there were enough cops in the area to keep her reasonably safe from the monsters. At any rate, it felt good to be part of a criminal investigation again, good to feel needed. Still, she couldn't help feeling guilty that she would be out of work in a heartbeat as soon as they caught the killer.

She remembered the first time the department had requested her expertise. Even now, years later, the thought made her wince with embarrassment. After all the classes she had taken at the Police Academy, she had been convinced she was prepared for anything, but no amount of training could have prepared her for the reality of seeing that first fresh vampire kill. At the Academy, the bodies had been dummies and, while they had been realistic, they hadn't come close to the real thing. Regan had turned away and covered her mouth, trying in vain to keep her dinner down. It had been Michael who had come to her aid, who had offered her a handkerchief and assured her that it happened to everyone sooner or later. They had been friends from that night forward.

Now, she stood in the shadows, watching two men wearing masks and gloves slip the body into a black plastic bag for the trip to the morgue while the forensic team tagged and bagged possible evidence from the scene. Maybe they would get lucky downtown, but she didn't think so. She had a hunch that whoever had perpetrated the crime knew exactly what he was doing and that whatever evidence he had left behind, if any, would be useless.

Regan watched the ambulance pull away from the curb. Once the body had been thoroughly examined, the medical examiner would take the necessary steps to ensure that the corpse didn't rise as a new vampire tomorrow night. She didn't envy him the job, but if there was one thing the city didn't need, it was another vampire.

Regan was jotting down a few notes when she felt a shiver run down her spine. Not the "gee, it's cold outside" kind of shiver but the "you'd better be careful, there's a monster close by" kind.

Making a slow turn, she peered into the darkness as every instinct for self-preservation that she possessed screamed a warning.

If he hadn't moved, she never would have seen him.

He emerged from the shadowy darkness on cat-silent feet. "Do not be afraid," he said. "I mean you no harm."

His voice was like thick molasses covered in dark chocolate, so deep and sinfully rich, she could feel herself gaining weight just listening to him speak.

"Right." She slipped her hand into the pocket of her jacket, her fingers curling around the trigger of a snub-nosed pistol. She never left home without it. The gun was loaded with five silver bullets that had been dipped in holy water. The hammer rested on an empty chamber. "That's why you're sneaking up on me."

The corner of his sensual mouth lifted in a lazy half-smile. "If I wanted you dead, my lovely one, you would be dead."

Regan believed him. He spoke with the kind of calm assurance that left no room for doubt.

DESIRE AFTER DARK

Cursed to an eternity of darkness,
Antonio Battista has wandered the earth,
satisfying his hunger with countless women,
letting none find a place in his heart.
But Victoria Cavendish is different.

"You wish something?" he asked.

She shook her head. "No. Good night."

She started past him only to be stayed by the light touch of his hand on her shoulder. She could have walked on by. He wasn't holding her, but she stopped, her heart rate accelerating when she looked up and met his gaze.

Time slowed, could have ceased to exist for all she knew or cared. She was aware of nothing but the man standing beside her. His dark blue gaze melded with hers, igniting a flame that started deep within her and spread with all the rapidity of a wildfire fanned by a high wind.

Heart pounding, she looked at him, and waited.

He didn't make her wait too long.

He murmured to her softly in a language she didn't understand, then swept her into his arms and kissed her, a long searing kiss that burned away the memory of every other man she had ever known, until she knew only him, saw only him. Wanted only him.

He deepened the kiss, his tongue teasing her lips, sending flames along every nerve, igniting a need so primal, so volatile, she thought she might explode. She pressed her body to his, hating the layers of cloth that separated his flesh from hers. She had never reacted to a man's kisses like this before, never felt such an overwhelming need to touch and be touched. A distant part of her mind questioned her ill-conceived desire for a man she hardly knew, but she paid no heed. Nothing mattered now but his arms holding her close, his mouth on hers.

Battista groaned low in his throat. He had to stop this now, while he could, before his lust for blood overcame his desire for her sweet flesh. The two were closely interwoven, the one fueling the other. He knew he should let her go before it was too late, before his hunger overcame his good sense, before he succumbed to the need burning through him. He could scarcely remember the last time he had embraced a woman he had not regarded as prey. But this woman was more than mere sustenance. Her body fit his perfectly, her voice sang to his soul, her gaze warmed the cold dark places in his heart, shone like the sun in the depths of his hell-bound spirit.

He felt his fangs lengthen, his body tense as the hunger surged through him, a relentless thirst that would not long be denied.

Battista tore his mouth from hers. Turning his head away, he took several slow, deep breaths until he had regained control of the beast that dwelled within him.

"Antonio?" Vicki asked breathlessly. "Is something wrong?"

He took another deep breath before he replied, "No, my sweet." Summoning every ounce of willpower he possessed, he put her away from him. "It has been a long night. You should get some sleep."

She looked up at him, her eyes filled with confusion. He expected her to sleep, now?

He forced a smile. "Go to bed, my sweet one."

Vicki stared at him a moment; then, with a nod, she

left the room. That was the second time he had kissed her and then backed away. Was there something wrong with the way she kissed? But no, he had been as caught up in the moment as she. She couldn't have been mistaken about that.

She closed the bedroom door behind her, then stood there, trying to sort out her feelings. She knew very little about Mr. Antonio Battista. She had no idea where he came from, who he was, if he had a family or friends, or what he did for a living. But one thing she did know: no other man had ever affected her the way he did, intrigued her the way he did, made her want him the way he did.

Tomorrow morning, she thought. Tomorrow morning she would find out more about the mysterious Mr. Battista.

NIGHT'S KISS

The Dark Gift has brought Roshan DeLongpre
a lifetime of bitter loneliness—
until, by chance,
he comes across a
picture of Brenna Flanagan.

After awhile, Brenna lost interest in the images she was watching. Instead, she found herself sliding glances at Roshan. He had a strong profile, rugged, and masculine.

She wondered if he liked being a vampire. He had told her he had no vampire friends. It seemed unlikely that he would have mortal friends. Did he then spend all his time alone?

She knew little of what that was like, could not imagine living without friends or family for hundreds of years. Such a lonely existence. She wondered why anyone would want to live like that.

"Brenna?" His voice scattered her thoughts and she realized she had been staring at him. "Is something wrong?"

"Everything," she replied. "I do not belong in this time or this place." She stroked the cat's head. "I do not think I will ever belong."

"Sure you will. It might take a little while for you to get used to it, but you're young. You'll learn."

A single tear slid down her cheek and dripped onto the cat's head.

"Ah, Brenna." Reaching for her, he drew her into his arms. At first, she held herself away from him but then, with a sigh, she collapsed against his chest. With a low hiss,

Morgana slipped out from between them and curled up in front of the hearth.

Brenna's tears dampened his shirt. Her scent filled his nostrils, not the scent of her blood, but the scent of her skin, and her sorrow. He stroked her hair, ran his hand down her spine, felt her shiver in response to his touch.

Placing one finger under her chin, he tilted her head back, his gaze meeting hers.

Though a maiden innocent in the ways of men, her eyes revealed that she recognized the heat in his.

She shook her head as he leaned toward her. "No."

"No?"

"Kissing," she said with a grimace. "I like it not."

"Indeed?" He cupped her head in his hands. "Perhaps I can change your mind," he murmured, and claimed her lips with his own.

Eyes wide open, Brenna braced her hands against his shoulders, prepared to push him away, but at the first touch of his mouth on hers, all thought of pushing him away fled her mind. His lips were cool yet heat flooded her being, arousing a fluttering in her stomach she had never felt before, making her press herself against him.

Closing her eyes, she wrapped her arms around his waist, wanting to hold him closer, tighter. She melted against him, hoping the kiss would never end, a distant part of her mind trying to determine why John Linder's kiss had not filled her with liquid fire the way Roshan's did. But it was only a vague thought, quickly gone, as Roshan deepened the kiss, his tongue sweeping over her lower lip. She gasped at the thrill of pleasure that engulfed her, moaned softly as he repeated the gesture.

She was breathless when he took his lips from her. Lost in a world of sensation, her head still reeling, she stared up at him.

"More," she whispered.

"I thought you didn't like kissing."

"I was never kissed like this." Feeling suddenly bold, she slid her hand around his nape. "Kiss me again."

A WHISPER OF ETERNITY

When artist Tracy Warner purchases
the rambling seaside house
built above Dominic St. John's hidden lair,
he recognizes in her spirit the woman he has
loved countless times over the centuries.

She wasn't surprised when Dominic appeared in the doorway. He wore a long black cloak over a black shirt and black trousers. His feet were encased in soft black leather boots. Though she had refused to admit it, she had known, on some deep level of awareness, that this was his house.

He inclined his head in her direction. "Good evening. I trust you found everything you needed."

"Yes." Her fingers clenched around the brush. It was hard to speak past the lump of fear in her throat. "Thank you." Though why she should thank him was beyond her. He had brought her here without her consent, after all.

He took a step into the room.

She took a step back.

He lifted one brow. "Are you afraid of me now?

"How did I get here? Why am I here?"

"I brought you here because I wanted you here."

"Why didn't I wake up?"

"Because I did not wish you to."

The fear in her throat moved downward and congealed in her stomach. She started to ask another question, but before she could form the words, he was standing in front of her, only inches away. She gasped, startled. She hadn't seen him move.

"I will not hurt you, my best beloved one."

"Where are we?"

"This is my house."

"But where are we?"

"Ah. We are in a distant corner of Maine."

"So, I'm your prisoner now."

"You are my guest."

"A guest who can't leave. Sounds like prison to me."

"We need time to get to know each other again. I will not be shut out of your life this time. I will not share you with another. This time, you will believe. This time, you will be mine."

"So you're going to keep me locked up inside this house?" She stared down at her hands, noticing, for the first time, that she was holding the brush so tightly, her knuckles were white. "And what if I believe and I still don't want you? Still don't want to be what you say you are?"

"Then I will let you go."

AFTER SUNDOWN

Edward Ramsey has spent his life hunting vampires.
Now he is one of them.
Yet Edward's human conscience—and his heart—
compel him to save beautiful Kelly Anderson.

After dinner, they drove to the beach and walked bare-foot along the shore. It was a calm, clear night. The moon painted ever-changing silver shadows on the water.

After a while, they stopped to watch the waves. Ramsey's gaze moved over Kelly. She looked beautiful standing there with the ocean behind her. Moonlight shimmered like molten silver in her hair; her skin looked soft and oh, so touchable. He wished, not for the first time, that he possessed a little of Chiavari's easy charm with women.

"Kelly?" He took a deep breath, the need to kiss her stronger than his need for blood. He knew he should turn away, afraid that one kiss would not be enough. Afraid that a taste of her lips would ignite his hellish thirst. But she was looking up at him, her brown eyes shining in the moonlight, her lips slightly parted, moist, inviting. He cleared his throat. The kisses they had shared at the movies had been much in his mind, but he had lacked the courage to kiss her again, afraid of being rebuffed. "I was thinking about the other night, at the movies . . . "

"Were you? So was I."

"What were you thinking?" he asked.

"I was thinking maybe we should kiss again—you know, to see if it was as wonderful as I remember."

"Kelly . . ." He swept her into his arms, a part of him still expecting her to push him away or slap his face or laugh out loud, but she did none of those things. Instead, she leaned into him, her head tilting up, her eyelids fluttering down.

And he kissed her, there in the moonlight. Kissed her, and it wasn't enough. He wanted to inhale her, to drink her essence, to absorb her very soul into his own. She was sweet, so sweet. Heat sizzled between them, hotter than the sun he would never see again. Why had he waited so long?

"Oh, Edward . . ."

She looked up a him, breathless. She was soft and warm and willing. He covered her face with kisses, whispered praises to her beauty as he adored her with his hands and his lips. He closed his eyes, and desire rose up within him, hot and swift, and with it the overpowering urge to feed. He fought against it. He had fed well before coming here, yet the Hunger rose up within him, gnawing at his vitals, urging him to take what he wanted.

"This is crazy," she murmured breathlessly. "We hardly know each other."

"Crazy," he agreed. Her scent surrounded him. The rapid beat of her heart called to the beast within him. He deepened the kiss, at war with himself, felt his fangs lengthen in response to his growing hunger.

Contemporary Romance by

Kasey Michaels

Available Wherever Books Are Sold!

Visit our website at **www.kensingtonbooks.com**.

Put a Little Romance in Your Life with

Lisa Plumley

__**Making Over Mike**
   0-8217-7110-8   **$5.99**US/**$7.99**CAN

__**Reconsidering Riley**
   0-8217-7340-2   **$5.99**US/**$7.99**CAN

__**Perfect Together**
   0-8217-7341-0   **$6.50**US/**$8.99**CAN

__**Josie Day Is Coming Home**
   0-8217-7696-7   **$6.50**US/**$8.99**CAN

__**Once Upon a Christmas**
   0-8217-7860-9   **$6.99**US/**$9.99**CAN

__**Mad About Max**
   0-8217-7697-5   **$6.50**US/**$8.99**CAN

Available Wherever Books Are Sold!

Visit our website at **www.kensingtonbooks.com**